Life tau
that mu
are the
that life
Except t
In an old textbook,
published by the Imperial Printing House
in the year of Vrclicky's death,
I looked up the section on poetics
and poetic ornament.
Then I placed a rose in a tumbler,
lit a candle
and started to write my first verses.
Flare up, then, flame of words,
and soar,
even if my fingers get burned!
A startling metaphor is worth more
than a ring on one's finger.
But not even Puchmajer's Rhyming Dictionary
was any use to me.
In vain I snatched for ideas
and frantically closed my eyes
in order to hear that first magic line,
But in the dark, instead of words,
I saw a woman's smile and
wind-blown hair.
That's been my destiny.
Behind it I've been staggering breathlessly
all through my life

Jaroslav Seifert Prague 1983
translated by Ewald Osers

A Lesser Silence

a history

A novel

Colin Walter

Published by Colin Walter

A CIP catalogue record for this book is available from the British Library.

ISBN 978-1-9996805-0-3

Book layout and design by Clare Brayshaw

Prepared and printed by:

York Publishing Services Ltd
64 Hallfield Road
Layerthorpe
York YO31 7ZQ

Tel: 01904 431213

Website: www.yps-publishing.co.uk

For my family

Erratum: The author is most grateful to Ecco Press/ Harper Collins for permission to re-print the poem by Czeslaw Milosz: 'Meaning'.

owledgements

; the large number of people and organizations I have k for their assistance in the making and telling of this 'e the following:

National Rail Museum/Science Museum, 'Science ciety' Picture Library, for permission to use their for the cover of the book. Carlton Publishing , lly, for allowing me to use Jaroslav Seifert's poem, a Poet' which introduces the novel; and similarly the Agency (UK), and Penguin Books Ltd., in respect of / Milosz's poem 'Meaning' which concludes it.

grateful thanks are due to Boosey and Hawkes for reeing to my reproducing Ilse Weber's poem/song, 'I through Theresienstadt'.

n indebted to the School Library Association for ion in respect of reprinting those book reviews rst appeared in *The School Librarian*.

Page 100 refers to a poem written by the nine-year-old Simon, now much older than when we first met. Unfortunately I have been unable to trace him to discuss the use of his poem here.

Throughout the narrative, I have referred to the work of a number of poets. In mentioning their lines and insights it has been always in wonder and appreciation; and because I think they help the story along. Any shortcomings in achieving that are entirely mine.

There are many other people who have helped me in this making, and in ways of which they may be completely unaware: particularly John Loveday and Maurice Rutherford. Of the rest? Well, they know who they are, and I know they will forgive me for not mentioning them individually.

Finally, I really must mention how the advice of Clare Brayshaw and Duncan Beal, at YPS., has been both patient and invaluable; and instrumental in bringing this project to fruition.

Colin Walter

February 2018

"The genesis of language is not to found in the prosaic
But in the poetic side of life"

Jesperson

"The Angel handed me a book, saying, "It contains everything
you could possibly wish to know". And he disappeared.
So I opened the book, which was not particularly fat.
It was written in an unknown character.
Scholars translated it, but they produced altogether
different versions.
They differed even about the very senses of their own
readings, agreeing upon neither the tops nor the bottoms of
them, neither upon the beginnings of them nor the ends.
Toward the close of this vision it seemed to me that
the book melted, until it could no longer be distinguished from
This world that is about us"

Valéry

"…'tis in my mind to tell you a story in which are mingled
things sacred and passages of adverse fortune and love"

Boccaccio

"The highest state that man can achieve is that of
astonishment"

Goethe

"I want to know where it goes, that moment of enchantment, to what
Heaven above, to the bottom of what abyss,
to what gardens growing beyond space and time.
I want to know where the house of instant seeing is …"

Milosz

This is a story made from stories

There is a child's mysterious journey in the world from a particular, and now vanished, place in Britain in the 1940s. There are stories around illegitimacy, around mental health crises in the young, and of an unwilling, and sometimes surprising, journey through parenthood. More stories still are of children and schools; and particularly of poetry, childhood and teacher education.

Most of all though and altogether, this is a love story –
made from wonder and terror.

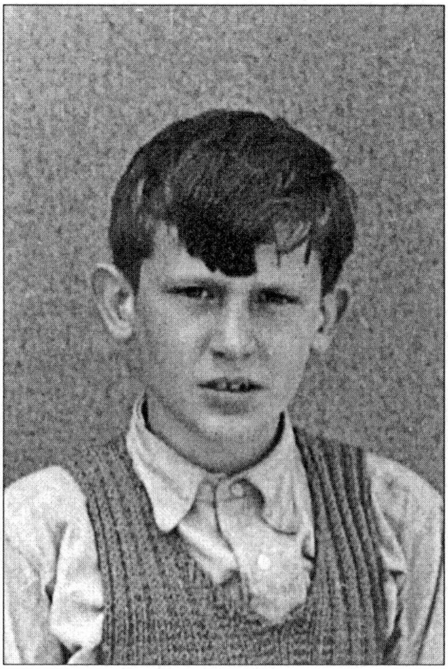

One of the narrators

SCANZIANI, Piero *The Adventure of Man*. Eureka. 1991, pp.267, £14. 99. Hardback. 1-873414-01-3

Coming upon this book is like picking up a bag on the 36 bus and finding it contains the philosophers' stone. Written within a distinctively European tradition, and drawing upon varied intellectual disciplines, it describes a view of the nature of human life from conception to death. It diagnoses personal and cultural ills which have their cause in an overemphasis upon logic as a substitute for human reason. Ills attributable to "the later decadent period of Greco-Roman civilisation" (p.68), and which make us good at discussion at the expense of understanding our lives.

The writing is crystalline: simultaneously scientific elaboration, narrative, and poetic. It runs straight, with musical properties: as by repetition of phrasing, echo, and refrain, it re-creates its subject.

Scanziani's reminder that we are born accompanied by our ancestors, is an arresting introduction to an analysis which has us related to all human beings past and present ... (and) to all living creatures" (p.19). His conclusion is that our human potential originates in our knowledge of our own death. About the "adventure" before, he is more useful than Freud on dreams as imaginative activity. Startlingly, unfashionably, convincing upon how it takes fifty years to make a mind – or, as he puts it, why we may be said to be ancient at birth, old at twenty, and able to live as ourselves at seventy (p. 230). He re-interprets the notion of the Unconscious to our age, which for many reasons, and with disastrous consequences, chooses not to acknowledge it. And he is limpidly clear as he demonstrates the essential compatibility of man and woman, in terms reminiscent of C.G.Jung: to societies which have developed a mis-understanding of statements such as: "There is no similarity between men and women: they are opposites" (p.223).

The insistence that "we are human and not Sileni in so far as we live in others" (p.186), suggests the relevance of social policy decisions to our achieving individual consolation. Scanziani's priorities for education, for example, are very different to those now dominant in contemporary Britain. To recognize our folly in turning our schools into corner shops, and for many other reasons, we should return to this generous and optimistic interpretation of our best possibilities.

William Holden

Nine year old children reading poems

Simon:	I read them to myself, and then I read one … to my mother
Daniel:	I read them to my family, to see what they'd think
Corinne:	I read them to myself, and read them to my friend. And then I read them to my sister
Linda:	Here's one I like because it's true … it really does happen
Peter:	I read some poems again and again
Sam:	Same with me. I read this five or six times at lunch-time …

VORSPIEL

Mysteries

What makes an overture sound like an overture?
What makes a conclusion more than an ending?

"A spell always guards something unexplained"

Stefan Zweig

It is now a year since my friend William Holden passed away. During his final months we had many conversations when he told me things about his life that I'd previously no idea of. We were talking about what he was actually writing down. It is his story, so I'll let him tell it through my recollections of our conversations, and through those of his own recollections that he recorded in other places.

I feel I have to get down what I have to say on paper, before that stuff kicks in again. It's a race. Six or seven months on, and then some months off before the levels rise again, and the tumour grows. Then to start again on the drug.

One of its side-effects, so my urologist tells me, is that concentration becomes difficult. Then, it becomes easier not even to try.

So I must get my story told before the fog descends. To sort things out. Understanding our own story can be difficult. But understanding it without interrupting it is more difficult still.

To understand what? That my life has been a most fortunate one. Yes, certainly. But fortunate in unusual ways, which makes the race worth entering.

I've just laid aside Zweig's novel, *The Post Office Girl*, discovered, unpublished, in his papers after his death, in 1942; two years after I was born. A novel that is about the effects of war and poverty.

Perhaps you may think it will tell you quite a lot about the events I shall relate, which in turn may explain why I so value that novel. Cultured, Austrian and Jewish, Zweig's time was his own, and very different to mine; but yet they are conjoined. Begun in Central Europe, it ended at the time of the Second World War, as his world was swept away. Both losses he anticipated, his world and his life – by suicide.

So, I know when my time began, but I don't know where. And I don't know with whom. I never knew my mother, nor my father.

I still have my time though, life continues. Of those often quoted "three score years and ten, (of which) twenty will not come again", none of my three score and ten will do so. And so there is comfort. It's not finished. But how different that line of Housman's seems now to when I first met it as a boy.

Speaking of comfort, how strange are those quiet, civilised, six monthly, conversations with the urologist. Like being in a confessional – I imagine.

Him weighing the best possibilities. Checking the odds. Not hurrying, as mortality itself is considered, and re-considered. How he gift-wraps optimism!

Happily, also, obligations and duties, pleasures and enthusiasms continue. So, the parcel of books arrives every three months from the reviews editor, always surprising even before I open it. Always expecting it, I still had forgotten that it would arrive. The reviews are for an arts' journal which has a particular interest in Education; whose title, *The Late Edition*, has only recently begun to amuse me by its appropriateness.

So, for many years now there has been another, recurring, series of little races, to meet copy deadlines. Becoming easier once I've made the selections.

I've just sent off the latest batch. Strange how the process of exchanging reviews for books, seems not even to have begun before the pieces are in the post. Then, suddenly and immediately, it's over; finished.

Because so many books come from which I have to select, I have been able to live by Matthew Arnold's advice: "Say nothing if you can't praise. And if you praise, explain!"

So, the pleasure has been to write about books I admire, in a conversation with an unseen reader. For, because I've been having these conversations for so long, the editor sometimes passes me letters from readers, or even authors, who write back. Always unexpectedly: a kind of review of a review. That, and the discipline which writing about a book, quickly in admiration, imposes, is why I've carried on doing it for so long. And of course I get to keep the books – even the ones I can't find space to do a review for.

Of the hundreds I've sent to the magazine over the years, I've done none with greater urgency, or pleasure, than that of Piero Scanziani's *The Adventure of Man*.

If there's something I hate, it's for what I've sent in to be altered – even a word. Luckily it only happened once in all the twenty six years so far. And during all that time, I've worked with three different review editors.

I made a promise to myself that if it happens again I'll pack it in.

Chapter 1

To be precise then, I have no knowledge of where and with whom my time began. Nor how this absence of knowledge came about.

My earliest memories are of warm days deep in the countryside of southern England. That was my territory, and has been internally ever since. My first store of memories: from the cocoon of a village in the Saxon Weald.

It would be more accurate to say that I was raised in two villages. Two villages at once. And perhaps it is that which, along with the mists that swirled around my origins, resulted in my not ever being able to identify with the idea of coming from anywhere in particular. For good, or ill, I never had a tribe – and gradually I came not to desire one.

But the idea of needing permission to stay, well that came to me early; and gradually I came to embrace it even. Paradoxically, it led to a love of being in a particular place – if it was congenial. To being more than willing to settle down where I was; of being aware of the charms of the present, and present companions rather than peering into the past. Of course this may easily become a fault, and I am still seldom without a sense of guilt.

So it is with these thoughts that I recall my earliest time; and I will explain about the two villages very soon.

For now, I can say only that there was a gap before I met those people whom I came to think of as my mother and father. An empty place. And I'm not even sure how long the gap was.

My first, earlier, village was big and deep in the country of hops and cherries. From the earliest time I can remember I was surrounded by hop gardens and orchards.

It was normal, then, for a local farmer to give a box of apples to my small village school. And old men would often offer me an apple from the pockets of their large coats as we walked past each other. And I never refused them.

The village had a long, broad, main street which seemed to contain many shops. At its centre was Freemans' the corn merchants. And there was a fine Norman church at the head of this High Street, its graveyard neatly presented to all the bustle or calm that was before it, like a tablecloth. At an early age, I had the habit of very carefully examining the headstones, pleased when I discovered long lives lived.

From all of this the road turned away abruptly almost at a right-angle and made off, quickly out of sight, to the county town of Westerford. Nine miles, and now sixty years away – but only half an hour by bus.

At the other end of the High Street, and ten minutes walk away, there was the railway station; on the main line to London. It had a long, wide, approach road; almost an avenue, as befitted the start of a journey to the capital. In those years just after the war.

In between, there were two grocers (with a third just away from this main street), a butcher's, three drapers, Mrs. Burden's seed shop, a saddler's, two newsagents, a greengrocer's, a bicycle shop, a chemist's, a hardware store – and of course the Post Office.

There were two blacksmiths, one by the High Street, and the main one a little away from it. Nor is that the full list, for there was also a baker's, and a fishmonger's shop, round the corner by the church. Not to mention two cafés and a number of pubs.

Just outside the village there was a Creamery. Everybody called the milk-processing plant by that now quaint-sounding name.

My simplest days began about two thirds of a mile from the High Street. In a white lap-board cottage where we lived. There was a large orchard, alongside a brook where I fished for sticklebacks with a jam jar. At the front of the cottage was a single apple tree. Its fruit was small, green and hard, but very sweet. And I believe it had the common name of "Irish Peach". I've never found that sort of apple since.

High up, under the eaves of the cottage, swallows and swifts nested every year; it was natural to note their arrival in the Spring and their departure in the Autumn. Baths were every Friday night in a tin bath sometimes in front of the fire.

The journey to the High Street is imprinted on my memory, for in every season it was my task to run shopping errands. Particularly to the Post Office to buy stamps for my mother, or to post letters. My mother seemed to write a great many letters.

First I passed the main blacksmith's at the end of our road. Then I could cross the road and follow it around the new council estate: later on passing a row of small, terraced, Victorian 'villas'; their front doors nestling warm under red sun-awnings in the summer. I recognized Tranströmer's "sun-heated doorsteps" when I met them again later. And so into the High Street by the butcher's on the corner.

Or I could turn right at the blacksmith's, where I would always stop to watch the work, the heat and the bouncing noise, on past the school, through the new recreation ground and village green, before joining the High Street halfway along by walking through the backyard of "The Ploughman"; or I could go across and around the green, joining the High Street past the church.

If I turned left at the blacksmith's, the road quickly passed George Meadow's farm; and then on to the always immaculate cricket field bounded by one of his hop-gardens. George was a particular friend of my father's.

Turning right out of the cottage took me to Upton's farm up the hill, where I sometimes went with my father to feed the pigs – with apples. Further up was Tatlebury Corner. Lonely.

There were many horses in the fields around the village. We had a horse called Kitty, and one of my jobs was to take her to graze the verges. She was brown and large, placid and gentle. She helped me always to take care when walking behind a horse. If my job was to take her to graze, hers was to pull the trap. Though I don't remember her doing that so very often, I can still feel, perched high up on the seats alongside my father, the hard iron-shod wheels on the road. Becoming a part of me.

Mostly the roads around us were free of motor vehicles; just a few cars and vans was all there were, with the occasional tractor and steamroller. Relatively though, there always seemed a lot of steamrollers – or perhaps it was just that their noisy and slow-moving presence stays in the memory.

Kitty and I visited the blacksmith sometimes for her to have a shoe replaced. I thought the red hot nails and shoes must hurt her, but of course they didn't. They smelt as if they should though, as the iron burned into her hooves.

My father was quite old even early on; and early on I worried about him. He must have been sixty at that time. Also in the house was my mother and my sister Eunice, whom I very slowly came to realize was not my sister. I knew it for sure because when birthday cards arrived for her, her surname on the envelopes was different to mine; just as my surname was different to the rest of the family's.

The details of all this, which appear so complicated and unusual now, were unimportant at the time. The grass verges were wide, green, and thick with milkmaids. In the summer the baked hard dirt-paths were studded with the small red and blue flowers which we called "birds' eyes". The brook was full of sticklebacks. The hedges were high and the ditches deep, full of wild roses and primroses. And if violets "smoked blue along the pack way in a haze", there were also white ones in the ditches – something that Sackville-West does not mention.

The world outside the cottage was a warm and perfumed front parlour. I went where I wished, and the adults I met around the village were friendly and welcoming – and I seemed to know them all.

I was a ragamuffin, a tatterdemalion in a world full of treasure, often seeing and feeling "the sun/smooth its hand across the corn". I asked local farmers if I could cut their willow branches for a bow, and begged the greengrocer to give me the paper wrappers from oranges. These crinkled and sparkled with brightly coloured images. And they had the scent and the magic of foreign places and names.

I collected everything then. Coins, because my father had served as a saddler in a horse artillery regiment in the British army in India. Some of them were very thick, with holes in the middle.

And foreign stamps, birds' eggs and car numbers. Bus numbers too. Westerford and District Bus Company numbers were to me what the numbers of trains were to Dvořák. How could he know of the sinister connotations that would become attached to trains in the twentieth century? How could I?

The afternoon sun, of summer, gleaned and gleamed on the hot shuddering mudguards of the hugely green double-decker as it grew around the corner of the High Street. Right in front of the graveyard, engine cover shaking. Eased round the tight corner by the driver, struggling over the steering wheel to where I was waiting in my jerkin; with a small, red, warm, soft-backed notebook, pencil poised. Taking notes on the world.

Every half hour during the day, it drew up outside "The Ploughman" where its passengers got off. Then it would drive a little further along the street, reverse alongside the butcher's, wait for ten minutes outside "Hubbles", the drapers, before setting off again to Westerford. First though the driver and conductor rested, chatting and smoking on the seats at the back by the open platform.

On that Summer afternoon it was a bus that had grown immense and slowly around the corner of the street. And not the muzzle of the gun-turret of a tank – appearing huge and shocking and rattling, and always without warning.

A little time before, tanks would have been easing around the corners of a myriad streets in Central Europe. Probably just as the bus was waiting outside “Hubbles”.

Later too. Naturally.

JÓZSEF, Attila *The Iron-Blue Vault : selected poems* : translated by Zsuzsanna Ozsvath and Frederick Turner. Bloodaxe, 1999, pp.160, £8.95. 1 85224 503 4

PETRI, Geörgy *Eternal Monday: new and selected poems* : translated by Clive Wilmer and George Gomori. Bloodaxe, 1999, pp.95, £7.95, 85224 504 2

Two books of poems. Two Hungarian poets. One died in 1937, the other is still writing. Lyric poets, telling of love and death. Both challenged totalitarian civil authorities, and suffered the psychological and social consequences. Both books are urgently relevant.

The persona in György Petrie's more recent poems is detached, harsh and ironic: 'Here I am, and the whole thing's beyond me, / The epoch expired like a monstrous predator. / My favourite toy's been snatched' (p. 90). The Communist regime may have collapsed, but his earlier declaration resounds: 'I do not forgive anyone'. Consequently he survives.

In pre-Communist Hungary Attila József could not be detached enough to survive. Aged 32 years, he laid his head on a railway line; an event discovered and broadcast by the village idiot.

József, it seems, was propelled to forgive – assuming others' guilt as his own. His father deserted his family; which was dispersed, and twice re-constituted through the efforts of his mother. Still, tragically, she was yet broken by an un-negotiable poverty before dying of cancer. The young József had been withdrawn from school to help his desperate mother, who ill-treated him by whippings. As a result of this early damage, further misfortune dogged him. Certainly that is what the poetry records: 'Each moment heaps on me those unhappy /years that destroyed my destiny, my hope' (p. 124).

During a self-devouring life, threatened by inner darkness and terror, searching for a love that would be denied him, Attila József produced a unique poetry. Two essays by the translators, printed at the front of the book, provide valuable biographical details, and a clear analysis of the philosophical system inherent in the poems. No short review can summarize the effects and felicities of these poems, and the pain they contain. Nor could a reader be prepared for the implications of the question: 'Ah, what strange stuff is that of which I'm made, / but that your glance can sculpt me into shape?' Addressed to 'Judit', it earlier or later might easily have been asked of 'Marta', 'Edit', – or 'Flora'.

And Petri? 'Well, 'Death will come suddenly to a life ridden / into the ground. Decisions, achievements, successes / could ripen inside it. But they won't' (p.77). And meanwhile? 'All that can save us now, all that can save, / is absolute distrust' (p.71).

Both poets are awkward customers. Both are 'misled neither by power nor orthodoxy' (Ozsvath of József) ; which is why they should be introduced to mature readers in the secondary school. Many of them may respond to the educative nature of these two books: intellectually, morally, emotionally, politically, socially, and individually; and recognize the beauty they contain.

William Holden

Chapter 2

One Christmas when I was nine I was given a bicycle. It was quite an old one, but solid and well maintained, smelling sweetly of light oil, from Mr Harding's bicycle shop in the High Street. And so I was released on to the roads, and into the lanes, between our village and the others all around.

And when I ventured further afield, and even to the sea from the summer that followed, it was to journey into what upon reflection now seems an astonishingly trusting time. When it was quite usual for me to knock on the front door on a hot afternoon and ask for a drink of water. And to be given it with a smile and without question.

Cheek? Probably. But the question and the response was a part of something more. Something significant.

Sometimes on the tarmac near the village that I now began to explore, I met a grocer's van, or the choir mistress's Austin 7, all of us struggling up a hill - I had a choir mistress early in life, though I could not sing at all well. Sometimes I met the butcher's bicycle delivering to scattered houses outside the village.

Up past Upton's farm I went, tyres whirring on the road, and on to Tatlebury Corner.

This was a large triangle of grass; in my memory often in a sea of dog daisies, its almost buried signpost almost giving directions; only pointing two ways, instead of three. As if it was assumed, by the great authority that governed signposts, that the traveller would know already where he had been. To me at nine that seemed fair enough.

Nearby, but away from the signpost, and out of sight from it, were two houses. One was a large Tudor Wealden farmhouse, with the usual pond in the front garden. Soon, but not yet, I would meet the two sons of the family that lived there; one a little older than me, the other a little younger, when I started school in my second village. When I met them, their mother had just died. I didn't know why, and I understood that neither did they.

Just before that house, as I approached Tatlebury, on the opposite side of the road, was another smaller house behind a tall hedge. In the hedge was a door. Not a mounted door. Just an old door filling a gap in the hedge, which was not uncommon then.

I knew the young woman who lived there, though only slightly. I knew that her husband was away overseas, in Kenya. At that age I was a silent participant on the edge of many conversations. Sometimes she said hello to me in a shop in the village. Sometimes I saw her in her garden, reading.

One day, in the summer after I had received the bicycle, as I was passing, she called out and invited me into the garden for lemonade. She had made it herself. Smiling, she laid down a basket of cut flowers: sweet peas and roses. As she walked towards me, warm sunlight glanced off her. It fell over her arms and shoulders, settling on her hair.

As we sat, with me sipping her lemonade, I was too shy to offer much conversation, other than thanking her for the drink - which tasted like the morning.

Looking up, I saw a dark figure, alone on the very edge of the garden beyond the flower beds. I thought it was a man. She must have noticed, as I looked up.

"He protects my beans", she said. "Do you like him? And then I realized that I was looking at a scarecrow. A very life-like scarecrow.

Before thinking much, I replied "He looks lonely".

And at this she laughed a light gentle laugh.

“Well he has me for company”, she said, filling our glasses again to the top with lemonade.

A few months before, I had set out to pick primroses for my mother. The best place for primroses, I knew, was Tatlebury Corner, where in the Spring there were banks of them. I found them that morning, shining in the sun - everywhere.

When I began to gather the flowers, taking care to make the stems as long as possible, the sun was out - bright and warm. As I bent over the many bright plants, however, suddenly everywhere around became very much darker. And cold. As if a shadow had passed over the sun; and as if a presence noticed what I was doing. And didn’t like it.

The place was green and growing, but I knew it always felt lonely; full of silent, slumbering energies. As the sun lost its warmth, I felt all around me a threatening disapproval. Yet I picked on, and as the sun came out, everything was flooded with warmth again; although the dark towering elms, and the shining horse chestnut trees still glowered down a warning. Up above, their many leaves were talking among themselves, earnestly, whispering. And even the restored warmth of the sun itself seemed forbidding.

Then, and ever since in my memory, that place was simultaneously full of light, and dark shadows. On summer mornings it contained an obvious darkness; on winter afternoons a lighter glowing promise. I wouldn’t have dared to go there after dusk.

Nor did I go there with anyone else. Never did I ever see any one else there.

Nor do I remember anyone ever talking to me about Tatlebury Corner, or even referring to it. Of course, someone must have, or I should not have known its name; there was certainly no sign to announce it.

Also, someone else must have been there before me. If for no other reason that the signpost had been turned around. This, to add to the joke I’ve already mentioned, of it only offering two possibilities, when as I have said there were three narrow roads leading away into their first corners of hazel hedges, honeysuckle, wild roses, and the bread and cheese leaves of hawthorns.

That morning, it was as if I simply wasn't intended to be there, or at best not intended to stay. I was an intruder in that place of lonely and intense silence; an interloper among the flowers.

And so, although there were more primroses than I could count, large and plentiful in the sun beside their long, dark, green leaves, I left with my basket very far from full. Taking only what I felt I was allowed to; banished by scarcely audible voices all around and above. Singing, but warning.

I left behind the shiny surfaces of the departing narrow roads, the pealing of silent bells, the dark elm trees, the brighter horse chestnut plumes, and the half-buried, ironical, signpost. To me back then, the place was obviously and invisibly peopled.

So, this was part of my world. A ragamuffin's world. Part of the winter days when the clay of the Weald was waterlogged and clinging, and the river on the other side of the village beyond the church was sometimes in full and threatening flood. Or the clay was frozen into concrete.

A world when in summer that same clay was baked just as rock-hard by a fierce sun, with cracks and fissures that you could put your foot in. "When June in festive garb/ pushed jasmine under our windows".

This June world included the cycle of the annual visits of horse-drawn gypsy caravans, which would pass our cottage every year to camp opposite Upton's farm. They too were part of the mysterious associations of histories and landscape. The smoke of their fires drifted down the road in the light evenings; strange fires, but not unexpected.

And in the Spring I dreamed of birds' eggs, because a friend whose father was a farm labourer in yet another part of the village, showed me his collection. Neatly, quietly, softly, stored among cotton wool, in a drawer of a chest of drawers.

He lived with his mother and father in a cottage which was adrift in a sea of tall grass whenever I visited. There was no road that led up to it.

He was wonderful at climbing trees, and could reach the nests of rooks high up in the elms. I wish I could say that we decided just to look at them and to make notes of where the nests of chaffinches, great-tits, hedge sparrows, and the song thrushes were - but it wouldn't be true.

Equally expected, yet surprising, was the sudden appearance of the Sikh travelling salesman, richly be-turbaned, knocking on our front door with his leather suitcase full of coloured silks. He was a serious man, and opened his case with gravitas. Which was no less than its contents deserved.

Nor was the young lady from Tanganyika, tall and elegant in robes of greens, oranges and reds at all unexpected either, when she was introduced at our school as a special visitor.

As I have said, part of my world, too, was staring into the blacksmith's furnace for hours, the steamrollers announcing their rumbling arrival remarkably frequently, and enforced attendance at Sunday School, church, and the choir.

The demands made upon me then were few, although that I should wash my face was one of them. If I didn't, it was washed for me - with vigour.

They were singing, urchin, days. Discarded cigarette packets thrown into the gutter, golden blue and white, were treasure to be collected. As were butt ends, picked up, re-rolled, and un-hygienically, furtively, smoked with companions.

School was composed of other days spent in the company of many of the same children whom I met frequently and variously around and outside the village. They were from finer and humbler homes than mine, often from farms around the village. Every day, just five minutes before everyone else finished school for the day, these farmers' children boarded a silver coach which delivered them to their widely scattered doors. That seemed to me a rare privilege. And the coach really was silver.

School was interesting or not. Pleasurable and frightening, comforting and threatening as events dictated. I enjoyed playtimes best.

At school I heard about Norse legends and myths; of how thunder was really Odin throwing I forget what down the stairs. About the Greeks and the Trojans. About King Arthur and the Knights of the Round Table. About the competition between Genoa and Venice. Of Vasco da Gama. Of Marco Polo and the Great Khan; of people coming from the East and going to the East. Of Tartar battles and Mogul emperors; of monsters and grotesque figures.

With the scented combs of the horse-chestnut trees outside, sprinkling wind-assisted shadows on to the walls of the classroom, school was a place that was full of stories. I learned of Saladin. Of the revenge of Echo, and of the sad narcissus flower; of what might have been had not Orpheus looked behind him. I learned that Orpheus was a fabulous musician, and I heard about the British Museum. And that just down the road Caxton had invented his printing press - or that's what I understood.

Warm afternoons at school would often smell of plasticine, especially it seemed when the room was flooded with sunlight. The glass partition that separated two classrooms would then have been pushed back, re-inventing our classroom for painting, modelling, or weaving lessons. We made and used simple looms. And wicker baskets too; learning how to first carefully soak the canes.

On Thursday nights, the travelling cinema would re-invent the village hall. At seven o'clock, when it was sometimes dark and sometimes not, the programme of films each week would include comedies, westerns and horror films. Peter Cushing's Dracula and Graham Green's

Brighton Rock squeezed together. Laurel and Hardy, Old Mother Riley, and Charlie Chaplin.

Sometimes, on the solitary walk home in winter, with the memory of some film still immediate, between tall hedges and in the moonlight, my step would quicken. Imagining "what rustled in the fern? I felt my flesh divide". Then I ran hard, pursued by images of Transylvania.

LATHAM, John, *All Clear*. Peterloo, 1990, pp.63, £5. 95. 1 871471

Reviewing is sharing, and so I recommend this third, cream-paged, Peterloo collection from John Latham. These poems are sometimes funny and they often hurt, for they describe a mutuality of love and pain. They sing as they weep of the characters and places of wartime childhood; of memories of parents and early home; of parental reflection upon life with children; of suffering and confusion in ageing and illness; and of the loss of love in death. Celebrating our love for those from life already lived, they describe, in sadness, the hopelessness of "retrieving" that life as it was. For "... its integrity / depends on never being found, for everything we see or touch, we alter". Humour is part of the regret, as when a child is "sent to bed for telling God / not to bless (his) / brother any more".

Characteristically quiet in tone, the poems work precise effects. So, a child displays a "tongue-extended care", "an un-used summer full of song" leaks from a dying bird, and a father describes in the night how his daughter's "shrill voice scissors me awake".

Surely young adults should be introduced to this civilised reflective poetry of human sympathies? For it will serve them, as it does us, as a whetstone. By the way, there's a poem called just that on page 50 - not to be missed.

William Holden

Chapter 3

One September I had a new teacher, and suddenly everything that happened in the classroom became as fascinating to me as what was going on outside it.

I learned later that this teacher only stayed a year, which was my last year in the school. He was tall, upright; and had a small moustache; and a black and white checked tweed jacket. He was in his early thirties, with black hair already flecked with grey. Quietly spoken, he smiled a lot; in fact he was not at all like the other teachers. And this was simply because he seemed to be able to smile and talk at the same time. I never heard him shout.

When many years had passed, I learned that he was also a novelist. The person who told me this went on to say that "So, he wasn't a real teacher then!". When he left, he went with his young family to Australia, and became well known there and here in Britain too. I still have several of his books.

But one morning, in the summer towards the end of the school year, Mr Parker wasn't in school. Rather, he was with the headmaster preparing the cricket field for the school sports' day, which was to be held that afternoon.

The headmaster's wife took the class that morning. Her lessons were usually about Art and Craft, or Hygiene. That morning the first lesson was Mathematics – as usual, and we did work that Mr Parker had left for us; and after play, 'Dental Hygiene'. Early in the morning there was already a large shiny poster illustrating teeth, pinned to the blackboard, arresting us as we entered the room. *Only a little menacing*, I thought.

Lunch came early that day. As the dinner ladies unscrewed the large steel canisters containing the food delivered to the school on a lorry, no smooth, polished, suet-pudding appeared to blight my anticipation of a warm afternoon on the cricket field where the races would be held. So I looked forward to the afternoon with a light heart.

Our class left for the field a little before the rest of the school. Walking in pairs past the forge and George Meadow's farm. The carefully cut grass of the field soon lay before us, under the hot sun of early afternoon, green and mown, scented and inviting. Mr Parker and the headmaster had erected a small marquee during the morning, next to the glaringly white low wooden cricket pavilion which I already knew so well.

Clear white lines had been marked out where the races were to be run, and piles of green, yellow, red and blue team bands had been placed at the end of each track. Next to these were piles of hoops; and also sacks for the obstacle races. And to one side there were rows of chairs, three deep, facing the lines; each chair with a programme on it. These were where the spectators, most of whom were the children, would soon be seated. There would of course be some parents – but very few in those days.

In the middle of the field, to one side, was a blackboard, and two large tables on which had been placed a jug of water and drinking glasses. Here the scorers would sit.

At two o'clock, all the children and the teachers were in position. The rest of the school had arrived. Just a few visitors from the village were in the seats put out for them.

The headmaster, Mr Stewart, was in charge of the scorers, and he started each race; and now he was making an announcement through a large speaking funnel. The blackboard was divided into four columns, Green, Yellow, Red and Blue.

Mr Parker was in charge of the finishing line. He held one end of the tape, and a member of our class held the other.

Near him waited three children, whose job it was to run to the scorers' table about fifteen yards away, with the names of those children finishing first, second and third in each race.

At two-thirty, everything was in full swing. I had already taken part in the 60 yard sprint and come second, and also in the obstacle race which our team, the Greens, had won.

I felt a part of the day as I had handed the baton to Janice, who then set out crawling under the net before climbing through a hoop, bouncing a tennis ball ten times, and finally jumping the last thirty yards in a sack, as I had done just before. The sack was very clean, and had that special smell that only sacks in the country and which had been left out in the sun can have.

After I had watched Allen taking Janice's ticket to the scorers' table, I went to the cricket pavilion to the lavatory.

On the way back I passed the open flap of the tea-tent, and looked in. Then I went in, attracted by the warm canvas-lit world inside, where the sun stirred together the scents of the newly mown grass and the light brown canvas of the newly erected marquee.

I laid down on the grass, peering out under the bottom canvas flap at the scene before me. Although I had not noticed it, the red light of the tea urn glowed on the table a little to my right, next to rows of white cups and saucers.

The hot sun beat down on the roof and walls of the tent; and all along its bottom a sharp white beam of light forced itself through from outside.

The infants' egg and spoon race was in progress, and the participants were picking up the tennis balls that had fallen off their table spoons carried out in front of them. For a little while then, they ran with a finger on the ball, before lifting it again – to keep to the rules. Usually the ball soon fell off and it had to be retrieved, whereupon the illicit steadying of the ball continued for a little while again. Periodically they lifted their finger from the ball to abide by the rules again – of course.

In the distance tall elm trees stood imposing in the strong sunshine, and behind them the lighter tunnels of the hop garden stood straight in their green lines behind the hedge. The sun shone down upon the white lines of the tracks, on the scorers' table, and on the rows of children and visitors. As I lay there with my chin on my hands I saw my teacher at the finishing line, and saw how the sun glinted upon the headmaster's silver shirt-bracelets And so I spied upon the afternoon, in secret and separate.

Then behind me I heard a scraping sound and a loud crack. Looking back I saw that the tea-urn had fallen from the security of the table, on to the grass. It lay there, fast emptying of water, and I realized that I must have dislodged it by knocking one of the legs of the table. Immediately the scene outside fled from view.

But almost immediately, I saw that the day outside the tent was continuing, and so I quickly moved to join it. Once outside the tent walking slowly to where my class were sitting.

Allen saw me and came up, "Hello Will", he said. "Mr Parker told me to ask you if you would take over from Janet as a runner for the scoring."

I was glad to have a job to take my mind off the tea-urn. Glad to have something to do. The races continued, and I set about the task of taking the names to the scorers' table with extra concentration. At the table, the headmaster's wife sat taking the slips of paper with their names and colours; and occasionally she altered the scores on the blackboard.

I could see the headmaster at the starting line, and how his steel shirt-bands flashed in the sun. Gradually the tea-urn began to be buried in the busyness of the afternoon. I thought, *No one is paying it any attention after all. It really is not of any importance.* And so things continued, uninterrupted by anyone else's knowledge of the tea-urn lying on its side, quite empty.

Soon the tree-legged race would start, and Allen and I were in it. While we were preparing for the race, I glanced up and saw Mrs Fennell, who was in charge of the refreshments, deep in conversation with the headmaster's wife. They were standing together by the scorers' table.

I returned to concentrating upon us tying Allen's left leg to my right one, with the long white strip of cloth we had been given. As I did so I invented new subjects of conversation with my friend, to drive away what I had just seen.

On the starting line, Janice and Janet were to our right, and Brian and Peter on our left. Brian was the headmaster's son. The race was going well for us; we were neck and neck with Janice and Janet. Then we began to pull away. Then the girls fell, and I knew the race was won.

Except, then, a thought entered my head, because of the tea-urn. *If the two girls were not to win, then I didn't want to either. Then, perhaps, if we didn't win, retribution for the empty tea-urn would not after all arrive.* I understood about retribution, and believed in it completely.

And so, as a result of this reasoning, I stopped. Simply stopped. The peculiar three-legged rhythm was upset, and Allen and I tumbled to the ground, rather like the tea-urn, just short of the finishing line. Peter and Brian passed us and won.

A little later, we walked passed Mr Parker. "Bad luck!" he said, "but at least you were third".

As my teacher spoke, the headmaster was also talking through his loud hailer. He was making an announcement. I heard him say that he was sorry.

"Ladies and gentlemen, and children, we hope that you will be patient. There has been a slight delay with the refreshments. We will arrange for tea and some cake, and of course some squash, to be brought to you shortly. Here are the scores in the competition so far."

So, I thought, with relief, *None of it mattered. The tea would be coming, and the sun was still shining. The tea-urn was already heating up.*

But then, I knew that although the headmaster was a kindly man, he did like things to run smoothly. And ... his wife had disappeared from the scorers' table.

Next morning soon after our Mathematics lesson had begun, the whole of our class were listening to the headmaster in our classroom. Of course Mr Parker was there.

Mr Stewart wanted to talk about the tea-urn. I heard him say,

"It is clear that a tea-urn cannot just fall off a table. So, I want you to fold your arms, sit very still, and listen". I obeyed. To placate fate.

"Mrs Fennell saw a boy coming out of the refeshment tent just before the urn was discovered on the ground. And I want that boy to think very carefully, and to come to see me at playtime".

My mind began to race away, and my head buzzed. But I thought,

No, it was an accident, I have nothing to admit to. If I went it would be an admission that I did it purposely. So, I wouldn't go.

"So", our teacher said, when the headmaster had left the room, "now I want to do some Mathematics with you".

I felt cheered.

It seemed, I reasoned, *that Mr Parker thought that the tea-urn was not so important too.*

During playtime I played football with a tennis ball, on the field, with Allen and Peter and the rest of the boys in my class. After play, it was a writing lesson, and Allen and I had been asked to plan some work together. A short while after the lesson had begun, with pairs and groups of children working around the room, Mr Parker called me to his desk.

"Will you go to see Mr Stewart please William?"

Inside, I was in turmoil now, but my course was set. And without saying anything, I immediately left the room.

The headmaster's office was bare, and painted cream.

It contained only a desk, and because it was at the front of the school the windows were too high to make curtains a practical matter. The windows had to be opened with a pole. It was the same with some of the windows in our classroom. The desk was at the end of the room, with a small mat in front of it.

As I went in, the headmaster took off his glasses, and looked up from where he sat behind his desk.

"Ah, William", he said. He was a short, serious-looking man. And he looked particularly serious that morning.

"I want to talk to you about this business of the tea-urn."

The expanding arm-bands glinted still, on his freshly laundered shirt.

"I wondered if you had anything to tell me?"

No sir!" was my shameful reply.

"For instance", he continued, "Did you go near the refreshment tent before you ran in the three-legged race?"

"Yes sir".

Mr Stewart's eyes brightened and narrowed, and he leant forward with his weight on his elbows.

"I went to the lavatory".

This was true, and I wanted to be truthful.

"Did you see anyone else near the tent as you went past it?"

"No", again truthfully.

"Did you go into the tent?"

Ah! I thought.

"No, sir".

"Did you look in?"

"No, sir"

Mr Stewart looked hard at me. "You didn't go into the tent where the tea-urn was?"

"No, sir".

The man leant back and sighed. Then, "Alright, you can go back to your classroom".

When I got back, everyone else looked up, as I went straight to my place.

"What did he say?", whispered Allen.

"Not much, he asked me if I saw anyone near the tent".

"What did you say?"

"No".

"What do you think's going to happen?", he asked.

"Don't know", was all I said. And the rest of the morning blurred away.

At half-past one, Mr Parker was reading to us from Kenneth Grahame's *Wind in the Willows*. This was before an art lesson.

The desks were pushed into pairs facing each other, so four of us would eventually face each other in a square. Already the desks were covered with newspapers, and in the centre of each square were four pallets, a number of as yet empty jam jars, and four large paintbrushes.

At the front of the classroom, on two tables, were boxes of powder paints, red, magenta and green, blue and yellow, filling the room with their bitter odour. Also on one of the tables at the front, were piles of large sheets of plain, grey, sugar paper, carefully cut to the same size. One for each of us. And on the floor at the front of the room stood three buckets of water.

For now though, all our heads were turned towards Mr Parker as he read, when there was a knock on the door, and the headmaster and his wife came into the room.

"Excuse me Mr Parker," said the headmaster, "I wonder if we might interrupt you and have a word with the class".

I knew that the speaker was not a bully. Rather, fair – but capable of becoming angry.

There was a pounding in my head.

It was clear that this matter was not going to be left as it was, I thought. *It's serious!*

"Everyone sit up and fold your arms", commanded the headmaster.

I folded my arms very tight, and looked over the heads of Janet and Janice seated in front of us, at Mr Stewart. In his shirt sleeves, his face flushed. The face of his wife was also red, redder even than usual.

"I want to speak to you again children about the incident that took place during the sports' afternoon yesterday. And to ask you all again if there is anyone here who knows anything at all about what happened?"

I thought, *I should put up my hand now, and say that I know about it. That it had been an accident. But, then … there was the very big difficulty of what I'd said in his room that morning. But it didn't matter. They could never find out. No-one else could get the blame. How could they? Only I knew I had knocked over the tea-urn. But I didn't mean to. I didn't even know it was there. I mean I hadn't seen it. It was an accident. I was safe, and so was everyone else.*

The headmaster's wife's face seemed to have become even redder, and her bosom was moving regularly. The whole class was still, and so was Mr Parker. The paint brushes were still too, bunched together.

I stared down at the print of the newspaper spread over the desks, and at the empty jam jars, to fight back tears.

"I will ask you once again", I heard Mr Stewart say, "to think about yesterday very carefully".

I looked at the headmaster's wife. Our eyes met, and I looked away quickly. Back to the print of the newspapers in front of me on the desk.

When I looked up again, I was aware that something must have happened.

Something was wrong. But what?

Everyone was looking at Roy. And at me too. *But why were they looking at Roy?*

"What did you say?" I heard the headmaster's wife shout. And I realized that she was speaking to Roy.

"It was me!", I heard him saying. "I did it. It was an accident".

All the colours of the room drained away.

"How dare you!", shouted, the woman. "Don't you realize the trouble you've caused by not saying so before?"

"We thought it was William Holden! How do you think he felt? And all because of you!"

Now, I knew why everyone was looking at me, but I couldn't see them. Allen put his hand on my arm. And Roy left the room with Mr Stewart and his wife.

Mr Parker began a new chapter of *The Wind in the Willows*. He read …

> "It was a bright morning in the early part of summer…".

But I couldn't hear him.

ROPER, Mark. *Catching the Light.* Peterloo. 1997, pp.66, £7.95. 1 871471 656

Well constructed, traditional in their forms, these poems have qualities that always surprise; whether in their subjects, or by an enchanting lyricism.

Some are fantastical; grimly ironic about the absurdities and destructiveness of our modernity. We find an angel in a field, Ireland overcome by a new Ice Age, and Pilate discovering the marketing opportunities of his decision. There are grim poems that record children needing to "survive" childhood. And the felicity of the collection's title is differently manifest as it shines through a very substantial number of powerful, carefully crafted, nature poems. So, in 'November' "Butter of leaves at its feet, the lime stands / astonished, holding nothing up to nothing." 'What the Deer Said' is "What makes me tremble so? / The world's infinite sweetness, / sweetness with fear ripened."

Other fine examples include 'Halcyon', 'Svala, Svala', and 'Snipe'.

As if to represent this section of the book particularly, the title poem is explicit about the ways in which writing can seem similar to painting: "In a world of light we are creatures of distinction / lost and found / as we speak".

The collection easily achieves the 'must own' category; as easily for mature readers in the secondary school as for us.

William Holden

Chapter 4

Sometime before the sports' afternoon, another day had come and the school was closed. Everywhere under the falling, long, combs of the horse chestnut trees was quiet. Feeling deserted.

But with a few other companions I still had to go to school; to the board room, just for the morning that Spring. When we were there, we filled in a lot of shiny papers.

In the board room there was a large glass-fronted bookcase; and behind the glass were soft, thin, soft-backed books with bright, differently coloured, zig-zagged covers. Blue, Vermilion, and Turquoise. These were books of music, and when Mr Stewart opened each one of them to play the piano in assembly, he did so in an especially deliberate, very careful, way. As if the act of opening the book would release what was inside. A kind of physical overture.

Then we had the rest of the day off. Later a letter would come, and what it said seemed to please my mother.

I was about to leave the school, and my mother had to select from a list of secondary schools which arrived. As she did this, she had to cross out 'Parent' where the letter asked: 'Parent' or 'Guardian'?

As a result of that letter, my mother and I caught the bus from outside 'Hubbards' in the High Street one morning. Aunty Evelyn came too. That my mother should be with me on the bus was very unusual, for I don't remember her leaving the house much.

We were to visit a school in another village for an interview. I had seen it many times from the Weald, high up on the escarpment. I had passed along the side of it in the years before also; on the way to Westerford to Saturday morning pictures; or to Westerford market to buy a box of chicks with my father. That was one of my earliest memories.

The Romans had populated the village when they arrived, and it faced south. Towards where they had set out. They planted vineyards to remind them of home – perhaps to comfort them.

The main school building stretched along the top of the sandstone ridge; in the centre of the village. Redbrick, facing the south, mellow and handsome, its front covered with Virginia Creeper which glowed deep crimson in the Autumn sun. At the building's centre was the clock tower, looking out over the Weald below, and France somewhere. Someone had told me you could see the sea from the top of the clock tower.

The green double-decker took us to our appointment at 11.30, and we all sat downstairs at the back near the door.

The day was very warm as we made our way that morning, through the wide gates of the school. Along a broad drive with the school chapel on our left, across a quadrangle and into the main building.

The entrance was through a small door to the side, and soon a long cool corridor brought us to the bursar's office where we were met with smiles by a small grey haired lady with a bun. She was very friendly, and I was glad I had on my Sunday clothes which I usually wore only for church.

She took us even further along and deep into the cool corridor, past a large hall next to a flight of stairs, and through another door – and out again into bright warm sunshine. Straight into the perfume of wallflowers. Now we were at the front of the school, which is what I had seen so many times from below. Now, the whole of the Weald from which we had just come was clear and bright in front of us.

Then down more steps by the side of a vast lawn in front of the school, along the perfumed, dark red and orange flower-beds, passing a gardener who smiled a greeting, and so to the Headmaster's house.

We all went in, and the lady with the bun knocked on a large panelled wooden door.

The man who opened it was tall, with a short grey moustache, and dressed in a brown tweed suit. He was not unlike Mr Parker.

He smiled, spoke quietly, and was not at all solemn. When we'd sat down, he wanted to talk about the papers I'd filled in some weeks before in the boardroom. And said that he particularly liked the things I'd written in the mathematics paper. I was pleased, though I couldn't remember.

He and my mother discussed a few things, and then quite soon afterwards he said that if I'd like to come to the school he would be pleased to see me in September.

His quiet courtesy would be a feature of the greatest majority of the staff I would meet at the school during the following seven years. But for now he said goodbye, shook my mother's hand, and mine, and we re-emerged from his study overlooking the Weald, to be met again by the lady with the bun. It was just before mid-day but I didn't see any other boys. Just the sun, and the warm welcoming ochred wallflowers offering their perfume as greeting.

And so that was it. My introduction to my second village was made. We went home, and I took off my Sunday clothes, and everything returned to what it had been before.

A little later a man came from the county council offices in Westerford, to speak to my mother. He talked quite a lot about the different clothes I should wear when I started at the school, and how I would receive a season ticket for the bus-ride to the school. He was friendly also.

When he left, my mother gave me a dark blue plastic biro pen. This revealed itself as something of a miracle to me, since unlike the pens with nibs that I had to dip into the inkwells at school when we did handwriting, it didn't suddenly spray showers of ink drops over the paper.

Biros were not allowed at my village school; and when I left for my new one it was with a fountain pen bought from the newsagents. I did a paper-round in the holidays.

In late September a new life began. Everyday, except Sundays, but including Saturdays, I would take the bus to school for the same fifteen minute journey we had all travelled together in the Spring. My first day there, was the day after my eleventh birthday.

No shutters came down. Just the opposite. Though I left at 7.30 every morning, and reached home again at 6.45 in the evening, the holidays were longer than for two of my friends who had gone to grammar schools. Lessons began again in the afternoon at 4.30, and there was always homework to be done.

Many of the boys I joined were not much like me, though most were quite friendly.

Suddenly I had new clothes, all at once, and I was given a leather satchel.

Every time I met a new teacher in that first week I was given books. So long as I wrote my name in them, and my form number, it seemed that I could keep them. The books were new.

Although everything was so very different, I don't think I behaved very differently. Not consciously, and not immediately. My tatterdemalion ways continued as the days of my two villages became fused; first when I left in the early morning, and then in the early evening.

When I said that things returned to how they had been, there was one very big exception. We had very recently moved from the cottage by the brook, to a house in the High Street. It was not really very much larger, but it had main drainage and a bathroom. The orchard and the brook were no more for us. The new garden was small, not much more than a yard; with a little scrubby lawn.

The house was next door to a café, owned by the grown-up son of my father and mother. His name was Victor. He lived above his shop, and he washed his hair in 'Tide' washing powder. I don't know why. He had been in the RAF., and I sensed that he didn't much like me after I changed schools.

Inside, as well as outside the house, there seemed less space than in the cottage. There were four bedrooms off a central landing, but they were not large. I slept at the back of the house in one room with my father, in the same bed. There was another bedroom at the back of the house in which there was no-one at first. I don't know why. Later it was periodically occupied by strangers, and I didn't know why that was either. Anyway, for much of the time it had a bed and a wardrobe but no occupants.

At the front of the house, but right next to our room, Arthur and Evelyn slept. Across the hall, and also therefore at the front, was where my mother and Eunice slept. I cannot explain these arrangements; that's just the way it was.

Downstairs there was a kitchen, and a scullery. The dining room was small with a brick floor, and there were two other rooms at the front on the ground floor. One was a sitting room. The other was furnished, but not used.

I liked my new school, even the homework. The three subjects a night was something I quickly got used to, though when a master forgot to set homework I rejoiced a little. Silently.

The long school days were exciting, perhaps because every one of my afternoons, except Tuesdays and Sundays, were given over to games. Football at first, and later rugby, in the winter. Later hockey. And always there was the less welcome possibility of 'cross country' if the pitches were unfit. And … in the summer, cricket. Tuesday afternoons we had Scouts, which quite quickly became the Combined

Cadet Corps.' afternoon. Of everything we did, I liked that the least.

I quickly became used to visits to other schools for various matches, and to their teams coming to us. When we travelled, it was by coach.

There was chapel every morning, and there were rules which were enforced by house and school prefects. But although our days were carefully ordered, yet our freedom was considerable. I began to make friends among my new companions, and I rolled down the banks of the school almshouses in the village with them just as I liked, in my new clothes. If anyone minded they never said.

The school grounds were very large. Above the quad. where we had entered first, there were several rugby pitches, and across the Westerford road but not accessible without going out the main gate, was the main cricket field – opposite the village recreation ground. To one side of what was known as 'The Lower', against the road, was a cherry orchard, and on the other side were cricket nets, a swimming pool and tennis courts. And cricket pitches.

Stretching up from 'The Lower', a long way up, were the rugby pitches. This area, I quickly learned, was known as "Bloody Mountains". Not in reference to any rugby matches, but because of the legend of a Saxon battle which had taken place there. In fact the legend is corroborated by reliable historical sources.

Down some steps at the front of the main building, towards the centre of the village, were other boarding houses, and the refectory.

And so as I passed my eleventh birthday I began to live in my two villages at once, and between them. When I was in one, I sometimes thought of the other. Looking back, my experience of the first was, you could say, of a sensuous life in childhood; whereas life in the second was to become, gradually, an aesthetic one. If life in the first was the subject for a ballad, in the second it would become eventually the subject for a lyric. Certainly my days were in a singing time.

This singing accompanied me unrestrained for up to about two years after my beginning at the school; and it's interruption came about because of my making new friends – and because of Belgium.

Philip and Peter lived in the village where the school was. Philip's father was a canon. One day they told me that they planned to go on a cycling holiday to Belgium in the holidays, for a week. They asked me if I wanted to go.

Their idea was to stay in youth hostels, which they seemed to know all about. They costed the trip, and when considered practically the figure was of course completely unrealistic for me. It was very many times greater than the 6d a day I was given to spend in the school tuck shop. And I knew even that was generous.

But the excitement of the idea carried me away, far beyond Belgium. In a way that I could not have anticipated, that country entered my life for ever; long before I set foot in it. The idea of such an adventure became overwhelming, and simply in the planning.

My friends explained to me that I would need a passport. When, consumed by this idea, I approached my mother about getting one she didn't say much. But I got the form from the post office anyway.

It explained that I would have to send in a birth certificate with the application. When I asked my mother about this she said she didn't have it. So I found out that I could apply for one to Somerset House, in London. Which is what I did.

When it arrived, it came with an official judgement. In the column for 'mother's name' there was the name of a complete stranger; in the name for 'father' there were simply the words: "Not known".

The cycling holiday to Belgium was never really even a possibility. It was just a fancy. I had no money even for the passport application. Not to mention for train fares, the ferry, and youth hostel charges. But it was not only the idea of the cycling holiday, which had so seduced me, that now so suddenly vanished.

Urgently I had to make sense of the birth certificate. I asked my mother, who now officially was not my mother, about it – and she was not pleased. My insistent questions were met with silence, and when I persisted she became angry.

Eventually, she said simply that if I wanted to know anything I should ask my mother!

My surprise at that, even outweighed the news of that my birth certificate had brought.

When I said that I didn't know where she was, she said she could give me her address. This was in Westerford, and when the summer holidays came I caught my usual bus, and set out to find it.

By asking passers-by, I found the area of the town I needed, and eventually the street and then the house. The day was hot, and the paint on the front door before me, blue and peeling, gave off a cooking smell in the heat of the sun. I knocked, and the door was quickly opened by a fierce-looking woman. She had the sort of face that Dickens would introduce to me later, and it was not at all friendly.

"Yes?" she said, glowering down at me on the step.

"I've come to see Mrs Holden", I stumbled.

At that moment I hoped that I'd come to the wrong house, or that "Mrs Holden" wasn't there. Perhaps had never been there.

"Mrs Holden is inside. Who are you?" was the reply I actually received.

"I'm her son", I said, "and I've come to see her".

At this, the woman's re-action astonished me. Even more than the other pieces of news that I'd had recently. More than what I had seen on the birth certificate. More than the news of this address from my mother, where I now stood.

"You wicked, wicked boy!", the woman screamed. "You've certainly taken your time. How dare you not come before!"

What she said was an explosion of which I felt a part, and from which I wanted urgently to escape. I thought of my singing villages, and everyone I knew there. I thought of my school, and I mumbled a rebellion. A rebellion which selected survival.

Or at least that is how I have justified what I did next.

"It doesn't matter", I said, and I left. Simply left. Walked away.

On the bus, I remembered that the woman seemed to be wearing a kind of uniform. Navy blue I thought.

When I got home, my mother didn't ask me about the visit; and I didn't tell her about it.

SIMPSON, Matt *An elegy for the galosherman.* Bloodaxe. 1990, pp. 128, £6.95. 1 85224 103 9

Oilskins, shipyards, grey rope streets, and family life without congruity, are the furniture of these autobiographical poems of disinheritance and loss. Arranged as a narrative, they relate the cruel effects of necessary choices in a life, The teller's refusal to go to sea, to accommodate his father's "ruined boyhood", bequeaths an addition to "home's accumulating bitternesses ". Like the wind from the docks, his father's "dreams that carve through oceans" assume a particular menace. The memory of resisting them, is kept keen by the gifts that the boy does accept. Of poetry from an English teacher, given as if it was his last half-crown, "because it was good to give away". The shared pleasure in angling, later in middle age, from a soon-dead friend, " ... wanting the joy of it for me".

A sympathetic eye looks into the wind always, and sees also the resistance of others. Tenderly, poems record a boyhood idealisation of a vicar's daughter, "... dogging her footsteps to bus-stops. And of choirgirls – in "investing" them "with / too intricate psychologies".

A book to share with secondary school pupils; they'll wince as well as "... grin / the other side of poetry". Try 'My Grandfather's African Grey', 'Who's Who in Bootle', 'Old Ma Lennon', 'Home from Home', and 'Letting Us all Down'.

William Holden

Chapter 5

When I arrived home in the early afternoon, my father was in the kitchen; sitting in his usual chair in the corner, reading his newspaper. Sally the bull-mastiff, was with him, sleeping nearby. She was his constant companion in the house.

Erect, calm, and grey haired, I remember feeling worried again that he was now already in his seventies. That was very old to me then.

Retired from being the village postman, as well as from his army days, he had recently retired also from looking after the boiler at the village school, and helping out there generally. His days were now spent visiting farmer friends around the village.

There was of course always casual farm work to be done: threshing, or hop-picking. When he visited, it was on foot. There was no place around our new home for the trap, and I did not notice what had happened to Kitty.

The kitchen was where I did my homework in the evenings during term time, often with my father reading a newspaper in his chair. It was always quiet and warm there; and the table was big. Sometimes we played cribbage, or drafts, on the kitchen table in the evening. Sometimes shove-halfpenny.

He looked up as I came in, "Would you like some soup?"

Meals in the house were not regular, and I was hungry. And my father's soup was always good.

As I sat down with the hot soup and a hunk of bread, I was thinking how it was Friday. Tonight was the night when it was my job to fetch the eggs from George Meadow's farm. This was in preparation for Sunday breakfast, which was easily the best meal of the week.

Then, my father would be in charge of breakfast for the whole family, and our plates would be loaded with bacon and eggs, liver or kidneys, and mushrooms – which he and I would have gathered ourselves when that was possible. The outfield of the cricket pitch was a very good source of mushrooms in September. And there would always be fried bread.

Now it was soup, but Friday.

"Will George be in tonight do you think? I asked, as I devoured the soup.

"Well, probably, if you go at about seven. But you'll need to go around the back". He always said that. He probably guessed the reason for my question, but said nothing more.

The farmer was a short, portly, red-faced man. I was always very interested in people's ages, and I guessed that he was in his early sixties. My memory is of the perspiration that flowed from his face as he measured the hops, bending with effort over the wooden-framed canvas bins in the hot, afternoon, September sun. Watching him, I would be praying that he wouldn't walk away because of the leaves I'd left among the hops I'd picked – and so leave them unmeasured. I had therefore practice in, and good reason for, a close scrutiny of George.

I cannot remember whether he ever actually refused to measure my hops, though I must have come close more than once. No doubt the farmer's friendship with my father was an influence upon his leniency, and no doubt I was unaware of that.

I watched his face closely as he dipped his measuring basket into the pile of hops, and finally lifted up the canvas corner of the bin between two fingers, to arrange those that remained in the bottom, as he came to the end of the measure. He would always give it a delicate little shake. I would look on anxiously, as more than once there would be just many too many leaves, unavoidably obvious and now exposed at the bottom of the bin. They would cause the farmer to grunt in disapproval as he shook the corner of the canvas.

The number of bushel baskets in the measure, which was carried out four times a day, decided our pay. I always left it very late to check for leaves in the bin, and to clear them out; usually right up to when the cry of "Get your hops ready!" rang out. How long I, and the other pickers, would have to remove leaves, depended upon where our bin was situated in the line advancing through the tunnels of the hop garden. And upon where George and his bin-men began the measuring.

George Meadows lived in a large, but run down, farmhouse which had a grey mock-Georgian façade. It could have been a handsome house but wasn't.

He lived there, almost alone, with his sister Miriam. My recollection of him was that he was always hot, long before and after the hop-measuring in the September sun.

He puffed as he walked.

When I was very young, I thought the reason for this puffing movement was the long, thick, leather gaiters that were always strapped to his legs. Either that or the snuff he used. Later, I realized that it might have had more to do with the large quantities of cider that he made – and drank.

His sister was a year or two older than him. She was a tall, very thin, woman with a pointed and grey face. Her hair was always arranged in a bun, though I cannot say I saw her often, for nobody did. And I never heard her speak.

That afternoon over the soup, Miriam was the reason for my question to my father. For it was the opinion of everyone in and around the village, that Miriam Meadows was insane. The story was that when their father died, the farm had passed to George, but only on condition that his sister continued to live in the house. In other words that she should not be committed to a mental institution. Was the story true? Who knows, though there was evidence enough that it could have been. At thirteen, I had no doubts.

Nor I think did Mrs Bonnet, who lived in one of the three or four houses which were spaced out between the forge and the farm. About fifty, she was a friendly, kindly, widow with a cleft palate that had not been corrected.

Calling at the farm one evening, on some errand a year or so before, this cheerful woman, whom I knew well was attacked from behind and beaten about the head with a broom handle.

The story told how she ran back down the road with blood pouring down her face, with her assailant in frenzied pursuit. It was more likely that after the attack Miriam had herself run off, leaving the visitor to struggle home as best she could – for her daughter to call the doctor.

When this good woman told my father of this incident in a conversation which I overheard, it was clear that the visit had been made out of neighbourly concern for the unfortunate farmer. And it was equally clear that what she had experienced had tempered, rather than deterred, her determination to look to his welfare. I can only reflect that I was nowhere near achieving such a nobility of spirit.

What was clear to me was that there was danger behind that front door. Especially when the sun was going down.

I even heard the new village postman telling my father how he pushed letters through the letter box on the farmhouse's front door with greater than normal speed. If anything needed to be signed for, he simply left a note without knocking.

As a result, the farmer's stout be-gaitered legs, leathered and shiny-brown, had to turn towards the post office in the High Street. There, the postmaster, also portly and puffing a lot at every exertion, would arrange the necessary transaction, never making reference to the reason for the farmer's tedious journey.

In our village many of the men seemed to have few words. Perhaps this was because lots of things were too well understood to warrant a mention. Why should either farmer or postmaster speak of this example?

Of course my father discussed none of this with me. And I did not broach the subject of Miriam. At least not directly.

I knew the farm well. To the side of the house, slightly back from the road, was a large barn. The farmyard itself was spacious and regular in shape, and there were always hens, ducks, and a few geese around. And of course at its centre was the oast-house.

My guess, looking back, is that the farm ran to 150-200 acres, mostly given over to pasture and sheep, with a little barley and wheat; and two good sized hop gardens. One beside the cricket field, the other just across the road from it.

I went to the farm quite often with my father. In the winter we would be at either end of a two-handed saw, cutting up a fallen tree to split for logs for the fire. Once I had helped him transport a dead and yellowing sheep on a cart. To my amazement, its stomach suddenly split open, and I saw that it was seething with maggots.

And so, at a little after 7 o'clock that evening, I was retracing the farmer's route from the High Street. The hot day had become a golden evening; warm, still and silken. When I reached the farmhouse, it lay quiet and seemingly deserted; a little back from the road and facing the warm, sinking, sun.

On the inside of each window casement, were piles of neatly stacked bricks. As if walls, but without mortar, had been built on the inside of the glass. This was Miriam's work.

Where the tops of these makeshift brick walls ended, along the tops of the bricks and up to the top of the glass of each window, sheets of newspaper were neatly stuck to the inside of every window.

Now the whole of the front of the house, the bricks, the newspaper sheets, and the front door, were lit up by the evening sunshine. The front door was placed centrally inside a small porch.

I knew that the bell was broken, so I knocked on the door three times. I didn't expect an answer, and there wasn't one. So, I knocked again, but everything was quiet and very still. I knew I must do everything I could to find George; for if I failed I should have to return for the eggs the next morning.

So again I used the knocker over the wide flap of the letter box, giving it three more loud bangs. And I took care to remove my hand quickly afterwards. On a previous visit to collect the eggs, the letter flap had opened from the inside; and when I bent down to look closer, my gaze was met by two light grey eyes staring back at me from the inside. Since then, I had always removed my hand from the door knocker immediately.

But tonight, there was no sign of life in the house. George didn't appear. Everything was quiet. Neither the door nor the flap moved.

I looked up at the house and walked around the front, as if I was being watched, since I decided I should have to go to the back of the house. Perhaps I could find the farmer in his large old kitchen. I reflected upon how dad had told me always to go to the back door, though I preferred to try at the front first. Sometimes successfully.

Not tonight though. So I walked along the stone flagstones of the path, looking straight ahead, out into the sun again.

When I came to the wide door of the kitchen it was open, which gave me hope that the farmer was at home and just hadn't heard my knocking at the front.

I knocked quietly on the thick wood of the door, which had a lot of its paint missing; but I did not move from the large iron boot-scraper at my feet.

There was no light on, but I could see inside the bare kitchen; to the broad, plain, wooden door leading to the rest of the house. There was no-one about.

Sometimes I had found the farmer in the barn, working among the farm machinery, on the tractor, bailer or on a wagon, and so I decided to try there. But instead of taking the direct path to the barn, which was in full view of the house but out of sight from the sunlit road at the front, and only fifteen yards away, I retraced my footsteps to the front.

Back along the side of the house, and out along the road. Then, into the farmyard, and through the huge, open, sliding doors of the barn.

Inside, all was quiet and cool, smelling sweetly of hay, petrol, and engine oil. As I came out of the sun, the inside of the barn was very dark, and at first I could see very little. Tools hung from the walls, and after a while I made out the tractor and bailer. Of course, I would know immediately if the farmer was there because I would hear him breathing – even if he wasn't moving around.

But everything was quiet, still, and deserted, save for a few hens clucking at their evening rest. As they did so, I could feel the chance of avoiding another visit receding.

Walking forward, I called out, "Hello, Mr Meadows!"

The hens squawked a complaint, and scattered further into the gloom of the barn.

There was no-one there, and so I turned to leave. Moving out again towards the sun, I then saw the tall thin figure of the farmer's sister, motionless, silent and erect, standing in the shadows, beside one of the thick supports of the storage floor. Quite nearby.

She was just staring straight at me, perfectly still. I felt frozen, and there was a ringing in my ears which tinkled. The bun at the back of her head grabbed my attention.

I spluttered out, "My dad says, can I collect our eggs please?" And as I did so, I decided to move slowly towards the large open doors of the barn.

But she didn't reply. Slowly though, she moved, and then … she turned her back on me, and then stayed exactly where she was. She didn't walk away, but remained there, perfectly still. With her back turned. Still and silent in the shadows.

For a second, I waited. Then, increasingly quickly, but deliberately, and watching her carefully, I walked out of the front of the barn into the yard, towards the evening and the sunshine and saying nothing more.

Looking back just to check, outside the wide door now, I saw her just where I'd left her. Perfectly still, erect, and standing where she had turned.

When I reached the door, I ran across the yard and out on to the road, where the tarmac was warm through my shoes; and its heat rose to my face, and the gravel was loud beneath my feet after the dried mud of the farmyard.

Now, the evening seemed more golden still. And I didn't look back at the front door of the farmhouse again as I walked along the other side of the road away from it. Towards the forge, and the village.

Had I done so, I should have seen that the house was now deep in shadow. Although I knew I should have to return next morning for the eggs, I didn't mind anymore.

As I walked on, I wondered if Mr Harding had repaired my bike yet. When I got home, I didn't mention Miriam to my father. Just that George wasn't in.

Henson, Stuart *Ember Music*. Peterloo, 1994, pp.69. £6.95. 1 871471 41 9

Stuart Henson's *Ember Music* is one of the best new books of poems I've read this year. A central, narrative, sequence records "the path to grace" of Guthlac, the Mercian warrior turned hermit – and saint. Before and after, are lyric poems about the countryside; full of those mysterious associations between human histories and landscapes within which may lie the roots of poetry itself. Poems that are fresh records of abandoned celebration, and regret at human mutability. Records that themselves will begin to slip away, for "our books fade with us as we age".

'The Players' can stand for section 1 – as a poem that many poets would be as happy to have made as any reader to discover. Summary being impossible, here is its opening:

> "Out of the green graves or the road's dust
> the dusk assembles them, wisest and least,
> like shadows gathered to a feast,
> and one by one in candle fall they come
> about the chestnuts and the tombs
> ..."

The play between "candle fall" and "chestnuts" is eloquent within the poem's recognition of

> the benevolent dead, since
> "...our intelligence
> is rhymed to theirs and hears as if the trees
> translated us..."

'Croyland' is the book's narrative middle section. And the poem 'Green Man' as aptly represents the last section of the whole book – as would 'Planting'. Reading them, and around them, is richly rewarding.

Putting readers in the secondary school, and everywhere else, in touch with contemporary poetry of this quality, is surely the point of English teaching.

William Holden

Chapter 6

War was declared one year almost to the day before I was born; and an industry of inhumanity engulfed Europe.

As I began school in England in my first village reluctant and five, and as the buses set out from Westerford to my village, the Red Army had continued its journey across Prussia to Berlin.

More paralysed and nervous than mine were the faces of women, boys and girls, on the sides of those other roads. One voice with its plea of "Don't shoot me soldier!" spoke then for many. Spoke with futility.

Then it was not a bus, but "the cannon of a tank / growing immense at the corner of a street". Women were fleeing invaders – as they had from the beginning of time. Girls only a little older or younger than those who held my hand to Sunday school as children do – or did then in those days in my village.

As I began school in my second village, half of Europe was still in ruins; and the other half was exchanging one tyrannical political system for another. And in Russia, Stalin was set upon the destruction of seventy or more million of his own people.

All of which I was completely unaware of, intent as I was upon the twelve minute bus ride between my two villages.

Looking back upon my home at that time, I can make more sense of it. Though there is much still that I cannot explain.

Then, there were many more puzzles; some obvious, some hidden. The obvious one was why my surname was different to that of those around me.

My mother told me that Eunice, whom I thought of as my sister, had been adopted, and so carried the family name. So, while I could understand, from very early on, the notion of adoption, that of fostering was completely beyond me in those early years.

Arthur also carried the family name but as he was married to Evelyn, I didn't realize until later that, long before, he must have been adopted also. He had returned from the sea, from service in the Merchant Navy when we still lived in the cottage, though that was via imprisonment in a Japanese prisoner of war camp. He had been a bosun, and was a handsome and quiet man.

Overheard conversations told of other names, mentioned as if they were familiar but unknown to me. My mother very frequently by mistake, referred to me as Maurice. She sometimes actually called me Maurice. And this happened so frequently that I asked her one day who Maurice was. She didn't answer

So I never found out much; never really even started to solve these puzzles. Naturally, I never met Maurice, At least I don't think I did. For all I knew for sure was that he had once been a member of the family also.

Later, throughout the years in the High Street house, the empty back room became occupied by strangers; by quite a variety of visitors. Not for a weekend only, and yet not for very long either. Just for five or six weeks in the summer usually. When they left they didn't return, unlike the swallows where we used to live.

One day, not in the summer, a young woman called Audrey arrived with a small baby. My mother seemed to know her, and expect her. She was about twenty three, and stayed for three weeks. When she left, it was finally. For most of the time that she was with us she was closeted with my mother.

Another sudden visitor was an elderly, stout, and very bad-tempered lady who also stayed in the back bedroom.

She seemed to have a hole in the side of her head, which gave off a very unpleasant smell. She stayed for quite a long time, and also spent much of it alone with my mother. Mrs Cheetham was intolerant of children; especially she disliked young boys. When she left, it was forever.

Aunty Elsie, my mother's sister, came quite frequently. About the same age as Mrs Cheetham, she too disliked young boys – and Americans. I didn't know the reason for either aversion.

Yet another, and more promising, visitor occupied the back bedroom one summer when I was about fifteen. He was two years older than I was, and West Indian. He told me that he lived in Holborn. He was unimpressed by life in our village, but had a portable record player on which he played Elvis Presley records. I was disappointed when he left after about four weeks. When I asked my mother if he would be coming back, she didn't answer.

I cannot say that my mother was not kind to me sometimes at that time. My father was always kind. Another question which remained unanswered was why my mother and father did not share the same bedroom. And yet another was why they spoke so little to each other.

I have mentioned how long it took me to come to terms with the notion of a 'foster parent'. Adoption was easy, parents also; even 'guardian' which cropped up on the bottom of my school reports seemed self-explanatory.

The more conventional family lives of everyone else I knew rather reinforced this difficulty, and tended to drive it underground. When someone at school asked me about my family, I didn't speak of guardians, foster mother, foster father, foster sister or foster uncle, but just mother and father and the rest. Increasingly though, I tended to avoid the topic of 'family' altogether in those conversations. Whenever possible.

When I answered the questions of friends I answered as they expected, trying not to surprise them; and by doing so I lied to them, and therefore to myself of course.

What I was only slowly realizing was that I lived in a foster home. I wonder sometimes if that may explain in some way the absence of continuous conversation in the house which became progressively characteristic of life there. In a way, perhaps, home was becoming, so very gradually, too much just a set of rooms where people lived. Though even that is not quite true.

Perhaps all this explained why my questions were ignored – simply not answered. The reason perhaps why for as long as I could remember, one of my mother's favourite warning – sayings was: "little pitchers have big ears!" This when I was obviously listening too intently to adult conversations.

Looking back upon that time, I realize now that other people in my first village knew of my situation. Indeed but for their knowing I should probably have perished, as I think will become more clear later.

I was learning that adults have some responsibilities but not others; immediate but circumscribed. That although I stayed, actually for a very long time, the arrangement that led to me being there was probably intended to be temporary. Perhaps more temporary than it turned out to be.

But however I had arrived there, and for whatever reason, I knew that I loved my parents; and on another level realized how my life would have turned out very badly had I not been given the shelter they provided. Simply because I had no real sense of my own history, it was easy for me to be reconciled to the puzzles and contradictions of the histories of other people in the house once we had moved. I learned to ignore those histories, for there was so much else to interest me.

The controlling business presence in the house was my mother. Her lieutenant and main worker was Evelyn.

At the cottage, with all its space outside, my mother had run a breeding kennels for dogs, mostly pekinese and bulldogs; breeds that were popular at that time. When we moved, many dogs came with us, but not to the benefit of outside kennels. Quickly the small walled-garden became poisoned by dog excrement and ashes.

There was an alsation, a chihuahua, a bull mastiff, a Manchester terrier, a long haired sheep dog, a pug, a greyhound, a great dane, and a whippet. There were more still; and of course the several pekinese and bulldogs continued to have litters. There was also a bloodhound belonging to Victor, which lived next door with him.

This number of dogs in the house patterned life at home, and greatly contributed to the exhaustion which gradually overtook Evelyn, although she was still only in her early thirties when we moved.

The dogs had their main meal at 4.15 every afternoon, cooked in the kitchen in a large pot on the stove.

Just as my journeys to the shops, when we lived in the cottage, had been for stamps and postal orders for my mother's letters, now my trips continued; to the butcher for bones and cheap cuts, to the fishmonger for off-cuts, and to the baker's where Arthur now worked, for stale loaves.

I had known all these shopkeepers, and the other customers that I met in their shops, for a long time, and they recognized me.

First, and every day, a dozen stale loaves had to be broken up; and if I was about in the school holidays the job fell to me. Then either the fish, or the offal and cheap cuts of meat were put into the large pot also.

Every afternoon the odours of this preparation permeated the house, and very likely other houses nearby. And they triggered a daily cacophonous chorus of barking, roaring, howling, yelping and quarrelling, as a large number of the assorted animals fought each other to get into the kitchen before their meal was ready. The most agile of them often succeeding should the kitchen door be left accidentally ajar.

Evelyn was responsible also for everyone else's lunch or evening meal in the house during the week. And because of the daily ritual of feeding the dogs, and her many other duties, the preparation of food for the rest of the family could not match the carefully organized afternoon ritual at 4.15.

As long as my homework had been completed, my bus journeys between my two villages patterned my life, just as the feeding of the dogs patterned the day at home; and although often solitary these journeys were always taken with a light heart.

One Easter holiday, the Tuesday afternoons with the school scouts meant that I had a task. And that was to play my part in the 'Bob- a- Job' scheme. In return for completing a job for someone, I would be paid a shilling, though they could pay more if they wished.

The card upon which had to be listed the jobs, the time they took, and the payments, along with the signature of the person making each payment, had the school's crest on its front.

Now, this would be called sponsorship. Then, it was very carefully controlled, and along with my other eleven year old companions I received strict instructions. Most of these companions, being boarders at the school, would discharge these duties in all manner of ways, and in many places.

In my case, since to ask at home for paid work was out of the question, I took my bicycle and set out to visit the farms around my first village. Though not to George Meadow's.

Had I thought to have fears of rough rebuffs, angry refusals, or long hours of toil in the hot sun or heavy rain for a measly payment, they would have been quickly dispelled.

As I approached each front door with my card and my explanations, my question was always met with other questions from either the farmer or his wife. I think I quickly came to understand that they knew very well about the scheme, although their immediate response was to appear doubtful – and accompanied by much head and chin scratching.

"Mm, well I don't know! You want me to pay you, you say?" and then they would appear to examine the card very carefully.

"What school did you say you go to?", and I would have to say which it was, whereupon they scrutinized the front of the card all over again. At first, when this happened, I felt doubtful myself.

"'Bob-a-Job', you say. And you'll do any job I give you?"

"Yes", I would reply, as at first visions of some of the less desirable jobs around a farm came into my mind.

"For one shilling?"

Upon my agreeing that this was also the case, I was then shown to some small task.

"Can you chop wood with an axe?"

I could, of course. So, shifting a small pile of timber, cutting it into logs and stacking them, would be that job.

Or perhaps making a bonfire of rubbish. Or clearing a patch of ground from weeds in the farmer's garden. Or one or another of a myriad possible tasks in the country, real or contrived. Simply invented, when some ragamuffin such as I came along with a request such as mine.

When the task had been set, and the deal struck between two such un-equals, the farmer would tell me where to report upon its completion.

Without exception, on the dozen or so of these visits, about half an hour into the task the farmer's wife, or perhaps the farmer himself, would appear with a tray of refreshment. Usually a glass of squash and a piece of cake.

And when I'd finished I would go to find someone, just as I had been instructed to.

If it was the farmer's wife I found, she would usually just sign the card,. She wouldn't ask me about how much to enter, but just write down an amount and give me the money. It was always more than a shilling, usually 2/6 or three shillings. And there would be more squash and cake.

If it was the farmer and his wife together, there would often be more light-hearted banter about the card and the task,

"You say you've finished?"

"Yes, sir!"

"Mm, well, I think we'd better come and have a look". And so my work would be examined.

"Yes, good. And how long do you think the job took you?"

When I answered this question, to which he already knew the answer, the farmer would then begin to examine the card again, and ask another question.

"I have to enter the time you took on the card, here?"

"Yes please, sir", came my inevitable reply.

These exchanges were always good humoured and kindly, and I quickly realized that they were a ritual in which I was expected to play my part.

"Now then, I have to pay you a shilling?"

"Well you don't have to, but you can if you like". I had been instructed to say that if necessary I should accept less than a shilling.

"You mean I can pay less?"

"Yes, sir".

"But I don't have to pay more than that?"

"No, sir", I answered. For those were my instructions.

Of course, they always paid more. Three shillings, then, was a very considerable sum. Then it would be smiles and thank-yous. And I would be off on my bike with card and the money in my jerkin pocket.

I quickly recognized that there was theatre in all of this. And that my only difficulty may be not being able to find anyone around, as I went up a new path to a fresh door or the entrance of a barn, to explain and put my question.

My new school had about 360 pupils, and had been founded in the 16th Century. As a day-boy, my life was very different of course to the lives of boarders. I was a member of one of the largest school houses and I had breakfast at home; and I didn't usually go to school on Sundays.

Yet, I recognized quickly that the boarders also lived within their own, sometimes sad, cycle of arrivals and departures.

I was to learn late in life, that Stefan Zweig had a fierce hatred of his secondary school, but for me the opposite was true. The customs of my new school seemed exotic, and it took me the whole of my first year to gain an introduction to their novelty. It was a time when days were still long dawns.

I quickly got used to the sudden half-day holidays to watch the first XV playing at home, or the first X1. To being given permission on hot summer days to remove my blazer to sit in lessons, and go about the school in shirtsleeves. And to feeling the luxury of this.

But first among the new customs, were those that attended the variety and eccentricities of my new teachers. My discovery was that I liked a lot of them a lot, and found them interesting. If there were some that I was doubtful of, I learned that I had simply to act cautiously and rely on my judgement.

One of the very first masters I met, taught us Biology; one of the first but actually quite untypical. For a start, I'd never met anyone before who had a double surname.

He had a very red face, a moustache, was quite short and a little fat, and spoke loudly with a booming deep voice. I could best describe him as a less extreme version of the Hapsburg Colonel Kraus in Hašek's *The Good Soldier Švejk*. Except his military background was in the British Army in India, where he had been a major on the North West Frontier. He was in charge of the Combined Cadet Force at the school.

We were of course, at eleven, very quick to notice any peculiar, special, characteristics in our new teachers. He had a very obvious one, which was that he often repeated the phrase, "When I was in Poona!", often in surprising contexts

– and completely without warning. The final syllable of 'Poona' would always be heavily accented.

He used the phrase often enough for us all to identify him with it quickly in our new world. We greeted it with carefully and judiciously disguised mirth.

My very first lesson with him was in a classroom rather than a laboratory, and initially caused me great puzzlement.

To my amazement, very near the very start of the lesson, he addressed me directly,

"What's your name boy?" he suddenly demanded.

'Olden sir", I replied.

What's your name? he repeated.

Thinking that perhaps I hadn't spoken loudly enough, I repeated my name, more forcefully this time,

'Olden sir!"

And then, to my even greater surprise, he asked me the same question yet again; as if I had made no reply on the previous occasions. As if he'd not asked before.

Intent as I was upon pleasing him, I swiftly ran through all the available options, as all the eyes of my new companions were upon me.

Not confidently now, I repeated my previous answers.

"Boy", came his reply, "your name is not 'Olden".

By now, thoroughly confused, I asked,

"Isn't it sir?"

"No, it isn't, … it's Holden," and he emphasized the first syllable of my name.

Now I understood. "Oh, yes sir", was all I could reply, as laughter tinkled all around me.

After a few weeks, however, his attitude towards me softened. I knew quite a lot about stamens and the structure of flowers generally, about the root systems of plants, and how they retained moisture. I was very familiar with moorhens, and duckweed on the black-glassed surface of Wealden ponds. The seasons of my time, up to then, had been those of the cuckoo, the curlew, partridges exploding in front of me, and yellow hammers running across the road in front of my bicycle. And the arrival and departures of swallows and swifts.

I already knew that we breathed in what trees breathed out. And so when my biology teacher asked general questions of us, my hand was always up first; with me bursting to tell the answer.

Surprisingly to me, most of my companions seemed to know very little of these things. But then, I knew no Latin, and my Algebra was non-existent too.

I came to have no doubt that this teacher's initial phonological, if public, instruction to me was well meant, and intended for my benefit.

'Speech day' was an important occasion, in late June every year. Our housemaster, and the house prefects laid great emphasis on smart appearance. Personal appearance was even more important on this day than usual, and it was very important always. We each wore a red carnation on that afternoon, pinned on the lapels of the blazers of the younger boys by house prefects – and carefully checked.

A special visitor was welcomed, who presented school prizes, particularly to the sixth formers. The quad. was full of very expensive looking shiny cars belonging to boys' parents, and the school stage in the hall was full of flowers, and cheerful and important looking, and also shiny, visitors.

There were speeches: by the Headmaster, the Head of School and the Chairman of Governors – and by the special guest visitor of course.

The newest boys sat at the very front of the hall, and therefore had a very good view of the proceedings. Year by year, they would move towards the back in their classes.

When the time came for them to leave the school, they would be seated at the back.

Except if they were a prize winner, for then they would be seated among those at the very front; first the upper sixth, and behind them the lower sixth.

And so to all of this I became gradually accustomed as it was introduced to me, and as I became absorbed in the life of the school; in its classrooms and in the many activities outside them.

In the classroom beneath the daily lessons there ran a careful, well established, system of measurement of our achievement and effort.

Twice every term, in every subject, effort was measured by the award of three colours: Red, Green, and Blue. Red indicated enthusiasm and the best effort that could be expected; Green: steady application; Blue: low effort.

Actual achievement and progress in each subject was measured by the award of numbers on a scale of one to five. So, a 1 indicated high attainment and progress, and 5 no progress at all.

So, an R1 was the obviously best outcome, and a B5 the worst possible, although an R5 was possibly even worse news. Three R1s at a time would result in an invitation to speak to the headmaster in his study, as would any combination of the less desirable assessments. In truth R5s did not occur, since the unfortunate recipient would no doubt have been withdrawn from the school before such a judgement was necessary.

These results then, announced twice each term, were eagerly awaited, or not, by us all; and read out by each subject master in class, in a matter of fact, quite neutral, manner. There was no further judgement indicated, or needed, by tone of voice, or change in volume. Neither by inflexion nor in expression. The result, for everyone, announced as it was in front of the whole class, carried all the necessary import.

In addition to this system, there were class examinations, which were held in each subject at the end of the second and third term each year from the very beginning of our time at the school, and there was a similar system that operated for Athletics in the summer.

Then, each boy attempted to reach an established list of times and distances on the athletics field, in each year right up the school; these were described as 'Standards'. So, in addition to competing against each other, we competed against ourselves to reach the set 'standard'. The achievement of each standard was translated into points in a house competition, but was first announced on the athletics notice board. Then also, depending on the time of year, there were house matches in cricket and rugby, hockey, cross country and swimming.

If in the classroom, as elsewhere, my schooldays were measured and patterned by these demands and sensations, when I reached the 6th form I came to love school. I was free suddenly from struggling with subjects for which I had no aptitude. What I have to thank the school for most, among many things, was that it encouraged us to feed our enthusiasms, to become immersed in those subjects that most interested us.

Now, I could concentrate on three subjects only, (apart that is from the demands of a new General Subjects course): on History, English Literature, and Geography. On the past, upon language and art, and upon the nature and variety of place.

The masters who taught me were genuinely interesting men with wide interests, scholarly, humane and absorbed in their subjects. Because my obvious enthusiasm and quiet application matched theirs, I had a ready passport to good relations with them.

The panelled library then became my sanctuary. Looking over the Weald, from where I had first seen its front; four miles away, and below, at Tatlebury Corner. Quiet, behind its wall of Virginia creeper: deep green and cool in Spring and Summer, glowing red and golden in the Autumn.

Sometimes our 'A' level English lessons were held there. And then it became a special kind of theatre, but one of muted sounds. Where the quiet reading together of the poetry in a Shakespeare play created a spell.

No acting in those days, just concentration, reflection and exposition. There the plight of Desdemona and the evil of Iago first held me in thrall; and the resolution of the conflict between Beatrice and Benedick made sense. They all captured me, just as the tales of King Arthur had captured me in the school of my first village.

This magic of absorption was created alike when the sun shone through open windows and down upon the Weald outside, or on winter nights when fog curled around the tightly shut windows. Whenever it was, that absorption in play, poem, or novel, was a gift; a territory in which I've lived ever since, along with the territory of the Saxon Weald itself.

It was probably from then that the countryside and libraries came to evoke each other always in my mind. Place and language. From two villages.

When not used for 6th form lessons, the library was always quiet. I came to love its atmosphere, and the smell of the books and panelling on the walls. It was certain that there would be no interruption there; the idea of anyone normally actually talking in the library was unthinkable. Equivalent to turning up to a school match with dirty kit, or no kit. It didn't happen.

Part of the order of things was that it was quite likely for a master to be sitting working at one of the large tables, alongside me, each of us intent upon our own affairs.

And so, during my last two years of school, my life at home in the Weald was conjoined with my becoming lost in the letters and poetry of Keats, the poetry of Housman and Thomas Hardy, Edward Fitzgerald's 'Rubaiyat', and Tennyson's 'In Memoriam'; in Wordsworth and Matthew Arnold, Hopkins – and all the rest. In the essays of Francis Bacon too.

I knew then that *"the cuckoo"* really did *"shout all day at nothing"*, though now I seldom hear it at all. I lived inside the recognition that "*The Bird of Time has but a little way / to flutter – and the Bird is on the Wing*". And I recognized the despair in Hopkins' question: "*Why do sinners' ways prosper? And why must disappointment all I endeavour end?*".

As I rode late and alone through dark summer nights, past darkened hedgerows and ripening hop gardens, I experienced too the fear as well as the cadences, of how

> "*huge and mighty forms, that do not live / Like living men, moved slowly through the mind / By day, and were a trouble to my dreams*".

Omar Khayyam seemed to speak directly, if metaphorically, to me, when he advised: "*Drink! for you not whence you came, nor why; / Drink! for you know not why you go, nor where*".

And I anticipated then, what I know now for sure, the pain of the insight inside his words:

> "*But see! The rising Moon of Heav'n again / Looks for us Sweet-heart, through the quivering Plane: / How oft hereafter rising will she look /Among those leaves – for one of us in vain!*"

Although I knew by now how illegitimacy got a bad press in Shakespeare, I noted more hopefully Chaucer's approval, in his Prologue, of 'the clerk' – poorly dressed as he was.

In such ways my journeys between my two villages would continue for just a little while longer, before I left them forever; and before taking the territories of each of them with me.

Chapter 7

As I have said, it was in late September, that elegiac month of contrasts, when bus journeys began to measure out my life. Fresh beginnings just as winter whispered its approach. Soon it would be dark when I left the house in the morning, and dark again when I waited outside the Chequers pub, at the top of the hill in my second village at around 6 o'clock to return.

At first in short trousers, with a new blue and red cap. In summer it would be a boater, a remarkable piece of headwear to which I quickly adjusted. I learned that there was a strict rule that caps and boaters had to be worn when travelling to and from school. In truth, in the summer in the morning, I carried my boater, and only put it on as I left the bus to walk up the drive past the school chapel.

And from the beginning, I possessed two shirts with collars that came off.

One advantage of these collars was that it was impossible to chew them when I was eleven. I had two new ones, and a collection of others which appeared at various times that I was at the school. They all had to be specially laundered and starched.

All my clothes had to have my name sown into them on a neat red tag; and it was so with my new collars. The other collars had another name sewn into them: 'John Aster'. I didn't question this though, and never thought about it.

As the day boys left for home, in various directions, the boarders continued on to supper in their various houses, followed by 'prep.': which was the new word I learned for supervised homework. Except they didn't go home, and I remember feeling immediately sorry for them that they didn't.

And I quickly learned, as I waited for the bus outside 'The Chequers' in the dark, in the rain and snow of winter, or in the heat of summer, that my wait was a public one. Just as when I left my own village in the morning.

The difference was that when I left in the morning, I was normally too late to make waiting for a bus necessary, for it was usually on the point of leaving.

By 'The Chequers', especially on a Wednesday or Saturday afternoon, when it was still light in any season, and masters or their wives might pass by, I also learned that we must exchange greetings. Always.

So, I thought, this was the reason that I must wear a cap or boater. How else could they be doffed? Of course all this changed later as I grew older, and greetings became less formal.

Over the years, the five or ten minutes spent outside 'The Chequers' in the afternoon or evening, quite often alone because of differences in individual timetables, were quiet moments of reflection or celebration, and very occasionally of crisis.

Bullying was very infrequent in the school in my experience, in my own house anyway. If there was a personal disagreement, among younger boys, they could in theory settle it by the ritual of a fight on the Lower – the first of the fields that extended up from the quad. at the back of the school. This took the form of a duel, in that a challenge would be issued and an acceptance given.

However, they were really very, very, infrequent, and I remember only two in all of my time at the school. Fortunately, neither involved me. But they could happen, and when they did, they were public events taking place in the centre of a group of other boys. Although sometimes managed for a very short while by house prefects, they were officially strictly forbidden.

The protagonists risked severe punishment if school prefects learned about such events; which were also frowned upon by staff. So, although the option was there, it was seldom used.

The school was small enough, and too well regulated, for any kind of bullying to go unnoticed, or once discovered to be tolerated. Although I knew little of life in the boarding houses, I knew for certain that any kind of fighting was strictly forbidden both by precept and custom.

However, one late autumn afternoon, my wait at the bus stop, leaning against the wall of one of 'The Chequers' outhouses, resulted in my only experience of the attention of one of the few bullies I encountered.

Minton had often expressed an intention of giving me a good thrashing. We were both about thirteen, though he was bigger than I was. His hands were large and raw.

I had the good sense to ignore his taunts of 'Daybug!', though that could have been simple cowardice. But on this afternoon he came upon his opportunity, and I was literally cornered. There was no escape.

Realizing that this was his moment as he walked towards me, he moved quickly to his task. Saying nothing, he aimed his clenched fist immediately at my face.

In the short time that passed between me realizing that here was a problem, and his moving in for the kill, I decided what I must do. The plan was conceived and executed in the shortest of possible moments. I had just to carefully wait, and hope.

His fist arrived just as I ducked. Although it missed my head, it couldn't miss the red brick of the outhouse wall behind me. It hit the wall with all the force that he could muster, powered by all the hatred he felt for me.

That weathered, dark red, wall outside the public house, high up and facing out towards the Weald, received his fist.

That old wall of the outhouse of the ancient inn which had been there for centuries; built so long before we happened past. Baked by summers, its surface powdered and serrated by frosts, washed by countless storms. Solid and roughened, it offered itself to the clenched knuckles of my would be assailant. All I had to do was move aside. Then my bus came.

I learned the next day that, a little after I caught the bus, Minton was admitted to the school sanatorium. When I saw him later in the first lesson we shared, I saw that his right hand was in plaster. We didn't speak, and he never bothered me again

There was no evidence that he had disclosed to anyone in the form how he had injured his hand; and I said nothing to anyone too.

Celebrations were more a part of my waiting at the bus stop though than this kind of crisis. For instance, they were part of my reflections about the pleasures of life in the sixth form, when I noticed the smiles of some of girls from the village as they passed and we exchanged glances.

There were many girls in my own village also, whom I had grown up with. Some of them I met on my Proustian cycle rides in the summer. Fortunately or not, my absorption in my last two years at school, and my own ragamuffin appearance for much of the time, excused, in my own eyes at least, these exchanges never getting beyond shy greetings.

My tatterdemalion appearance did not much alter in the holidays, as I exchanged school clothes for work clothes. Even during school terms I changed out of school clothes immediately on arriving home, in order to preserve them.

A major source of farm work, for me, was hop-picking. Fortunately the school's Christmas term began on or around the 22nd or 23rd September, by which time the hop-picking at George Meadow's farm was just completed.

George only employed village people to gather his harvest of hops. He was quite different in this from the other hop farmers; their farms were all much bigger than his – scattered around the other quarters of the village, to north and south and east.

To the west there was the river, and one its tributaries These were interesting because the one was full of pike and the other full of trout – both of which eluded me. Here the land was unsuitable for hop-growing, being too liable to flood.

All the other farms employed pickers from London, the appearance of whom in the village made three weeks of September days seem like no others, before or after.

My father's friendship with George, ensured that we would share a bin, and the pay.

During these years the picking machines were beginning to appear, but George still employed hand-pickers. Just.

This was very fortunate for me, for it was by hop-picking that in my later years at school, I earned around £25 in three weeks. This was sufficient for new school trousers, or a new blazer, and a replacement pair of good and comfortable shoes.

The hop-picking mornings were often cold and sometimes wet. If there was rain, the hops could not be picked. But when the sun came out and the clouds cleared, and the hops were big, and the price was still high, everyone cheered up. Then the garden was full of gaiety and chatter; and the day became "saturated with the light of hops". Sunlight reflected off the fruit, its leaves, and throughout the long unpicked tunnels of glistening green bines.

The pickers were mostly women, and they were quick to let George know if they thought the price he was paying per bushel was too low. This communication was effective, for the price was always quickly adjusted. The picking was a family event.

I listened intently to the conversation all around, largely ignored, as we picked away the day. The gossip flowed on as it recorded, dissected, or otherwise reflected the lives that I lived among.

Each measure would be recorded by the bin-men on my tally card. At each of the four measures, seven or eight bushels would be the most I could hope for, if the hops were big. The price the farmer paid would rise as the size of the hops diminished, but it was always best for us when the hops were big. Their size reflected the weather earlier in the year, and the success or not of the cultivation methods.

Large hops resulted in a price of around 10 pence a bushel, but with George it was always a little higher than on the other farms. This was no doubt influenced by the forthrightness of some of the women, directed at him as he perspired his way through measuring their hops with his basket. Banter and negotiation were mixed together, much like the hops and leaves in my side of the bin; and together they flowed from the women over and around the farmer.

"Don't think much of the hops here, George! Easier measuring than picking these buggers, I reckon".

Or, "Some of these hops are so small I can't find 'em!"

But, in truth, it was a general good-nature that defined the relationship between farmer and the women. Though he actually said very little. A large cross-section of the working families of the village were represented there in the hop garden. They and the farmer had already shared many years; and they had shared backgrounds. They depended on each other; and the older women knew his circumstances well enough.

One afternoon, after the picking was finished, everyone would visit the farm again to collect their pay for the three weeks work. Just in front of the oast-house, and flanked by his binmen, George would sit behind a trestle table. The tally cards would be checked again, and the payments made.

There was always an atmosphere of late celebration, particularly if the harvest, and therefore the pickers' rewards, had been good. George was a fair, even generous, employer and everyone knew that; and so the air was full of a kind of relief, and of laughter and friendship. Or so it seemed to me.

The hot afternoon sun of late September could be better enjoyed still when the women accepted the farmer's invitation to a glass of his cider, from the barrel beside him on the trestle table. Perhaps even more than one glass sometimes, although of course the cider was not offered to me.

As the chatter and the laughter increased, the return to their homes of a good few of the happy women along the road past the forge, became a slow procession. Interrupted more than once by one or other of them falling over on to the soft grass verge, where they remained awhile in the afternoon sun. Unable or unwilling to move immediately, through laughing and the effects of the cider.

And so my school holidays, extending well into September, and long after my friends in other schools had begun their terms again, became a very great help to me in solving the real problem of achieving clothes for school. Not unreasonably, the new clothes of my beginning at the school could not continue, and the visit of the gentleman from the council in Westerford was not repeated.

Looking back, this seems a trivial concern now, but in recollection counterpoints rush forward nevertheless. Just as years before, the deep, ordered, and scented beds of wallflowers of the school in my second village had reminded me of the hedges of September honeysuckle, and the white violets in the ditches of February in my first, so I now recognize other counterpoints. That in Poland the hop was, and is still, regarded as a symbol of marriage. That the furnaces of the oast-houses which were all around me, burned as the furnaces of Buchenwald, Dachau, and Auschwitz had so recently burned. Of all this, of course, I was then entirely unaware, and only the flames of the oast-houses singed the manuscript of the years of my childhood, and quite harmlessly.

Because of George, I could also earn money by joining my father on the threshing machine. He was on the top, tying up, an old piece of sacking around his lap, well into his seventies. My job was carrying and stacking the sacks of chaff from under the machine; this was uncomfortable work because the dust and the chaff got everywhere. Down my neck and all over me, prickling and itching.

Then, I was part of a small team working quickly, and I knew I was lucky to be there. These men depended on this work for their living, and they pressed on hard at their task. They had no interest in anything but that I should also. And I understood.

Sometimes I initiated my own farm jobs. There were many fruit farms around the village, and I knew them all. My bicycle therefore took me to them at plum-picking and apple-picking time, to ask my question – just as it had with my scouting tally card.

As the answer was usually positive, I spent a good many August days in orchards.

In a nearby village, Stapleford, there was an apple-packing and cold-storage unit, where I went with my question one year when I was in the sixth form. First to pick apples, but later to work in the packing shed.

I got to know the young manager and his small family very well. His tiny house was owned by the company, but the living room was full of books that were his. He possessed many Russian novels. Handsome and strong, he would often drive the firm's lorries up to Covent Garden market in the early morning.

He laughed with delight when I asked him if he knew the legend of why blackberries tasted so foul after Michaelmas, and why it was therefore best to avoid eating them. Of course he did. The reason is that the bad taste is due to the fruit's gradual deterioration and fermentation on the bush. Red Admiral butterflies got drunk on them. I hope they still can.

The legend though has another explanation, which is that when the devil was cast out of heaven he landed in a pile of brambles. He then spat upon the blackberries in disgust, and that's what accounts for their bitter taste after Michaelmas, John surprised me by also knowing that the leaves of the hawthorn bush were often called 'bread and cheese' by children. I had thought that only I and they knew that!

Whether on the farm, or in the packing shed for a few short weeks and long days, I became therefore part of a number of completely different communities to those of my term-time. And I had to adjust to the rules of these communities just as I had to early on at school.

The movement of a long fruit ladder around a plum or apple orchard required a technique that had to be learned and applied. Trees could be easily damaged; and the treatment of the fruit also was of the greatest importance to the farmer, whether it was on the tree, or after it was picked. Such tasks had to be done in one way and not another, and I learned the need to respect that. And I welcomed that I needed to learn to do so.

Within these communities I joined in negotiating the weather, wet clothes, the need for shelter sometimes, and the quiet pleasures of conversation with older people in shared breaks during the day. Mostly as a listener.

In these few weeks, for a couple of summers, I lived among middle-aged and also sometimes quite young women, who were working to help support their families. I knew how this was for them a serious matter, and that the money they earned was essential – just as the way the trees were treated was important to the farmer. They tolerated me, and treated me kindly, as we worked away the day.

I understood and identified with all of this, just as I sympathized with the seriousness of my masters in the sixth form at school. As a result we got along in a gentle fashion, and I enjoyed living inside the various moments of the August days with them in the orchards.

By this time, Arthur and Victor were working on night shifts at a toffee factory in Westerford; and I became aware that my bus journeys to and from my public school, were very different to their bus journeys. Although they travelled together to work, they never seemed to talk much together; and I think their pre-occupations were very different. Arthur had a young family to look to. Victor was unmarried, and lived separately next door, though my mother was assiduous for his welfare; and he spent an increasing amount of time with her.

Perhaps it was for this reason that she so often emphasized the need for me to find work, though it was scarcely necessary. The advantages did not need emphasizing. My mother's references to working and leaving school often became mixed up around the time of my sixteenth birthday with my questioning her again about my birth certificate.

It is possible also that the visitors who came and stayed in the house for a short time before leaving for ever, prompted my questioning.

I began to wonder, now more consistently, about my father who wasn't my father, but an empty space on my birth certificate. And so, unreasonably, I persisted in asking my mother, who wasn't my mother, who my father was.

Her reply was by now always the same, that I should ask my mother. If I said that I couldn't, the conversation that had hardly even begun, quickly deteriorated. So I was told what I already knew but had scarcely begun to understand, that:

"If I you don't like it, you should get out!"

Uncle Victor's silent disapproval of me was as haughty as it was abiding, in the small house. And it seemed to increase.

I didn't spend all the money I earned on school clothes. Some I spent on food – and books.

At the beginning, many of the books were second-hand from Westerford market. They were unlikely stories of South African farmers and Zulu warriors; I even picked up a book that explained how I could teach myself Swahili, but I made no progress with it in spite of great efforts.

Another, I remember, was a collection of the speeches of Franklin Roosevelt which I absorbed by torchlight under the bedclothes.

In the early days I often visited Westerford market on a Saturday morning. One day to buy a second-hand wind-up gramophone for 9d.. It quickly broke, but I played it still by working the turntable with a finger at the centre of the records. These were old 78s selected from boxes at the same stall.

The trader came to recognize me, and gave me the records for practically nothing. To him they were junk; but to me, still in their brown paper sleeves, they were pieces of magic. Mostly, they were records of 1920s' dance band music, and First World War songs. With melodies which were sources of new wonder, they had titles such as: 'You're The Cream In My Coffee', 'Violet Can Do It Why Can't You?' and 'Farewell Isabelle, Isabelle. I've Got To Leave You, I've Got To Go'. And then also , and quite different, there was a record of 'Tales from the Vienna Woods'.

But most of all through those years, I collected books, carefully selected books. These special ones were new – with one exception. And this was an original 18th Century volume that recorded Captain Cook's voyages in the South Seas. I think it was written by the ship's doctor.

It was very big, and resembled a family bible in its bulk. And it cost me £4 in an old bookshop in one of the backstreets of Westerford. This was of course a vast sum, and I disclosed the transaction to no-one.

My small collection was eventually joined by Pasternak's *Dr Zhivago*, which I learned of in a review in *The Listener* in the school library, and with which I was immediately transfixed. There was a scholarly history of smuggling in Kent, the name of the author of which escapes me, along with books I received over the years as Christmas presents. Among these were a fine edition of the tales of King Arthur, a volume describing the travels of Marco Polo, and a single volume encyclopaedia for children – published at the time of the Festival of Britain.

I had a cardboard box under my side of the bed in which I kept this treasure – just a little away from my father's chamber pot and his tin of biscuits, which I raided regularly but carefully. Dishonestly.

For some reason that I cannot now explain, I became passionately interested in ethnography and anthropology. The public library in Westerford seemed to be full of popular volumes telling of the history and colonisation of the island groups of the South Pacific, which I borrowed and devoured.

The tribal distinctions of the inhabitants of Polynesia, Micronesia and Melanesia absorbed me. Ironically, looking back, since what I most lacked was a tribe. These books recorded the destruction of the indigenous cultures following the arrival of missionaries; from England, Holland, and to a lesser extent France.

Arthur Grimble's *A Pattern of Islands*, was typical of the many such books on the subject, which fed my adolescent wonder of foreignness and history. At about this time, for Christmas, Arthur bought me a copy of Richard Dana's *Seven Years Before the Mast*.

At this same Christmas, a drop-handled racing bike replaced my old bicycle which had finally disintegrated. Of course it was not actually a racing bicycle, not like those to be seen then on the roads in the summer around the Weald. Whishing past in large groups, ridden by members of French cycling clubs, as well as by those from our own country; in special clothes, and behind goggles.

My bicycle was not especially light, but it was still light for me, with quite narrow wheels. It came from Mr Harding's shop in the High Street, and was in very good condition.

And so, in the summer, my solitary rides became more far ranging, and now more frequently as far as the sea. And even when I was not actually on the way to the sea, the many villages I visited became in my mind part of the archipelagos of the South Pacific; on hot Wealden days as my school days began to draw to a close.

One of my history masters, remarked to me gently, and with some amusement, upon how the treatment of the native peoples of the Pacific seemed to creep into my essays on British Constitutional History, or upon 17th Century Poland. He advised me to consider being aware of this when the 'A' and 'S' Level examinations finally arrived. In the same conversation, he asked me if I had considered applying for a university place, which I had not. It was not an ambition that seemed even a remote possibility for me. Perhaps somewhere, deep down, there was a memory of Belgium.

When I said that I hadn't, and that I wouldn't actually know about how to set about applying, he suggested his own college, which had been Brasenose. "I think it would suit you!", he said. But of course he was unaware of my life in my other village, and the complete impossibility of making such a suggestion at home. How could he know, too, of my long established habit of living without future plans?

If I was somewhat unreasonably concerned about what I accepted were the misguided actions of missionaries in the Pacific, this was definitely not a reflection of some adolescent revolt against the authority of the church. It was simply a sympathy for islanders dying from tuberculosis, or having to swim fully dressed in 'Mother Hubbards', the dresses provided by the missionaries to hide nakedness. I had become aware of the writings of Rousseau.

My dismissal of the idea of Oxford, was therefore part also of a complete mental involvement with what I accepted was an injustice. For me the real subject of the conversation about Brasenose, was the suffering of the Polynesians; whereas for my history master it was my applying to his old college. And this was an example of how sometimes my lives in my two villages remained separate; this to complement the instances when they over-lapped.

Perhaps part of my response also, was that I had long before learned the futility, even the wrong-headedness, of aspiring to the shiny Jaguar cars in the quad. on Speech Days. Now to do so would perhaps be seen as justifiable ambition, or envy. For me, then, in my naivety it was simply neither. Particularly, I had learned very early on the complete futility of envy.

My interest in Polynesia, was simply that. Similarly, my interest in the past, in place and in art, was visceral; it had no extrinsic purpose. I was just engaged by History, Geography and English Literature; that was the whole story. Looking back, it was perhaps an echo of the wonder I felt when I was given so many new books during my very first week at the school. Then, also, I thought that was the only point.

Certainly, I had no reason to be antagonistic towards the Church in my village. For me, from the beginning, it had been a source of light and optimism, of colour and music. Even of shelter and hope.

This attitude could be aptly summarized by my being welcomed into the choir, without having a singing voice that was at all appealing.

The church itself stood like a rock at the head of the High Street where the bus turned. The 'cared for' smell of its interior belonged to my earliest days, and yet remained immediate. If the hymn books, 'Ancient and Modern' smelled of the perfumed Weald, that might have been because I was always, somehow, aware that the bus that turned by the church when I was eight years old, and turned still, could have quite easily been a tank. Its shuddering mudguard, the muzzle of a gun turret.

I loved the summer garden parties in the large garden of the large Victorian vicarage in the very centre of the High Street, a little along from our house; and I was in love with one of the daughters of the vicar; about my age, and very pretty.

I had grown into being a ready, if somewhat detached, audience for the cadences of hymns and carols throughout the church year. But naturally, simply as part of the order of things. If I had sometimes to be cajoled and almost 'driven' to evensong, when I got there and encountered the smell of the soft and clean surplice, the smiles of the prettier choir girls, the order, and the solemnity of voice and music, I entered a world that had long been familiar.

Sitting in the choir stalls, almost in the dark, yet aware still of the hushed colours of stained glass windows, among the music, and the measured language of familiar yet patinated readings, I experienced the value of being alone, and yet with others.

So my version of religion was of passed years of annual choir outings to the sea in summer, choir practice in the cool of August evenings, and parties at every time of the year – but especially at Christmas. Just as earlier it had been defined by the large brightly coloured stamps I had received for attending Sunday School. On ecclesiastical subjects, they could be stuck into small books.

Carol singing really had been for me at ten years old, something experienced at a time of snow which actually was "deep and crisp and even". When the earth really did stand as "hard as iron". When very young, the festivities had included tableaux in the village hall, when the preparations had always been frantic, and always successful.

My role then was simply to do as directed, though I strove to interpret these instructions. To stand on the lighted stage, dressed as a shepherd, nearer than was required to Pamela who was astoundingly pretty – and of course was Mary.

So my memories of the church in the village, along with everyone else, was of somehow being on the inside of something. Of belonging. And of being among many grown-ups who were on my side without ever saying so.

Chapter 8

If the Church was a continuing and diminishing influence on my life in my first village, cricket was a continuing and increasing one. At around the time of my life in the sixth form, though when not in school, I embraced it.

I have mentioned already the cricket field, a little away from the centre of the village, flanked by one of George Meadow's hop gardens. In my memory it was used for no other purpose, other than on the village school's sports day. No-one, to my knowledge, walked upon it except to admire it, play upon it, work on it, or watch a match. I have mentioned the mushrooms which later in the year grew upon the outfield, but even this seemed restricted knowledge.

The square at the centre was completely flat; mown short and marked out, loved and coaxed into match-readiness, it was always roped off when not being played upon.

The village fielded three sides on a Saturday in the summer, one on Sundays, and yet another on Wednesday afternoons. Wednesday was early closing day for the shops in the High Street. There were long fixture-lists against other villages, and clubs, which we played twice in a season – at home and away.

Since I played cricket at school, I had a pair of whites, boots, and a sweater; and I loved everything about the game. This was not because I was any good at it, but with cricket that doesn't necessarily matter; or it didn't to me then.

I loved the elms that stood high around the pitch, and that the old men sat on benches to watch in their shade. I loved the cricket teas on match days, and the Thursday evening net practices. But most of all I loved being a quiet member of whatever team I was playing for, composed of men from every station in life but sharing one purpose. And I loved the trips to other villages on match afternoons in team members' cars.

I belonged for an afternoon, easily the youngest; and in the evening in the pub afterwards, for there was always a pub, and home or away I was always included in the round. I couldn't contribute to it though. A pint of shandy has never tasted so sweet since those days.

There were many characters among our teams, partly formed and defined by the contrasts between their prospects in life. For instance, the garage owner tall and lean, who always opened the batting for the 2nd XI, and always seemed to be given out lbw.. And always shook his head in disbelief as he walked slowly back to the pavilion. Each time aghast at the fallibility of human judgement other than his own.

The Wednesday afternoon side was captained by a very wealthy member of the village, who owned a large farm to the north of the village. With his necktie girdling the extensive waist of his flannels, and with his side on the very brink of victory at the end of a long and hot afternoon, he would bring himself on to bowl at the critical moment. Always. Or so it seemed then.

Poised for victory, our fortunes would immediately begin to slide. The immaculate line of his slow trundling off-breaks, and his ability to turn the ball sharply off a perfect length, were recognized by no-one but him. Certainly not by the opposing batsmen. They helped themselves in joy and disbelief. On those Wednesday afternoons when I was free in the school holidays.

Mid-week would usually see Fred Freeman, an important person in the village, knocking on our front door. As I have mentioned he and his brother owned the corn merchants' business in the centre of the village. Someone would have had to cry off at the last minute, which prompted his question: "Are you free for a game on Saturday?" As if I wouldn't be if it was in the school holidays. Or on Sunday, or on Wednesday, for that matter!

I was seldom down on the team sheet originally, because of my commitments at school. I didn't pay a subscription to the club. And yet I was seldom without a game.

Cricket was a serious matter for our 1st X1, who always played on Saturdays, and in an early-season two day match at home around Whitsun time. It contained two batsmen in their mid-twenties, who had previously attended my school. They were very good players with a sound technique. The attitude of the members of the 2nd X1 was serious also, for each aspired to the recognition that would lead to their joining the 1st X1, perhaps permanently. The spirit in the 3rd X1 tended to be more relaxed, though still very serious. Cricket was simply an important business.

Mr Williamson, who like me, appeared for all the teams from time to time, had a batting technique which was at best unconventional, and depended upon a very good eye. He wore glasses, but they must have been good ones. For whereas the earlier batsmen had carefully negotiated the fast bowlers, cutting and glancing patiently to build a sometimes over-small score, Mr Williamson arrived at the crease to lay about him immediately, with never a care.

However furiously the opposing bowlers steamed in, and whatever guard he carelessly took, Mr Williamson's cross-batted swipes had the effect of fielders having to search for the ball in the hedges of the hop-garden, or in the overgrown grass around the pond at the back of the pavilion.

If our cricket ground was carefully kept and prepared, so were many of the grounds of other villages around and about. Usually but not always; for at Stapleford we sometimes had to remove sheep or hens from the pitch before the match could begin – it was even ducks one year. But the match, it was always a 3rd X1 match, would start eventually so long as rain allowed.

Very occasionally I would meet school companions at these village matches in the holidays. Day boys like me, who had also been pressed into service by the villages in which they lived. I was not a good cricketer though, just as I was not a good chorister.

ii

Sometimes my methods of getting to school varied very slightly, though not often and not intentionally. As well as the service bus leaving at 7.45, the London coach also stopped outside Hubbard's store on its way through the village to the capital.

It was modern and fast, with very soft and clean seats; everything about it smelled new. However, although it was always on time, and left at 8.05, it was not theoretically possible for me to catch it and arrive at school on time.

Although it was quick, it did not arrive in my second village early enough for me to attend my house meeting before chapel. Another, no small matter, was that my season ticket was not valid on the coach.

On the rare occasions that I had to catch it, I would then proceed straight to chapel; and that was not only forbidden, but was a very public transgression. Lateness was frowned upon even for 6th formers, and could have uncomfortable consequences if noticed by a house prefect.

Fortune might be kind, but other house members would know immediately; and later on some of these were school prefects.

However, sometimes, I simply missed the service bus, and on those occasions the driver scrutinized me and my season ticket closely, but still let me on. On one of these mornings that generosity was even greater than I, or he, could have possibly anticipated or known.

Not only was everything about the interior of the coach warm and smelling clean, but the ride was smooth beyond imagining, not stopping between my villages.

That morning the driver had the radio on as I settled, still sleepy, into a soft seat before negotiating my unavoidable lateness. By a happy chance, orchestral versions of Dvořák's five **Prague Waltzes** were playing; and as I listened, and as the morning countryside flashed passed, I felt a peace and a joy that I could not previously have imagined. Possible retribution for my lateness was of no consequence now; and simply because of that coach driver's taste in music.

I had stumbled upon a beauty that was beyond my comprehension, and which still is; and so began my untutored but loving dialogue with music. And, I began to love especially the music of that most optimistic and lyrical of composers. I believe he once remarked that he regretted that he wrote so much, though that was a regret that I have never shared. When I reached school and went straight to chapel, nobody seemed to notice. Or perhaps it was that I didn't notice their noticing.

iii

My mother was anxious still about my needing to get a job upon leaving school, to earn money. I was still anxious about my birth certificate. By now I had sorted out the previously blurred distinctions between step parents, adoptive parents and foster parents.

Her anxiety about my getting a job, and my continuing questions, made our relationship worse. By now she had health problems because of a seriously ulcerated leg, and her frequent wincing indicated that she was in increasing pain. This alone was enough to reduce her tolerance of my renewed questioning. And, perhaps also, any justification for my continuing to question her.

Whatever the reason, relationships at home became more fraught and increasingly tense.

Whenever I started to question her about my father, her reply was always the same. It referred me to my mother, and … . What characterised this conflict most was that it was never resolved by an answer, and then not mentioned subsequently. With the result that resentments grew on both sides.

There was one important event which propelled me towards the future, the end of my sixth form career, and hence my school days, and that was the last Speech Day that I would attend. And I should explain how it was that Gladstone, a German Field Marshall and the Archbishop of Canterbury all had walk-on parts.

One of the most prestigious school prizes, awarded to sixth formers, was the Grizelle Prize for History. This was for quite a considerable sum of money, to be spent on books. Or a book.

At the end of my first year in the sixth form, to my complete astonishment, I had been given this. To my astonishment, and never expressed pride. Then, sitting in the library and combing through the pages of *The Listener*, I had selected a book that was praised there: Sir Philip Magnus's *Life of Gladstone*. And it turned out to be a good choice. A very good choice.

When I eventually read this large volume, handed to me by General Ironside, I felt that someone was saying to me that after all I was good enough to read it; and indeed the book fascinated me from the outset. And not only was this a gift, but a public gift.

The inscription plate carrying my name, the title of the prize, and the date, announced that here was something that could never be taken away. I didn't need permission to keep it. And so, I stored it in the box along with the other treasures, but wrapped in brown paper, under my side of the bed.

Occasionally, during the year that followed, I would remove it, unwrap the brown paper, and examine the inscription plate. Vanity and weakness of course. But more than that, it seemed to represent to me a kind of permanence – or at least a temporary permanence!

Anyway, it was a gift to me from people at the school that I admired; and no doubt that it was a gift caused me to admire them even more.

As the end of my final year in the school approached, and with 'A' and 'S' level examinations looming, the day of red carnations approached again. This year the visitor, we learned, would to be the Archbishop of Canterbury.

Intent upon revision, Speech Day had not been in my thoughts. But one day I heard that there was a notice on the Sixth Form Notice Board which someone said that I should go to read. It announced the year's winner of the Grizelle Prize – and there was my name again.

One member of the history group was very upset that I should have the award for two years in succession. He considered it very unfair; and who is to say that from his point of view it wasn't?

He was the elder son of a very famous entertainer, and his brother was also at the school. I learned very many years later, and quite by accident, that he became a successful barrister. An occupation for which, I imagine, he was very well suited.

However having the Grizelle again, was a kind of affirmation. It cheered me, and amused me, as I sat in the library reflecting, and leafing through the pages of *The Listener* for possible titles to give as my selection to the history department. Perhaps, I thought, something by Simone de Beauvoir? Or Sartre. Or Camus? Or Zola: perhaps *Germinal* – as a kind of souvenir. I considered, too, Milovan Djilas's critique of Tito's Yugoslavia, *The New Class*.

There was however quite a large problem which presented itself to me as a result of my having the prize; one arising entirely out of my own weakness. It had to do with everything about the shiny cars in the quad., and with my own threadbare clothes; which although very acceptable to Chaucer in his Clerk, seemed very threatening to me at seventeen and about to meet the Archbishop.

As I sat in the library reviewing my options, they seemed unpromising. My blazer was not too dilapidated, and should last until the end of term if I had it dry-cleaned. And I could always find a reasonably white collar to make a shirt look respectable.

But my trousers were a problem. They were too short, were threadbare, and hopelessly shapeless at the knees. Also my shoes had been just too many times repaired; the last time, and quite recently, I had used tacks and my father's last. In short, I realized that I did actually mind now that I looked a ragamuffin.

The appearance of my clothes was viewed by my antagonist in the history group, as proof of a slovenliness which indicated moral failure. His dress was as immaculate and polished as one would expect from his background; and no doubt it has remained so in his professional life.

Sitting in the library, with the sun shining down upon, and up from, the Weald, I thought about the assembled school, and about the elegantly dressed people who would be on the stage. The simple fact though, was that as a result of the demands of revision, and because it was still early in the summer, I had no funds; and it was unthinkable that I should mention anything of this at home.

My mother expected me to leave school and earn money, not to ask for new trousers and shoes. In any case to do so was unthinkable. I had mentioned the prize, but she would not have considered there to be a problem – even if I could have found the words and the wit to explain.

When I discovered the remedy, I applied it immediately, as I had once before on the doorstep of the strange house in Westerford when I had been thirteen. Having selected a copy of *Lost Victories*, Field Marshall Erich von Manstein's account of the German defeat at Stalingrad, as my prize – along with the text of a modern French play called *The Egg*, by I forget whom, the following weekend found me in Mr Harding's bicycle shop.

In an act of cowardice, not unprompted entirely by the mockery of my complainant in the history group, I asked Mr Harding if he would buy my bicycle back from me, without of course mentioning the reason for my request.

He gave me enough money for it for me to buy a new pair of dark grey worsted flannels and a new pair of shoes, which when I wore them made me feel as if I was walking on a serenade of strings – now that the tacks of the old ones no longer bit into my feet.

The immediate physical pleasure of wearing soft, light, new trousers and shoes, seemed an immediate vindication for my selling my bicycle. It was another example of the power of the moment, to which I had surrendered; though later it became something that I was not proud of. Rather, I felt guilty almost immediately.

All I had bought was the possibility of meeting the Archbishop with a quiet mind, and in comfortable shoes. And all I could do was hope that my cowardice may be viewed mercifully by more kindly souls, as no doubt it always had been.

The history prize gained for a second year, was nonetheless a source of silent pride, given to me, as it was, by people I identified with and respected. Meeting the Archbishop of Canterbury in one pair of trousers rather than another, was simply one consequence of that.

iv

One night, two years later, in December 1961, the poet, critic and editor, Alexander Tvardovsky, surrounded by the perils of Stalin's Russia just bequeathed to Kruschev, was at home in Moscow. It was late, and he was reading the manuscript of Alexander Solzhenitzen's *One Day in the Life of Alexander Denisovitch*. He was in bed in his pyjamas, as he started to read.

After reading the first two pages he got up, dressed, and went downstairs, to continue his task there. Later, he confided that he did so because he felt it was an insult to read such an author in his pyjamas.

My point has nothing at all to do with the author of *Lost Victories*, which just happened to be the book I chose almost randomly to receive. It was rather that I was choosing new trousers, at least in part, out of respect for my teachers in the 6th Form; not even because of a particular desire to please the Archbishop I was about to meet for the first time and very briefly. And not simply, I hope so much still, out of fresh cowardice. They had helped me, without the remotest possibility of knowing quite how, to stay at home until my schooldays were done.

I stored the second Grizelle Prize, with its inscription inside, under the bed, wrapped separately, carefully, in brown paper on top of the first. As I did so, I believed, as before, that it could never be taken away.

Later that summer, one weekend, I would lay on my side of the bed, on a hot July afternoon, having just left school. I had on again my old pair of trousers. Days of August fruit picking lay ahead, and I was reading Norman Mailer's *The Naked and the Dead.* A narrative largely set in the Pacific, though with more than missionaries for the indigenous peoples to contend with.

Soon enough there would be no place even for the box under the bed, which contained my treasure. And I'll come to that.

PART 2

Harmony

Twenty Years Later

The music endures but not the music maker

Milosz

Sometimes the music stops
But mostly they accept the score
And play the harmonies
That exorcise the demons at the door

Tim Cunningham

Chapter 9

I sat in William and Carol's small garden with them, during a sunny weekend early in October, approximately ten years after I'd first met William. He had been talking about how impressive he found the students at the Open University. He had begun working as a part-time tutor with them the previous year. On Thursday evenings.

His room in the faculty building at College was just across the corridor from mine. We shared a background in the Philosophy of Education, as it was being developed in our universities in the UK during the late 1960s and 70s.

At around the time I was staying for the weekend with my friend, some new members of staff had been appointed after years of a freeze on new appointments at the college. In a faculty meeting, I remember now, one of these new members was proposing that tutorials should henceforth all be conducted with the tutor's study door open – in case, they argued, female students, of which we had a great number, felt uncomfortable in the room alone with a male tutor.

The proposal made questionable assumptions, refusing to acknowledge for instance the importance of the promotion and development of trust between men and women. It was therefore thrown out. The practice became an option though, for that was the Goldsmiths' way. I remember catching William's resigned looked of amused forbearance as I glanced around the large meeting, as the new staff member's over-long harangue drew to a close.

William had returned from the US. a fortnight before, and the conversation between us turned to his trip. He talked about a theory of poetics for the classroom which he'd been working on with children and students for a couple of years. At last, I thought, the invitation he'd received to go to the States showed that people were starting to take some notice, and I recall how, almost innocently, excited he was about that.

I'll recall that conversation, in as nearly as possible his own words. If I tell you as he told me, you may get some idea about how he worked, and the kind of person he was. So, he told me how,

"It was just getting light. And there was a noise. A low roaring sound. It was hot as I began to wake up. And I didn't recognize the window through the curtains.

Then, in the Sheraton hotel room on Jacksonville Beach, I realized that the noise must be the sound of the air-conditioning system.

But that was wrong too. If it was the air-conditioning, why was the room so stiflingly hot?

The room in the gathering light was large, and as I got out of bed my feet sank into its deep carpet.

Opening the heavy draped curtains at the three huge windows, I suddenly understood the sound which I had woken up to. It was the ocean. Not the air-conditioning. And not the sea – but the ocean. The difference is the difference of scale.

What I saw with my ears as I looked out was the bright, vast, Atlantic Ocean. In the warm sun of a clear morning, sky met water, and white sand met sound.

Perhaps part of my first confusion was that I'd never woken up in a hotel room right on the beach before. I looked around for the air-conditioning controls before laying down again on the huge bed. It was so hot in the room.

As I continued to wake up, I thought about how I had come to be here. It was all because of voices; young voices in Goldsmiths, where I now worked and which I would have passed had I stayed on the London coach that morning over twenty years before; after first hearing Dvořák's *Prague Waltzes.*

It was all about students' voices, and the still younger voices of the children that they had been working with – in college, and out in local schools.

The voice of Maria, who said:

> ***"It wasn't that school turned me off poetry – it just didn't bother with it"***

And of 9 year old Sam:

> ***"You ought to be able to write what you want. If you're told all your life to write what other people tell you, you'll find that you won't have anything to show that's really yours".***

It had all begun because of the new course that I'd got agreement to run. Something I'd managed to negotiate in exchange for agreeing to move from the Postgraduate Secondary Department where I'd been very happy for seven years, to work on the planning, design, and teaching of a new undergraduate degree. The small poetry teaching course was quite on the margins of my normal tasks in the department; and I imagine that at first some colleagues thought of it as an indulgence. I was happy about that though; that is just the nature of things.

The course had been running for two years when a letter arrived in my pigeon hole from the U.S.. From a graduate student at Berkeley, who'd read some articles I'd published.

That letter led quite soon afterwards to an invitation to speak at a conference in the US., not in California but in Florida.

It would be the first time that I'd been to the States, and I was certainly new to this kind of attention. I remember how excited Carol and I were when the invitation arrived; and later when another came from the British Council – with news of a grant to cover travel expenses.

Sitting on the Eastern Airways flight up to New York for the connection back to London, very early in the morning, I looked back on the previous ten days. Back upon the lead lecture, the seminars I'd run, the various meetings and visits that followed, and a surprise interview for the local television station. And I wondered if my hosts realized what a novice I was to all of this.

As I sat back in my seat, I heard the folksy southern drawl of the voice of the captain introducing himself over the address system. Telling us at what time we would arrive at JFK airport, and insisting upon how New York was "just the very greatest city in the world".

The university staff at the conference had seemed so young, and engagingly optimistic. And the sun of every day, so unusually and exotically hot.

As I spoke to my audience, I had let other voices speak with me, on audio recordings which I had collected in college and in London classrooms.

Voices and laughter of second year students of Education. One: ***"I never thought of it as a course, but just my time".***

A second: ***" The way we could work, makes it more true. You feel happy about yourself".***

A third voice my audience heard, said: ***"There's a warmth. Everybody's feeling floods you. You feel connected with other people".***

And yet another spoke with me, as I spoke:

> ***"The course was academic, and necessary to our professional knowledge, but because it was so enjoyable it by-passed the staid and the apprehensive, which ensured that every task we undertook was a***

pleasure and seemed effortless … . I feel I've been introduced to a great resource".

So, for my talk, I had brought those other voices with me. Particularly, Elizabeth told them:

> ***"Just for fun, at home, I checked with my husband which ones (poems), he thought I should read today … . Also we've been reading to each other over coffee, before we came today".***

I played them Maria, saying:

> ***"I share a flat with two other people, one doing Nursing Studies, and someone else doing Architecture. And we spend a lot of time sorting through the anthologies you asked us to make, picking out the good ones (poems). Sometimes I think they're even more interested than I am!"***

And Jean joined in :

> ***"Jane and Beverley are in the same hall (of residence) as me, and we compare poems we've found, and read them to each other – often late into the night. It's almost one of the best things we do".***

Returning, still sleepy, from these reflections, I heard the captain continuing to crack his jokes; as the sun shone around the aircraft's cabin, and breakfast arrived.

I thought of the scorn, and the doubts, and of the accepted wisdom about the difficulty of doing something effective about poetry in school which could reach more than a very few children. And I smiled to myself, and was still smiling when coffee arrived.

Why did it matter so much to me? I couldn't say at that moment, 30,000 feet above North Carolina. It just did. Just as it did to the students and children whose voices I had brought with me, and to whom I was now returning.

Most of all though, what mattered to me now was seeing Carol, Claire, and Anna, again.

Chapter 10

> …
> And be happy in your love
> it's not too late
> never too late for those
> who read a poem together
>
> Josef Hanzlík

> You have to inhabit poetry
> If you want to make it.
>
> Anne Stephenson

There was a single plum tree in William and Carol's small garden. At the bottom, near the low fence in front of the corn field, sloping up to the church in the distance.

I remember one evening, in the summer, we all sat under it and talked after dinner; and William spoke quite carefully about a place from his childhood: Tatlebury Corner.

He spoke of a signpost that someone had turned around, and he saw this as an example, somehow, of how we should not always accept conventional directions, but rather go the way we knew instinctively was right. Of course the idea of going in the opposite direction is always worth considering; nothing remarkable about that, in itself. What was significant, he insisted, was that the signpost had been turned around.

Somehow when he spoke of that signpost, it was connected for him with a 'poetics' for the classroom where the notion of 'composing' as 'fashioning and making' is central. But also that composing is just as much about children reading and listening together, and speaking in conversation – telling each other what they are understanding – as about them actually writing. Most of all, 'composing', for him, in what he was trying to formulate, was in quite a special way definitely not only about children writing on demand in the classroom.

It was still an hour before we were to land in New York that I remembered Tatlebury Corner for some reason. From so long ago. It came back to me as I thought again about the students' and the children's conversations.

I saw that signpost again, and so clearly, almost buried in dog daisies and ragged horse-parsley, or almost invisible in snow; and how it had been turned around. Nobody knew who had done that. Nobody corrected it. Nobody much bothered.

Of course the fact that the instruction it gave to the innocent or the unwary traveller, would not help them to arrive at their intended destination, was plain.

But then everyone who lived in those parts knew how to get where they were going anyway, so they could ignore the signpost. And then I remembered Heidegger's reminder to us that poetry is the opposite of something special made from everyday speech. Rather everyday speech is a forgotten poem, where words are just working on reduced power.

Usually, but not necessarily always, which is where the extracts from the conversations I had played the audience in Jacksonville, in all that Floridian warmth, comes in. Sometimes, poetry can enter conversation again, and the melody which ordinary speech once had becomes restored.

And the simplest example of this happening can be when someone wants to quote from something they have found, and which they know someone else might want to listen to. Partly, perhaps, because they remember having offered something similar to another listener themselves – and hope to do so again.

It was so when Maria, said:,

> ***"After you read that poem by Carlo Levi last week; you know, about his friends and hoping for a long autumn for them. Well my husband and I looked at another of his books about the camps: Moments of Reprieve. This is not written out as a poem, but I think it is still poetry".***

And when she'd finished reading to us, the silence that followed seemed to last for so long that everyone struggled with what to say … or when to say it. Perhaps because of the tears which I saw in the eyes of at least two of her companions when I looked up. The tears which were part of the silence, after she had chosen to read out:

> ***"'Like Rumkowski (a character described by Levi at the end of the book) we too are so dazzled by power and money as to forget our essential fragility, forget that all of us are in the ghetto, that the ghetto is fenced in, that beyond the fence stand the lords of death, and not far away the train is waiting'".***

Maria was reading Natural Sciences as well as Education. She wasn't studying English Literature.

What I'd stumbled upon, on those stolen Wednesday afternoons working for a year in Barking with nine year olds, supported what I'd known from the very first school I'd worked in. And what I had experienced in winters and in summers in my own school's panelled library overlooking the Weald.

The two years of the course, so far, simply confirmed and reinforced what I already knew. The difference was now I'd discovered a transferable method that would work as well with twenty year olds as with nine year olds; and one not unconnected with their once having been nine years old.

It was a methodology built upon Octavio Paz's reminder that "human beings not only use language, they *are* language that produces language". Put that insight into how to proceed with poetry and children, and perhaps, I mused, we may after all be able to sing our way to where we belong.

These reflections were interrupted by the Eastern Airways' stewardess, young, tanned and cheerful, rustling her presence. Offering more coffee, muffins – and peanuts.

'Yes, thanks!'

She smiled as she served them.

When we find a way of putting together young people and poems, as readers and listeners, talkers and then writers, their conversation about what they are doing will inform each other, and their writing also. In each, each will merge with each; and the children will observe this happening also in their companions. Then, we can begin to recognize best possibilities. After all, the trade that we are in is about recognizing those best possibilities.

Thinking and communicating can, in these situations of generative exchange, become almost simultaneous. Students together, or children together, can hear and answer each other almost at the same time, because each is attendant upon something of which words are only the outcrop. Just the beginning. Just as with improvisation in jazz, or in a string quartet, there is something vital running beneath. The character of the spoken communication achieved, suddenly has the same newly minted quality that Heidegger recognized at the very birth of speech itself, and as at first poetic.

The coffee tasted so good!

And what I thought, as I looked out of the window, down upon the sun reflected back from the top of the clouds beneath, *could be less abstruse than that, less abstract, more relevant – and more simple?*

Then, it makes the most perfect sense for us to speak

of nine year olds, or twenty year olds, in the classroom or seminar room, listening to each other listening; reading with their ears; composing as readers and listeners as well as writers; composing in conversation, composing themselves, and indeed composing each other. All such seeming paradoxes are perfectly explicable – and necessary. Necessary in situations where poetry becomes, again, workaday.

Voices can get into each other, and as they do so they can take a poem with them. It happened when I asked the children at the end of the year, in the summer, whether they would like to come to college to read to, and talk to, a group of Postgraduate Secondary students, who were at the end of their course – and the beginning of their teaching careers.

There would be the same number of students as children, and although some of the students were my own, the rest were selected from other tutor groups. All were graduates of English, Music or Drama, and all had volunteered their Wednesday afternoon. Of course, I told the children none of that; only that they were friends. But then they knew of course where I was from, and where I worked.

On this afternoon, it was the voices of nine year olds and twenty four year olds together that could merge.

Usually on Wednesday afternoons the children would go for their weekly visit to the local swimming baths, something they loved. But they insisted that they didn't mind forgoing this.

And so, they crossed London on a dusty, sticky, summer afternoon, with their teacher, to talk to a bunch of strangers. Their teacher spent the afternoon with one of my colleagues, Barbara; and they relaxed together for an hour and a half around the college. There was plenty for the visitor to see.

The 'strangers' though were young, and they and the children ran things for themselves, while I simply listened to their conversations as they all discussed the reading and the listening, the writing and the talking that had gone on during the year, in and out of school. Listened to the children saying why it all mattered to them, and listened to these strangers' reactions to them doing that. And so the afternoon was composed of children reading to graduate students of Education, as the recording equipment collected everything that was said.

It later noted Kelly, as she said when I met the children on the following Wednesday afternoon:

> ***"They smiled at us. And laughed when we read our poems. And then Corinne sang, and they laughed again. I liked Fiona. I hope I can see her again".***

And they listened with those smiles, when Simon read his poem about questions, without knowing that it was his mother who had asked the questions, or that Simon had heard, and read, a few poems by Robert Frost. Perhaps his listeners had not thought either all that much recently about water butts. Nor could they have known how many times Simon had read this poem, among others he had written, to his mother; and to the companions who came with him that afternoon. Nor how many times he had chosen to read it, and they had asked to hear it, in our previous meetings at school. And how many times other people had chosen to listen to it, in or out of the classroom:

Have you been outside?
I have not. I said.
Then why are you wet?
I'm not. I said.
Then what are those drips?
What drips?
Those drips.
I've been playing in the water butt.
So you have been outside.

But these strangers did hear for the first time how Simon thought:

"It's very different when you are able to write at home as well as at school ... the more time you get the more ideas you get".

They heard Sam agreeing:

"Writing does matter because its interesting. It's important, it's fun, it makes you happy. You enjoy it when you have a choice, you can decide what you want to do".

When one of these strangers asked the children whether they ever read their poems to themselves, Linda burst in:

"Yes, I keep reading them. I read one, and I remember when I did this or that".

Later, after the conversations had moved quickly on, Linda returned to what she'd said:

"Say I went on something at a funfair and I thought it ... this is really exciting. I think when I get home, or at another time, I've definitely got to make a poem about it – and make sure I've got it. If I think I'm enjoying myself too much, so I might not remember, I get a piece of paper out of my pocket and write it down. So when my mum washes my coat she takes all the bits of paper out"

And so, these young teachers laughed with Linda as she read to them.

They heard on that afternoon just some of the results of these children having become used together, to hearing and answering seemingly at the same time. Used to living in a situation where the inner world of thought really can lead to a social world of being. And that they may govern this themselves. Must govern it.

They all recognized together, fleetingly of course, how singing can get into reading and into writing – and into conversation. The children had experience too of how conversation may contain inaudible as well as audible voices; and that there can be a silent chorus of listening.

In such conversations, rhythmic thinking becomes easily intelligible, and understood. As does an unspoken understanding of the relation of re-listening to re-reading; and of children choosing to re-listen because they already know about the repetitions of hearing and listening again, in the playground. And all of this is harnessed immediately to the necessary re-reading which successful engagement with a poem requires. Because pleasure insists upon repetition. In the playground and sometimes, hopefully, in the classroom also.

As I bit into a muffin, I thought of how what went on that afternoon was built upon how poetry is a basic, elemental, thing; and that teaching it involves promoting the kind of reading it entails. Where the reading itself is the only point. And that in spite of the origins of poetry not actually being literary.

The method of achieving all this was like the box that I had once had under my bed. Yet much bigger, a whole storehouse full of treasure. It was as simple, or as difficult, as the origins of poetry within language. True the stages of the method I had discovered were systematically arranged, and their effects were progressive, but the means were still simple.

Describing the method by writing about it was not so simple though, not least because when writing about Education the constituency had become so large. Perhaps because, as with poetry, Education as distinct from education, may have fewer friends than flatterers.

On the one hand, there is the rock of needing to somehow explain the linguistic and anthropological background. The risk here is the charge of being unpractical – cut off from the classroom. Or there is the hard place, of explaining what to do, step by step, in the classroom or seminar room. Here the risk lies in being over prescriptive, and leads to the danger of reinforcing the very difficulties I am trying to remedy.

Then the stewardess returned with more coffee and her tan.

The need was to help the young teacher achieve their own theory of poetics for the classroom, informed by their own experience and reading. And a very important means to beginning this was to use what children actually say – and I had plenty of instances of this happening, on many hours of audio tape. They just had to hear the children's voices: clear and committed. To hear that the children were doing the same as they were.

The rest would gradually be taken care of by the stages of the method itself, which I had outlined in a number of places. This introduced them to their own predispositions; and allowed them to become confederate in what they were engaged upon.

Then I remembered that I had agreed to speak about the course at a teacher education conference in Maastricht in a few weeks, and I resolved to use children's voices again.

The proof of the worth of the approach was always in the response of the audience, whether at conferences, or in a variety of schools with teachers – where I was finding myself increasingly describing the course.

I was becoming confident that it could all actually work; with children, with students, and for teachers.

I knew it, when students I'd not met previously, smiled a greeting on a college corridor, or in the refectory. Or when they held open a door for me, which I often, ironically, jokingly, refused to go through first. For, "a little courtesy glows/ like lemons on the underside of leaves".

This, in truth, was something of a new experience for me. My nature leads me to eschew any suggestion of over-ready, over-familiarity with students at work, unless it was firmly grounded in a teaching/learning situation already well established. In what would be defined within the Philosophy of Education as the "discipline" of co-operative work. In a large college full of young and attractive young women, such a resolve was a necessary one, to avoid the fraudulent – and the dishonourable. Perhaps this is a weakness, I don't know.

Whatever. I had worked out that what led to students' response to my little course, at first at least, was just surprise. They simply had not expected to be asked to consider the things that they found themselves suddenly addressing. True they were led to consider them only obliquely, but the effects of their doing so were simply not what they had expected.

They understood well enough, and immediately, that they should be prepared to teach poetry with young children. After all no one could see that as a bad thing! What they did not anticipate was their own level of involvement. That it could become important to them personally – and to so many of their companions. So I realized that their response was governed by a kind of astonishment; and a realization that the treatment of poetry in the classroom would become important to their children because it was important to them.

So, colleagues would joke over coffee to me, at that time of the week when the various so called 'Professional Studies' courses were running, that all their students seemed to want to talk about was poetry. When they were expected to focus on other things. Science, Mathematics, Nature Study, Art and all the rest. Then I smiled just a little – but a great deal inside.

And it became noticeable at odd times, how small groups, or pairs, of students had to be negotiated sitting on the stairways of the Education Faculty building, intent as they were on books of poems. And I noticed how often young eyes smiled as I passed.

The manager of the Waterstones bookshop in the concourse of the college, spoke to me, in some surprise and amusement, about how her staff were having increasingly to field enquiries about poetry collections, from students in pairs or singly. Not because they were set texts on English Literature courses, but because the enquirer was intent upon reading for pleasure. Indeed these unsophisticated enquiries were not from students reading English in their degree.

She was pleased of course. And so was I.

The invitation of the course was one that they could accept just a little, or completely, but since they were all together, they re-discovered again the social origins of poetic response, and so were encouraged by each other. And most importantly, there was nothing else in their college work, their overcrowded days, which so addressed their most personal pre-occupations.

And so, it was in this surprise that their un-stated but deeply experienced confederacy lay. When they spoke of what they were doing, what became obvious was the involvement of husbands and boyfriends, girl friends, flat mates, and room mates. Just as the participation of parents, and classmates, brothers and sisters, friends in the playground, uncles, aunts, and grandparents are important for children.

Put simply, in being prepared to teach poetry with young children, they were being asked to address their own natures. And so it really did, for just a few moments but quite often, become one of the most important things they did. It really felt, in those moments, that the way they worked, in a special way together, was simply their time.

As a result, they recognized together something that by inclination they were prone anyway to recognize: that one of the pre-dispositions of young children is towards joy.

The strategies of the course required them to travel the same roads along reading and public response, participation and presentation, listening and exploration, that they would ask the children they would teach to take. In doing so, they would recognize without being told, because of the choices of reading they would make privately and publicly, in many places other than the seminar room, that the bedfellows of joy and wonder are decay and terror.

The letter from that graduate student from California, which had led me to my now imminent arrival back at JFK. airport, had referred immediately to how the course worked with young teachers in the same way as they were expected to work with children. She understood immediately that you cannot expect children to value something that you don't value yourself. And that the young teacher and children share the need to travel the route from social to private and back, and from speech to the literary – and back.

She used the term "re-education" in her letter, to describe what she thought I was doing with these young people. I didn't much like that way of putting it, and preferred instead to see the methodology of the course as about "repair". What they were being asked to consider was something they couldn't happily avoid, because they already knew a lot about it.

In a kind of way, it was this that lay behind the sudden smiles of welcome in the corridors, as we passed. Those smiles had an ancient source. As soon as the course began, most of these young people quickly recognized that it was essentially about them, although that could never be made explicit. If it were to be, the whole enterprise would collapse. That part of it had to be hidden, and I think they even understood that.

News spread that here was something a little different to everything else that was required of them. It spread as only some news can in the student community, to those who eventually would join the course later in the year.

Once these chains of recognition and response, participation and sharing, had been set up, the rest was not my business on a day to day level. My only responsibility was to keep the repair going, by attending with them to those processes that had started to run.

As the Boeing 747 prepared to land in New York, these reflections upon the sounds of the voices of nine year olds and young teachers, were interrupted by the instructions of the cabin crew.

My final reflection was upon how these voices actually validated my job, and yet belonged to a small course which had almost not existed; and which as far as the faculty authorities were concerned, existed only on the margins of my week. But then that's just as it should be, as I've said. Like so much else, it was best that its importance to me should be hidden.

That way, other people as well as my students could be surprised. For, not for nothing is poetry subversive!

For me, as well as for some students, "it was almost one of the best things I did". At work.

I remember wondering, as I listened to the cabin crew's announcements, where else I would go with the course; and whether the visit to Maastricht was not something I should be thinking about quite urgently.

After the early start, the heat of Florida, and all that had happened in the last ten days, I felt suddenly tired. Yet it was still only 7.30 in the morning, and my flight back to London did not leave until the evening. So I had a day to spend in the city that had been so fulsomely praised by the pilot.

I planned to visit the Rockefeller Building, and the World Trade Centre. Now, since then, partly rebuilt.

A day in the city was before me, and I felt excited about that, and about all that had happened in Florida. Relieved and contented also. About the voices of the young teachers that had accompanied me, and about the responses to them that I had met.

I remembered the report I had to write for the British Council, because of their support.

But thinking about all that could wait for now. I was in New York!

Chapter 11

William once confided to me how light had listened when he first met her. And it was listening still when he met Carol at Gatwick Airport. I think it listened during the whole fifty years or more that they were together.

He said that he knew that when it came to finding that kind of love he had been more than lucky. In a number of ways life had prepared him for choosing well. From his beginnings, that weren't beginnings, right through to his becoming a student at Goldsmiths' in 1960.

The melody that he had heard early would play on until the end. And as he flew back from New York, of the alternating light and shadows of Tatlebury Corner only the light shone at this time.

If the everydayness of language that he often spoke of was at the heart of what he had been describing at Jacksonville, it was the everyday of their life together that he loved even more.

Although he knew that some people would consider it a weakness, he simply hated being away from her. If the young women he met as a child were sources of astonishment to him, his life with Carol was full of an astonishment that was mature, alert, and full of delight.

He was aware that this happiness was simply the pathway of mutability and transience. He had always been aware of it. But their days were days of sharing and innocence.

They had been married one afternoon in early October; "between summer and the end of summer." Then it was that he began to love the sharing and the innocence. He loved going to bed at night with her, and waking up with her. He would often wake early and watch her as she slept.

They were at a stage of life when "youth lay sleeping on the breast of youth / Where life was love, and not a brief desire". He knew what heaven was then, I think, because he lived there.

He told me of the special meaning that Elgar's **Enigma Variations** had for him, and how it dated from that time. The piece was on the programme of the first concert he and Carol had attended together, in the very early months of their marriage. The place was the Festival Hall, the orchestra was the London Philharmonic, and the conductor was Constantin Silvestri. Almost unbelievably also, in the second part of the evening a young Vladimir Ashkenazy played Rachmaninov's **2nd Piano Concerto**.

It was another bus-radio moment, full of poetry and wonder from the cheapest seats.

She was a little over three years younger than him, and they had met at a wedding. He had been best man, and she the chief bridesmaid. He had never been to a wedding before. She had often been – as a bridesmaid for various friends. Everything about her was feminine, and it engulfed him immediately.

The early 1960s were not those of popular media legend for everyone, and they weren't for William. They were years of awakening and freedom though, for light and shadows, wonder and terror, had continued to alternate during the years since he had left school.

When he had come to London as a student first, it was a little after the opening of the Festival Hall; where he could hear, for instance, Otto Klemperer, already elderly and ill. A generous local authority grant, temporary work on building sites, or in factories, easily come by then, meant that he had money enough to start to explore the capital.

So while the college was in New Cross, guided by various new and young companions he discovered the Everyman Cinema in Hampstead, and the still sparsely attended Sunday afternoon recitals at an, as yet, un-restored Wigmore Hall.

Then Bergman's melancholy was stimulating and exciting; and the dust motes that danced in the afternoon sunlight filtering in during a recital, appeared just the result of the pianist releasing Chopin into the hall. Part of the performance.

He never went alone. The years since his leaving school had taught him to value company; to love it almost above everything.

And so he became as familiar with the Royal Court and Sloane Square as with the Gaumont and Lewisham. With New Cross as with Bloomsbury; with the terraces of Highbury when watching the Arsenal, as with the Festival Hall and a myriad West End theatres; with Blackheath as with Hampstead Heath. London was not as crowded then, and was generally much cheaper; and as the song goes the living was easy. At least for a young student with his essential costs taken care of. At least during term time.

In London then, jazz was everywhere. In the record shops, in its cafés, in the cinemas and on the radio. Everywhere in the college; in the study bedrooms and in the public events of its eight or nine halls of residence – and at the mammoth dances held throughout the year in its Great Hall. And also at the private parties, to which he found himself quite frequently invited.

Now that he had the time and the opportunity, William regretted that he could not play a musical instrument; that his love affair with music was so uninformed. That the school, and his home life, to which he owed so much, could not have helped him to remedy this absence. It was an inability, I think, which he was to feel increasingly, throughout his life.

The music department at school had been one man, Mr de F., a most gifted organ scholar. William had imagined that this unfortunate man's loneliness was revealed by the trail of cigarette butts which appeared behind him each morning in the quad.. As he crossed it each morning on his short, stooped, journey to the school chapel. Those journeys, along with his isolation, ended for ever during one school holiday, after Mr de F. was found gassed in his room by his own hand.

William had already experienced a shard of the same kind of loneliness for himself.

But now life was full, though when the college terms ended, there was a recurrent problem. He had always, each time, to find somewhere to live before the next term began. The very reasonable request to everyone to clear their room to allow for maintenance and cleaning, inevitably only led to a foreboding in him.

Later, their wedding night was spent in the vast Midland Railway Hotel in Sheffield, before leaving the next morning on a train for Devon. Staying in a hotel was a new experience for William, so that night was one of firsts.

As I said the 1960s were not those of popular legend for everyone.

When they were in Brixham, a letter from Dorothy, Carol's mother, arrived. It told them that the vicar had been to see her, and that they must go to see him immediately upon returning to Yorkshire. The news was that they had to have their marriage certificate altered – "to make it legal", as William's new mother-in-law put it in her letter.

He had of course told Carol about his origins as he knew them, of his unconventional childhood; and had taken her to visit his foster home. When he answered the questions for the marriage register, he had written his foster father's name as his father. After all, he reasoned to himself, it was right that name should be recorded. And since the difference in surnames was plain for anyone to see, he was hiding nothing.

Of course he guessed that the old problem would surface. It could not of course be that easy to avoid it. Never that straightforward.

When they kept the appointment, the Reverend Wall said little. He simply amended the entries in the register and on their marriage certificate, by striking through his father's name. It was replaced by ------------. Just as on William's birth certificate. And then they left. William was too familiar with the inevitability of it all to do more than regret it. It didn't surprise him.

There had been very little discussion. William tried to explain why he had made the original entry, but the vicar was business-like and in charge. He did not need to listen, and so he didn't.

And then William turned away from all that, in resignation. His love for his young wife had been anticipated in the green and the gold of September hop gardens, in the sun-baked High Street of his first village in all its Julys; and out in the middle of cricket pitches as clouds scudded. And it had been anticipated also, during the early evening 6th Form English lessons in the library on the escarpment high above the Weald. And it was all that mattered.

He had anticipated it when looking up from the school quad in January, upon

> "Fields of Snow and tranquil trees in snow
> Through veils of twilight, northern, still and sad,
> Waiting for night …"

So, he turned confidently away from that interview with the vicar, to married life. And to a new job three hundred miles away. Down south again.

When the plane touched down, Carol and the children were waiting; ten and seven years old and in their best frocks. And his wife dazzled with her welcome.

The nearly completed journey home, repeated the earlier first journey back from Yorkshire to their new home and his new job. The forty minute drive from the airport to their house on the outskirts of South London was full of questions and the chatter of the children. And yet it too was just the latest of a series of journeys around the country. Journeys made as jobs changed, as he sought to earn enough by teaching to support marriage and even a small family.

The first one had taken him to the Essex coast to a class of seven year olds, his first after leaving college. It was a brand new school, where the classroom floors were waxed and polished during each holiday for the beginning of the school term. And where, every morning, everything smelled as fresh and new as the children themselves appeared.

The Head there arranged a discount upon a radiogram at a local electrical store for William. He paid for it by instalments, and it was installed in a room which he rented from a young couple near the beginning of their marriage – a little away from the school, and near the cockle-sheds on the coast, at Leigh.

He was lucky to come upon this arrangement; for when he'd first arrived in the town he had lived for a month in a quiet boarding house with other working men. But although the landlady was kindly, the company of four or five older working men bore down upon him. These middle-aged men said little, pre-occupied as they were by the details of their bachelor lives; watching television and queuing for the bathroom. The contrast with the youth of the company which he had just left was just too great.

Then after just a year he found a job in the north near Carol; a journey which took him to a pre-fabricated classroom, and a class of nine year olds. "Temporary". Built after the war, it had yet remained. Large cracks in its walls let in November rain and snow, and winds which soon began to blow straight off the Pennines. In through the same cracks that the heat leaked from.

He told the children to keep their coats on when they were dry – if they had coats. The room was heated by a large coal-burning stove by his desk, surrounded by a metal safety grill. It was old, and emitted doubtful fumes into the room and over the children.

The Head, a coarse, short, taciturn man. was unconcerned about the condition of the classroom, and this became a source of conflict between William and him – and the conflict grew.

The classroom had a storeroom, in which researchers from the university had installed equipment. This was there to measure the levels and types of the air pollution blown to the classroom from the large British Steel works along the valley in Foxton; and from steel plants in Rotherham in the other direction. Each morning and afternoon young people in white coats came to inspect and change the filters.

Just as these visitors became part of the school day, William's long walks over the moors around Foxton, with Carol and the family's dog, quickly became part of his week. Looking down upon the small gardens full of the colours of chrysanthemums and dahlias, overlooking or just out of sight of the giant three mile long steel works. Colours lovingly coaxed into those small gardens from and alongside blackened moors.

How green the moors seemed just a little further away from the huge steel plant. And in that October he went with Carol one evening to hear Stan Barstow give a talk about how he had begun his life as a writer. And about how he came to write *A Kind of Loving*. At the local secondary school.

William's struggles with the Head to get him to address improvements to the classroom, continued; and continued to be unsuccessful. They became part of his new life at school. Every evening he met Carol, and often ate with her family, before returning on the bus to his digs in a nearby village, halfway between her village and the school.

The Head's secretary, a small, kindly, woman of around fifty, smiled her support gently when they met, for she must have overheard his discussions with the Head about the classroom. She would have heard her boss say,

"If you don't like it go back down South!"

A little after that she came to his classroom on some pretext, and before leaving she told him not to worry.

Near the end of the school year, as his departure for the new job drew near, she came to the classroom again. As they talked, she wished him good luck, and added:

"I knew you wouldn't stay!"

And then he felt guilty about leaving the children. But these were the 1960s, and finding work as a teacher was as easy as it was un-remunerative. And the new job would enable him and Carol to be married.

And so the new journey back to the South really was to a completely new kind of job; even William's employer was a newly created London Borough. The post was as the only teacher in an experimental, open, remand home. And its main building was an old hunting lodge set in extensive parkland.

William's responsibility was for designing and teaching the school curriculum for boys aged between eleven and fifteen – sometimes sixteen. Though, as he would learn, some of the children would be even younger. And in addition he ran evening classes for senior boys aged up to seventeen; classes about English Literature – mostly poetry.

With the job came a newly converted and renovated mews cottage with two bedrooms, for which William and Carol would be charged a nominal rent of a few shillings a week. The rent even included a garage.

All this was provided because William was required to carry out what his contract described as "extraneous duties"; on three of the five weekdays, until ten o'clock at night; and on one in every three weekends. In addition his annual leave was restricted to eight weeks, including all bank holidays.

The extra work included the organization of psychological tests for some of the boys, in co-operation with a visiting psychologist from the Home Office. He also had to conduct attainment tests with all of the school-aged children, for the courts; and write reports for them upon every facet of the stay of each child that was in his care in the classroom.

The psychologist's visits would always provoke comment from the children he interviewed.

Summer and winter he would arrive for his weekly visit during the afternoon. Noisily, in his red sports car; scattering the gravel of the sweep of the circle at the front of the house. His arrival was always noticed by the senior boys as they were working in the gardens, because of the sports car. A good many being there for stealing, or rather 'taking and driving away' various makes of cars. And nor was this transgression confined to the senior boys.

All the school-aged children interviewed by the psychologist were anxious; in a state of inner turmoil. Away from home and lonely. So, his methods of introducing himself to them often surprised them; and when they returned to the classroom from their interview it was usually in a state of some moral indignation.

The resultant conversations with William would follow a familiar course:

"Here sir", they would re-tell. "That bloke's mad if you ask me". William would always look up from what he was doing, and with the same question,

"Why?"

"Here, what are you grinning at sir?" Not to be diverted, the boy would continue,

"Anyway, I goes in, and this geezer says, 'Hello mate, sit down!'

"So I sit down". Then he says, 'Would you like a smoke?' And he pushes this box of small cigars towards me. I couldn't believe it. He's smoking one. So I says "Yea, okay thanks", and I takes one. And he carries on writing like he was before.

Then all of a sudden, he looks at me, and starts shouting". He says, 'What the bloody hell do you think you're doing smoking my cigars? Are you stealing my cigars?' And he takes it back.

But sir, he offered me one!"

Give or take minor details, this would be the story that the boys returning to the classroom would tell after their interview. Always, William would reply something to the effect: "Oh don't worry", he's just a little eccentric. We're not all of us the same, are we?"

"Mm bloody mad you mean! Got some nice wheels though!"

"Well there you go", William would reply. And the conversation would end, and the boy would return to what he had been doing before the excursion upstairs which had so surprised him.

In his discussions with William, the psychologist had explained what he was trying to do, and what responses he was expecting. He left it to William what response he would give when the boys returned to the classroom.

As you can see, the work was very different to teaching in a conventional school. Full of incident, challenging certainly; and often harrowing and hard, because of the home circumstances of many of the children who had fetched up with him. He always tried to treat them with consideration and courtesy – and with the sympathy he felt for them.

Sometimes former college friends came to stay for the weekend. They seemed puzzled by the choice of job William had made. And often William's conversations with them were laced with the kind of dark humour that often attends people, especially young people, when they are describing other peoples' crises.

Though the job made the annual leave welcome, even a necessity, it also demanded of them that when a weekend was free they should get right away whenever possible. Often that was to Carol's parents in Yorkshire. After a short time, they had bought a demonstration model Hillman 'Imp', from the garage in Carol's village. From the garage used by her father. So they would leave on the milk run at four in the morning up the A1, and arrive by nine o'clock. Returning quite late on Sunday night.

As William would joke to his visitors from the past: "You must remember our low rent, and the additional allowances which allow us to save!" For Carol worked also; at a large American publisher's office in a small town nearby, which had recently moved from central London. His friends didn't look convinced.

And he got the impression that their judgement of him was not dissimilar to those boys' of the psychologist. "Bloody mad!".

But the darker side of it all actually worried William quite a lot; for reasons connected with Carol's safety – in spite of her working off-site in the week, and their often being away at weekends.

He never, ever, discussed personal matters with the boys, though they were always asking him whether he was married.

Although the greatest majority of his pupils presented no kind of risk, some of the boys with whom he worked in the evening had committed crimes of violence. Serious crimes. They were at the home only temporarily, because the courts had fewer options than were ideal about where to place these young people for a short time. They would be quickly transferred when it became possible.

A very few of these older boys, who were not his responsibility during the day, had serious psychiatric disorders. Although medicated, they nevertheless, for however short a period, could present a real threat, adding to William's fears for his young wife.

The home was run on genuinely open and liberal lines. Some of the senior boys did run away and had to be retrieved by the police, but the children for whom William was responsible during the day very rarely absconded. At least not during school hours.

Because the grounds of the house were so extensive, he was able to add cricket to the curriculum in the summer, just as it had been introduced to him. Fortunately during the time he was there, the summers were long and warm. The games took place frequently, in the afternoon. The Superintendent supported the idea of the cricket, and ensured that there was a generous budget to provide for good equipment. Just as the support for books and equipment for the classroom was generous.

It was surprising perhaps that no-one ever ran away during those afternoons. It would have been easy for them to have done so, for only William was with the boys. In fact they could all have run off together, over the fields and away. Fifteen or twenty of them. That would have put paid to the cricket. But they didn't, and so the warm summer cricket afternoons continued.

On one occasion Carol and William took a nine year old to a nearby cinema for the evening, to see a James Bond film. His home circumstances were particularly grim, and he had few visitors; and when Carol heard about him, she suggested the trip to William – who at first was sceptical. He pretended to protest that it would be on one of his evenings off!

The Superintendent listened carefully when William put the idea to him. He agreed though, and surprisingly quickly, turning his back upon of how it would look to the police if the boy had run away in fear, and had to be retrieved; or what the local paper might have had to say had such news come to its notice.

So, although the evening could have ended badly, it didn't. The young lad was relaxed and childlike.

Still, some of the senior boys continued to worry William, because of where he and Carol lived; though other married staff would have similar concerns of course. And some of them had children to think of. There was an excellent outdoor swimming pool, and on summer evenings, when all was quiet and William was at work, Carol used it for half an hour or so. By herself.

Insofar as working in such a place, with children who at best were in turmoil, could ever be a happy experience, it was within its own strict parameters a happy time. William, however, had insisted to Carol that they could only stay there for a limited period – however pleasant their cottage and cheap its rent.

He got on well with the Superintendent who had appointed him. And also with his Deputy; who when Mr Perkins transferred to the Home Office Inspectorate, took over at the home as Superintendent. Both showed a close and genuine interest in the work in the classroom, and were supportive in many ways.

But William was determined that he would not be there when their own children arrived.

The promotion of Mr Perkins was, however, significant because of the necessity for the appointment of a replacement Deputy Superintendent. I should mention that it was a condition of the post of Superintendent and Deputy Superintendent that the holders should be qualified teachers.

When the new Deputy arrived, he brought conflict with him. First it was with a number of the senior care staff, and one in particular, Henry, with whom William had stayed in the first few months of his own appointment as the cottage underwent extensive alterations and improvements.

Henry and his wife were from the East End and had two young sons. They were, it seemed to William, almost an ideal family, and he had got on well with them from the beginning. Violet was strikingly handsome, and her husband was straightforward, honest, and committed to his work. He was a strong man who had no trouble with the young people with whom they all dealt.

Their sons were aged twelve and thirteen, and attended a local public school as dayboys on a scholarship.

One very tangible result of William's short, but absolutely essential stay with this family, was a lively, black, Labrador puppy; the family pet had a litter while he was there. He thought she would be good company for Carol when he was at work during the evening. Perhaps when she grew, she might become a good guard dog even.

When after only a year the dog was killed in a traffic accident in the grounds of the home, it was Henry who quietly buried her, so reducing the sadness that the loss of the animal caused Carol.

Henry's disagreement with the new Deputy had its roots in the new man's bullying manner with the boys – and for that matter with staff also. He wasn't used to it. He was a quiet man who went about his days in a quiet manner; he was not used to sitting down beneath an aggressive imposed authority.

On one early occasion the two of them were on lunch duty together, and there was an incident with one of the more troubled boys to which the Deputy, let us say, responded with extreme harshness. Henry was outraged, and tempers were quickly roused. Afterwards he let his opinion be known quickly, as soon as was appropriate, with the result that even a physical confrontation between the two men seemed likely.

This would have been serious for both men. For the Deputy because Henry was a very strong man, who had run a gym in Poplar for some years before beginning this work. For Henry because any sort of physical disagreement between a Deputy Superintendent and a Care Worker could only have had serious permanent consequences for the Care Worker. Luckily however, Henry cooled down; and an armed truce was established.

It was essential that the children in the classroom should not be left. The first part of the teaching day began at 9.00 and finished at 12.30. The second began at 1.30 and ended at 5.00. In between was lunch, which William always had at home.

There was an arrangement, for both the morning and the afternoon, whereby William would have a ten minute break to visit the bathroom perhaps, or have a cup of tea. For instance, in the morning, the usual arrangement was that the Superintendent or the Deputy would come down from the office at 10.30 to sit with the class.

This routine had been inherited from the previous teacher. It met a physical need for William, and no doubt provided his superiors with opportunities to assess the learning activities that were taking place in the classroom, and the boys' responses generally.

It was not uncommon for William to send a boy up to the office, just to remind whoever would come down, not to overlook him. Partly because they would often be heavily involved in what they were doing. Or partly so that a reminder would allow whoever came down to adjust what they were doing to allow for the imminent visit to the classroom.

And so one morning in December, just before Christmas, at around 10.45, William sent a boy up to the office. The Superintendent was out that morning, which was something that William didn't know; although if he had, he probably wouldn't have given it much thought. And so it was the new Deputy who received William's message.

Quite quickly, the boy returned smiling,

"Cor", he said, "he's not half annoyed with you sir!"

William looked up at the returning messenger, as the boy continued,

"And he said sir, that you should tie a knot in it."

William thanked him, and asked him to sit down again, and get on with what he'd been doing previously.

Hardly had the boy done that, than the classroom door flew open with a loud bang, causing eighteen pairs of eyes, along with William's, to looked up as the peace and order of the classroom was disturbed.

It was the Deputy, who splutteringly demanded of William,

"What the hell do you mean by interrupting me?"

Now there were was a keenly interested audience to this question, waiting for William's answer. Very aware of this,

William simply excused himself for his break, taking care to return within ten minutes. When he came back, the children were working in silence. He thanked the Deputy, who left clearly still enraged.

It was not in William's nature to let matters rest, and before leaving the building for his lunch he went to the office to speak to the Deputy. His intention was to point out that the system for cover in the classroom during the morning and afternoon was just a necessary custom. Although he did intend to arrange a time to discuss the Deputy's dramatic entrance to the classroom.

Obviously, he was keen that any further discussion of all this should take place later – simply to preserve his lunch break!

But the man was still in a temper, and as William began to speak to him about how the system of classroom cover had come into being, he became further incensed.

Rounding on William, he spat out,

"It seems to me that you should get some nappies on the line!"

To which William replied,

"And it seems to me that you should consider how you address staff members in front of children".

The effect of this reply of William's was electric.

The male Secretary, an ex-Royal Sergeant Major, the only other person there, stiffened at his desk.

The Deputy shouted at William to get out, and further told him that he was suspended.

Now it was William's turn to experience rage, feeling both deep offence and alarm, mixed together. Now almost white hot with anger, he simply left the room and the building, convinced of the wisdom of saying absolutely nothing more in reply to the Deputy's fresh outburst.

So, now suddenly, unexpectedly, he had the whole afternoon to himself.

The first thing he did after preparing a quick lunch, was to ring the local secretary of his Union, whom he didn't know personally, but whom he knew worked in a local secondary school. Then he lay down on the settee to listen to some music. Brahms. He felt very hot still, and adrenalin was pumping around his body.

When Carol arrived home, he broke the news about what had happened, gently. Her response was,

"Okay, so we can spend the evening together. Good!"

As he was telling her about what had led up to his dismissal from the building, the Union man rang back, and arranged a time to visit next day. He said that he'd also be arranging for a Field Officer to come with him, when he visited again early the following week. And that he would be in touch soon about this.

William felt much better after the call. Less isolated.

That evening there was a carol concert in the home, and although it was William's evening off, they had planned to attend it together. The concert began at 7.00.

Carol sat beside him on the settee.

"Do you know what I think?", she said.

"Go on", said William.

"I think we should go to the carol concert as if nothing has happened".

And William agreed to this. The idea immediately appealed to him. Why not? It would be a good riposte!

But then, he thought again, "Are you sure. It might not be easy?"

But she was adamant.

They arrived early, and sat in the empty hall: it was the large dining room converted for the evening. They sat at the end of a row, halfway back.

As various staff members who were not on duty came in, it was clear that the news of the morning's drama had spread. Younger care staff, directly responsible to the Deputy, exchanged greetings with them both, but sat on another row.

Just before the concert began, Henry and his wife came over to them, and sat down beside them.

"We heard what happened", Violet said.

William nodded, and actually felt quite near to tears as his initial assessment of what had happened was beginning to wear off. Carol squeezed his hand.

The boys were entering the room and taking their seats, and he noticed how the new Deputy and the Superintendent sat together deep in conversation. The Superintendent appeared to be listening intently with his head slightly on one side. His face impassive.

William returned his attention to Henry and his wife, and thanked them both for coming over. But went on,

"Are you sure you want to do this? It might better for you if you sat somewhere else. You can see how it is!"

The older man smacked him on the back, "No", he replied, "these seats are just fine"

And so passed that unusual carol service, in those unusual circumstances, in that unusual place.

With their faces burning, Carol and William wished their companions goodnight – after thanking these brave souls again. And as they left, he felt glad that he had listened to Carol, and that they had come.

The next day, Saturday, found the Superintendent sitting on their settee with them both, asking to hear from William what had happened the previous morning. In the afternoon, the Union representative came, and the following Monday afternoon he came again accompanied as promised by the Field Officer.

If the truth were told, William and Carol were now feeling their isolation, which this quite elderly, courteous, man helped to dispel. He took careful notes of everything he heard from William. He listened with a close interest to the details of William's working week; and when he left he said that he would be in touch again soon, after speaking with the Borough's Children's Officer. The Children's Officer was

William's boss at the Council. The meeting the Field Officer referred to was scheduled for the following afternoon.

After the visitors from the Union left, William sat for a few minutes on the settee in their small living room. He leant his head back, closed his eyes, and reflected upon where he would be without their support.

On Wednesday, the Field Officer was again sitting on their settee, this time with the Children's Officer. The council official seemed embarrassed, although he said that he felt that he must mention how serious the whole matter was. William said that he agreed; though at this the Field Officer smiled him a warning.

At the end of the meeting, the Children's Officer declared, suddenly, that he thought it important that William should return to work as soon as possible; and he suggested that the following Monday would be best.

"We have to remember", he said, "that the children are without a teacher at the moment".

And so, two days later, a letter arrived from the Children's Department confirming this decision. As a result of the negotiations conducted by the Field Officer, it was agreed that there would be no loss of service days, no loss of earnings, and that no mention of the suspension would appear on William's service record.

On the day before the letter arrived, Henry and Violet came to see the two of them. And so the episode passed, with a week off work as the only consolation for the worry and anxiety that had almost completely engulfed William and Carol.

William returned to the classroom just a few days before Christmas. The Superintendent never referred to the matter again, and their amicable relations continued as before.

But now William had decided not to stay beyond the summer. By May he had applied for, and got, another job. When he left, it was on cordial terms with everyone; except, it has to be said, with the Deputy whom he had simply avoided whenever possible.

At the beginning of the following September, he and Carol were making another journey, to a small mixed secondary school of about three hundred and fifty pupils, in Essex again – for William to run his own department, as Head of Social and Remedial Education. Yet again, a new kind of post.

The school was a very happy one, and his department would consist of three full time members, including William. It was established as part of the local authority's response to the recent publication of the Newsom Committee's Report: *Half Our Future*

And so in another town a little way away, our travellers took out a mortgage on a house on a small, brand new, Wimpey estate, and so began another life.

His new Head was Mr Hughes, a kindly man in his early fifties; his Deputy, Mrs Hilton was a history graduate from King's London, about the same age as the Head. He liked them both from the beginning.

Yet it could hardly be said that the first term in his new post began uneventfully, for within the first few weeks Mrs Hilton came to him with a request. And that had to do with the school's annual prize giving ceremony.

She asked him to arrange activities and classes on the afternoon of the ceremony, for those children for whom his department was responsible. The school premises, were modern, composed of one large single storey building, and a three storey classroom tower at one end.

It had been decided, said Mrs Hilton, that the ninety or so children who were William's department's responsibility, should work in the top classrooms of the three storeys during the prize-giving. Well away from the school hall, and the ceremony. She was asking him to make the arrangements.

Last year, she said, some 4th Year boys had caused a disturbance, by being generally rowdy, and clapping ironically when the names of prize winners were read out. And in any case it was, she thought, she said, demoralising for pupils who would never win prizes to have to sit through a prize-giving ceremony.

With the optimism of youth, William smiled disbelievingly at his imposing colleague, with her seemingly reasonable and innocent request. In the first three weeks of his new appointment, by which time he had read and re-read the Newsom Report.

And to the request, he said … "No!"

He explained that he thought that the children they were discussing should attend the prize giving, because they too were part of the school. So, although he was sorry, he couldn't do what she was asking.

Mrs Hilton was shocked. And at first quite speechless.

"But you have to!" was her immediate response to this refusal. And she flushed a deep crimson.

That afternoon, after the end of classes for the day, in a warm sunlit corridor, he met Mr. Hughes, who usually was to be seen walking around the school at that time. Clearly he knew of William's conversation with Mrs Hilton. But the Head seemed friendly, asking how the day had gone.

They went together to his study, and when the matter was raised, William agreed that it was unacceptable for pupils to disrupt the prize giving ceremony. Upon which, the Head asked him what he suggested.

Although William's memory of his previous quite recent brush with higher authority was still raw, he couldn't but be aware of the great contrast in the approach of this man to that of the Deputy in the Remand Home. And of course there were educational issues involved here, which had a different resonance altogether than bathroom breaks.

And so he pressed on, and let the moment govern his arguments. He suggested how the two classes from each of the four years attending the prize-giving would, in the longer term, prevent discipline problems rather than lead to them.

William raised the interests of the eleven year old boys and girls who had just joined the school, some of whom were taught by his department; and suggested that their parents might expect that their children would attend an important school function.

The issue of the wearing of school uniform was raised by the Head; and again it was the early-leaving class of 4th Year boys who were prone to be rebellious about that. He mentioned again the disruption which occurred at the previous year's ceremony, and said it was simply a matter that these pupils did not want to attend. William sensed the chance of a resolution here, and so suggested that he should speak to these classes, and ask them if they wanted to attend the prize giving. And that if they did, they must give certain undertakings.

There was then a silence. A long silence.

Mr. Hughes continued, "You do understand the importance of this prize-giving ceremony to all of us? And that I cannot have it spoiled?"

William felt sorry for this reasonable man, for he knew already how difficult some of the older boys were. Indeed that was part of the reason for his appointment. He certainly did not want to be in conflict with his new boss.

"Will you be personally responsible for ensuring the good behaviour of all the classes we are discussing, and that if they attend they wear school uniform?"

To this, William had to reply that he would be. And he added,

"And if any of the fourth year leavers don't want to be there, then they can opt out and I'll supervise them during the prize giving." Obviously it had not escaped him that if such a large number of pupils were not at the ceremony, nor could he and his two colleagues attend.

And so it was left, on that early evening, that William would speak to the classes involved, and would report back to the Head the following afternoon. He jumped in his Renault 4, and set off for home.

His two colleagues in the department had joined the school at the same time as William, and were John, a psychology graduate from Exeter University who'd come straight from service in the Hong Kong Police Drug Squad, and Melanie an extremely able and experienced former primary school-trained teacher, who worked with the younger children.

That evening, William telephoned these colleagues and told them about Mrs Hilton's request, his meeting with the Head, and about the undertakings he had given. He knew that they would be in agreement with what he had arranged – and they were.

Next morning, William spoke to each class, asking them if they wished to attend the prize-giving or be set work for the afternoon away from the school hall. He spoke of the disruption by some fourth year pupils last year, and how important it was that everyone should behave well, and that they should wear school uniform. In fact the greatest majority of them did anyway.

And naturally they opted to attend the prize-giving!

The uniform was simply a white shirt and grey trousers for the boys and a white blouse and grey skirt for the girls. With a navy blue sweater or cardigan. There was also a navy blue school tie. William had found some spare ones in one of the cupboards in his room, and he saved these carefully – they would be useful as spares just in case … .

And then he had a meeting just before lunch with the class of fourth year pupils who would leave the following Easter. He reminded them of the inappropriate barracking that had occurred in the previous year. They would have witnessed this as younger pupils. He said that everyone wanted them to be at this important school event, but only if they wanted to be. They could of course, if they wished, work with him at the top of the teaching block for the whole afternoon.

They all said they wanted to be at the prize-giving. Naturally. And they gave an undertaking to William and his two colleagues, just as William had given his to the Head.

When he met Mr Hughes later in the afternoon, he told him of all the undertakings he'd received, and particularly those by the fourth year boys. He told him that, when given the choice, all the fourth year leavers involved had elected to attend if they could, and that they understood that they must wear the school uniform.

The older man's reply was simply, "Okay!"

Just that. "Okay!" The meeting was short.

During the day, William and his two colleagues in the department had discussed everything that had happened since the previous day, and what William was proposing. Both his colleagues were enthusiastic about the arrangements.

John was particularly indignant, having not met this kind of dilemma in the police in the Far East. He would leave at the end of the year to move to Manchester to train as a Probation Officer. He was also to be married. Several times, later in the year, he would come out to dinner with William and Carol at their home twenty five miles away. He and William became friends for that year.

On first hearing of the Head's proposal, John's anger led him to declare,

"Well if these children cannot attend, then I'll not either!"

"Mm", thought William, *that is actually true!*, for the proposed separation of these children from the rest of the school for the afternoon certainly involved him and his colleagues also.

But he didn't remind them of this. He simply assured them both that it wouldn't come to that.

And so, a wider stage was set as the afternoon of prize-giving approached, where the school stage itself would become the focus for everyone. For visitors from County Hall, for all the children in the school, for the staff, and for three staff members in particular.

Unsurprisingly, the uniforms of all the children William had spoken to three weeks earlier, were immaculate – as was their conduct as they applauded in all the right places, as other children were awarded prizes for attainment. And at just the right volume. Nor was there anything about the demeanour of the fourth year early-leavers to suggest that the idea of barracking had ever occurred to them.

Only one boy, Brian Willis, did not attend, but then he often didn't appear at school; preferring instead to support the family finances by pea-picking, or some other casual farm employment.

So William, and his two colleagues, got to attend the prize-giving also.

Perhaps it is worth considering the context of these small events. A former member of the staff of one of the Paris universities had just joined the staff of the school, albeit only for a year. Quite a mature lady, she came to the school to teach English, having been dismissed from her post in France for supporting the student protests which had engulfed Paris. So, large as well as small rebellions were in the air. They were a part of the times.

Next day, when he arrived at work, William was greeted in the foyer by a beaming Headmaster. In a good school "much goes to little making" sometimes; and essentially he was a humane and kindly man who cared about his work. Carol was to become a favourite of his, and later on he would quite often invite them both into his study to chat when she came with Claire to collect William. She had to drive past the school on her way back every week from spending a day with her parents. They had by then moved from Sheffield to another Essex town nearby.

Claire was only fifteen months old then, and on these occasional visits she entertained William's boss with her chatter in his study.

But that was for later. Now William had another idea, and thought that today might be a good time to put it to his boss.

That particular afternoon in Mr. Hughes's study, the two of them were discussing how the prize-giving had passed off;

and it was then that William pressed home his advantage. After all it could all have gone so differently, and now might be the best time to ask.

He was mindful, he said, of the position of the very youngest children who had just joined the school, and who needed to feel a part of things in spite of any difficulties they might be having at the present. And as he sat facing the Head, sitting in the armchair normally reserved for visitors, William suggested the value of prizes being awarded for effort and individual progress, as well as for examination success.

The older man smiled, nodding his head as he did so; and then to William's surprise and delight agreed immediately. Immediately. "One prize for each year!" said the Head. When William asked if he and his colleagues could let each class know of these new arrangements, as they met them during the week, the Head agreed to that too,

"Alright, Alright!", and he continued to grin, as he added getting up from his desk: "I think you should go home to your family!"

Of course, it was a very small thing, and William knew that, but when he came to look back upon that first term in his new job, it was with something like real affection. That beginning could have worked out badly for him, but it didn't.

As he left the study that late October evening, the Head touched his arm, almost affectionately. And Mrs Hilton? Well she and William became quite good friends. Her husband was a good cook, and was very interested in narrow boats.

Two years later, William would be seconded by the local authority for a year on full salary, to complete a degree course at his old college, having first given an undertaking to Mr. Hughes, that when he returned after the year he wouldn't leave for two years. William actually was to break that promise, although the way that came about could not have been anticipated by either man, the older or the younger. And I'll come to that.

When William looked back at his time at that school, it was always with pleasure and gratitude. Out of a problem, at the very beginning of his time there, came the possibility that any of the children would receive prizes for progress. Which was not something available to them before. Not much, sure, but it might very easily not have happened. In that it was very like the poetry course. Both were about possibilities only. Best possibilities.

Now, eight years on, William and his little family, turned into the small drive outside their home. Back from the airport. William jet-lagged. The house was opposite the primary school which the children attended; they were still chattering of course, and William was tired now.

In the early afternoon, Carol closed the door of their bedroom quietly as she whispered to the children. William lay down. A warm breeze caught the curtains, and they billowed into the room from an open window. Soon he was asleep.

Chapter 12

Now it was that time of year again – between the end of summer and the beginning of autumn. Yet for William, as always, it was also the start of the year – when school and university terms began. Beginnings in late sunshine.

It was an exciting time, which in a peculiar way came to represent the love he felt for his wife. The season's elegiac colouring, when he was to look back on this time, framed an understanding that all he wanted of life was to be with her.

The perfume of the buddleia which had tapped upon the kitchen window in August, had faded. Now only a few of its large purple plumes remained.

It was Friday, and he wasn't expected in work until Monday; and this was the first thing William remembered as he woke up and heard the birdsong around the still open window. It could just as easily have been the sound of traffic at that time in the morning, as children were being dropped off at the school. But it was birdsong that he heard first.

Carol was already up, for it was quite late. So he dressed quickly to join everyone at breakfast. They always started the day together in the kitchen; then the children were too young to object.

Their 1930s' house being so near the school had advantages. Sitting down on the low settee, and looking through the front bay window, with its wooden sill that he was for ever patching up at this time of year, the scene before them was all roses in the front garden, and plane trees at the front of the school.

This was something of an illusion. The front garden was actually very small, and separated from the school by a sometimes busy road. However the road was wide, with pavements either side and generous grass verges. And it was tree-lined.

The previous owners of the house had been expert gardeners, and they were responsible for this impression of bucolic peace and colour.

The small, just detached, house had a long extended sitting room at the back, and a dining room at the front. The kitchen had originally been very small but now, since the alterations, was large enough for breakfast altogether. Off the hall was a new shower room and lavatory.

There were fluted whole glass doors connecting the three living rooms downstairs, which William greatly disliked but had not found the funds to replace. The hall was cramped and narrow.

Upstairs, there had been two reasonably sized bedrooms and a box room. Now, there were three bedrooms, with the box room serving as his study; at the front, looking out over the road to the plane trees and the school buildings set well back from the road. The landing was now larger and more interesting than the hall, and there was a bathroom and separate lavatory.

The back garden still paraded the skill of the previous owners, five years on; facing south it was both open and sheltered. Sheltered because of a low fence at the bottom behind the rockery, which ran the whole width of the garden, and because it faced south. Sheltered and open because a little path divided the rockery, and led up to a raised grassed area which looked out upon a large field sloping gently upwards to the village beyond.

In the summer the field was full of wheat or barley. But always only the spire of the church was just visible, and the rest of the village was hidden from view.

The back garden gave the house its sense of rural peace. The character of the field belied how the house was in an unfashionable part of town. Now, as often, house and garden were tranquil and warm.

They had first seen it one March, when the back garden was crammed full with daffodils, seeming to flow everywhere.

When they moved in that August, they erected a swing at the bottom of the garden in front of the rockery. At first there were three solid days of rain. But when the sun appeared, everything shone. As soon as she saw the swing, Claire, their older daughter, and then three and a half, adopted it. Trying but always failing to touch the branches of the plum tree with her feet.

Now it was a little rusty and neglected, but in those first few weeks of that first summer she had rarely left it; sometimes naked in the warm sunshine. Her sister, two years and a half years younger, was not old enough to use it by herself and so had a small swing of her own.

So, right at the edge of the capital itself, indeed theirs was the last row of houses before the Green Belt, they also lived on the edge of the country. In the back garden they felt part of the countryside; in the front they felt they were in the town.

Every April they heard the cuckoo's shout. William would later recall how since their moving away they never heard it.

William joined his small family in the kitchen that morning, where it was sitting over breakfast. The sun lit up the room; and through the plain glass of the kitchen door the recently harvested field seemed part of the room. The bales had not yet been collected and were waiting upon the farmer, who only rented the field.

The children were ready for school and were chatting with Carol. They looked up as he entered the warmth and peace of the kitchen, into the smell of bacon cooking. He had some coffee before quite soon seeing the children across the road. Afterwards he and Carol sat for a time in the kitchen, talking into the morning.

Although the buddleia's perfume had gone, and with it most of the butterflies, the perfumed manuscript of their still young marriage remained. She often said that the years when the children were young would be the best years. And indeed, it was a time when they assumed together that Spring would always return; and when they never really noticed if it was raining – beyond when they got wet.

As they sat there, the day outside was warm though the year was well advanced. While the heat of the sun had lost its promise, the harvested field was still lit up. And the stored warmth of a long summer reflected back its late comfort into the house.

(ii)

He knew that the Monday return to work after an absence right at the beginning of the academic year would be fragmented, and more disordered than he really liked. But he was grateful that he didn't have a first year group this year, for that could have led to difficulties. New students needed careful explanation and support at the beginning of their course. They needed to be set upon their way carefully, or problems could arise. His train would get him to his room in the Faculty building by 8.30.

When he arrived at the entrance of the building, the first person he met was Len, on duty behind his desk. After a brief chat he went straight up to the General Office on the first floor to pick up his mail.

Quite a lot had accumulated in the fortnight that had passed since he had been in. Any urgent departmental and Faculty notes had been isolated by Linda, in one pile held together by an elastic band. The rest was in another pile, held fastened by two elastic bands and placed on the table under the pigeon holes. He thanked her, and left almost immediately for his room on the third floor.

The Faculty building was modern, and its corridors and stairways were carpeted. When he entered his room, he saw how clean and ordered it was; warm and smelling of polish. Smelling still of the dye of a new carpet which had been laid sometime during the vacation. There were a number of chairs stacked neatly in a corner. Outside, he saw the roof tops of South London. Through a single picture window lay Waterloo and the City. Both seeming very close in the clear bright morning.

The room was regular in shape; not particularly small, and had a regulation, modern, black, imitation leather, armchair for individual visitors. His desk looked unusually empty except for a photograph of his family, and Sandra had watered the petunias that were in a pot next to it. He must remember, he thought, to leave a note to thank her, before he left that evening. And he scribbled a reminder on the pad on his desk. The petunias had been a gift from a student who said that the room should have a plant in it.

He put down the two packets of mail on his desk. They would have to wait until later. There was no time to knock on doors nearby, to speak to me or Pamela; in any case we weren't there yet. His first task that morning was to give a block lecture to around 200 second year students on 'speech acquisition' by young children; in one of the main lecture theatres in the administrative building on the back field.

After collecting together everything he would need, he went straight to the Audio Visual Department in the main building, to check that the equipment had been set out. Then, over to the lecture theatre to make final preparations, greeting a few colleagues and students he met on his way through the corridors.

Carrying books he would need to read from, and his briefcase, he had another chance meeting, one that was typical of how the college worked. Hurrying through one of the heavy doors at the rear of the main building, thinking about the lecture ahead, he found himself, and suddenly, face to face with the Warden; and colliding with a question. The head of the whole college was standing in the sun of the October morning – just outside the door. Both were surprised.

The Warden had been looking up at a newly erected Victorian lamppost; one of six or seven which had appeared along the back of the building during the vacation.

As William was about to greet him, this international scholar, the boss of the whole place, spoke first,

"Ay up! I'm very pleased with those. What do you think?" He was standing back, admiring the lampposts – gleaming, freshly painted, elegant and black, in the morning.

In fact they were easy to admire, and William agreed therefore that they fitted in well with the back of the building; reflecting upon how their installation could only recently have been completed.

It was typical also of the place that it had fallen to William to introduce the new Warden at a lecture for the Education Faculty in the previous year. This came about because of the system of 'co-ordinator' roles which distributed administrative responsibilities for organizing lecture events in the Faculty.

So, when this inaugural event by the new Warden, about his recent work as Deputy Director of UNESCO was planned, it fell by chance to William to introduce it on one of the dates for which he was responsible. This in spite of his very junior role in the Faculty. To propose a welcome on behalf of five hundred or so students and staff in the theatre that morning. To a part of his own institution.

And that had been in the very same lecture theatre that he was headed towards this morning.

Unsurprisingly, this man was a very relaxed and engaging speaker, who nonetheless was searching and analytic in what he was describing about the post he had just left in Paris.

Hearing him was like listening to a story-teller at a kitchen hearth.

When planning his short introduction, and how later to frame the obligatory note of thanks which would follow questions at the end of the hour, William had decided to use a personal recollection

It was of a conversation, years before, with Carol's younger brother James, who happened to have just read the seminal *The Uses of Literacy.*

They had been sitting together on a soiled, blackened, hillside looking down upon the chimneys and furnaces of the British Steel plant in Foxton, just outside Sheffield. William illustrated his few words of welcome by referring to parts of that conversation with a fifteen year old about that book. This seemed to work, and the Warden had asked him later about the reference to Yorkshire.

Now, he reflected, he was discussing Victorian lampposts with the book's author.

The older man asked him where he was off to in such a hurry, and upon receiving the reply, he went on,

"Oh well, I'd best let you get on then! Good luck."

In the years to come, after this Warden had retired, William would ask him if he was willing to act as the external examiner for the MA course he ran. After that they remained in correspondence periodically. And yet I knew how so surprised he was one winter's day after that retirement, to receive in the post a signed copy of *A Local Habitation. Life and Times: 1918 – 1940* – the first part of an autobiography.

By co-incidence that gift arrived at the very same time as Ewald Osers sent him a copy of his translation from the Czech, of Jaroslav Seifert's *The Plague Column.* I happened to be with William in his room at college when he opened the parcel containing Osers' book. He'd thought, as we chatted, that the package contained an inspection copy of some textbook sent by a publisher. And he seemed so innocently pleased, ecstatic almost, when he discovered what was really in it.

He just could not understand how respected men of letters would take the trouble to send him copies of their books. Though I knew how much he loved Seifert's poetry, and admired Osers' work, I don't know where they had met. What I do know is the effect of the book's unheralded arrival upon William; just how it cheered him. And how he treasured it!

But I am digressing. As they parted, that October morning, the Warden turned back again to him, and asked,

"Can I take it that your Jacksonville trip went well?"

William was surprised that the head of the college should know about his visit to the US., or at least that he would remember it; but later thought it was probably because of the involvement of the British Council. He would have had to endorse the application by the US. conference organizers at their end of things.

Attempting to disguise his surprise at this fresh unexpected question, William thanked him for asking, and added something to the effect that it was enjoyable and absorbing. Which was the truth.

The college was that kind of place, and Richard Hoggart was that kind of man, and William momentarily reflected upon both, as the two of them went on their way. The whole exchange had lasted no more than three or four minutes.

Having found everything prepared in the lecture theatre, he retraced his footsteps across the field through the bright sharp morning, which had now become brighter and sharper. And now his destination was the students' refectory, a cup of coffee and a final, solitary, look through his lecture cards.

This was his usual practice when he gave a 9.30 lecture; and it had become a ritual for him. It always relaxed him, cleared his head for the hour ahead, and allowed him to anticipate possible audience responses for what he had to say. Everyone of his colleagues worked in their own way. This was his. He believed in preparing carefully for what could carefully be prepared for, and letting the rest take care of itself.

The course was a new one, as was the degree of which it was a part. Both had been two years in the planning. It was very important that the lecture should go well – though naturally it was always important that things should go well!

Returning to the lecture theatre by 9.25 he found it almost full. As he walked in, he greeted colleagues scattered around the room; and exchanged a few words with students who looked up at his arrival, and as the room became quieter.

The lecture would be followed by coffee in the quiet hum and comfort of the Senior Common Room. Then the seven staff members who worked on this course could catch up, and do the odd pieces of business for the rest of the morning ahead. At 11.00, the group seminars would begin, and the content of William's lecture would be amplified and developed with their own groups; in whatever way the judgement and expertise of his colleagues made appropriate.

The hour had passed, and the responses in the lecture theatre seemed satisfactory. Afterwards his own group had prepared as he had requested them to, in a brief meeting at the end of last term. And so the morning finished productively – and the week had begun. He was back.

At 12.30 he had arranged to meet an in-service part-time student in his study, for a tutorial on her Education Special Study; she was a colleague's student on another undergraduate course whom he had agreed to supervise. Although usually for William one of the greatest pleasures of his day was lunch with particular colleagues, today he knew that would not be possible.

The afternoon would be spent in a nearby school, which he would be visiting because two of his 4th year group were there beginning their term long final teaching practice. This visit was only possible today because the Junior Mixed and Infant School was right next to the college. Usually his school visits were much further afield. So, a sandwich and another cup of coffee would allow him to be at the beginning of the school's afternoon at 1.45.

He had arranged this visit today on this first day back especially, partly because he expected everything to be going well for these students. He knew that both were conscientious and capable. He had discussed their schemes of work very carefully with them and their teachers at the end of last term. So, although the usual pre-practice meetings had not been possible because he had been away, he had done everything he could to allow for that.

To his relief he found things at the school were much as he'd hoped. The afternoon as usual was full – with observing two lessons by each of the students, discussing with them how things had gone, and leaving copies of his comments and summaries of what had been discussed with the two young women. Everything he'd seen was encouraging, and he felt contented.

Most important, also, were discussions with the two class teachers and the Head, to ensure that there was nothing troubling them. These meetings followed others held at the end of last term when the students' work was still at the early planning stage.

Monday evening was the first of two weekly meetings of the MA (Language and Literature) course. This was a two year part-time course for serving teachers, who came to the college after a day at work. They were drawn from every school age-range; from infant, junior and secondary schools. One course member in this 2nd Year group worked in a Further Education College, and yet another was an Advisory Teacher in a London borough nearby. This evening's meeting was the first of the term for the group.

The breadth of the teachers' experience was one of the tenets of the course, and the university's approach, when planning higher degrees for serving teachers. This group was pleasant, hard working and well motivated, and William looked forward to the evening.

The subject of the first seminar of the term was the language functions model of Roman Jakobson; work which William greatly admired. From the so-called Prague School of Linguistics. The meeting would begin at 5.30.

Before that, he had arranged at 5 o'clock, to meet the young teacher who was to give the paper and lead the group during the first part of the evening; to check that all was well with her.

Like all the rest on the course, men and women, she juggled its demands with a full time job, and in her case also with the demands of a young family. She was Head of English in a secondary school in Camden.

After something light in the refectory, for he would be eating at home, he kept the 5 o'clock appointment; and just before 5.30, they walked together down to the usual seminar room on the first floor of the Education Faculty building.

His evening train was at 7.45, and he had decided not to join everyone in the bar afterwards. Some staff liked to do that, but it was something that he usually tried to avoid. It was not that he was averse to socialising with students over a beer, but rather that it always felt too late in the day while home was waiting.

At this time of night the train terminated one station before his own. Therefore Carol usually came out to collect him in their old Lada, to save time. The distance between the two stations was a little over a mile, so as long as the evening was fine he would set off walking, usually meeting her coming down the hill towards him.

On Mondays and Thursdays, Angela came in from next door to baby-sit the children who were long asleep by then. Just for a few minutes. And so by this means he would usually be back home on those two days by 8.45.

On this evening, as William sat on the train for the twenty five minute journey, he continued to sort through his packets of mail to attend to the next day.

He looked forward to the week ahead being more ordered, and to catching up with friends and colleagues again. He had scarcely had time to talk to any of them today. He was thinking also of the other school visits he must fit in over the next few weeks, and he made a note to telephone the schools and the students to arrange each visit – as soon as possible.

(iii)

Now, you may wonder how exactly it was that William came to be looking forward to meeting new colleagues in his old college, so I should fill in some of the details of how that came about.

A visit from an elderly gentleman was how it began; or almost how it began. At the start of this journey of return, to the unconventional place that had become early on so important to him. Which if he had stayed on that London coach that morning on the way to school he would have passed, as it sped on its way to Victoria Coach Station.

This return to his college to work, was eight years after his leaving it.

At the time, they were living in their hamlet on the Essex-Suffolk border, with William's work still twenty five miles away towards London.

Mr Hughes had already agreed to support his application for secondment, following an earlier interview at the college when he was offered a place on a degree course.

The visit was by a County Inspector one afternoon following a few days notice; and it was one upon which a very great deal depended. Without secondment there was no chance of his joining the course. At this stage, therefore, the idea was nothing more than just a possibility.

The visitor joined first a class of fourth year boys and girls, who that afternoon were preparing for a three week period of work placements around the town: these placements would lead to the possibility of later training, full apprenticeships or employment. It was a project that William had been appointed to initiate, and for obvious reasons it was popular with the young people. This was fortunate, because as we have already seen, some of them didn't always show such enthusiasm.

Later in the afternoon found him working with a small class of first year children, who for various reasons were having problems with their reading; difficulties which they had brought with them when they joined the school. It was a happy little group who were keen, and making real progress. William's responsibilities included identifying and seeking to remedy these children's difficulties before they turned into frustration and disappointment with their new school.

There was no time for him to feel nervous, or to dwell upon whether there was a need. In any case their visitor was relaxed and friendly, and seemed genuinely interested in what was going on. And in both classes William's pupils answered the very different kinds of questions the inspector asked; in their different ways in a spirit of co-operation.

Later on, William would learn that the visitor had been the Headmaster of one of the County's largest and most successful secondary schools. That afternoon though, between the two lessons that he observed, he was closeted with Mr Hughes in his study. And then he left.

A few weeks passed, and the days in his department sped away, before a letter arrived from County Hall informing him that his application for secondment had been successful. Even more heartening for William and Carol, on their tight household budget, was that the authority had awarded him a book grant; and also a travel grant to cover the costs of his daily return rail journey from home to the college.

This was in effect a temporary pay rise, for at present his journey to and from school entailed a fifty mile round trip in an ageing car.

When the summer break came he was released from the usual preparation for the year ahead at school. Instead he embarked upon a programme of intense reading, using the lists that had been sent him from the English Department, and the Philosophy of Education Department, at Goldsmiths'. He tackled this on day-long visits to the University of Essex library nearby, throughout all of August and most of September. It had been emptied by the summer, and was full of peace. So he was quickly able to establish a solid work routine.

Soon a train journey from the small local station at 7.30 would begin his completely new routine early that October. And because the trains then were not as crowded as now, he could easily read as he travelled.

In the morning, Carol even dropped him off at the village station in the car; sometimes with their young daughter in the back, and sometimes not. In the winter months, the two year old would stay with Margaret next door. She had three children of her own.

In the evening he would walk home the mile or so from the station. He needed a torch at first, if he wasn't to walk into a ditch, for the darkness that winter was often even more complete than usual. Power cuts were frequent; for much of the country was on a three day week.

At thirty one, being a full-time student, and on full pay with a family to go home to at night, was a very attractive novelty. He enjoyed the company of the serious, attractive and obviously able young people who were his new day-time companions. And he came to understand, as the year progressed, how anxious they felt because of the demands of the course. In spite of the differences in their age, they quickly accepted him – and for the most part his groups got on well together.

In quiet moments, William certainly felt his own set of pressures. He was attempting to complete the degree in a year, whereas his companions were in their fourth consecutive year. While he was away on full salary, his colleagues worked on at school. Carol was at home all day, and by this time was pregnant again, and with a toddler to look after. How would things be, he wondered, if he returned to school next year having failed the course? Without a degree?

Although he did not think so much about it, he felt the impossibility of failure, and that prompted a constant, sometimes feverish, energy. But most of all, he felt exhilaration, due largely to a fascination with the subjects he was reading, and the atmosphere and patterning of his now very different days. Half of his week was flavoured by the international work and teaching of Richard Peters and the Philosophy of Education Department at the university's Institute of Education, and the quality of Patrick Wilson's writing and teaching at Goldsmiths': the other half was a familiar and entirely pleasurable immersion in English Literature.

Always though he looked forward, once on the train in the evening at Liverpool Street, to returning to Carol and Claire.

One Saturday morning, driving back from their weekly shopping for groceries in the town nearby, he and Carol were discussing some incident, or character, from his past week. No doubt prompted by a detail he had just mentioned, and in her enthusiasm and interest in what he was doing, she suddenly said,

"Wouldn't it be terrific if they offered you a job there?

But he just laughed and thought nothing more of it. He had a job already. And a generous employer; moreover one who was making all this freedom possible.

It is surely one of the strangest features of life that when things are going well they seem without warning to become better. The opposite of that other tendency of things going from bad to worse.

And so it was for William when one morning, just a very few weeks later, in what seemed a chance meeting with Mr Kay, who had been his tutor when he was first a student at the college, he was asked if he was able to meet him over lunch that day. I should mention that Mr Kay had nothing at all to do with the course William was on now.

Courtesy was in the genes of this man, who was now the head of a large department in the Faculty. And it was characteristic of him that he should suggest a meeting in the form of a request.

Conversation at their lunch together in the Senior Common Room ranged over old times, and then came to rest upon the planned expansion of Mr Kay's department. And then upon a vacancy therefore, in October, for a Junior Lecturer. And then came a second question, which was whether William would be interested in applying for this kind of post.

William's first response was a kind of elation, which he was careful to contain, as a March sun poured over the table at which they sat. Of course he would be, but then he remembered the terms of his secondment from his local education authority. And the personal undertaking to stay at his school for at least two years, which he had given to Mr Hughes. And so he mentioned these immediately.

His old tutor thanked him, but then said,

"Well, yes, of course, that could be a difficulty if you were to be offered the appointment". And then he added, "But probably not an insurmountable one".

And then their conversation turned to how William was finding his course – at least about that he could be unequivocal. As they left the dining room of the Senior Common Room with its white table clothes, shining cutlery, waitresses and buzz of conversation, William moved to pay for his lunch as his old tutor did his. But he was interrupted.

"No, No, the department's paying for this!"

And so ended a pleasant and surprising lunch. And that evening the journey out to the country on the other side of London seemed even more hopeful and celebratory than ever. And after that, he concentrated even more strenuously upon his course.

He did apply for the post, and a meeting with the Dean of the Faculty followed almost immediately. Then came a formal interview at the college; although this was organized so that the candidates attended on various different dates and times.

Notice of the date of William's interview came with little warning, and it was on a Wednesday afternoon. And so there was no time for anticipation or nervousness about it to divert him from his work.

The interview panel consisted of five people, including the Warden – who had been at the college when William was first a student there, the College Registrar, and the Dean of the Faculty of Education. The meeting was directed by the Warden, who remarked gently and early on, as he was seeming to examine the application form that was before him, how William's teaching work so far was with children who were experiencing some kind of crisis.

William's immediate response was that this was not entirely so. And further that although he could see how it might appear that way, he didn't view things like that. Rather, he went on, he thought that crises would come to us all sooner or later.

This reply was not considered. Not planned nor prepared. And it came readily. And, who knows, perhaps that was the intention of the questioner.

Everyone in the room immediately looked at him fixedly, and there was a long pause in the proceedings. A silence. It was as if what he'd said had not been at all what they had all expected. After that beginning, he was asked about the work of his current department at school, and why he wanted to join the college. There was discussion about the terms of his secondment, and the undertaking he had given to Mr Hughes – which William raised again. And then after about half an hour, the relaxed and cordial interview was over.

Immediately afterwards, he wondered if he should have phrased his early reply to the Warden's remark differently.

Whether his response had been just too unconsidered. And then he became confident that his and Carol's expectations had been unreasonable. They had got carried away, thrown off guard by new possibilities.

As he sat alone after the interview, over some coffee in the unusually quiet students' refectory, he thought how he still had his job to return to. And he thought about the children whom he had known since they joined the school. He still had his department, and he would be returning to colleagues that for the most part he liked, and to afternoon conversations with Mr Hughes – who had helped him and shown confidence in his work.

And if he got a reasonable degree, his return would be to a quite large pay rise, and the congratulations of his friends at the school. Now he just had to get on with the job of achieving that. He remembered Carol at home, and he went straight to the library.

He remembered how at the end of last summer as he had left for his year away, some of the younger children had asked him if he was leaving for good. And how he had replied,

"No, of course not!"

And he recalled how they had seemed happy enough about that. He thought how they would have grown since then, and how obvious that would be to him when he saw them again.

That Wednesday afternoon, sitting in the refectory and afterwards, he discussed the interview with no-one; for there was no one there that he could talk to about it. Certainly he could hardly discuss it with any of his young companions on the course.

Finals would arrive all too soon after the Easter break; and he must concentrate on those.

Finals did arrive of course. They came and they went. He had stayed on Blackheath, in one of the halls of residence, from one Sunday night to going home on the following Thursday evening. In between, he negotiated eight successive

3 hour papers in the University's Examination Halls in the centre of London.

Before that, he had received a letter from the College Registrar informing him of an offer of an appointment to the College staff, on the grade of Junior Lecturer. And much later he had another from the university authorities informing him that he was also, consequently, appointed to various committees of the university's Institute of Education. Carol and he found it all a bit overwhelming, and William resolved again that he must focus on the Finals still to come. Many things might have changed, but their importance remained.

After the written examinations, and a viva voce on his English dissertation on D H Lawrence in a church in Piccadilly, which followed soon afterwards, William visited his school, to ask his question of Mr Hughes.

As he drove into the familiarity of the school car park it was as if he had not been away. He saw a number of children he knew, and they chatted together briefly. Fortunately they were on their way somewhere, and were in a hurry. Lessons were still in progress in the early afternoon, and so he was able to avoid questions about when he was coming back.

He had decided not to stay beyond his meeting with the Head, not being sure how to present his news to his former colleagues.

He had delayed this visit until after the letter from the college confirming his appointment had come. And now that it was here, the visit was layered with both sadness and elation.

The College's Registrar had told William that he would be writing to County Hall, explaining the offer of the new appointment. This official of the college seemed very certain that the authority would put no obstacle in their way; that given the nature of his new duties it would release him from his contract. William had decided to write to the LEA requesting this release as soon as possible after his visit to the school.

But his promise to Mr Hughes really was a different matter. He knew how much he owed this man; and that his promise to him last year had been unequivocal. Now he was asking to be released from an undertaking that he had freely and firmly given. And he felt very uncomfortable about breaking his word.

Yet he need not have worried, for his boss, soon to be his old boss, was as good-hearted and as indulgent as ever. William tried to explain how the offer of the new job had come about, as truthfully and in as much detail as possible. And the response he met was simply that he must accept the offer. There was little doubt that County Hall, having received the Registrar's letter, had already been in contact with the school.

The meeting wasn't long, and William explained that he wouldn't be staying to wait for the end of afternoon school. He asked the Head, who seemed to understand why he had decided to leave straight after their meeting, to pass on his best wishes to everyone. And so it was that William left that happy school perhaps feeling a little ashamed. Feeling that this departure was not entirely satisfactory, but not knowing how it could have been any better.

The summer that lay ahead would be taken up with fresh, and until recently quite unexpected, preparations. The course would be over. He had only to await his results, and then a new job lay ahead. Depending on his degree, he had agreed to explore preparing part-time for a higher degree – which would be in Linguistics and Comparative Literatures.

In November, Anna was born.

(iv)

So in another year, between the end of summer and the beginning of autumn, it certainly appeared that "the gates were open, and the pathway clear".

Their house was on a small development in the Essex/ Suffolk hamlet. There was just one little shop which sold many things, all of them too expensive for William and Carol's pockets. And it was not near the house, being down on the main road.

All around them the lanes wound off in all directions, into open skies. The country was open without being flat. The small roads twisted about, up and down gentle slopes, passing small triangles of grass as they joined up with each other again. Through tunnels of high hedges, and past pink-washed farm houses set back behind ponds which in the Spring sat in their own lakes of daffodils.

The distance between where William lived and where he had worked had been twenty five miles; and now from Goldsmiths' in South London it was far greater. Both were a great contrast to his job at the Remand Home. He had come to fear a too close proximity of home and work, as carrying a kind of threat. But here, deep in the country, work would be just too far away.

Although a stranger in this part of the country, he would in later years associate its landscape with his and his wife's optimism at that time. With a sense of good fortune and progress. And with their still young marriage, and very young children.

The seasons seemed softer then in this new, washed, territory. Spring came early, and the Autumn was long. Life here was at once enclosed, and yet lived under open skies; perhaps enclosed because of them. Even when the winter dark from outside came early in the afternoon.

And in the following Spring as they walked the lanes, Claire alongside on reins, and Anna in her pram, the farm houses shone pink again, freshly set in the new season. And landscapes and inscapes were both flooded with light.

William knew that he could not escape his rebellious tatterdemalion nature, yet here now, he began to feel less of an outsider. Love was introducing him to legitimacy.

Memory was not perfecting life. It really was like that. Youth was revealing more and more possibilities.

Their first child had been born in the local maternity hospital. He thought his wife could not be more beautiful, and their excitement was their life.

Husbands did not yet usually remain at the birth of children then. But they had both devoured the good sense of Grantly Dick-Read's book *Childbirth Without Fear*. When they had first asked if William could be present at the birth, it was an unusual enough request for a letter of permission to come quickly.

Carol's admission to the hospital was very quick. After so much anticipation and planning, suddenly there was no time at all. When they arrived he was ushered into a waiting room.

When Carol looked up in alarm, he explained to the matron about his permission to stay; and produced the letter. She seemed quite shocked. But quickly composing herself, she said:

"Alright, but if you faint, we'll just step over you!" And she grinned.

"I won't faint", William said, with unjustified confidence. And he was quickly kitted out with a long green gown and cap.

That was when they lived in another village nearby.

Now, nearly three years later they were walking the lanes in the sunshine with two daughters. He had missed Anna's first cries upon arrival in the world, getting there only a few minutes after she had.

As they walked towards the sky, it and the greening hedgerows framed the small family.

When William, eighteen months earlier, had left for London for the first day of his secondment, it was not from the old house – or any house.

Their old one, which was also their first one, was sold. The new house was still three days short of being ready enough for them to move into.

The solution was ready enough though. The easy optimism and distinctive character of the times extended even to the builder of the small collection of houses; for he paid for them all to stay for two nights in the White Swan Hotel – in the High Street of the old town nearby. Their furniture was simply stacked, and covered up; and left in one of the downstairs rooms of their new home awaiting their arrival. Waiting for the decorators to lay down their brushes.

William reflected upon how the builder's gallant gesture was probably not unconnected to his beautiful wife, and Claire's chatter; when they had all met on the site and first heard of the still unfinished internal decoration.

So, when he left for London on the first day of his secondment that Thursday, from the town's station nearby, it was after breakfast in the ancient coaching inn, with its beamed and very low ceilings, its alarmingly sloping floors, and leaded windows. And it was here he returned to, on that first evening. On Saturday morning they joined their furniture in their new home.

But now this house was simply proving too far from his new job. And after a few short months, they would have to move to somewhere much nearer the college. At last William's home and work would be just close enough to each other; and Claire could start school nearby; as it turned out, very close nearby.

The house would be smaller and older, but the garden larger and open to sunlight. And the daffodils they left in the lanes around and about in Essex, were matched by those that were everywhere in the new garden – when they first saw it on that early Spring afternoon.

(v)

We all know, and William knew too, that dwelling upon personal happiness in a self-congratulatory way is a kind of impertinence. And not without risk. As the Russian proverb has it, 'If you want to make God laugh, talk about your plans'.

His meeting Carol, and his immediate love for her was within the Zeitgeist of the 1960s. Their tapestry and their manuscript were London; and by 1965 they were married.

The sense of freedom, release and youthful wonder, that he discovered in the capital, had seemed to permeate and define their first meeting. He met her at the very end of his first period as a student at Goldsmiths'; and the spirit that lived in its corridors, of colour and freedom, was with him at that first meeting.

If chance, and the purposes of other people at a wedding had governed their first meeting, the direction and timbre of their life together once married was definitely their own. And so it remained.

The conventional was not a reserve that he could ever draw upon, and Carol was immediately influenced by that. He had the resolution, or perhaps it is better described as stubbornness, of all outsiders.

The Vietnam War, the Cold War, the American missiles resting in their East Anglian silos, and the thirteen-day-long Cuban Crisis all coloured the edges of everyone's life then. They were their crucible. Michael, just down the corridor in William's hall was convinced that the end of everything was imminent. And haunted by that thought.

Dances small and very large, in all the college's halls of residence and in its Great Hall, echoed with the melodies and pleas of anti-war and protest songs. At once elegiac and youthful, they entered everyone's consciousness – and spread. And so, Pete Sieger's 'Where Have all the Flowers Gone?' became an ironic song to dance to – with the lights dimmed.

For William at that time, Bergman films with no hands on the clocks, and beautiful Scandinavian women whose lives were scarred by angst, had an almost obsessive appeal. One that was exotic, but only because he was young. This at the time that the 1960s didn't even recognize themselves.

These events, and the atmospheres and feeling tones which they created, left their mark, but William's and Carol's time together from the start, was outside all of that, which was not perhaps so unusual.

So, that first sense of freedom in the capital helped William, and spread to this beautiful young girl who would become his wife, as they explored together its theatres, its plays and musicals. That was when she came down from the north by train at weekends, or in the school holidays during the year when William was at work on the Essex coast – during his first year after leaving college.

Her natural sense of life, gaiety and openness, captivated William immediately. He loved her honesty, and with it that special innocence which was so obvious from the beginning. And he was engaged by her beauty, for who could not have been? And he loved her large green eyes when they smiled at him. It was just a simple love story.

She loved dancing, which he did too – except that he couldn't dance at all well; he'd somehow never got round to learning. But then he loved music without being able to read music. And he had spent much of his childhood in a choir without being able to sing. But at least he knew how to organize dances, which I'll come to.

At the time when he had moved jobs to be near her before they were married, he was something of a curiosity in the large but closely knit steel town. Just as the huge chimneys, the noise throughout the night, the sulphurous air, and the beauty of the nearby moors, were curiosities to him. Her father had arranged for him to witness a furnace as it was tapped. Visually and audibly it seemed to him like a vision from Dante.

He heard a story of a furnace man recently committing suicide by jumping into a furnace of molten steel. He witnessed the strain on the gaunt faces of all the furnace men he saw that afternoon of his visit; and when he heard that it was common for them to drink ten, twelve, or even fifteen pints of beer after work or at the weekend, he knew that it was true. The beer replaced the lost liquid of their bodies, moving around the deposits in their lungs which had been breathed in during their shift.

But nearby Sheffield had the attractions of its Playhouse, which along with Nottingham's, was one of the country's last and finest repertory theatres. Carol and he had a season ticket, and it was at the Playhouse that they became engaged. Their Saturday visits on the bus often included afternoon tea at 'The Roman Room', the most fashionable place then in Sheffield for tea and something light to eat. In that city which was often affectionately referred to as a dirty picture in a golden frame. And then the Hallé Orchestra visited the City Hall regularly.

(vi)

When William joined Goldsmiths', on both occasions, as a student and a staff member, it was led by Sir Ross Chesterman who was a devotee of Carl Jung. And that was perhaps a contributory reason for the quite uniquely expansive and inclusive atmosphere which lived in all those corridors. For that special atmosphere which everyone immediately felt, and spoke of, when they first visited the college.

Carol had sensed it immediately. And if the essence of the place could be immediately recognized, this in its turn was informed by the infinite variety of the great capital city which gave its name to the university of which the college was a part.

This college was not a conventional place, nor a bureaucratic one. And it insisted on being un-authoritarian.

It would have not favoured the turning around of signposts in malice, nor indeed the slavish pursuit of arbitrary directions.

William often reflected, later, how he imagined that he could hear the same hidden voices in its corridors that he had heard so many years earlier at Tatlebury Corner. If at that earlier time, at nine years old, William had premonitions of alternating light and shade, here now before the sixties realized that they were the sixties, there was suddenly and only light.

The college was owned by the university, and yet its constitution was something of an anomaly, the result of which its degrees were validated by boards of study in the university – rather than in the college. And perhaps it was this anomaly which lent the college a further spirit of independence, and a sense of its own difference.

It had a national, even an international, reputation for its work on the education of children in school. By the quality, the depth, and the range of this work, it was then a defender of childhood itself. Situated in an inner-city area in an unfashionable part of London, it was yet near to everything in the capital. And it viewed youth as the best possibility – as the country emerged from the grey 1950s.

Along with this reputation for the study and practice of Education, its Art School had a worldwide reputation, its other departments taught the usual range of subjects and disciplines, and its Music Department possessed internationally known teachers. It was soon to become host to other unique institutions, including the Laban Institute of Dance; and every evening its Evening Department welcomed nearly 2000 part-time students engaged upon a seemingly limitless range of courses at every level, up to external degrees of the University of London.

And so the place was large and remarkable in its influence, both in its history and its work, and was widely recognized as such. Set back a little, the front of the main building overlooked a busy trunk road which ran straight to the heart of the capital. Those many corridors possessed a cloistered quietness, which had a lot to do with the architecture of the main college building itself. For at the front of the building, and at its very centre, was the Great Hall, with its huge organ, stage, and galleries.

The Great Hall was known by this name to distinguish it from the Small Hall which lay further into the building. It was however very big; one of the largest indoor spaces in London at that time. Originally the parade ground of a naval college, it had been covered and converted with some style. And so this large space at the building's centre, provided a pervading calmness – a cool and cushioned hush. During the day and in the evening.

A further contrast to the busy road at the front of the building was the peace of the large 'field' at the back of the college. Anything but untended, it could yet have been anywhere – many miles from the capital.

Perhaps particularly appropriately given the college's character, the size, colour and scope of the student dances held in the Great Hall, at that early post-war time, were almost legendary in student London. In those still straitened times.

And so, naturally, William became quickly absorbed by the many new possibilities he met, and recognized that the college was celebratory of a unique approach to education; serious, unapologetic and full of optimism.

He knew that here, unlike say in Brasenose, there would be no dividend of social cachet as a result of being one of its students. No introduction to any network of social influence, advancement, or worldly status. Nor indeed any promise of eventual wealth or worldly privilege. The advancement on offer was simply the opportunity to live within a suddenly discovered excited enlightenment. And later, the opportunity to live by values to which he was now being introduced daily.

He realized how fortunate he had been to arrive at this place. And he found that it suited him. The young men and women who were his new companions, were drawn from all around the country, and the Commonwealth. He joined them with Housman, Hardy, Tennyson, and the Rubaiyat; and together with them was introduced to Freud and Jung, Milton, Synge, Webster, Milton, Lorca, D.H. Lawrence, T.S. Eliot and Yevtushenko among many more. It was a time when he re-experienced the glamour of personal study. And when he found Erich Fromm's *The Fear of Freedom*, during his third and final year that first time around, it seemed just a synthesis of that spirit of the place which he had experienced from his first day there.

When, before making his first application to Goldsmiths', he had re-visited his old school to ask for a reference to support the plan, his welcome was positive and supportive. The Head was not the one who had interviewed him so many years before, and when the testimonial came, it contained no reference to the 6th Form Grizelle prizes. It mentioned that William was little known to the rest of the school, but that this was not to his detriment, since "he had made his mark in an academic way".

With his course in seeming good order, William decided at the end of his second year that he would enter student politics; but in a very practical way. In one that would erase for good that judgement of his former headmaster. And because he was affected by the energy he felt was all around.

The post on the Union Executive for which he, and his new friends on his behalf, campaigned, was that of Social Secretary for the College. It carried responsibility for most of the major social events on the College Calendar; organizing dances in the Great Hall, by chairing the Union's Social Committee. This body was composed of representatives of every hall of residence, along with two representatives of those students living in digs or at home. Because of the help he received, he was to his own surprise elected.

The frequent Union Council meetings were not much to William's liking. Their deliberations, reported at length in the widely bought and read, weekly, college newspaper, often extended well into the night. They were political in every sense. And the wordiness and divisiveness of some members made the long meetings feel very long indeed. The dryness, and extreme formality of the proceedings especially repelled him.

But the dances were another matter, and promised an especially public set of consequences – in either success or failure. The social year began with the Freshers' Boat Trip up the Thames from Greenwich; and the Art School Ball in the Great Hall. This fancy dress event set the standard for the year; extravagant and filling the hall with colour, music, and the imagination and energy of young life. But this dance was not, as it happened, William's responsibility. However, the great majority of the rest which followed definitely were. Every detail of them. At every stage.

One of his earliest responsibilities was a Fresher dance in Chislehurst Caves.

Throughout the year, the booking of bands, arrangements for the printing of posters and tickets, their sale, the organization and staffing of a temporary bar, and the general administration of the evenings from 8.00pm. to 1.00am. the following morning, were entirely for him to be certain about.

The new Social Committee, elected at the same time as William, was hard working and conscientious, and William soon established a machinery for the smooth running of the dances. At the heart of this was publicity, and the distribution and the regular sale of up to 2000 tickets.

He quickly realized that the money immediately generated had to be carefully and swiftly managed. Luckily the Union Treasurer was a member of his hall, and together they quickly set up a simple system of receipts and general accounting. Or rather the Treasurer did; for which William was very grateful. He did not want to be bogged down by that. Not his thing at all.

The Great Hall, which was such a wonderful space, nonetheless presented its own challenges. One of these was its constant use for other purposes during the day; and so making it ready for dances, very quickly, was a major logistical task on the day of each dance. Luckily this could be achieved by liaison with one of the most influential officers of the college – who simply made it happen. Along with a great deal else.

This gentleman was a wonderfully efficient and effective, former captain in the Royal Artillery. And he was in charge of college services. Quietly spoken and clear headed, with a large staff of porters at his command, he listened to William's requests. Mr Pritchard made clear what he thought was expected of him; and he made clear also his expectations of William. And so they got on.

Because William understood their relationship so well, and because of Mr Pritchard's administrative abilities, when hundreds of chairs needed to be moved from the hall very quickly, it happened as if by a thousand elves. William respected him, and enjoyed their meetings – which were necessarily frequent, always to the point, and brief.

And then there was a second challenge. The large hall had ten entrances, apart from its main doors; and each of these double doors opened on to corridors around it. Because of the fire regulations of the Local Authority, which were very strict, these doors had to be attended throughout the whole evening of the dances – from before the start to the very end. There could be no exceptions. From time to time, a memo. arrived from the college authorities reminding William of the importance of these fire regulations.

He met these demands by a simple device. He issued complementary tickets to carefully chosen men; mostly, but not exclusively, from his own large hall. In return for an hour's service on the doors, after which they returned to their partners for the evening, they received two complementary tickets. This arrangement had the further advantage that many members of the college, other than members of the Social Committee, became involved in the running of the evening.

Their other task was to check that everyone who entered the hall possessed a ticket. Although often they already knew those who arrived at the doors, this was not always so, because William ensured that the dances were well publicised in the rest of the colleges of the university. And in any case Goldsmiths' dances had achieved a certain reputation long before William took on his responsibilities.

Should anyone try to gain unauthorized entry, they could either be sold a ticket – or so many young men on all the doors of the hall would provide a line of immediate security in the event of trouble.

This system also became quickly established, and seemed to work well from the very start. There was no obvious loss of revenue, no-one failed to turn up for their session on the doors, and there were no emergencies – particularly there was no fire!

William booked the bands through a well known agency, and it was always a jazz band at the heart of things. Whatever the group, they were always excellent musicians, and therefore not cheap. The Alex Walsh Band appeared regularly. This insistence on a good band was a priority of William's, and the Social Committee soon accepted the initial extra cost of this policy.

Then there had to be an interval band, in order that the main one could have a break. And this was always the college rock band. They were good, had a distinctive style, and were therefore popular. Everyone liked the idea of having their own band. The group of four members with a male singer, received a fee; and were therefore able to supplement their grant.

On these evenings of the dance, all that mattered for William was the dance itself. It was its own world. Illusory of course, but the only one for the evening. A piece of confection certainly. But a public and absorbing one. And its own justification. Something made.

One of William's pleasures was to sit up in the gallery which spread all around the hall, for ten minutes, at sometime on each of these evenings – as the dance was in progress. When the floor was full, and the evening well under way. Leaving his partner for a short time, he would go up to the gallery, and just sit there in the dark.

The gallery was of course officially closed, but he was allowed the key by his confederate in charge of college services. Sometimes Mr. Pritchard would join him – for that gentleman was always about, and knew about everything that was going on. And they would sit there together, looking down on the scene below. Just for a few minutes.

Down upon the stage and the musicians, and upon the dancers on the floor of the hall. Upon the movement and the colour. And during this short time William felt that he and the very experienced older man became almost friends. And then, always quite suddenly, they would leave, and lock the gallery door behind them. Or if William had been there alone he would return the key to the Lodge immediately.

And so looking down upon the dances when he could not himself dance well, was one of the pleasures of William's sortie into student politics. Now he knew that at least no one could say he was unknown in the wider (college) community!

When he returned to the dance, to the bar, the corridors, or the hall, he was immediately recognized by many people; and with that came a satisfaction that he had never known before. He enjoyed the sense of being public property. The Head's school testimonial had been modified in at least one respect. This was a new pleasure. Sitting in the gallery, he would recall another smaller one. That gallery at the back of the chapel, where the dayboys sat every morning. And where he sat too – whether late or not.

A third of the way through his final term that summer, final examinations were looming. All of the social events for which he was responsible for the year had passed. And he felt a strong impulse to withdraw from the tedium of the Union Council meetings, and to concentrate upon his course – which he had inevitably neglected. And so, a little ahead of time, he resigned his union post.

A completely unheralded consequence of that decision was that the college newspaper printed a fulsome estimate of the success of the dances held throughout the year. William could not help smiling to himself as he anticipated the few weeks of freedom ahead. The editor and he had not always been on the best of terms; he thought the editor self-important, and the editor thought William was too prone to take criticism personally.

So, William had not anticipated any kind of acknowledgement from the keenly read newspaper. When it appeared, it spoke of large profits made for the Union, very high attendance at college dances, and William's conscientious membership of the Union Executive. And he was surprised – though silently pleased, as he looked forward now to some privacy.

Although, it has to be mentioned, this peaceful and private conclusion to his first three years might easily never have occurred. And it was all because of Althea.

They had met halfway through the Lent Term of this final year. On a Wednesday afternoon in the refectory, just as William was about to walk into Deptford to go to the printers with a design for tickets for the next dance.

It was a crisp and clear early March afternoon, and they walked to the printers together. She was a chemistry student in her final year and they had very little in common. Except that they were both young.

But she was friendly, and feminine, and it was nearly Spring. He had lots of feminine company, but none of it could be allowed to be serious for William at that time. He felt, in any case, that he was near the conclusion of something as his course came to an end and he looked for a job. Not the beginning. Also, he had no funds whatever. Nothing to offer anyone.

He would see Althea a few times after that afternoon, before the end of term. And she invited him to stay on two successive weekends, at her parents' home in the Easter holidays. She lived in a small town on the Sussex coast where her father was an engineer at a small airport.

The family owned a pleasant, well furnished and comfortable, beach hut to which Althea took him on the very first morning of his stay that Springtime. So they could be alone. And they spent a lot of time there also on the Sunday of his first visit. She obviously wanted to be there, and on the beach, and normally this was something that William would have welcomed. Except … .

There was something else that caused him to be reluctant. At the time, he had no idea what. And so could not have explained it.

Naturally his background would have made him cautious. Not likely to accept the obvious invitation, unless the temptation was overwhelming, the girl irresistible.

But the truth was that neither was the case. Rather he found that by the time of the second weekend, he was growing less rather than more attracted to Althea. And perhaps there was something of the prude in William's character, to add to his naïvety.

Whatever the truth, William found himself engaging in a series of small diversions, to distract her. On the Sunday of the second weekend this resulted in a crisis in their obviously waning relationship. He took refuge in the task of trying to remove some tar from a new pair of sand trousers he was wearing. Discharged from a ship out in the Channel, he'd picked it up by sitting on the beach.

She was exasperated by his continuous and various ways of concentrating on this task. With a different girl a bit of tar on some trousers would probably have been the least of his concerns. But on this warm Sunday afternoon it simply seemed very important to him. He resolved that it should be.

A short time after that they broke up, though in truth it could not have been said that theirs had been a close relationship – had ever actually developed.

Soon afterwards, near the start of the next and final term, William learned from the Senior Student of Althea's hall of residence that Althea was pregnant. She made a point of saying that she felt he should know. And although his informant gave him no further details, it was clear that she knew the name of the father. That however was a confidence.

When he heard this news, William was genuinely shocked. And he pondered how, had things proceeded differently in that warm and inviting beach hut, he would have automatically assumed that the responsibility for the pregnancy was his.

On the one hand he was grateful that he had followed his strong intuition during that last weekend. On the other, he couldn't help wondering about Althea's intentions.

And yet, and so, on a warm summer evening after all of that, in that final term, he was settling down to work on an overdue essay – on 'characterization in Homer'. He was sitting reading alone under a plane tree at the bottom of the large Victorian garden at the back of his hall of residence. As he worked on, the garden he sat in shaded into the garden of Alcinous. The next day he would continue his final teaching practice at a school in Southwark.

It was a time still of youth and elegy; as the urban and the bucolic were joined together, and were all about him in South London.

He had learned during those three years that love has a natural place in education. That the concerns of the teacher are essentially with vulnerability in the young.

He was on the way also to accepting the wider relevance of what Leavis saw in the work of George Eliot: "the weakness and ordinariness of us all", which "she did not find contemptible". William had begun to recognize that the best hope for each of us is not to be thought contemptible. And at the end also.

Another of those best possibilities?

PART 3

Altruism

"… when
we hear some note of kindness
innocent of its courage amid
the clamour of lies, it seems after all
there might be open to us, even now,
a chance to evolve."

Denise Levertov

"…freedom isn't granted,
We win it from ourselves"

Gabriel Fitzmaurice

Chapter 13

Re-wind to Norman Mailer. Remember him?

(i)

I was not meant to be there now that school days had passed. I couldn't know what the contract had been with my foster mother, nor whom she had made it with. All I knew was that it had expired.

I was not her responsibility. Her obligation had been discharged. From her point of view that was reasonable and fair. Whatever the bargain had been, she had kept her side of it. I'd had a wonderful childhood, and because of the school in my second village much more besides.

But now I knew that I was not welcome. I wasn't expected to stay – and it was up to me to discover where to go. My presence was, if not suddenly, then quite urgently a nuisance to her.

She made this clear in her silences; in her refusal to speak to me for long periods. It was clear in Victor's repeated replies of:

"Really?"

to my every attempt at conversation. Victor was close to his mother.

I had saved about fourteen pounds from money earned in orchards and in the hop gardens, and I withdrew them from the Trustee Savings Bank in Westerford. And with some of the money I bought the largest cardboard suitcase I could find in the only departmental store in the town. My destination was Grimsby.

I had to trust that it would be alright to leave my box of books under my side of the bed.

It isn't possible to explain why I had chosen Grimsby. It could have been anywhere in the country, but that fishing port on the North Sea was my choice. It had a large fishing fleet still, and I had a notion that I could find work.

In any case the decision to leave was more about the imperative that I should go, than it was to do with any thought through, worked out, decision about where I should go. When I mentioned to my mother that I would be leaving, she didn't asked me any questions about my destination.

She only said,

"Right!"

So one bright September morning I said goodbye, as if I was leaving for the shops. And I caught the London coach up to Victoria coach station, and from there on to Grimsby. And of course it felt like an adventure.

Late in the afternoon, the coach passed through a village which was very close to my destination. It was bathed in soft September sunshine. And I took this to be a good omen – something which augured well for my optimism about Grimsby.

The early evening was still warm when we arrived. As I collected my new suitcase from underneath the coach, and with the smell of the sea everywhere, I became aware that someone was talking to me. He was small, and I guessed was about thirty five.

He was asking me if I knew where I would stay. And did I know where I would eat? This immediate kindness and consideration from a stranger, reinforced my feelings of optimism on that September evening. And of course I felt grateful.

That was how Jim introduced himself. He told me he was a seaman, and that he worked on the trawlers. His talk was all of the Ross Group – the company that owned most of the boats, how much the skippers earned, and how he had just returned from a six week trip to the White Sea. And he told me that when you signed on for a trip, the company issued you with a ration of Park Drive cigarettes.

He said he could show me where the offices of the Ross Group were, and suggested that I could perhaps sign on for a "pleasure trip". This would be a six week voyage, working on a trawler. He told me that although there would be no pay, there would be full board. He said, I'd have plenty to eat. And he explained that the company provided this arrangement for people whom they expected to accept on to their training scheme.

All of this information, so freely given, made me grateful for my good fortune in meeting Jim. And I thanked my benefactor.

He continued,

"But you'll be needing a bite to eat and a cup of tea after your journey. I know a seaman's café. I'll show you if you like. And you'll need somewhere to stay. I know somewhere!"

When we entered the warm café, we were greeted cheerfully by a large friendly woman who called me "Dear". She seemed to know Jim, but didn't speak much to him.

We had fried eggs and toast, some bread and butter, and a large mug of hot sweet tea. It all tasted very good, for I had not eaten all day. When I had paid, we found a table and Jim told me about the company's training scheme. Then we left to find the bed that he had spoken of before. He asked me if I would like him to carry my case, which seemed to be growing heavier as the evening wore on.

After a short while we arrived at a large, dark red building, with a notice over the door which read 'Salvation Army'. "You'll be fine here!" my new friend assured me.

He took me to the desk, and explained my position to the man seated behind it reading his newspaper. In his turn this gentleman, somewhat annoyed at being interrupted, told me how much it would cost to stay the night. "Payable in advance!", he snapped.

When I'd paid what he'd asked, he showed me to my room, while Jim came along to check that all was well. In fact what we had all entered was a small cubicle. One of a number partitioned off within a large dormitory. In it was a bed and a small chest of drawers, and I noticed there was no window. There was a lot of background noise, mostly coughing. There was the sound of men talking, but not in conversation with each other; rather, the statements they made were fractured, spasmodic. And I noticed a quite loud hissing sound.

The attendant mentioned,

"You might be right to keep your door locked, and your suitcase. Lights out at ten!" And then he left.

As I wished Jim goodnight, he said he would collect me in the morning, and that we could go to the trawler company's offices together. He mentioned also that he was a bit stuck for money because the payment for his last trip had not come through. He wondered if I could possibly lend him five pounds. He'd let me have it back almost immediately of course. At just eighteen I was happy to do as he asked, simply out of gratitude for of all the help he'd given me – although it meant that my own funds were now reduced to around seven pounds.

He seemed very grateful. I thanked him, and as he left he said he'd be back to pick me up at eight o'clock sharp next morning.

By now it was nine-thirty. As I returned to my cubicle, darkness was falling and the night was still warm. I lay on the bed, and thought over all that had happened during the day and since I'd arrived in Grimsby. I looked forward to the next morning and visiting the trawler firm's offices; and then I must have dozed off.

When I woke with a start, it was eleven o'clock. The noise all around the darkened cubicle seemed to have increased. There were loud intermittent shouts, the coughing was continuous. Men were talking in their sleep, shouting complaints at invisible companions who didn't reply. Other neighbours did reply, but with curses. And the hissing I'd heard before, was louder and seemed to be coming from the cubicle next door.

I felt very warm, and as I lay there I wondered how likely it was that I would get back to sleep quickly. Then the door handle rattled as someone tried to open it – and I was glad that I'd remembered the attendant's warning about using the lock.

The coughing and the cursing seemed to get even louder; shouting and complaints were all around – and all of them very near.

I remembered that I'd not changed into my pyjamas, and was grateful for that. I just didn't feel like sleeping now; so I got up, unlocked the door, picked up my suitcase, and went along to the desk where the attendant looked up from his newspaper. I told him I was leaving. He didn't comment, but simply got up and unlocked the front door – and I stepped out again into the warm September night and the smell of the sea.

I soon found a bench on a quayside, and made myself as comfortable as possible. I used my coat as a pillow, and made certain that the suitcase was under one of my legs before I went to sleep. When I woke up it was six o'clock in the morning, and I was surrounded by the cries of seagulls. I felt cold and stiff; and remembered immediately that the café opened at 6.30 for the dock workers. Soon I was walking again through its doors for buttered toast and hot sweet tea.

After only about half an hour in the warmth of the café, Jim came in.

"They said you'd left", he said. That was all.

"Yes", I felt I had to explain, "I couldn't sleep".

"You want another cup of tea?" He asked.

"Yes please".

He fetched the tea and some breakfast for himself, and we talked about going to the trawler company's offices.

"We'll go at half past nine", he said.

On our way there, we walked through the fish market, and everywhere men were hosing down the stone floor. He described how some catches had already been landed and sold to dealers.

When we arrived at the Ross Group's offices Jim did most of the talking. About me wanting a career in the fishing industry.

The middle-aged woman gave me a form to fill in, which I did there and then, straightaway. She talked about what "pleasure trips" were for, with what I thought was just a trace of irony; and we talked about how long it would be before I could join a vessel. She explained about the training course, which I could apply for if I still wanted to, after the six weeks on the trawler.

She then looked directly at me, before saying,

"It really is very hard work you know".

"Yes", I know" I replied, though of course I didn't.

I felt I should wash my face, for I felt tired still. Excusing myself, I went into the toilet, cleaned up and combed my hair. And then we said goodbye, and left. The woman had said that since I didn't know yet where I'd be staying, it might be best if I looked in after a week, to see if there was any news about my application.

The rest of the day was spent walking around the docks and the quays of the fishing port with my new companion, whom I already felt I had known for a long time. As we walked, he told me many stories of life on the trawlers.

Late on in the morning, Jim said,

"Now that you've signed up with the company, you'll be able to stay at the Seamen's Mission. And he took me to it, and we went in.

The entrance hall was very bright, and everything about this building smelt clean and fresh. Jim explained why we had come, and the man who ran the mission showed me to a room. Jim stayed downstairs.

This room was large, and different in every way to where I'd spent part of last night; and it would cost me more. The polished wooden blocks of the floor shone, under two clean coloured rugs. The bed linen was white and gave off a cared-for perfume, and there was a bible on the bedside table. There was a large wardrobe, a chest of drawers, and the curtains at the two windows looked bright and new as warm sunshine flooded through and around them. There was a large wash basin, a mirror, soap and a clean towel.

The mission was where fishermen, or any seamen, might stay for one or two nights when they needed accommodation. Perhaps before joining a vessel, or when their personal circumstances dictated at the end of a trip. There was a small chapel on the premises.

In short, the room was inviting; and I calculated mentally and carefully, how long my remaining money would allow me to stay.

As I looked around, the manager then asked me,

"How long do you expect to stay with us?"

Thinking of my dwindling money, I said I thought four nights.

"Okay then!" he replied. "You don't need to pay now, and we'll see you at around seven o'clock this evening. Do you have any questions?"

I thought of my suitcase to which I felt I'd been shackled for too long, so I asked if I could leave it in the room all day.

"Yes", came the reply. "I'll give you your key now, and you can leave anything you want to in your room".

As I left the mission I was full of hope again, and anticipation, now that there was the prospect of having somewhere clean to stay that evening, and being able to sleep. And I felt relief at being free of the heavy suitcase for the first time since arriving on the coach the previous evening. This was shelter, and much better than I had come to expect.

The following days passed in Jim's company, along with a growing awareness of how quickly my funds were reducing. It was unclear when his money would come through; but very clear that I would not be able to stay at my comfortable lodgings for longer than the four days I'd agreed to with the manager of the mission.

This piece of reality must have cropped up in our conversation, because Jim suggested that I should "Go to the Social". When I looked at him in puzzlement, he simply said,

"I'll show you".

We went. I tried to explain why I was there, in embarrassment. I had made contributions during periods of farm work. I was interviewed, and had to fill in a form. But then I was told that I didn't qualify for any money immediately.

"Sorry", said the woman I spoke to. "You haven't made enough contributions. If you wish to apply for a hardship grant, you must wait six weeks".

I thanked her and left, saying that it wasn't possible. When I told Jim about this outcome, he seemed genuinely disappointed for me.

My fourth night at the mission approached, and with it the end of my days walking the docks with Jim discussing the fishing industry, and his life. I'd not heard from the trawler company, but then it was still under a week since my visit to their offices.

I told him on that last afternoon, that I would have to leave. And he told me about the lorries heading south; and where to go to ask a driver for a lift.

This was surprisingly easy, and the only question I was asked by the second driver I approached, was "Where are you trying to get to?" When I told him, he said that he was only going as far as Tilbury, but could give me advice about the best place to go to get a further lift into Kent.

And so as I sat high up in his warm cab, as the road sped away beneath our high perch, I could ponder upon the abject failure of my trip. We chatted away the day, and when we were quite near to Tilbury, we stopped at a transport café, and the driver insisted on buying sandwiches and tea for us both. Of course I hadn't mentioned I was out of funds, but perhaps he read the concern on my face when he said we'd be stopping soon for food.

Near the end of our short meal, he left the table of the transport cafe to speak to another driver seated nearby, and they came over together to where I was sitting finishing my mug of tea.

"I hear you could do with a lift" this other driver said immediately as they sat down together. "I'm going as far as Boughton Ewell, which is near enough to where you're headed".

I thanked him, whereupon he stood up, "Right then, if you're set we can get under way".

Then we all stood up, and I thanked the companion of my return trip so far. He winked, and said, "Good luck!" and so we went our ways.

Boughton Ewell was five miles or so from my first village. I'd quite often cycled there in the summer holidays on the way to Beulton. It was a small village then, but with a number of medium-sized, mostly packing, processing and road transport companies on a small industrial estate.

When I climbed down from the cab of my second lift of the day, thanking another benefactor, and saying goodbye, it was four o'clock in the afternoon. And although it was still warm and fine, I thought immediately of finding shelter for the night; and how immediately heavy my suitcase felt.

I came very soon to a yard which seemed completely deserted, and in front of me were the large open doors of a warehouse. A couple of fork lift trucks stood about, but there was no other sign of life.

When I went in, I found that the building was packed from floor to ceiling with large flattened corrugated cardboard casings. Inside it was warm, and the cardboard gave off a not unpleasant, welcoming, smell. The stacks were of varying heights, because some had already been partly dismantled.

It was easy for me to climb up two of them, even with my suitcase; and very soon I was at the top of one of the partially dismantled stacks, encased, private, surrounded by cardboard and completely out of sight from the floor; away from the afternoon sunshine and the large open doors. There was plenty of space up there for me and the suitcase.

It felt pleasantly warm and enclosed here, high up and sheltered. I had nowhere to go at that time, and if I returned to the floor, I'd probably be seen and be told to clear off. Not that I could hear anyone about. Everything was quiet. I decided that since I needed to sleep, that's what I should do now. High up on top of the piles of cardboard casings I made myself comfortable, and curled up with my suitcase next to me.

It was six o'clock the next morning before I woke up, and still everything was quiet. What a luxury it would be to sleep so soundly now.

I realized that very soon, men would be arriving for work – I thought probably around 7.30. To avoid discovery I should really be away as soon as possible.

On the previous afternoon I had noticed a tap in the yard, so taking my flannel and the towel from my suitcase, I climbed down from my hiding place. Although the doors of the building were already open, there seemed to be no-one about.

The water was cold, but I washed as best I could, brushed my teeth, and was finishing off before returning to my cardboard retreat. Then I heard a voice behind me, just as when I was collecting my suitcase from the bottom of the coach only a week before.

Startled, I looked round. The voice belonged to a short man, of late middle age. He was smiling, and was carrying a toolbox.

"How would you like some breakfast?" he asked.

I was dumbfounded at first, expecting a quite different response on being discovered. I thanked him, and spluttered, "Yes please, I would"

His question was so unexpected that I simply repeated my answer. I hadn't eaten anything since the previous afternoon's sandwich. But I knew that didn't matter.

"Yes, please", was all I could say again – and I thanked him again.

He indicated the way to a small cream caravan, which I had definitely not noticed the previous afternoon. With me still carrying my towel and toilet bag, he showed me inside, where his wife was cooking bacon and eggs. "We have a visitor for breakfast", was all the man said as we both entered the caravan.

His wife gave me a large plate of bacon, fried bread, and eggs, and a mug of tea. "Do you take sugar?" she asked, pleasantly

"Yes, please", was all I could think of replying. I was beginning to realize what an antidote hot sweet tea is for the lonely and the hungry.

They didn't ask me who I was, nor how I came to be washing my face in the yard. They didn't ask where I had appeared from. Perhaps they already knew.

They didn't tell me that I shouldn't be there. They just offered me a large breakfast in their small caravan.

I felt guilty and ashamed, and not for the first time. I had read enough, and thought enough, and been told enough, and now I was learning first hand, that I was being offered undeservedly, without question, a very great deal by people who didn't have much for themselves.

Because I knew this, and because they were so friendly, and because of my shame, and as I thanked them, I remember still how I had to fight back tears. And as I left, still in this rather wretched state, and as I thanked him again, the man gripped my elbow as I said goodbye.

"You be careful how you go!", he said. That was all. Just that. And I left him. There was no time to discover his name. And I didn't feel that I had the right to ask.

I returned to my suitcase high up on the cardboard, repacked my towel and toilet things and climbing down, left the warehouse the way I had entered it the previous afternoon.

There was still no-one else about yet. Walking along the road towards the village, I saw a transport café with lorries parked outside. I guessed that sooner or later I would find one that would be passing through my first village. The villages around, all had a number of small cold stores and packing companies for fruit, and they depended on lorries. I had often seen vehicles with the owner's name, and 'Boughton Ewell', advertised on their doors, around my own village. And in any case, were it not for the suitcase I could walk. I was now so near to home.

It had become easy to ask, and to expect a generous response, and by ten thirty I was back in my own village, and wondering how I could ask now if I could stay back at home. That would not be easy, and everything seemed suddenly bleak; my failure would be public and obvious. And I knew what Victor would say – though not to me.

(ii)

I knew very well that without my foster home, which I had been so slow to recognize for what it was, I should have perished. It was just that I had thought and hoped it was more than that. Yet without its shelter, I would have joined the legions of the young throughout Europe at that time, who because of the widespread dislocation caused by the war, and for other reasons too, were not at home.

I learned, from when I was very young, to love my parents, and like all children who loved their parents I worried about their health. And I knew I was lucky because of the part of the country where I was allowed to live.

I loved my father the most because of his quietness, his civility, and his gentleness. For what Shakespeare would have termed his 'human kindness'.

I had tried to leave, because I knew that I should. But it hadn't worked. And now I was standing at the front door of the house in the High Street again, my suitcase beside me on the pavement, knocking on the door.

Nearly always, when someone was "at the door", it was Evelyn who answered it. And so it was that morning. When she saw me she didn't look surprised, or unsurprised. Just busy.

"Can I come in? I asked.

She didn't answer, but just walked away, leaving the door open. I knew I should have to see my mother straight away to ask if I could stay again. And so I went into the downstairs front room where I knew she would be.

When I entered the room, she looked up from the letter she was writing. She didn't say anything, and waited for me to splutter out my request. When she replied, it was by a slight wave of the hand. But she didn't say "No!" At least she hadn't said that straight away.

She didn't ask where I'd been, nor why I'd come back. That was just not her way, and hadn't been for a long time. Yet her answer was simply inclusive, with the result that I took it, with relief, that I could stay.

And so life became again something like it had been before I'd left. First I went to the kitchen, where I knew my father would be, and we talked a little. Victor and Arthur were both in bed, after their night shift in Westerford. Later that day Victor was not enthusiastic when he'd learned that I had returned. He just sniffed, and ignored me as usual.

Arthur spoke to me, but he had many concerns, with his two young daughters, and new baby son. And surely also, he was concerned about the ever increasing duties of his wife in the house, though he would never have discussed such things with me.

Early the next week I decided to go into Westerford on the bus. It wasn't a good idea. Perhaps what I did there, was because of Norman Mailer and some misguided feeling of affinity with suffering humanity. Perhaps it was because of my love for my father, and my knowledge of his long service in the Royal Horse Artillery in India.

The one part of the week at school which I had come close to disliking was Tuesday afternoon. At that time, after thirteen, when Scouts had given way to the activities of the Combined Cadet Corps. To the smell of weapons' oil, blanco., and webbing, brass-cleaner and boot polish. A time of parades and inspections. A time of coarse khaki uniforms and rough shirts, which never felt as if they fitted.

When I entered the recruiting office that warm afternoon, I walked into the same warm smell of weapon oil, blanco. and webbing. Why did I enlist in an infantry regiment at just eighteen? I don't know for sure. Perhaps it was for the same reasons that I had left for Grimsby. Because it seemed that was all there was. Partly too it seemed an adventure – and certainly it had the advantage of offering somewhere to live. And so the Royal First Regiment of Foot became the answer then to all of the questions I had been facing.

Of course it was a bad idea, but didn't seem so at the beginning. It was, after all, a definite move, although I had no special aptitude or physical characteristics to indicate that I would make a success of being a soldier.

I heard after signing on, within only a few days, that I had to report not to Westerford, but to the regiment's HQ at Christfield, forty miles away. And I was sent a travel warrant for the journey.

My army career is swiftly told. There were two platoons in our intake. My platoon was 'Talavera'; I knew about that battle in Napoleon's Iberian campaign, because Napoleon's life and career had been the subject of a special paper on my 'A' Level History syllabus at school. The name of the other platoon was 'Albuera'.

I knew about that battle too.

All of the men in my platoon were National Servicemen; being in the barracks was not their choice. They were, as the saying goes, from every walk of life, and there was no-one there that I did not like or find interesting.

When our six weeks of basic training had begun, and it became known that I was a regular who had signed on for six years, no-one could hide their surprise – or rather their complete incredulity. Sometimes even their sympathy.

The training began immediately and at full speed, and we did all the things that was demanded by it. Marching, cleaning, undergoing incessant kit inspections, guard duty – with a pick axe handle at first, night exercises, PE and long runs (which I was used to), and early morning small arms training on the range. Down on the coast. Once the new Belgian rifles were issued, there was bayonet practice, and instruction on how to throw live grenades and survive. With my new companions, I learned how to avoid cook house duty wherever possible, and all those transgressions which might result in being 'put on a charge'. The guard house was a place of foreboding for us all. Or at least for most of us.

And I learned also how my companions were missing their families and their girl friends, though these were seldom regrets that were expressed openly. Rather only in a feeling they had of the futility at being there; sadness at the interruption to their lives that this two years would entail. And all of it expressed in how they looked forward to, longed for, the forty eight hour pass which would eventually come to us all (probably) one weekend, four weeks into the training.

The platoon sergeant had recently returned from a tour of duty in Korea. He was always immaculately turned out, no more than thirty years old, sported bright, new, translucent, campaign ribbons on his tunic, and was a model soldier – quiet, efficient and dedicated. Not in any sense fitting the stereotype of popular culture; but intent upon, and serious only about preparing us for the real possibility, at the end of this period of basic training, of being posted abroad to theatres of war. This was after all an infantry regiment, and a very proud one.

If the company sergeant major was closer to the popular stereotype, he and the platoon corporals had in common with the platoon sergeant, that they were fair, intent upon their task, and disciplined. Yet although they could recognize all of this, it did not temper the regret my companions felt at finding themselves in these barracks.

The platoon commander, Captain West, was a lean, erect, man of about forty two. Scrupulous, quietly spoken, serious about what he was doing, he carried with him an easy calm informality along with his officer's shiny wooden baton. He too had recently returned from Korea. Like his non-commissioned subordinates, he was secretly liked and respected by everyone in the platoon – however much its members might be reluctant to own to it.

We were fortunate that our NCOs and the officers who dealt with us, shared this certain, quiet, even earnest, aesthetic.

Naturally, every minute of every day, and often night, was accounted for. Nearly but not quite every minute. For between two and four o'clock every Wednesday afternoon, the education classes were held.

Everyone had to attend these; everyone except Alistair, whose bed was next to mine in the barrack room, and me. We were excused on account of our 'A' level passes. And so, for these two hours every week we could do nothing if we chose. Absolutely nothing. Usually we went to the oasis of the NAAFI, or lay on our beds chatting or reading.

In this proud regiment, where everything had to be done just so, our period of relaxation during basic training was a curious anomaly. No mean-spirited minor military bureaucrat had closed this loop-hole, and so we were left with our short two hour holiday in the middle of every week.

Sometimes, completely without warning, the platoon sergeant might stroll into the barrack room, and we would spring up to attention beside our beds leaving our books still open. He would say a few words, glance at the books or sometimes even pick them up. And then he would leave. Or one of the two corporals might similarly suddenly appear, and with the same result; although they would not usually bother with the books.

One afternoon, when we stood to attention as a corporal visited, I was ordered to report to the platoon commander's office immediately. In fact I was marched there by the corporal. Having escorted me, he left me at the door; left me standing to attention alongside the desk of an NCO stationed outside the platoon commander's office.

This kind of 'invitation' was usually reserved for a miscreant; for someone who knowingly or accidentally had offended in some way. And of course as I was marched to the platoon commander's office, this was in my mind. Obviously it also governed the perception of the NCO. at the desk by the door of the officer's room, who examined me doubtfully.

After I was marched in, and had saluted, the captain who was seated behind his desk dismissed the NCO.. Then after telling me to stand at ease, and to my very great surprise, he told me to take off my beret and sit down in the chair facing his desk. Throughout these seconds I was trying, frantically, to anticipate the reason for this summons.

The captain then offered me a cigarette from a smooth silver case which he'd taken from his tunic pocket. I accepted, at the same time as trying to disguise a pervading astonishment.

“Private Holden”, he began “I should like to ask you a question, which I want you to answer as truthfully as you can”.

“Yes, of course sir”, I replied.

As my imagination raced on, the captain continued, but not with a question; rather with a softly nuanced command.

“Tell me how you came to join the regiment.”

So I told him, as our cigarettes burned down, about my school, about the end of my sixth form course, and how I thought that by serving for six years I would broaden my education. It was all I could think of in the time available, and faced with the surprising request.

He waited a while, and seemed to be lost in thought. Then he continued,

“I just wanted to ask. It’s not so uncommon”.

And then, “Thank you, you may go!”

I stubbed out my cigarette, put on my beret, stood up, thanked him, and saluted. Turned to the right, and marched out of the room. As I passed the NCO. at the door, he looked up enquiringly, but I said nothing.

As I returned to the barrack room, I tried to make sense of what had just happened.

Alistair was reading on his bed.

“You okay?”, he asked. “What happened?”

“Yes, I think so”, I replied, as casually as I could. “I thought I’d had it, but he just wanted to ask me some questions”.

“What sort of questions?”

“Well, I suppose they were about how far I thought I was meeting the expectations of the army. You’ll probably get a call too. So be prepared”, I tried to joke.

“Can’t wait!” was all he said.

It was nearly four o‘clock. Our short respite was over for another week. Everybody came back from their classes, and we had a sudden kit-inspection conducted by one of the platoon corporals. There would be a night exercise later.

Life at the barracks was governed by a very strict regime, and it was fascinating to observe how individuals adapted to it. They did so in such a number of different ways. And in spite of some popular misconceptions about service life, my short experience of it led me to recognize, almost above everything else, its precision; and that it was a precision that was directed at the preservation of these new recruits of the regiment's.

Strict and ordered, these six weeks were directed at the strong possibility that in a few weeks any of us could be serving abroad – in the jungles of Malaya, or in the deserts of Aden. Or in Korea. Everything we did during this training, intense if short, was driven by the intention of preventing our heads being blown off, if at all possible.

After four weeks had passed, the longed for forty eight hour passes arrived, and I had to go home like everyone else. I even looked forward to it, perhaps just because everyone else had been doing so for so long. And yet when I arrived there off the train, I found everything much as I had left it.

I felt self-conscious in my uniform. Uncomfortable, and even a little ridiculous. I knew of course that I had not made a sensible choice. But now at least I had somewhere to live, and somewhere I was expected to be again. Late Sunday afternoon when I left to catch the train back to Christfield, it was with a mixture of relief and sadness. I had bought my father a regimental scarf made of silk; and giving it to him was the best part of the weekend.

The passing-out parade was drawing near, and we knew that each of us would be posted to other places, as the army determined. Some would join the regiment, others would be transferred to specialist units – the engineers perhaps, or signals. Perhaps the Pioneer Corps.. We had been asked to express our preferences, but of course we knew that everything depended upon the needs of the army. And this was an infantry regiment.

Along with everyone else, I sensed how changes lay ahead, and that I should be appearing to make a choice. But I hadn't addressed it. Not faced up to it.

One day Alistair asked, "Have you thought what you'll be doing after the passing out?"

"Not really", I said.

"Don't you think you should? I have", he continued.

"Well, okay, I thought I might apply to the 'Education Corps'".

I really had thought about this as an option. And I knew that upon being accepted, and after training, everyone was made up to the rank of sergeant. At least that was the talk.

Alistair persisted, "Do you know what they do?"

"Well yes, but not I suppose in detail. We've never been to a class have we?"

He laughed.

"Do you know what I think you should do?" he continued.

I looked at him, "Tell me!"

"I think you should buy yourself out while you still can".

I cannot truthfully say that I hadn't heard of the possibility, nor that other companions had not referred to it in conversation. None of these companions, all National Servicemen as they were, understood why anyone would want to sign on as a regular. Or that's what they said. But then none of us knew the other's circumstances.

I answered this defensively, "So, you don't think I'll make a soldier then?

"Well, you've got on as well as most of us. But since you ask , no I don't. I think you'd be mad to stay in for six years. Anything you did would be better".

I thought about the debacle of Grimsby. Of course being in the army was not an ideal solution, but it was still a solution of a kind.

Then Alistair asked, "Have you got twenty pounds?"

"I've got seventeen", was all I replied.

"So, you're short?"

"Mm", but nothing else was said. I said nothing more because I recognized the shortfall as being a decision made by default. That was the choice made.

The preparations for the passing out parade at the end of next week were now more than frantic; and they occupied us day and night.

Saturday nights however were still sometimes free, and on one such I was in the NAAFI, by myself at a table. Here at this time, it's very cheap and good chocolate cake with thick coffee cream on top, along with hot tea, was ambrosia. And a quiet moment alone was an added luxury to match.

I looked up, as one of the members of the platoon came over, and sat down at the table. Everyone called him Taffy, and he was indeed from Cardiff. He was a quietly spoken, thick set, man, who in civilian life was a carpenter. And he was well liked.

As he sat down, he said quite without any preamble,

"I can lend you three quid if you're short!"

Completely taken off guard, I just didn't know what to say. Of course I knew what he was referring to, but what I didn't know was how he knew I might need the money.

When I asked "Why?" it was partly that I was asking him why he was offering to do this, and partly because I felt suddenly moved – and suddenly depressed.

"In any case", I asked him, "How can I pay you back?"

"Don't you worry about that! Do you want it? I tell you, I wish I could get out!"

And that was all he said.

I realized then, at that table, that yet again I had made a mess of everything. And how everyone except me recognized it.

"Okay!" he said. "I can get it to you by next Saturday. If you take my advice you'll get your application in as soon as you can!"

So, within just three months I had failed hopelessly twice. It was an early lesson, and now I had to begin to live with the knowledge.

"Thanks", was all I was able to say.

When I made my application for release from the army, I heard very quickly that it had been passed. The news came in a letter from the platoon commander. He didn't ask to see me again. Why should he?

I left knowing that I'd been treated very well. Much better than I deserved. And I knew that I'd been more than lucky.

Gradually, quietly and yet quickly, I said goodbye to everyone, as Christmas approached. I wondered how many of them knew what had happened. Almost to a man, they seemed genuinely pleased that I was leaving the army, and I didn't know why. One of them said,

"Wish it was me! You lucky bastard!"

The latter without realizing, quite, how what they said was true. I had a long talk with Taffy before leaving, took his address, and promised to repay him the money as soon as I could.

My goodbye to Alistair was a long one too. And we wished each other luck.

When I walked past the guardroom for the last time, and outside on to the street, it was without a travel warrant this time. But I'd hitched a lift before; and in those days it was still quite easy to request and be offered a ride, even in civilian clothes. By now I was used to the procedure. Used to this kind of begging.

(iii)

At Christmas, I was back in my foster home having achieved a second failure. My mother didn't comment upon how I came to be there. My failure, and the events leading to my return were outside any conversation, and so were swallowed by the same silences as previously.

She made it clear to me that I must pay for my bed and board, and she put the figure at three pounds and ten shillings a week, So I got a job in Westerford, as a junior clerk in the branch of a well known insurance company. I travelled there on the bus which took me past the school in my second village. Now again in civilian clothes.

The branch was not large. The branch manager, Mr Simmons, had his office on the top floor. There was a Senior Clerk, Mr. Moles, a small and very timid man whom everyone seemed to disregard until they needed his advice. This was quite often, because his knowledge of the insurance industry was voluminous. He was the best qualified of anyone in the building, and he almost vibrated with enthusiasm when discussing any matter to do with insurance.

His room was next to the General Office, where I worked with nearly everyone else.

Whenever I entered his office, he would share his enthusiasm, recommending very often that I should begin studying immediately for professional examinations. It was his favourite topic. So, apart from the room where the typists worked, that was the geography of the building.

The General Office served as the enquiry point for those members of the public who had questions about their policies, or about anything else connected with their insurance needs. My desk was next to the enquiry desk, where I sat with my back to the door, facing across the office looking towards the two windows and two desks opposite. To my right was Mr Trent's desk; he was the office manager.

A very well dressed, fastidious, grey haired bachelor of forty five or so, he dealt personally with any member of the public who came in. He had a very great fear of germs, and periodically, certainly if any one came in with a sniffle, he would spray all around, often all over us all, from a bottle of green antiseptic liquid. In this way he conducted his own peculiar policy of health and safety at work This general sweep of spraying, this assault on all bugs, occurred at least twice a day; more often in the winter if there had been a rush of visitors from the outside.

Perhaps his fear of respiratory infection lay in a quite rational judgement that any kind of illness would spread easily in our cramped, warm, working conditions. From a concern that any absence from our desks might upset the efficient running and the productivity of the office.

From where he sat, close by, Mr Trent could keep an eye on me the whole time – and for that matter upon everybody else. Tall and imposing, in his county herring-bone tweeds, he had a barely disguised contempt for Mr. Moles, the Chief Clerk. It would be difficult to imagine two more different men. And this added to my liking for Mr. Moles, who in truth was my immediate boss – just as he was Mr. Trent's.

Opposite, facing me in the office, and therefore to the right of this gentleman were Brian and Ted., the one dealing with all matters do with Buildings and Fire Insurance, the other with Personal Accident and Life Insurance. Each had a telephone which was in constant use. However, they had both become, over time, so expert in modulating their voices, that their quiet conversations shaped and coloured the silence that would otherwise have reigned, instead of interrupting it.

At times the somnambulance would be disturbed by Mr Trent clearing his throat at some length, or taking a throat lozenge from a small tin in his pocket, slowly and deliberately, and putting it just as carefully into his mouth. Or when he flicked an invisible speck of dust from the lapel of his jacket, and as he did so looking over the top of his half moon glasses at me with disapproval if I looked up involuntarily. And as if he considered me a definite and continuing possible source of infection.

My job consisted of general duties. Mainly though, it was working out premiums for insurance applications, and entering the calculations on pink forms. There were a great many of these, a very great many, because although our office was quite small, it served as a regional office. It therefore dealt with applications, and policy holders from a large area.

The work was mind-numbingly boring, a fact that I had to disguise under the ever watchful gaze of Mr Trent. At times there was some detail which I was uncertain about, and therefore I would have to leave the room to consult Mr Moles. On these occasions, the Chief Clerk would keep me in conversation, as he discussed at length some arcane point about insurance. And when I returned, it was always to Mr Trent's suspicious glare and his not quite inaudible sniff.

In a way I was grateful for these short interruptions to the tedium, although any time out of the room meant that I fell behind with my task of reducing the pile of pink forms on my desk which was always being added to. And Mr Trent was ever watchful.

When he left for an early lunch, notice of which he would give not by speaking to anyone in particular, but rather by addressing the walls of the office, everything changed. Conversation burst out like a plant responding to sunshine and the rain. The typists would immediately appear with urgent items to discuss with Ted and Brian; an urgency which evaporated immediately upon the Office Manager's return.

There were two significant and regular visitors to the General Office, and these were the Inspectors. I don't know why they had that title, for they were actually insurance salesmen, who were responsible for generating new business, and following up any enquiry about taking out a policy. Their suits were sharp, and they drove large company cars. Because of their commission, they had the prestige of earning the most money of anyone in the building except the Branch Manager; both for themselves and for the company. Mr. Trent was in awe of them.

When my lunch time came, and I walked down the stairs and out into the street, it was as if I were walking up on to a sunlit plain.

I was paid monthly, but my mother wanted me to pay her weekly, something which required immediate management and negotiation. This was not a puzzle that I could solve immediately.

On the second morning at my new job, I ran up the stairs to the office whistling, although this was not something that I was aware of doing. I don't know why I did it that morning. Whistling was not at all something that I was prone to do, probably because I was not particularly good at it. Perhaps I was simply happy at having a new job. Perhaps it was because it was a fine day, or the bus hadn't been late. Perhaps it had simply become a habit.

A little while into the morning, a sudden hush fell over the office and Mr Trent sprang to his feet. As if an errant lozenge had become stuck in his throat. My back was to the door as usual, so I became aware only slowly of the sudden change in atmosphere. A chilling. The reason was that Mr Simmons, the Branch Manager had entered the room. The silence deepened and intensified.

"Good morning, Mr Simmons.", said the brisk Mr. Trent.

This greeting was ignored. Instead the Branch Manager replied:

"Mr Trent, will you please ask Mr Holden to come to my office in ten minutes?"

How could it be, I thought, that I was the reason for this visitation, even when no word was actually addressed to me? When I looked up, it was to meet Mr Trent's scornful gaze, as it slowly dawned upon me that I had been summoned to the Manager's office.

The other two looked at me enquiringly across the space between our desks, once Mr Simmons had left. I said nothing, partly because I hadn't been addressed, and partly because I was at a loss to understand what was going on around me.

At my interview, I had tried to explain why I left the army because that I had done so was apparent from my application form. Of course when I spoke about it, it was with obvious embarrassment. I could only say that I had made a mistake, and that the regiment had generously allowed me to leave. I was intent, at least, upon not adding lying to my shame.

Mr Simmons was not a lively nor engaging man. Rather he was someone who lived behind his spectacles, and seemed to be held together by his immaculate suits. There was always a white handkerchief, arranged horizontally to the millimetre, in the breast pocket of his jacket. He wasn't a man who seemed to expect anyone to warm to him, nor apparently was he interested in their doing so.

When the ten minutes had passed, carefully measured by Mr Trent, I left my piles of pink forms, and climbed the stairs to the Branch Manager's office. My brief knock was answered by a low, authoritative command, "Come in!".

As I closed the door behind me and stood before a large and very empty polished, dark red, cherry wood, desk there was no invitation this time to sit down; nor was there any kind of preamble. Simply,

"Mr Holden, two things! First your dress. Will you kindly ensure that it is more suitable? And as quickly as you can?"

Taken aback by these statements, which I had first thought were questions, it was obvious to me that no opinion of mine was either sought or expected. And so, I could only reply, lamely, "Yes sir". But his next detonation followed quickly, " And I'd like to remind you that this is not a barrack room!"

I was still adjusting to his opening statements, when the next which I had anticipated would require no fuller a response from me, was delivered. I must have looked at him in a way that showed my surprise, even puzzlement, for he elaborated,

"This morning when you came in to work, you were whistling. Will you kindly ensure that this does not happen again?" I took it that this was definitely not a question, but I treated it as one nonetheless.

I agreed that it wouldn't, hoping that he realized that I meant the whistling rather than arriving at work. And so, he concluded,

"I should be grateful if you would return to your work immediately."

When Mr Trent left for his lunch, Ted asked me, "What did the old man want?" And I had to explain that he didn't like my whistling. He and Brian grinned.

Although my first pay day had not of course arrived, I went to a men's outfitter's in my lunch hour, and I bought a dark grey 'Weaver to Wearer' suit. Or rather I should say that I arranged to buy it. I chose the colour because I thought it might not show the dirt.

The price was seven pounds and ten shillings, but if I paid by weekly instalments it would cost ten pounds. And if I took out the hire purchase agreement, I could take it away immediately.

The shop assistant gave me a form to complete, and pointed out that I would need a character reference. Later in the afternoon I asked Mr Moles about this, and he suggested that I put his name down.

And so I was introduced to the insurance industry, and my new job. I had shelter again, a job, and a new suit, albeit one that I had yet to begin paying for. Had I been asked, I should probably have said that I preferred fruit picking, but no one asked.

Food however was an abiding pre-occupation of mine; even more than my clothes were for Mr Simmons.

I was paid at the end of each month, and therefore had to budget for the month ahead. In a four week month after I had paid the gentlemen's outfitters, my season ticket to get to work, and my board and lodging, I had a little over £1 left; in a five week month there was less.

I had breakfast in the morning before leaving home, and dinner in the evening when I got home at around 6.00 to 6.15. The time did not much matter, because Evelyn had prepared the food at lunch time; and it was left all afternoon to steam on a plate over a saucepan.

I ate alone, yet when it came to it I couldn't manage that so easily – because the plate was usually floating in separated water and fat from the meat. I ate as much as I could manage; but was always grateful later for the soup that my father continued to prepare in the kitchen.

My budget excluded any kind of social life outside work; in any case all my former school friends were embarked on careers, or were away at university. But I still had books, my own and the library's, and I had the countryside all around me; and one other small opportunity.

I could just afford to eat lunch for three days every month in a small restaurant in the town, which I did immediately after being paid. I always hoped that this practice could last for four days but it never did. The restaurant served a cheap but wholesome set lunch for nearby office workers and occasional shoppers. After those few days this luxury had to be postponed until the next month, and it was sandwiches for lunch. I tried to space out those few meals in the restaurant more evenly throughout the month ahead, but my will power always failed.

In this fashion, Spring came and the year passed into Summer. Listening to the conversation in the office when there was any, admiring or not the typists; and hearing the rustle of their dresses brushing by when they came to talk to Ted or Brian. I continued, throughout the summer, to plough through the pile of pink quotation forms, the nature of which was that it would never diminish – devouring my three lunches a month in the haven of the small restaurant.

But I had a job. I could read and walk at the weekends, I had my father's company, and that of Arthur's small children – particularly Christine with whom I often talked. About nine then, she had the same quiet intelligence as her father.

My season ticket could take me to Westerford on a Saturday morning occasionally, for a cup of espresso – and the chance to imagine that I had something important and interesting to do during the rest of the day. More often though, I could look forward to being called upon by the cricket club.

The summer that year was a good one, often warm and dry; and sometimes hot. All around me the Weald bloomed, and the clay was baked into rock, and cracking open into large fissures.

Then one warm June Sunday afternoon, something very surprising happened as I was out, walking – though not to anywhere in particular. Musing, and simply enjoying that this wasn't a weekday, and when a cheerful, beaming, middle-aged lady came towards me on a bicycle. I suppose what happened next came about because when we're young, if we're fortunate, things like it do happen. Or they could then, in my village. This occasion introduced me to someone whom I had seen but did not know; certainly I didn't know her as well as she knew about me.

Mrs Aster was a widow, her husband having died without any warning, when they were home on leave from his job in the Indian Civil Service. She had one son, with whom I had a peculiar connection that I have already mentioned.

Her son had been at my school, three years ahead of me, and it was his name which appeared inside many, or indeed most, of the collars that I wore. I really don't know how that came about. On the morning in question, as I met his mother on her bicycle, John Aster was away serving in the merchant navy, where he was an officer on oil tankers.

After she had passed, she called back to me, dismounting from her bicycle, and walked back towards me, wheeling it.

"Oh, William", she said, "are you able to pop in to see me sometime? When can you manage?"

She wasn't someone who believed in unnecessary hesitation, nor much in wasting time. Very likely life had instructed her out of that.

There was no reason that I couldn't visit her whenever she suggested, for as I said my social life was hardly a full one. And when she suggested that evening, I agreed.

I knew where her house was. Her nephew had also attended my school, although quite a long time before me. He had been a boarder. Sometimes I met him, and his young wife, when I filled in at the last minute because someone had dropped out of the village first X1. He was an excellent opening batsman, and his wife organized the teas, which were also excellent. And for reasons I have already explained, very welcome to me. Both of them had always seemed very friendly, and this in spite of my contribution to the side being not exactly glorious.

James ran the family fruit packing and cold store business, and it often seemed to me how very tired he looked. At the time however, this was just a passing impression, though it became much more when two or three years later he suffered a massive heart attack, and died. However that was in the future on this Saturday – though not so much in the future.

Mrs Aster's house was a little outside the village, on the main road towards Stapleton, and I could easily walk to it.

When I knocked on the door, she opened it immediately, smiling and welcoming.

"Come on in. Shall we go in here? I was just watching something on the television". And she showed me through a large square hall and into the sitting room, where the covers on the settee and arm chairs were cream, and full of large flowers. Red bougainvillaea flowers

When I realized the television was still on, I thought I was too early and apologized, "I'm sorry, I'm early".

"Of course you're not", she replied. "Sit down. Would you like a glass of sherry?" I thanked her, and she poured out the drink.

I was nervous, since I had no idea why she wanted to see me.

She put the sherry on a small table to one side of the sofa on which I was sitting, and sat down opposite me in an armchair.

I knew that Mrs Aster was a teacher in the village school, in the infant department. She hadn't been there when I was at the school, but had come some time later – though quite when, I was unsure. So I didn't know her well, and hadn't even seen her much in the village shops or around the village. But then, lately, I was not much around the village either, being in Westerford during the week.

"Now then", she began as she sipped her drink. "I don't quite know how to put this, and you must forgive me if what I'm going to say is not something you will like".

My sense of foreboding rather increased, but then she still seemed very friendly.

"No, please, go on", I said. "Please… "

She seemed to chuckle. "Well first, I wondered how your job was going".

The question, though surprising perhaps, came to me as a relief. It would not take me long to think about an answer to that at least.

"Well, it isn't very interesting, though I'm getting used to it" was all I could reply.

"Is it something that you see yourself doing as a career?" she asked.

"No, it isn't, but I have to do it for now", I said.

If I was a little embarrassed by the questions, it was not because I minded her asking them, but rather because I was all too aware of my recent failures. Those I definitely could not talk about.

"Why haven't you applied for a university place?" Mrs Aster continued. And at this my embarrassment increased.

"Well one day, I hope I might. I have some prospectuses".

I had in fact applied to Leicester to read Geography, but had heard nothing. Why Leicester, and why Geography? Who knows what determines our choices when we're young? Geography had always interested me; but then English Literature interested me more – and History more still. And I knew nothing of Leicester.

"Have you considered teaching as a career?" she persisted.

"Well, I thought it was something I'd have to choose later, after I'd got a degree, if I got one."

Although my answers were not untrue, I actually had no expectation of being able to go to university.

But this was the very first conversation of this kind that I'd had. Nobody had ever asked me so many of these kinds of questions. Forcing me to face the choices and possibilities that other people of my age were facing.

She continued,

"Is it something that you might be interested in trying, do you think?"

"Well yes", I offered, before adding rather rashly, "it has to be more interesting than what I'm doing now".

And then she asked, obviously because she had something else in mind,

"Do you have a bicycle?".

At this, my embarrassment returned, as I recalled how I had, so ingloriously, parted company with my racer. Foolishly, and thrown off guard, I assumed that she needed one.

"No, I'm sorry, but I don't have one now, because I sold it". Of course I did not say why.

She laughed again, and her reply to this was something that surprised me, even in this surprising conversation.

"I meant I have a spare one which you can borrow if you like"

"Oh thank you, that's very kind of you", I said immediately.

And then came another question, and very quickly,

"Don't you think it's time that you left home?"

Of course I knew it was, and I agreed. I wished I could be more forthright, and could say outright, "Yes, I know it is, and I want to".

In any case Mrs Aster was not to be diverted, distracted, or put off,

"I don't know if you know, she continued, but I have just finished a course at Goldsmiths' College, which is part of the University of London".

I didn't know, and I had not heard of Goldsmiths'.

"You know, I think it would be just the place for you. It's very lively, and there would be a huge number of people with you of your own age."

I struggled to think about what she was saying, to take all this in. Her interest, her questions, and now a specific suggestion.

"What would you like to read if you went?"

"Probably English", I answered.

"Well, with your 'A' levels, you'd have a good chance of getting in. Why don't you think about applying?"

Of course I already was, though I didn't know how she knew about my 'A' levels.

"I have been talking to Mr Stewart about you, and if you would like it he would be happy to discuss how to become a teacher with you. It might be possible to get a temporary post before you went up to college, and he could tell you about that as well".

And so it was, that as I left Mrs Aster's front garden, and carefully latched shut her wicket gate, I thought how so suddenly the pace and grain of my life had changed yet again. It had been only two hours before that I was opening it, before knocking shyly on her front door.

When I went to the insurance office on Monday morning, it was much more willingly, but only to enjoy all the more the prospect of leaving sometime soon. And I nursed and nourished that prospect as I tackled the piles of pink forms, carefully observed as always by Mr. Trent.

The following weekend I went to visit Mr Stewart and his wife, which I re-called was the first time I had actually approached the school since leaving it at ten years old. The school house was joined to the school, next door. I knew one of their sons, Brian. He had been in the same class as me and left at the same time.

They were very welcoming, and Mrs Stewart overwhelmed me with her offers of cake and tea. I asked after Brian. I knew he was at Oxford reading Geography. He would later work for the UN., as an Agricultural Officer in India.

As we talked, and as I munched through their cake, Mr Stewart explained to me that it was possible to apply for 'unqualified' work as a relief teacher, to cover the absences of staff through illness. Of course the periods of employment in each school would vary, and might sometimes be quite short. He said he thought it would be good experience.

That meeting over cake led to another soon afterwards, at the Divisional Education Offices in Westerford, which turned out to be a kind of interview, though a very informal one. Though not with cake. And soon after that, everything had most definitely changed.

When I took my borrowed bicycle home, my mother was very suspicious, particularly because it was a lady's model. She asked me where I had got it, perhaps fearing that I might have stolen it. When I explained about the bicycle, she listened carefully and doubtfully, and then seemed really quite annoyed.

After a short while, I received a letter from the Education Offices, with a contract to sign, explaining that I was to be offered relief teaching work for a year from 1st September. The letter referred to my intention to enter a teacher training course in October the following year.

My days at the insurance office became more bearable still, since now they were numbered; and all because of the intervention of Mrs Aster.

An excursion on my borrowed bicycle took me one summer's evening, a little later, to nearby Stapleford three miles away. While there, I saw a small card in a newsagent's window, advertising a room to let. That was my introduction to the necessity of knocking on doors asking for digs, although I didn't enquire immediately. Before leaving, I looked around the small village which I already knew well, and found the address that was on the card: it was a small cottage near the churchyard.

I cycled home that evening in the warm sunshine, with yet something more to think about. Turning into the setting sun around the corner just outside the village, I rode by a very handsome cottage where, someone had told me, lived the mother of a famous cricket commentator who was often on the television and radio covering Test Matches.

Whether the story was true or not, I found it re-assuring, as the cottage basked in the warm evening sun. Then past the cider-making factory, on under 'cuckoo arch', which was really just a railway bridge, past the bungalow where another friend from primary school days lived, and then following the railway line back to my village. And all the time I was considering the possibility that I might knock on the cottage door, and enquire about the room.

The following evening, I mentioned my discovery to Mrs Aster, who was very enthusiastic; and said I should go ahead as soon as possible. And then she surprised me by saying something that I didn't really understand,

"You know William, it's not what you've done so far that matters, but what you are!"

I think she must have sensed my awareness of failure, and was trying to make me feel better about it. It was evidence also that that she knew more about my life, and cared more, than occurred to me at that time.

The result of that conversation was that I resolved to return to Stapleton as soon as I could; and the result of that resolution was that the beginning of September found me living in the small cottage by the church with a very thin, elderly, and kindly lady. Three miles away from my first village, and in the other direction to my second.

I had slipped away quietly from my career in the insurance industry, leaving the pile of pink forms almost exactly at the level that I had first found them, and after thanking Mr

Moles. And almost immediately, I entered my first school as a replacement teacher.

It was a mixed secondary school on the western side of Westerford. The young woman teacher I was to replace for a fortnight, had to enter hospital for an operation for a goitre. We had quite a long talk together on the morning that she left.

After another more brief and very careful talk from the Headmaster in his study, my very first class was an English lesson with a fourth year class, all of whom would be leaving the school the next Easter. There were about twenty pupils, mostly girls.

During this first lesson, I followed the guidelines and suggestions for work that the departing teacher had left me, and I did the same with the other classes throughout that first day.

When four o'clock came, and as I began my journey back to Stapleford, it was in warm September sunshine and floating among the impressions of the day. My first, was how quickly it had passed. And as the afternoon sun flooded the inside of the bus, I reflected upon how far away the Head's introductory talk now seemed, how welcoming and relaxed the other teachers were; and I thought about my timetable for the following day and the various groups of children and young people that I had met so far, so suddenly. Some of them I would meet again the next day, and some not until later in the week – and of course there were classes I was yet to meet.

Mrs Aster had suggested that I could leave the bicycle at her house in the morning, before walking along into the High Street to catch the bus to Westerford at around 7.30. I could then pick it up at the end of the day before riding back to Stapleford and my digs.

When I arrived back, at around five o'clock, my benefactress and guide asked me immediately how the first day in my new occupation had gone. I tried to explain about the teacher I was replacing, the Head, and something of the rest of it.

I think she knew that I had to get back for my evening meal at six. So, she suggested,

"Look why don't you look in when you pick up the bicycle tomorrow night, and you can tell me about it all in more detail?"

Perhaps she thought there would be more news still by then, and of course there was.

As I cycled back to my digs, on the lady's bicycle, along the side of the railway track, through the soft September evening, in my 'Weaver to Wearer' suit that didn't show the dirt, plans for the next day were running through my mind.

I could of course follow the guidance and notes given to me by the teacher, with the new classes that I would meet. There were specific things that she wanted me to do with them; work to continue. But she emphasised that I should also do things of my own that I thought might interest them; and she asked me to leave her notes about anything different that I specifically chose to do.

The very first class of the next morning, at 9.15, would be the one that I'd met at the beginning of the first day: the fourth year young people who would be leaving at Easter. As I cycled back to my digs, I sensed a need for me to do something with them that I had thought of for myself. And my choice, quickly made, was to talk to them about Matthew Arnold's poem, 'Sohrab and Rustum'. I had met it at school, during 'A' level work, and it had left an immediate impression on me. I thought if I liked it so might they. And so I read through the poem again, in bed that night.

My days now began at around a quarter to six, with breakfast at six o'clock. Mrs Lacey had asked me when I needed to leave in the morning, and she insisted upon getting up at that hour to prepare breakfast, so this routine became quickly established. The table was laid out neatly and generously, and we ate breakfast together. Outside it was still quite dark; inside as the day was only just beginning, it was warm and light.

Leaving at around a quarter to seven, meant I had time to drop off the bicycle at Mrs Aster's, and catch the bus; once in Westerford, there was a twenty minute walk to the school. As I got near to it, I began to meet pupils who were also on their way. I was startled when one of the girls in the class upon which I was to inflict Arnold's poem, suddenly appeared alongside me.

She had a friend with her, whom I recognized was from the same class, "Good morning, sir", she said and giggled, and then they left me.

The school was well run, and all the pupils that I met had been influenced by the successful work done by the popular English teacher whom I was temporarily replacing. No doubt also, though it didn't occur to me at the time, the Headmaster had made his expectations very clear to every class that I was to work with. He would have known that my inexperience was almost as great as theirs.

This first lesson of the day would, like all the rest, run for forty minutes, and I began by telling these young people whom I had only met the day before, the story of Sohrab and Rustum; and they listened, probably because it didn't occur to me that they might not!

They listened to how each was the champion of the opposing Persian and Tartar armies; and how it was agreed that single combat between them would decide the outcome of the battle. And they listened intently, to how Rustum killed his son without realizing who he was, and how that only happened because Sohrab did realize who Rustum was, and had stopped fighting.

As I finished this summary of the story, there was complete silence in the room; a long one which took me by surprise and was a little unnerving. Then, the girl who had wished me good morning without warning, and who was sitting with her friend near the back, said, but very quietly,

"Sir, that's really sad!"

"Well yes, it is", I replied. Into the silence.

So, then I continued by asking them if I could read them bits from how Arnold tells the story in the poem. And I read them the parts of the poem that I'd selected the previous evening, and particularly examples of its extended metaphors to fill in the sketch that I'd given them. And they listened. Probably, as I have said, simply because I expected that they would. Such was my inexperience.

When I think back now from over fifty years, I shrink from my temerity, and still wonder at my good fortune in the tolerance of those young people. I was protected in large measure, of course, by my own ignorance, and by the power of Arnold's poem. Those were my unlikely guardians that morning.

I finished reading my selections from the poem to them only a minute or two before the bell announced the end of the first period. And when those twenty or so pupils left the room, they did so in almost complete silence. Not something, as I was later to learn, that I could reasonably expect in other schools; when I would be much older. A few of them whispered to each other as they left; and a few wished me goodbye almost absentmindedly. And so, the rest of the day passed very quickly, as before.

That evening, as I sat upon Mrs Aster's sofa of bougainvillaea flowers, facing her, I told her about my first two days, and about what had happened with the Arnold poem in particular. She laughed and laughed, before saying thoughtfully,

"Yes", but remember that they are very little younger than you. The young will always listen to the young". And she seemed to say it with a mixture of generosity and regret.

Perhaps she was right, I didn't know.

This incident at my first school, among others, my regular conversations with Mrs Aster, and my early days as a 'teacher' (though you could scarcely call me that), became my escape from isolation – and silence. They were the means by which I became introduced again to living in the everyday, among Everyman and Everywoman.

When the young teacher returned from her hospital treatment, I was sent the very next day to a brand new primary school on a new estate in a different part of Westerford. Then, next, back to the primary school in my own village for a fortnight, under the guidance of Mr and Mrs Stewart. After that, for the final three weeks of this first term, the Divisional Office sent me to another secondary school in Westerford to fill in, to teach English and Games. And I reached this by a combination of Mrs Aster's bicycle, the usual bus that I had known for so long, and a trolley bus. It was a boys' school, set in parkland, a little out to the east of the town.

Only a week had passed in this new school, before it seemed that disaster had struck; but it turned out to be an incident which only served to further define my positive view of my new occupation. An occupation for which I was entirely unqualified.

Halfway between Stapleford and the bus stop in my village, the pedal of the bicycle came off. The November morning was very wet with driving rain; and having no waterproofs I quickly became soaked. Too wet to bother further about sheltering.

By the time I had walked to my village, my suit was blacker than it had ever been, and heavier also. I was now very late, and waiting for the next bus I had time to telephone the school from the box in the High Street; and to try to explain why I would be late. The School Secretary, a jolly and efficient lady, simply told me not to worry, and just to get there as quickly as I could.

By the time I had caught the later bus, and a trolley bus, it was well past eleven when I finally arrived; and the morning break was over. On my way, sitting on the buses, dripping over the seats, I had time to wonder about the response of the Head at this new school to my failure to arrive on time; indeed to my arriving quite spectacularly late.

When I arrived at last, The Secretary said that Mr Chambers would like to see me, and she showed me straight to his office.

As I entered, he got up from behind his desk, saying,

"Oh hello, Mr Holden", as I stood dripping all over his carpet, trying to apologize, and attempting quickly to explain the reason for my lateness.

"You seem very wet", he interrupted me.

He walked over to a wardrobe which was in his study, and took out a pair of trousers on a hanger. "Try these on", he said, and held the neatly pressed trousers out to me.

"You have a track suit top, don't you, and a football shirt? he asked.

I replied that I had.

"Well take these to the cloakroom, and see if they'll fit. I think they probably will. And when you've changed out of those clothes, get a cup of tea from the staffroom, and we'll get your clothes down to the boiler room to dry out".

The trousers did fit, and surprisingly well.

And so I faced my new classes in the Headmaster's trousers, while my own were despatched to the boiler room to turn again from their sodden black to a lighter shade of dark grey.

Before the Christmas holidays had quite arrived, Mr Chambers asked me if I'd like to remain at the school for the following two terms before going up to Goldsmiths'. The result of this was that I received a new contract from the Divisional Office; my 'relief contract' was replaced by a 'temporary contract'.

So now instead of having to get separate Head Teachers to verify and sign for my attendance at the end of each day, before I could submit my claim for pay to the Divisional Office, I was now paid automatically, both in term time and the holidays. I now had a monthly salary and just one Head Teacher.

This contract would take me right up to the following 1st September, and although the hourly rate for each school attendance on my old contract appeared better, now, all things being equal, my hours and payment for them were now assured; and indeed much better because there would be no interruption. I should add that when Mr Chambers came to verify and sign for my attendance on the day of my lateness, he suggested that I enter hours for the complete morning. And so it was.

Soon after the incident of the broken pedal, I was lent another item of clothing, which was an 'Observer Corps' greatcoat belonging to Mr Stewart. This loan was a real gift, being very thick and warm. And looking back, there is little doubt this fresh benefit derived entirely from another intervention by Mrs Aster.

Throughout the early Winter months of that first term, as I collected the repaired bicycle at the end of the day, before setting off back to my digs, I was often invited in by Mrs Aster. For conversation, a glass of sherry, some cocoa, or to watch a television programme with her. Looking back, I doubt that I adequately expressed the gratitude that I owed her, and felt. I know that I didn't. Whenever I knocked on her front door, her response was always the same; but I did worry about seeming to impose upon her kindness.

We had long conversations about teaching, she lent me many books and, again in retrospect, it was clear that she kept a close eye upon how my application to Goldsmiths' was progressing. But when my school term began again after Christmas, these regular daily meetings became less frequent.

The mishap with the bicycle pedal demonstrated how the morning journey from Stapleford had become impractical, now that it was certain that I would be working in Westerford for most of the rest of the following year. We discussed how much better it would be for me to get digs nearer the school in the New Year.

And so I returned the borrowed greatcoat, and the borrowed bicycle, and left Mrs Lacey and her cottage by the church, and moved to Westerford. And in doing so, I learned how there was a procedure to be followed when finding digs; which essentially was all about knocking on the door of someone I'd never met before, and asking them if I could live in their house. At the beginning it felt humiliating, and perhaps later too. But the need was inescapable; and now I had an actual reason to ask. This was that I needed to be near my place of employment. That seemed to make the difference.

The local newsagent's was always a good place to start, and so were local shops. I discovered quite quickly that usually somebody knew somebody, who knew somebody, who knew somebody. And it was in this way that I achieved accommodation; somewhere to live while waiting for the future. Somewhere to shelter, to preserve the balance of wonder over terror; the terror that was loneliness.

First I stayed with a small family of a husband and wife and their young daughter of ten years. The lady of the house was Scottish, and rather older than her husband who worked nights in a local factory; one of the town's biggest employers.

Their house was small and smelt very new, which was because it was being continually decorated inside by my landlady's husband. It was immaculately clean and spruce. When I knocked on their door, I was like the Sikh salesman of coloured scarves of my childhood, except that I would have nothing so exotic in my suitcase. Rather it was what I was to meet that would be exotic – and warm, and ordered, and comfortable with wonderful cooking. I ate with the small and happy little family.

But of course I was to learn, even at this stage, that good things sometimes come in small doses. I gained the impression that longer than a fortnight was not what my landlady had in mind for my stay; or perhaps it was her husband who thought that. After all, I understood. Why would he want a stranger living in his home?

From the beginning of my stay, I set about finding somewhere else in preparation for the day that I would have to move out of these comfortable lodgings. And when I found somewhere, with not so much difficulty, it was very different. It was a grey room in a grey street, just up from the local Salvation Army hostel – which was a reminder of my good fortune. Whenever I walked past the hostel I was arrested, always, by the acrid smell of a recently extinguished house fire. And I was never to learn the reason for this.

Undeniably, there was nothing homely about my new digs, where I was to stay for eight months in all. But the house was convenient for the school, and the bed and board a little cheaper than my existing warm and homely shelter.

I came to realize, whenever I moved into new digs, that there would be the same questions to answer. And in a way they were not an unpleasant novelty. Now these were asked by a middle-aged, unmarried, lady who owned the small terraced house: about when I needed breakfast, and when I wanted an evening meal. She put them in an abrupt and business like way. When I answered, she replied,

"I'll have to leave the dinner for you sometimes, because I have to go to look after my sister". I didn't ask her why. I felt only relief that it looked as if I had again found somewhere to live.

When she showed me the room, it looked neglected and bare, as without life in its greyness as my existing digs were bright and cared for. It was clear from the beginning, that living here would be simply a matter of utility. Necessity. Somewhere to wait for something. So it was upon this understanding that we arranged a date for me to move in with my suitcase, and a new deal was struck.

Paradoxically therefore, I returned to my existing digs to tell my Scottish landlady my good news; and to enjoy the company, the conversation, and the order of the small family's home while I was still able to. The few remaining days there, were to have the same quality as my earlier short stay in the Seamen's Mission; a quality that had its origin in transience.

When I moved, there was an immediate need to adjust to the hard, bare, unwelcome, strictures of solitude again, but at least my resumed work at the school was a return to the familiar. And I became immersed in the days of the school, even on Saturday mornings.

Ron, one of the masters, ran the town's senior youth football team. At that time, things were not organized as comprehensively as now. And I helped him generally, and with refereeing duties. The Saturday mornings took me all around and about the town, and were to some extent extensions of contact with people I knew. A few of the boys from the school were in the team, and some of its members were extremely good players. One, I remember had a trial for Charlton Athletic, then a major force in top level football.

During the half-term of the Easter holiday from school, I went for an interview at Goldsmiths'. On a fruit lorry on its way to Covent Garden. A lift offered by the young manager of the fruit farm at Stapleford; the one with the shelf full of Russian novels. The one who knew why blackberries tasted so bad after Michaelmas. I travelled back to Westerford, late in the afternoon on the coach from Victoria. It stopped near the college.

A little later, I took the bus one evening, to see Mrs Aster, to tell her that I'd been offered a place. She was very pleased, though I had the impression that she might already have known.

As we talked, she said,

"You did put down on the form that you wanted a place in hall, didn't you?"

She had advised me to do this because, she said, of the social life.

"Yes".

"Good", she replied, "that would be much the best".

Perhaps she already knew that I would be allocated a place. Looking back over the years, I suspect that she did. Perhaps she even knew how lonely life could be in some digs. I think she knew about loneliness.

"And you've applied for a grant?"

I assured her that I had, and as I did so I felt how essential to me her detailed practical advice had been.

A week or so later, I had another piece of news to tell her, of which she could have had no inkling. And it came to me one morning during break-time at school.

Mr Chambers took me into his office. He told me that the school planned to take a small party of the older boys to Rome, to the Olympic Games. The trip was to be organized by Ron. And then, he said,

" I wonder if you would be interested in going along? It would cost you the same as the boys are paying". And he told me the cost.

"Do you think you can manage that?"

Without taking time to think, I said that I could, thanked him and left, scarcely believing what he had just offered me. I'd never been abroad, and my failure to reach Belgium seemed to belong to another world and another time. I liked the group of masters that were going with Ron.

Yet the money was a problem, as always. I had nothing much left over at the end of every month. But I could work in the Easter holiday, and so I decided to try my luck at the bus station, which was quite near to my digs. The Westerford and District Bus Company, was the very same that ran the buses that I had known since my earliest days; even the same that ran the coaches to Victoria. The same that employed the driver who introduced me to Dvořák. And I had heard that it was possible to get temporary employment as a bus conductor.

The result of a visit to the bus station was that when the Easter break from school came, I exchanged my suit that never showed the dirt, for a bus-conductor's uniform. I had explained when I visited the bus station, that I was to go up to Goldsmiths' in October, was working as a temporary teacher in one of the schools in the town, but needed a job during the three weeks or so that the school was not in session. They asked me where I was in digs, and seemed satisfied at my answer.

I remember the delight I felt when they told me that I could report for duty on the morning after the school term ended. This was perfect. Now I really could go to Rome.

For the first two days that Spring holiday, I worked with another conductor, so I could see what was what. He showed me how to go about things, though his ways and methods were ones that I had to interpret rather than follow slavishly.

He was a sharp and wise-cracking Cockney who had been in the job for quite a number of years. He had a wide range of jokes and repartee, and for instance often addressed a crowded bus downstairs, with the question,

"Right you lot, who wants to pay twice?"

It was an approach that worked very well for him. I doubted that it could work for me.

He always helped the young and attractive young women up to and down from the bus, and he helped the elderly ladies also. Sometimes he got a warning look from the elderly ones.

But after these two entertaining days, I was out on my own.

The bus routes took me to the towns and villages around Westerford. Some I had not visited previously, but many I knew, though in different circumstances. Often there were very early starts, some at around 4.30 am., out to the docks at Portham, and as I recall those days I remember how Stefan Zweig mentions, in several places, how it is the poor who get up early.

One day I was 'teaching' boys 'English', and helping them with Games, and literally the next I was collecting their bus fares around the town. And yet they were so civilised about it. There was no mockery that I heard; and they seemed to adjust as I had to. Perhaps their attitude was a feature of those very different times; perhaps they just understood. Some of them knew that I would be joining them on the trip to Rome; whatever the reason nothing spreads so quickly as news of that kind in a school. Whatever the case, there was not the slightest problem as I asked them for their fares; not the merest unpleasantness.

When I told Mrs Aster about the opportunity I had to go to Rome, and my job on the buses, she laughed and laughed. And then she laughed some more. And then she asked me whether I had heard that I had been given a place in hall in October. I could tell her that I had.

A little while after I had given her my news about the trip to Rome, a crisis presented itself, and a small disaster was narrowly averted.

It happened when I was approached by another conductor in the rest-room. I enjoyed the company of my companions over a cup of tea and a cake always, and so was taken completely by surprise; thinking that nothing could be amiss when he sat down next to me. I knew that this conductor was a Trades Union Steward, because I had been introduced to him in the locker room on my first day. I don't think he had taken a lot of notice of me then, but now he sought me out.

He came straight to the point.

"Have you got two jobs? he demanded. Before asking a second question, "Are you being paid twice?"

At first I could not help but hesitate, being taken by surprise.

"No!" I replied.

I explained that I was a student waiting to begin a course of teacher training, and that my work at the school was only temporary, just as was my time at the depot. That I needed to work in the holidays to pay for my digs.

He seemed a little happier.

“Only I was told that you were a teacher, and you were working here in your holidays!” He said this with musical and Welsh tunes.

“No”, I said, “that’s not quite right.”

“Okay then. I understand now. You don’t mind me asking do you?” came the musical question.

It wasn’t a question, but I treated it as if it were.

“No, of course not!” .

The Union was strong at the depot. Perhaps it had to be. But if this impromptu interview for which I was completely unprepared had gone differently, I should have had to leave. Immediately. My trip to the Olympic Games would have been abandoned at the second hurdle.

As it was, the Shop Steward bought me a cup of tea in the canteen.

There were many characters working on the buses, but I realized almost at once that the best course was to be on time, and follow my own judgement. Certainly not to copy the manner and methods of any one else. I departed from this rule just once in the three weeks as a bus conductor, and I regretted my mistake immediately.

The occasion was early one Saturday afternoon on the way to Meddingham, where a little later an important football match would be played. Meddingham were a league side in the old Third Division of the Football Association. The bus was very crowded, and there was little time to collect fares before the bus emptied of passengers on their way to the match. People were getting on and off all the time; and perhaps because I was a little flustered, or perhaps because I simply misjudged the situation, I joked to one set of fans, as I collected their fares,

“I don’t know why you don’t support a decent football team anyway!”

This was not a joke that my listeners were prepared to share. Luckily we had almost reached the ground, and when they left me it was only with a few choice comments. I’d got away with my indiscretion, but I'd learned another lesson. Football fans are unlikely to exhibit a sense of humour in discussions about their favourite team.

When I told Mrs Aster about the union shop steward, she looked serious; and when I told her about the football fans she laughed. Her only reply was to repeat something she had said previously,

"William, I've told you before, the important thing is what you are, not what you've done".

But I was still not sure that I completely understood what she meant.

My short, and innocent, time on the buses presented me with a whole series of other impressions, and further unexpected dilemmas. And the one that sticks in the memory, still, occurred one other afternoon and involved a relief driver.

Sometimes I found myself on a bus that ran out of Westerford past my old school, and then through to my first village. On this route I inevitably met people whom I had met before in quite different circumstances. Usually they were women, and sometimes they acknowledged that they knew me, and sometimes they didn't. Perhaps sometimes they simply did not recognize me.

To set the scene, I should emphasise that when a bus leaves a depot, the driver and the conductor were a small team – for however short a time.

The unheralded appearance of an Inspector, who might join the bus suddenly and usually at a request stop, was one reminder of the main responsibility of the conductor, then, which was to collect fares. That was the reason for their existence. If the Inspector found a passemger without a ticket, he would immediately collect the fare himself and issue one. Then the consequences for the conductor could be an official warning, or even dismissal.

Another less obvious responsibility of the conductor, was the good time-keeping of the bus. If it arrived back at the depot late, the station manager would want to know why. But for it to run early was an even greater crime, because that would lead to loss of revenue, passengers being left at bus stops, and a rash of complaints to the company. In either case, the efficiency of the conductor would be addressed by the station manager, for whether a she or a he, it was the conductor who had control of the starting and the stopping of the bus. Simply because it was they who used the bell.

One afternoon as I left the locker room to join the service bus to my first village, I discovered that the driver who was on the log had not appeared. And so a relief driver took his place. The number 12 was the bus of my schooldays, and would take thirty five minutes on the outward trip of nine miles or so. There would then be a ten minute wait outside Hubbles store, before we began the return journey back to the depot.

The driver was new, and when he arrived I saw that the lens of his spectacles were particularly thick. He was a Yorkshireman, and I learned later that he was still serving his probationary period with the company.

The route had many stops along the way, request stops and compulsory stops. But whatever their nature, it made no difference that afternoon. The bus seldom stopped at either kind, unless I rang the bell for someone to get off. When it did come to a halt outside the Chequers pub in my second village, I had a chance to knock on the back window of the cab from the inside of the bus, to warn the driver that I was coming round to the front.

I had to let him know that we had arrived at this stop very early. Already the bus had driven straight past queues of patiently-waiting would be passengers, who could only look on in disbelief as it sped away from where they waited. Quickly disappearing from their view.

Of course it was possible for me to stop the bus by using the bell, so that passengers could get off at request stops. Stopping it to let passengers on however, was not something that I could do; that was up to the driver.

We waited at the top of the hill outside the Chequers to use up six or seven minutes, and left only at the appointed time. The remaining three and a half miles of the outward trip ran through open countryside to my first village. Though there were fewer of them, nearly all of the stops were request stops. Hopefully and diligently, single passengers and passengers in pairs or in small groups, held out their arms, but for the most part to no effect. The bus simply continued straight past them all. And so again, we arrived very early at my first village.

I should say next, that apart from the collection of fares and the good time-keeping of the bus, the conductor had another important responsibility. This was to assist the driver when the large double-deckers had to reverse. Obviously, the conductor or conductress, was best placed to see what was behind the bus as it reversed, and to participate in this operation by standing on the open platform at the back, and signalling from there to the driver.

This reversing was a simple procedure usually. That afternoon, as always, the bus had to stop in the High Street, just alongside Forge Lane by the Pinker brothers' butcher's shop, reverse and turn back to draw up outside Hubbles store. Bus drivers had been completing this manoeuvre in their sleep for many years, certainly throughout the years of my childhood. And to my knowledge, the side of the butcher's shop was never thought to be at risk; chiefly because the bus would naturally reverse on the opposite side of the road – where there was a draper's shop. The butcher's shop was definitely not in the way.

On this particular afternoon I took up my position on the platform in the hot sunshine, to start to signal, when with no warning the bus shot backwards on the wrong side of the road and into the side of the Pinker brothers' shop.

That afternoon I was not sure whether I felt lucky or not to have known these gentlemen since being a very small child. I had often seen them delivering meat on their bicycle. For some years I had lived next door to them.

There was a lot of damage to the bus, and to the side of the building, and when one of the Mr Pinkers came out of his shop, I had to ask him if I could use his telephone to phone the depot for advice. I did this between apologies and extended silences. The voice from the depot explained that we would have to complete an accident form when we returned, that someone would come out immediately to view the scene, and that we should return as usual to complete the service.

I had to explain to one Mr Pinker what would happen next, and then I had to leave him, looking very hot and worried; and looking as one would if someone had driven a double-decker bus into the side of their house and shop.

Even though we left late for the return journey back to the depot, we still arrived back early. It was as if we were beginning the afternoon all over again.

On arriving again at the depot, we were met by the station manager. We were given accident report forms, and told to fill them in immediately – in our respective rest rooms. When I got to the conductors' room, I heard that there had been many complaints; telephoned in from the irate passengers left stranded on the outward journey.

I expected a summons to the station manager's office, to justify what had happened, but it didn't come. Later I heard that the probationary driver had left the company, almost as swiftly as he had completed the two journeys we had shared. My time at the company was near its end also, and I left a little while afterwards. With the money for my trip to Rome.

Now that her house was not on my way home, I was able to visit Mrs Aster less often. Although I thought that I really should visit her more, I also didn't want to be a nuisance, or for her to think that I always wanted something from her. Also I no longer had a season ticket, and it was not easy to find the extra money for the bus fare. And so I hoped she would understand. Hoped that this was what she expected.

I missed her advice and practical concern, and I also missed filling in the gaps at the weekend with the village cricket teams. Now that I no longer lived in the village, I was no longer able to receive those personal invitations from Mr Freeman.

It is worth saying something more perhaps about those Saturday and Sunday visits to villages all around, and sometimes to the foreign land up on the North Downs. Worth saying more about the home matches also.

As I have mentioned, a few of the village pitches at which we arrived in the various cars belonging to team members, were just ordinary fields. How sometimes the ducks or sheep had to be driven off before play could begin. These however were the exception, for most of the grounds were carefully and lovingly cared for.

And as I have also said, our own cricket field was immaculately kept, and was used for no other purpose. Although the pitch, a little outside the village as it was, had itself an outfield that was smoother and more carefully cut than were the actual wicket of a few of the pitches in some of the villages we visited, its condition was not so unusual then.

The table from which one of the three or four wickets would eventually be prepared, was always fenced off. The new wicket would be made and tended with a care that was almost impossible to describe, or imagine now. The grass was cut to an incredible shortness, and the pitch marked out with the greatest precision and accuracy.

Out in the middle, in the sun after rain, after the walk out, padded up and determined at the lower end of the batting order, the overwhelming and absorbing impression was of light sparkling all around the results of the recent shower. The shower that everyone had willed would quickly pass over.

The sharp immediacy of the short grass of the wicket, the surface with the earth showing through from beneath, breathing out warmth and new moisture, has stayed with me until now.

Around the ground, the elms still stood then, distributing their shadows anew as the afternoon wore on and was translated into early evening. George Meadow's hops glistened on their bines, fattening after the rain, to one side of the ground. And the old men sat on their benches in front of the hop garden, an attentive if often silent chorus.

If the runs I scored were few, depending upon the quality of the bowling, so too were the wickets I took; there were some but not so many. Yet, it was my fielding that by chance had quite accidentally become a source of quiet, unspoken, pride to me. And as so often, such reputations can be made quite fortuitously – and undeservedly.

Particularly, I had increasingly found myself fielding close to the wicket, usually on the leg side, sometimes almost within touching distance of the batsman. On a few occasions in that position I had been able, on a few good days, to pick up an unexpected, and necessarily lucky, catch.

At that time, spin bowling was still something of an obsession in Test Matches, and in the county game. It was natural therefore that some senior members of our various sides wanted to walk in the footsteps of these national and county heroes. With just a hint that something extraordinary was about to happen, they trundled in off a short run with the ball carefully hidden at the end of their bowling arm. Hidden behind their shirt cuff, in the manner of Tony Locke the Surrey and England leg-spinner. Locke was a hero of mine also, and especially for the quality of his fielding – close in on the leg side.

Mostly my more senior team-mates bowled off breaks though, which sometimes turned and usually didn't; and if the ball did turn, it didn't turn much. Very few of them tried to imitate Locke in bowling leg breaks – these being rather too technical a proposition.

There was always the promise that the next ball would be quite deadly, presenting just too many problems for any batsman, however wary, skilled, and experienced. Usually the promise was not kept; the hope and the illusion quickly dispelled as the gleeful batsman despatched the ball, quite unaware of its quality, to the long grass. Or into the thicket at the back of the pavilion. Or into the pond, from which it always took a little time to retrieve. The clay of the Weald meant that there were many such ponds, and as I've said the cricket pitch had one of its own.

And so, because of the prevalence of senior members, because one of them was Mr Lineham the captain of the 2nd X1, and just because of the law of probability over a longish period, I acquired a small and undeserved reputation for snapping up unlikely catches close to the the wicket. When this happened it was to the delight of Mr Lineham, the bowler, who obviously had been planning, striving, and scheming for just that result.

Mostly, this small success of mine was just a matter of good luck; the pure chance which rules in cricket as in the rest of life. The language of cricket itself speaks of the batsman offering chances. That they are taken, is often frequently the result of chance in quite another sense of the word altogether.

One occasion will serve to illustrate the point. The 2nd X1, one afternoon, was playing a local village, away up near my school on the escarpment. Mr Lineham put himself on to bowl, and moved me in close on the leg side. It happened that the batsman was from my school, actually a member of my house. He was filling in that afternoon, just as I was. But there the resemblance ended, for he was a very good player; particularly he was a good batsman.

I should add that Mr Lineham apart from being the captain of the 2nd X1, was also the owner of the village fishmonger business. He was one of the best known members of our large village community, and was well respected, and for good reason. It was he who made the announcements every year at the August Bank Holiday fête. And it was from him, from our earliest times, that we had collected our small prizes after the short sprinting races held on the field next to the church.

He gave a great deal of his time to village affairs, and ran the November 'Crazy Night', which was a huge Guy Fawkes event, with spectacular firework displays and a large bonfire. On that late afternoon, and evening, each year, there would be a large influx of people into the village's broad High Street, from all around. It more than matched the flood of newcomers which descended upon the village earlier in the year for hop-picking. 'Crazy Night' raised a lot of money for village funds, and for various charities; and its success was far ahead of its time.

But on that Saturday afternoon, as he set his field, Mr Lineham, signalled me to move in a little closer still, and of course I felt honoured to answer the call. Finally, he held up his hand to signal that I was close enough.

Unlike Mr Lineham, I knew of Richard's abilities as a batsman, and I knew too that my position so close now to the bat, was not without an even greater risk to me than usual. As Richard took guard he gave me a long look, eight feet or so away from him.

In my optimism, and in the sun, I expected anything to happen; even that I might snap up something, as the grass exhaled its scent upon the escarpment high up over the Weald.

The first ball was an over-pitched off-break, which was begging to be hit through the off-side. And so it was by the delighted young batsman. The second ball was a better length, straight, and pitched on the middle stump. I realized immediately what was about to happen, and it did. As it pitched, the ball turned a little, spinning in my direction.

The batsman stepped down the wicket, and drove it straight through me. As he struck, I span away to take evasive action, in a reflexed attempt to avoid the ball, or rather to assist the ball in avoiding me. Partly as the result of the same reflex, but mostly by a complete fluke, the ball somehow stuck in my hand as I span round and fell.

As a result of this piece of pure luck I had contributed something. As he walked past me back to the little pavilion, Richard grinned broadly and muttered something about a good catch. And as he did so, the delighted bowler and captain ran up and slapped me on the back. All he said was:

"What a wonderful catch!"

When I looked up, everyone was smiling. I accepted the praise without a word, with no mention that I had not the faintest notion of how it had happened. With no mention that I really deserved no praise at all, just as the bowler didn't mention that there was nothing about the delivery that deserved a wicket. And so, I suppose, in that we shared a confederacy.

Another part of the truth was that I liked to field close in to the wicket because I was slightly short-sighted. I had therefore a better chance of success there than in the outfield, waiting underneath a skied shot hurtling down from the heavens.

Looking back upon all this, across more than fifty years, I think it is more than possible that those four or five catches, picked up close in on the leg side, over a few years, may have had a greater influence upon my fortunes in life than I could have possibly realized at the time. Transcending even the pleasure I felt on the field. With a greater effect even than the pleasure I felt when the captain bought a pint of shandy "for the lad" after the match – which incidentally we had won. And I have come to that conclusion for the following reason.

Later in the year, after I had left the village, and sometime since I had last turned out for any of the village's teams, and after my short time on the buses, I visited Mrs Aster one evening. And as we chatted, she mentioned that Mr Lineham, that very same captain of the 2nd X1, would like to see me if I could drop into his shop sometime.

When I went to see him the following Saturday morning, he greeted me immediately, obviously knowing that Mrs Aster had passed on his message.

"Ah William", he said smiling broadly. As he did so, he stopped what he was doing, and put his arm around my shoulder. And we walked together into an area at the back of the shop where boxes of fish were usually unpacked.

He confided, as he walked beside me,

"We thought you might like some news".

And he told me that the 'Crazy Night' Committee had decided to award me £40 to help me start my career, as he put it, at Goldsmiths'. He told me that £20 of it was a gift, and £20 was a loan that I could pay back as soon as I was able.

This money was a huge sum to me and, after thanking him undoubtedly inadequately, I walked away from his shop in a daze.

Here was another example of the kinds of things that could happen then, and which I hope still can. It was proof also now that the Summer was well advanced, and as I travelled back on the bus to Westerford, that my days in my grey room were coming to an end. As, more regretfully, were my days at the school.

Towards the end of the summer term, there was a staff party that was held in the evening at an old hotel, now long since demolished, in Westerford High Street. During the evening, Mr. Chambers took me to one side and handed me an envelope, saying as he did so,

"I thought you might find this useful one day!"

Inside was a generously written testimonial about the time I had spent at the school.

Mr Chambers, I had come to realize, was a remarkable man in a number of ways. For a start he was a devoted cricket fan, at a time when it was still possible for a Headmaster in a state school to announce that an afternoon would be a sudden half-holiday. Co-incidentally when the county team were half way through a match at their ground nearby; something that he also reminded the whole school of before we left for our afternoon off.

A scientist by education, he was held in quiet affection in the staffroom; though he did have a reputation for being excessively thrifty. Of not being too quick to buy a round. I don't know how justified that opinion was.

I have mentioned already his several pieces of generosity towards me, and there was yet another representative example of how unconventional he was.

He was a member of the Communist Party; something he never discussed, but which was apparent for a particular reason. And this was that from his own pocket, every day during term-time, he bought a copy of 'The Times' and a copy of 'The Daily Worker', which he placed side by side on the table in the centre of the staffroom.

From a lack of opportunity, I never was able to ask him how he felt later about the rule of Stalin in the Soviet Union; and about the havoc wreaked by the party in Central and Eastern Europe, something which was in full cry at the time. I am sure he didn't know about that; and perhaps his quiet, seldom announced, enthusiasm, eventually faded into a sense of betrayal. I would have felt sorry with him, and for him, when it did.

As I thanked him for the testimonial in the envelope, he remarked,

"And there's still Rome!"

Also, and after that, I was looking forward to a new life beyond the grey room, into which for eight months or so, the light of dawn had slid silently, through the grimy lace curtains at its single window. And I knew how glad I should be to leave it for ever, in spite of the shelter it had provided.

(iv)

Rome came and went, and with it many explosions of new discoveries, sensations, and light; and Switzerland, seen first from the train in the early morning after little sleep. When I returned, I first had to return to work in a local canning factory, a last temporary job in Westerford, which I had arranged before leaving. I still needed to pay for the digs that I was soon to leave, and to accumulate what further funds I could. In preparation.

The departure when it came was one for which I was now prepared, and this was entirely as a result of the various interventions of Mrs Aster, and the small constellation of people whom she had quietly organized and influenced, mostly without my knowledge. As a result I was better placed to leave successfully, than when I had left for Grimsby and Christfield. I had discovered that just deciding to leave was always unlikely to be enough.

In the interim I had accumulated debts that I could never repay. Acts of kindness, which I did not possess at the time the knowledge or reserves to acknowledge adequately; for which I was unable to express an adequate gratitude. In such situations it is always too late, and so it was, and has been, in my case.

The few weeks at the canning factory were unremarkable, though at the time they were in very sharp focus. The work was largely moving and stacking boxes, wooden and cardboard, and supporting the work of women working on a sorting-belt.

We worked in a small gang, and our foreman was very curious about what I was doing in the factory, though I don't know why; and was insistent in his questioning. I largely dodged this, and in answering him stuck to the essentials of what I had been doing for the past eight months, and where I would be off to in October. My five other workmates were middle-aged men, with whom I shared our breaks, and got along with well enough.

When at last my departure from Westerford came, I travelled on a one way ticket to Goldsmiths' on the London coach. The one to London run by the Westerford and District Bus Company, following the familiar route. On that afternoon, the driver did not have the radio on, although I could still hear Dvořák's **Prague Waltzes** with only a little effort. As the coach glided along, it was as if I was on that warm, clean, and swift journey to school all over again.

When I got out of the coach, it would not be to arrive late at chapel or, wondering on my way to a now almost defunct fishing port; but rather into a new world which I could scarcely have imagined. And moreover one to which I had been invited. Where my presence was legitimate.

What I had learned, since that introduction to Dvořák's music, and have come to recognize now that sixty or so years have passed away, is something about the burden of unpaid debts. Did I, at the time of trying to get some sort of foothold on the early foothills of life, ever really show to those that helped me, rescued me even, that I understood the generous treatment that I was receiving? I fear I did not, and truthfully, I don't know how I could have done. But I did recognize it, in my most private thoughts. And I remember it still, now that most of those to whom I had such cause to be grateful have long passed from this world.

The immediate effect of becoming "a relief teacher", was that I was offered a pathway out of isolation and loneliness. By itself this would have been quite the wrong reason for becoming a member of that profession. Rather, it was the example of those I met at that time which made it something that I chose, and not because there was no option. My time at the insurance company was that.

When I arrived at Goldsmiths', after successive pieces of good fortune, it was definitely not, largely because of the prompting of Mrs Aster, to go into digs again. I had at least learned from life, so far, that the matter of living accommodation was not something to be entered into lightly, in-advisedly. Nor carelessly.

In retrospect, I think I realized even at that early stage, that I was member of the confederacy of the blessed. Of those whom others had treated better than I could ever have expected. Better than usually happens. And better than I deserved. Perhaps, after all, that was not such a bad preparation for life, for it established the verities at least.

More important immediately, even than the matter of my new accommodation, was something that was yet intimately connected to where I would live for the next three years, and to how I should earn my living later. And it was that I recognized immediately a quality about life there, which would lead me to feel great affection for the place.

Its appeal was one that I could feel even in the air that I breathed there, then. And the form it took was within an understanding that what we were engaged in was the 'primacy of teaching' as an occupation. It had by definition almost a kind of quiet urgency, which was all about the discovery of important secrets that it was imperative to pass on. Teaching, then, was self-evidently about revealing important things to the young that could otherwise have remained hidden. It was about necessary interventions.

This primacy had its justifications not only in the social deprivation of the inner city area in which the college was situated. It lay in the opportunity to pass on what had been passed to us, because that was a good thing to do. Alongside the primacy of teaching lay, therefore, 'the sovereignty of good' – which is what Iris Murdoch was to address later – and at another time altogether.

This urgency pulsed in every aspect of the college's life, during the day and in the evening; in all its teaching departments, and constituent parts. It was in the life of the Art School, and in the dogged application of the very large Evening Department which welcomed everyone for many purposes and reasons as the light outside faded. It beat in its large music department, and in the Laban Institute of Dance. And it was continually and variously reflected in the life that was all around me in the company of other students.

Most of all, for me then, this energy and urgency pulsed in the Education Department. And this primacy of teaching was for me a reply to the hiss of the cold cosmos; to which I had been introduced, and had learned at least temporarily, to recognize and accept.

And of course it was this same urgency and goodness that had informed and motivated Mrs Aster.

Stanhope, Rosamund *No place for the Maudlin Heart*. Peterloo, 2001, pp. 53, £7.95. 1 871471 92 3

Good poets have a characteristic love of language, and Rosamund Stanhope's is especially notable. Reading her poetry is a peculiarly linguistic pleasure, such is the novelty of its lexis. Unmodish, literate, and sophisticated, it is at once gentle in tone and clear sighted.

A chess metaphor in the poem '*The Knight's Move*', well represents the novelty and the timbre of this collection: "*Approximating things by sudden obliquities / is more rewarding than the forthright advances / of bishops, the square honesties of castles*". How true this is, and how stunning is "*sudden obliquities*"; but please see the rest.

There is then the gift she has, of using almost lost words to present almost lost ways of understanding; in a way which conveys that they are only almost lost. For instance, of apples, "*that depend from sprays*"; of Spring, which "*puts live slips in the brakes*"; of Winter, when "*a blast curses the bent*"; but ... please see the rest.

Appropriately, there is a poem in praise of synonyms, by which "*we come close/ approximate, approach, set in to, gain on truth / (which has no synonym, I think) – it is the way / we ... lighten the black holes among the stars*".

Retaining wonder in both its subjects and its construction, this poetry is its own recommendation; to the young, mature, reader as to anyone.

William Holden

Chapter 14

Sudden Obliquities and No Synonyms

That Christmas Eve, when the ruthless chance of things again intervened in William's life, it was cold. Very cold. It snowed. The county newspaper mentioned the extreme cold of that winter on its front page on December 29th, before the New Year began.

It spoke of it when reporting: **"Three Injured In Icy Rooftop Drama"**, over another sub-heading: **"Father and Daughters in Hospital with Burns".** And most of that front page expanded upon a headline announcing: **"Christmas Blaze Leaves Family Homeless".** In black type above pictures of the snow.

Remarkably, William only read this newspaper account many years later; learning of details which he had no knowledge of at the time.

He had known nothing for instance of the scale of the wider impact of the fire around and about the town. The newspaper reported how "eight fire appliances attended the savage fire". And how "the raging inferno caused the diversion of bus services, as they fought the blaze".

He hadn't realized how severely the two houses on either side of the family's narrow and tall, terraced, house were damaged that Christmas Eve. How their occupants also had to move out.

He had not known that Evelyn, and little Owen, had stayed during the rest of Christmas in the home of the local

Congregational church minister. Nor how the congregations of two other local churches had "started a fund to provide for the needs of the family". The front page of the newspaper would inform him of all of this twenty years later; when he read a facsimile in Westerford's library.

Under a sub-heading: **"Burnt Out But Friends Were There",** the newspaper printed an open letter from William's foster mother, set at the very centre of its front page, surrounded by bleak photographs of the effects of the fire.

In the letter she "wanted to thank all the wonderful friends who came to our aid on Christmas Eve". It said that "we will never forget how everyone vied with each other to help".

This letter spoke of how "the police and firemen were outstanding in their efforts". And of how the Reverend Spaul (the Congregational minister), "had proved the most wonderful of friends". It mentioned, and thanked, many neighbours by name. Neighbours who "made great efforts to bring the spirit of Christmas back to us in our adversity". The letter did not refer to those neighbours whose houses had been so badly damaged by the fire.

And so the front page of the newspaper described the public details of a private tragedy.

William's mother had provided the reporter with all the details that he needed to construct his report. Telling of how her adopted son "had rushed upstairs to save his young daughters aged fourteen and eight". Of how when he came to return, "the stairs were in flames". Of how once they were all on the roof, the younger child had slipped from his grasp; and how in his attempt to hold on to her he had to release his hold on Christine – in spite of her being quite slight.

The reporter was therefore able to describe how Christine had lay on the scorching tiles of the roof, and so had received severe burns.

His foster mother told the reporter how "the smoke was so dense". And how the fire was started by an oil heater which she had lit to warm a bedroom for her unmarried sister who was staying with the family for Christmas. She mentioned to him how five dogs and four birds, had perished in the fire. But she didn't mention that two of the aged and quarrelsome pekinese, together in the room, had most probably knocked over the oil heater.

She told him how Eunice, "an adopted daughter", had returned home on Boxing Day to find the house in ruins.

The reporter did not speak apparently to William's foster father, nor to Evelyn whom he described as "Mrs -- junior".

In the unreality which always results when private disasters become public events, the main piece ended with his mother saying:

"We've lost everything, but we were insured".

The reporter ended by telling his readers how "her parting words" to him "with their home completely destroyed", (and part of the family in hospital) were: "It could have been worse!"

The reporter left, he said, as his mother was awaiting a visit from the insurance company; before travelling to Downsgate on the coast to stay with her sister. And he commented upon how that final phrase seemed "to sum up the courage the family have found in their moment of adversity".

It was not necessary for him to mention that he visited Downsgate to speak to her there, so that he could collect all these background details in time for his piece.

When all this occurred, William had been at Goldsmiths' for just over a year. It was sometime shortly before, that his foster family had moved to this house in Westerford. He had not stayed with them since leaving for Stapleford; though he had visited from time to time to see his father, and Arthur's children.

When the administrator of his hall of residence asked everyone at the end of each term to take all their belongings with them for the vacation, so that the rooms could be cleaned, William was presented with the usual problem. The assumption behind this very reasonable request was that the vacation was most desirable, and that everyone would eagerly anticipate each holiday. But for William the old matter of having somewhere to live always returned. Always he was anxious that he would be forced to ask his mother for permission to stay again at home.

He suspected, looking back over all the years, that various members of the college may have been aware of this dilemma – perhaps informed by Mrs Aster. And he thought this because of the various and repeated accommodations they made for him. And because physical accommodation also was made available.

On one occasion he was offered a labouring job for the vacation on the building site which was the emerging hall of residence next door. Of course he had to stay up to do this. On another he was asked by one of the tutors to cut a path across the back field after everyone else had gone down. The path was scarcely necessary, and he was definitely not the best person to construct it. However, it was a task for which he was paid, and for which he was provided with a college room to complete. And for which no charge was made.

The summer breaks were his biggest problem. During the previous long summer vacation, he had joined an NUS work camp in Northern Spain, across the bay from Santander; and that used up six weeks. Organized by the Spanish Student Union, the task was to work with a group of other students mostly from the rest of Europe, upon renovating a large, old, manor house. This was in Laredo – then not even a tiny village. When the renovations were finished, it was intended that the house would serve as a student hostel.

He washed with the others out of a bucket from the well, and they slept in dormitories; the men in one and the women in another. The progress of the work was fitful, and there was no pay. But bed and board were provided, as was the company. If he wanted to, he could visit the small cantina, where a glass of Spanish brandy or a bottle of beer, a plate of fresh sardines and a chunk of bread, cost the equivalent of a few pence. And nearby there were empty sandy beaches, where it was not wise to stay too long in the sun, nor to walk upon with bare feet because of the hook worms.

At the weekends they visited Santander on the little ferry, in varying-sized groups, where he could observe Franco's Civil Guard – swarthy and with pistols on their belts. With one hand on those pistols one afternoon especially, when they saw one of his companions, from the United States, walk across the grass of a Santander park. Although this visitor's Spanish was excellent, he had not seen the notices forbidding encroachment on to the grass. And William was able also to visit nearby San Sebastian; and see real, abject, poverty in hovels on the hills above Bilbao.

During the same summer, he was invited to stay in the Westerford home of Frank, one of the masters with whom he had gone to Rome. When he and his wife heard of William needing to write a child-study for his course, they offered their own and only son as a subject – and accommodation for two weeks also. This generosity seemed only to become the greater the more William recalled it over the years. He wasn't even in a position to find a child to study. Just another consequence of his unusual circumstances.

Nor was his unwillingness to make another request of his foster mother for somewhere to stay, the only guide to his decisions at the end of each term. For the absence of home is after all an un-fillable void, and he missed his father, and Arthur's children. He missed Christine, and their long conversations when he had visited for a day, at a weekend.

Another reason that he didn't welcome the end of each term was that he simply enjoyed term-time so much. He was almost enthralled by life in his hall, and in college, for it had everything that his former life in his previous digs in Westerford had lacked. The company of many friends of both sexes, the concert halls, the theatres, and the chance to attend any cinema; all were the antithesis of his earlier isolation. And a clean bed. William throughout his life, never took a clean bed for granted.

He had discovered in this new life, a peculiar domesticity, which was communal. When the vacations came and everyone left, his old isolation came back.

And yet … , after all, ahead of that cold Christmas, he had written to ask his mother if he could stay for the holiday – and she had agreed. And so it was that he would visit and stay in the family's Westerford house for the first time.

At first he spent nearly a fortnight working in the main sorting office of the Royal Mail in Westerford. Working on the Christmas Post was then a common student vacation job, and he knew that some of his friends would be doing the same kind of thing all around the country. And he was relieved that he could earn money in this way.

Perhaps he would have preferred to have been outside delivering letters and parcels, as he had done a couple of times in his first village; rather than sorting them inside. He remembered that then he had even delivered post on Christmas morning in his first village.

But the pay in the sorting office was good, and now it was Christmas Eve, and the ten days of working were behind him. He was grateful that he hadn't been put on night work, and today he would finish for good at 4.30 in the afternoon.

William described to me how the room in which he was sleeping that Christmas was in the attic, at the very top of the house. First, after getting back from work, he went to wash, and change his clothes, which he did as he looked forward to the family festivities of that time. He had presents that he needed to finish wrapping, and cards to fill in; apparently the family always opened their Christmas cards on Christmas morning. That was their custom.

Just as he left the bathroom, one floor down, and just as he was climbing the stairs again towards his room, the lights suddenly went out. All of them. It became completely dark. And at the same time he heard cries and shouting in the blackness from below him in the house. He told me about a loud rushing noise, and that he suddenly couldn't breathe. And that as he struggled to climb the narrow stairs at the very top of the house somebody rushed by him in the dark.

By the time that he got back to his room, he was breathing in liquid smoke from the burning rubber based composition which covered the stairs. Once there, he smashed the single window, and as the ice-cold air of the night rushed in, almost threw himself on to the window sill; from where he could hoist himself up above and on to the pitched roof of the attic room.

And there he sat, with legs astride the ridge tiles, coughing and trying to breathe in the suddenly chill night. Down below in the street he saw lights and vehicles, and then he made out what he only slowly recognized as an extended fireman's ladder inching up towards him.

Moments later he was being carried across a fireman's shoulder, slowly step by step towards the ground.

"Whatever you do, just keep perfectly still", was all the fireman said. William was silent. And still.

When they reached the ground, the fireman put a blanket over him, and told him not to move. He felt suddenly very cold, out now in the night, dressed as he was only in his work trousers and shirt after his visit to the bathroom; and as he tried to make sense of what was happening.

He stayed where he had been put down, rigid, and perfectly still. He couldn't stop coughing for a long time, from the effects of breathing in the molten fumes of the stair covering, and smoke. He could still hear the noise rushing up the stairs.

Now, his hair was hard and stiff with smoke. Singed and black. In fact he was, he gradually realized, completely covered in the residues of smoke, from head to toe. Inside, he felt as if he was still choking.

He wondered who it was that had rushed passed him, and understood that it could only have been Arthur. And he wondered where he was now. Where could the children have been? He hadn't seen anyone else around him at the top of the house as he had been preparing for Christmas Eve.

Then, as he sat there on the ground with a blanket around him, he heard a voice nearby, and understood that someone was speaking to him. He heard,

"Are you alright sir?"

And when he looked up into the face bent over him in the half light of the street lamps, and amongst the activity all around, he recognized that the voice belonged to the young girl who had once wished him "Good Morning". The girl who had thought Arnold's poem really sad, in that first school he had ever entered as a relief teacher nearly two years before. It had just not occurred to him that the school was only just around the corner from where he now sat on the pavement. Obviously, she and her family lived nearby.

William just nodded. And they were both silent. The silence of the rapt. He didn't see her again, because an ambulance man came up and started asking him questions.

The newspaper's front page would describe him as "a nephew in the family".

William's recollection of what happened during the rest of that evening was only partial, perhaps as the result of shock. Important detail, along with much else, had disappeared. For instance he had no memory of where he spent that night, or even of Christmas Day.

He remembered being in a dormobile on Boxing Day, driven by Victor to Downsgate. And he remembered Auntie Elsie's house, cold and small and smelling of the gas mantle. Surprisingly, he recalled again how she hated Americans, all Americans, and even at that moment found himself again wondering why.

He was with his father, mother, Victor and his mother's sister, – just those; and he remembered sleeping on the floor in his now filthy clothes.

When he asked his foster mother what she thought had caused the fire, she replied with no hesitation that it was an electrical fault.

He asked her about Arthur and the children, and she replied simply that they were "Quite alright!"

He knew there was no point in asking further, and so they fell into their familiar silence. Instead he turned to talk to his father, and tried to comfort him as best he could. Apparently, he had been in the basement when the fire broke out, in the kitchen, and was not physically hurt. As always he was quiet and calm, and said little.

With no clothes, and encrusted with smoke and soot, and knowing nothing about the fate of Arthur's family, it was impossible for William to know what lay ahead. The moment was just too solid.

How he later returned to Westerford, he could not remember. But he did, to collect his money for his Post Office work. It was strange, he thought later, that he just could not recall any of the details of just how that journey came about either. He returned also, that day, to look at the wreckage of the house, half expecting to find some of his own or his family's belongings.

But the fire, and the act of extinguishing it, had turned the whole site into a tangled, fractured, and black and grey, mush. Over it all, the skeletal charred joists of the roof of the house stood high up against the late December sky. Everything, from and in the house had been processed into a pile of detritus and rubbish, which was now piled up in the front garden of the building. Nothing was recognizable as anything in particular. Where his bedroom had been there was only sky.

As he stood gazing bemused at the scene, he could not understand how so much had just disappeared.

Though again he could not recall how it came about, William was given an emergency hardship grant from the Council, which enabled him to buy clothes. He had no recollection, in later years or indeed ever, of how that could have happened so quickly. Immediately. Nor could he recall how he actually returned to Goldsmiths' early, after that Christmas. He knew only that it had nothing to do with his foster mother, for he was not at all her responsibility. The family had pressing and immediate pre-occupations of its own.

He knew only that he did return to college early that New Year. When he explained as best he could what had happened, the administrator of his hall agreed immediately that he could return early. It was fortunate for William that she and her husband were not away for the holiday over the New Year.

And so for the next few days before the new term began, he joined them for his meals; though again in truth, as with much during that period immediately following the fire, he could not recall well the details and sequences of events. It was as if these days at the end of the old year and at the beginning of the new, could not be easily ordered nor arranged in the memory. Eventually, gradually, the days that followed would be; but never those immediately following the fire. Memory became established again, around the requirements of the second teaching practice for which he was expected to prepare. He had clothes again, and somewhere to live.

In the shelter and order of his room in hall, he wrote several times to his mother to ask about news of Arthur and the children, but at that time he did not receive a reply. He was to learn a little later how the shock of the burns she received resulted in Christine developing diabetes.

The fire had ruined her health just as she was about to begin her approach to adult life. He thought, and with such sadness, how her gentle and alert nature must have been so overwhelmed.

A consequence of the fire was that a number of books which he had borrowed from Mrs Aster, and which he had taken to Westerford to use in the holiday, were lost. They disappeared along with everything else. He was not able to visit her to tell her of this for quite a long time. Her response, when he did, was that she had no need of them anyway; though their loss was felt by William as another failure.

A month or so later, when he returned quietly to Westerford again, to look at the shell of the burnt-out house, the scene was much what he was to see years later in the photographs which appeared in the newspaper's report. There was the hole still in the roof where his bedroom had been, and the pile of rubbish in the front garden. Except of course it wasn't really his bedroom. How, he wondered again, could the destruction have been so complete? So total.

As he stood there, he thought of the fragility of treasure. His copy of Sir Philip Magnus's *Life of Gladstone*, and Von Manstein's *Lost Victories*, were now somewhere just part of the detritus, the mush, piled up still in front of the wrecked house. Or not even there. And in the cold he thought of Arthur and the children – and his father.

And all of this as his attention had to turn again to the final week of the second teaching practice. He had been fortunate in his school, where although the small staff knew nothing of his circumstances, he was able to become lost in the work with the children. Because of their support and assistance.

As a result, and by good fortune, the practice was going well, as he travelled each morning to this Charlton school with one other member of his tutor-group who was doing her practice there also. She was from Devon, was soon to be married to a farmer, and her quiet explanation of her life in the West Country, to which he had never been, somehow cheered him. Made him realize that life could be ordered and hopeful, because it was for others.

William's blackened, stiffened, and charred hair, had become clean again. But although previously thick, it had now imperceptibly begun to thin. Naturally.

PART 4

Terror

TRANSTRÖMER, TOMAS ***New collected poems***: translated by Robin Fulton. Bloodaxe, 1997. Pp219, £9.95. 1 85224 413 5

There are many good reasons to read fine poetry from another language. Tomas Tranströmer's poems are so well translated from the Swedish by Robin Fulton, that the English reader may recognize immediately how this poet *"look(s) upon existence as a great mystery"*.

The book includes poems from up to 1996, an 'Introduction', and some autobiographical prose by Tranströmer about his childhood and schooldays. This last section is illuminating. The 'Introduction' is disappointing, because it belongs to quite another book altogether, viz. the poet's 1987 Bloodaxe *Collected Poems*.

In the words of one of the poems, the poetry is concerned with much *"... that can neither be written nor kept silent"*. Yet it is written ; and thereby existence *"through form can be raised to another level"*.

Visually bright, and musical in its forms and colours, it is of forests and rivers, mountains and islands, snow, winds, the sea and woods. It is of isolated houses, and the city. Of human souls: from a great distance, and inside moments of awareness within existence.

Between ecstasy and oblivion. Remembering *"the sun-heated doorstep"* or pondering *"the secret in the migrating flock"*, its paradox is that it exists because of the poet's understanding that *"The only thing I want to say / glitters out reach / like the silver / in the pawnbrokers"*. That's not so surprising, rather just a feature of the mystery!

In art, as hopefully in life, we are left with a sense *" that a strangeness has crossed our path"*. It can be so for mature readers in the secondary school also.

William Holden

A Case Note

In the hospital
You frown, as I try to explain,
Doctor.
You ask about what
I cannot understand
Myself.
They do it differently
On the
Television.
At home again, I see the photograph:
A pretty girl, a child, with pigtails still.
Nine, blond, fine hair drawn back,
Polished clean with shampoo.
Light in straight lines, and
Innocence.
Seventeen,
She crashed into her mother
With fists flashing.
Into her mother's head.
Swore, screamed,
Ran
Down down our road, with following
Ambulance quietly cruising;
Knocking on neighbours' doors,
Complaining.
"He's molesting me.
Help!"
"Please … sorry, it's okay,
Don't worry, I'm her
Father!".

Chapter 15

> To know and not to speak
> In that way one forgets
> What is pronounced strengthens itself
> What is not pronounced tends to non existence.
> Our human kind persists by warmth and kindness.
>
> Milosz

When William was nearly fifty, he came face to face with an entirely new possibility, which was that some storms cannot be ridden. As storms sometimes do, the one that engulfed the little family and which he described to me over a couple of weekends, came out of a clear blue sky. Or almost. If not suddenly, then unexpectedly.

If one day the sky belonged to a hot Summer day, the next it belonged to a warm Autumn one. That time of year again! Yet still the Winter seemed far away.

I should remind you how our two girls are separated in age by almost three years.

Claire, as a child of up to twelve years old was, as one of our friends remarked much later, "so very engaging". And now as an adult many people would acknowledge that she plays the oboe very beautifully. We are very pleased about that. Very. For one of my regrets is that I never learned to play a musical instrument. I can't even read music, though Carol can.

Many years ago Carol had overheard the children talking to each other. I think Anna was almost nine, and her sister was just starting at secondary school.

As they chatted, the younger one asked,

"Now that you're a lady,
Will you still play?"

So you see, in that childlike way, Anna was also engaging. But not socially; not conventionally.

On another occasion, years before, Claire had asked her,

"Why do you have to tell mummy everything?" To which her sister replied,

"Oh, I have to.
Because if I don't, I get
A pain in my head".

One day, as we all sat having breakfast, Anna had suddenly said,

"I had a dream last night". "Yes?", I answered. And she continued,

"About God.
He was a freckled-faced boy".
Who knocked on our door.
He said,
'Has anyone died?'
'No they haven't', I said.
'Go away!'"

Carol and I looked at each other, and laughed. Claire sniffed.

At around the time that the sky darkened over our house, that late summer, Carol's mother became ill; her father had died some years before. We therefore drove up to Yorkshire at weekends, sometimes with the children, and sometimes without them. Then they spent their day with friends and neighbours. Because there was no-where for us to stay, we always returned the same day. The children tended not to be with us when we visited Dorothy in hospital, after the first few occasions. It really wasn't that kind of hospital. That Christmas, I remember, Dorothy came to us.

When Anna changed school at eleven, and we began to attend parents' evenings, we would leave in wonder and surprise. The many difficulties that there had been at her primary school seemed now very distant. And this was simply because of the optimism we heard from her teachers, and their positive opinions about Anna.

We were so relieved, then, that Anna was happy at school; and we silently and separately wished that her sister would apply herself with something of the same diligence. For Claire, things seemed to come so much more easily.

In the immediate years that followed, Anna seemed untroubled by the usual turmoil of adolescence; when there were flashes of aggressive behaviour, they were very mild. But it was in the May of the year that she was sixteen, that a storm broke. At the time that Claire was in her second term at the Academy, and therefore living away from home in term-time.

There was to be a party at Anna's school one evening, to celebrate the beginning of a revision week for the class's GCSE examinations.

I arrived at about ten o'clock to collect Anna. As usual I parked a little away from the school to wait for her. This was to make our old Lada less conspicuous among the many expensive cars of other parents' in the school's car park. The car always embarrassed Claire, and we assumed it might be the same for Anna. Especially at her school.

As that evening turned out, such a concern was a small one; for the daughter that I picked up that May evening seemed a different one entirely to the one had left the house in the morning. And I cannot over-emphasise the difference.

There was no usual greeting when she got into the car. Instead she slammed the door once inside, cursing and swearing; ranting furiously – about a shoe. Eventually I worked out that she had lost one of her shoes. Apparently it had been thrown into a pond.

I learned gradually that a number of boys, from a similar school nearby, had been invited to the party, though this was by no means immediately clear, so incoherent and rambling was Anna's speech.

She repeated several times,

"What he doesn't realize, is that she's no good for him. You know, she's no good!"

She seemed so distracted that I was simply astonished.

"Okay", I thought, *"so there's been conflict over a boy, and somehow her shoe ended up in the pond"*.

So I just tried to reassure her,

"I shouldn't worry about it, you can get it back on Monday". Before joking, "though it might be a bit wet!"

If that was all there was to it, I would have expected her to see the funny side of the shoe in the pond. For her to laugh, and return to her usual self.

But she didn't. Rather she continued to swear and curse. Rambling, and still incoherent. Really making little sense. And I began to feel uneasy.

As I listened, it occurred to me that there may have been alcohol at the party. And so as we drove home, I tried to steer the conversation around to what had happened during the evening.

I asked her what the food and drink was like.

"Alright", was all she answered. It seemed that only lemonade and coke were available.

But, so aggressive did she seem, so disoriented, that I wondered if because of a disagreement, or prank, something had after all been put into her drink. She really seemed so greatly changed.

I tried again to get her to talk about the details of the evening, in the hope of learning something useful. Something to explain this behaviour.

"Who was there?" "What was the party like?" "What else happened?" "What did everybody do?" General questions. Anything that might offer an explanation for her manner. But I couldn't really find out anything more.

Now we were nearing home, and Carol came to the front door as we drove up. She must have seen Anna's face in the car, and probably concluded that we had had some disagreement.

Anna got out, and slammed the door hard in a rage, before brushing passed her mother without speaking.

Carol looked at me,

"Whatever is the matter?" she asked.

I tried to make light of things,

"Oh, there's been some disagreement at the party I think. She's lost a shoe. It'll turn up on Monday. She can collect it then".

Before we went to bed I told Carol about the strangeness of the conversation in the car.

"Trouble is", she said, "those shoes were new – and expensive!"

"I know", I replied, but we can't do anything until Monday anyway".

And so, … and so, after Carol had looked in on Anna, we went to bed.

Anna had stayed in her room, although we could hear her still moving about next door. And we heard her music playing as we went to sleep.

Chapter 16

Next morning Anna was up early, before us, which was very unusual, especially for a weekend. At breakfast she said she was meeting a school friend to discuss some school work. So she wouldn't be home until about six.

I offered to run her over to the friend's house in the car, but she said she preferred to go on the bus.

Perhaps, I thought, in spite of my misgivings last night, we could forget about it all. Perhaps it was just all about living with a teenager.

But when Anna returned in the evening she brought another surprise with her. As she came in, she announced immediately to us that she had a job in a shoe shop in the High Street of our small town.

"Oh, you mean a Saturday job", said Carol

"Well yes, I've been working today, but I'll be working all next week too", came the reply.

Carol looked hard at her. Enquiringly.

"Now Anna, if you want a Saturday job, that's fine. But in the week you would normally be at school. It's school time. You have study leave for revision. They expect you to be revising!"

"But they want me next week, not just on Saturdays".

I came in during this conversation, just as Carol was saying,

"You cannot work in a shoe shop when you should be preparing for examinations at school. And that's all there is to it".

Anna was furious, and she rushed off upstairs to her room where she locked herself in with the telephone. Mobile phones were not a part of life then.

On the following day, Anna had a visitor. Mr Needham was a mathematics graduate who was the Deputy Head of a primary school in the borough. Claire had not been confident when she was preparing for her GCE Mathematics examinations, and he had helped her successfully with extra tuition.

He was a married man with teenage daughters of his own, interested in his subject, well organized, able to provide genuine and very practical help. Fortunately his charges were modest, and we knew that we were very lucky to have found him. So when Anna had shown the same lack of confidence in Mathematics as her sister, we had arranged the same extra support for her GCSE papers.

Mr Needham had called around that Sunday afternoon to drop off some questions for Anna to run through, and to give her some written pieces of advice at this late stage.

Anna seemed to be talking to him quite calmly in the dining room, where Carol had shown the visitor. They could work on the table there if necessary.

On Monday, Anna went to school to enquire about her lost shoe. And I rang the shoe shop, in a spare minute at work, to explain that there had been a misunderstanding: that Saturdays for Anna were fine, but working in the week was not, because she was timetabled at school. This was not strictly true at the time, but it became so; in the following way.

As the week progressed, Anna seemed not able to sleep well. Her radio was playing until very late; until one of us had to insist, at two or three in the morning, that she turn it off and got some sleep. She seemed to be becoming increasingly distracted in everything she did.

She talked a lot about the boy she had mentioned previously in the car, though we never learned his name. She forgot what she was saying halfway through a sentence, and black rings began to appear around her eyes. The shoe was not recovered.

It quickly became clear that Anna's revision week would come to nothing at home. Carol could only be around during the first part of the week; and I usually not at all during the day – nor until late on Mondays and Thursdays.

Carol therefore telephoned Mrs Evans at the school. She was responsible for the revision arrangements, and we knew her quite well from our visits to the school. Her suggestion that Anna should spend the rest of the revision week at school in the library seemed a reasonable one. There Anna could perhaps arrange her day better, and even see some of her friends who were doing the same thing. The quiet time in the library would perhaps help her to concentrate; and justify her being at school when most of her year weren't.

However, this arrangement quickly fell apart. Anna went, but we later learned of some violent disagreement with another girl; and that she had walked out of the library – and the school.

Our first knowledge of this was when Carol had a telephone call at work from Anna, at around 12.30 one afternoon. She was in the office by herself, her boss being away for the day at the Hertfordshire branch of his accountancy business.

"Oh mum, I'm at school. I can't get home. I've got no money. Come and fetch me now, would you?"

Carol was puzzled at the call,

"Anna you have got money, because I checked with you this morning. I'm at work. I can't come now".

The school was about twenty minutes drive away at that time of the day.

"If you carry on working at school, I'll be there at around 4.30".

At this the phone went dead.

Two or three minutes later, Anna walked into the office. She had been telephoning from a box just across the street.

It was in this way that the fresh revision arrangements collapsed. But that night when we thought she had settled for the night, late again, Anna burst into our room in the small hours.

As we staggered awake, we saw her in the light of the street light outside, standing at the foot of the bed.

"Mum, mum, she announced, I've decided what I want to do as a career. I'm going to be a disc jockey!".

And … she began to dance in the half-light – but not gracefully. Rather, very jerkily.

I remember saying,

"It's 2.30 in the morning. Can we discuss it in the morning?" And she went back to her room.

On the train to work in the morning, as I thought over these events, it was becoming clear that something was surely wrong. I thought back to that Saturday evening when I had collected her from the party, and wondered again if something more might have happened. Something we knew nothing about.

When I got home that evening, we decided that I would ring our doctors' surgery. When I did so the next evening, I was put through to Dr P., a young male doctor whom I had never met. Perhaps he was new, I thought.

I tried to explain the reason for my call, and that I was ringing on behalf of Anna. I mentioned the party, and wondered whether a blood test might be wise, if she were to come to see a doctor.

He agreed to see Anna, and Carol went with her for the appointment the following morning. When two weeks later, there had been no change in our daughter's distracted, erratic, and sometimes quite bizarre behaviour, I rang the surgery again to enquire about the results of the blood test that had been conducted. I was put through to the same young doctor, Dr P., who in reply to my question simply replied,

"There's nothing to worry about!" But he said nothing more.

And so to some degree, we felt reassured.

Except that the next day a local florist rang us from the High Street. The caller said that they were ringing to let Miss Holden know that the garden ornaments and figures, which she had ordered, were ready for collection, and that the cost would be £72. 80. Not a small sum to us.

I took the call, and learned this news with yet more surprise; and had to go into the shop the next day to explain this further "misunderstanding". With some reluctance, they agreed to cancel the order.

The examinations came and went, though the very obvious disarray in which Anna had been since the night of the party had not disappeared. Sometimes she seemed elated and full of energy, and sometimes silent and cast down. Sometimes frenetically talkative, sometimes morose and withdrawn.

Her eyes were by now ringed by black circles through lack of sleep.

There had been no evidence that she had been able to prepare for the examinations, and we had to be reconciled to that. Carol had taken her to school in the car. Particularly, on the day of the Mathematics papers, Anna seemed overwrought, was constantly mislaying things, and was generally very forgetful. As previously, she seemed to lose track of what she was saying halfway through an utterance.

But with the examination period over, all that was left for her was to await the results. Everything that could have been done to support Anna at the time, had been done; though nothing augured well. What, we wondered, would be her response if she had done particularly badly?

With the results came a further surprise. Indeed surprises now seemed only to increase, in their number and intensity.

She had achieved good passes in both Mathematics and English, and three more good passes including in French and German.

And now Anna began to talk constantly about what 'A' Level subjects she would choose for the 6th Form. Delighted though we all were, I had become increasingly doubtful, though I only mentioned these misgivings to Carol.

My doubts centred upon Anna's announcement that she had chosen three subjects: English, French and German. When she mentioned this to me, I tried to put it to her that she didn't have to choose three; that perhaps French and German would be good subjects to do by themselves.

She was adamant though, chiefly it seemed because everyone else was choosing at least three! I tried to point out that the three she had chosen were a particularly demanding combination, but I couldn't get her to listen. She simply refused outright the possibility of only selecting two subjects.

At the end of the summer term we were to attend an evening meeting at the school, along with other parents of girls who were staying on into the 6th form, to discuss their choice of subjects. All we could do was to depend upon the opinion of the teachers she would have, if she stayed with her chosen combination.

I knew the French teacher very well, because she had been a student of mine on the postgraduate course. A native speaker from Boulogne, she was an extremely competent, sympathetic, and able young person. She was very well thought of in the French department at college, and was someone for whom I had the greatest respect. I knew we could trust her judgement completely.

The German teacher was much older, and not apparently a native speaker. From all accounts she was somewhat eccentric, but Anna spoke of her with affection.

I knew least about the English teacher, but because of my own background I tended just to listen to what Anna said about her. I had no doubt that she was more than competent.

I also knew the Head of the school slightly since meeting her quite by chance at a conference on educational innovation, in Strasbourg, organized by the Council of Europe. This had been just before Anna started at the school.

We needed to speak to them all, and then perhaps we would be more clear about what Anna should do.

Carol and I had decided that we must be absolutely precise in the advice we sought during the evening of this set of meetings. All three teachers referred to our previous visits, to Anna's difficulties during the revision period, and to her GCSE results. These results, although enabling her to choose to continue to the 6th form, to do the subjects she liked best, had not been as good as they had all forecast. It was encouraging, we thought, that these discussions seemed realistic at least.

The French teacher thought Anna would cope well enough in the 6th form, though she drew our attention to reasons for a greater caution than she had previously thought necessary to speak of. Our own memories of the summer were still all too clear, and we understood completely what she was saying.

The German teacher was very optimistic, and was in no doubt that Anna would do well in what would be a small 6th form group. But she didn't seem fully aware of the difficulties that Anna had recently experienced.

The English teacher, who would be responsible for a much larger group, expressed no serious doubts about the wisdom of Anna choosing her subject.

With all of them we mentioned our doubts about the combined demands of these particular subjects, but heard nothing that supported my misgivings. And so, not for the first time, we came away from the evening feeling reassured; and against all the evidence. The following evening, I again raised with Anna the advantages of choosing just the two subjects, but she was determined upon her three.

And so the three subjects became her choice. Who else, after all, could choose but Anna? Any onlooker might wonder why I was so doubtful. Why, they might have thought, was I interfering? But then they could not have known the intensity of the sensations and surprises that we had experienced earlier – and recently.

Now the school summer holiday lay ahead. Anna found a holiday job for herself. This was in a picture-framing and art products shop in the High Street, but she was very soon asked to leave. We never discovered the full details of why.

Claire was home for the vacation, and the rest of the summer passed slowly – and warm. Eventually, they both worked, as Claire had done previously, on a large local 'pick-your-own' fruit farm nearby – on the tills. The two girls seemed to get on well enough, and the routine of the house returned to what it had been much earlier.

When school began again, Anna was calmer. Claire's term re-started soon afterwards. Everything seemed to have settled down. Anna caught the bus to school at the start of a warm autumn, as before. When we attended the first parents' evening at the end of Anna's first term in the 6th form, each of her teachers seemed encouraging and positive again in everything they said.

The school had a new Head but when we spoke to Mrs Evans, who now had overall responsibility for the 6th form courses, she seemed relaxed about Anna; as well organized and encouraging as ever.

As we left the school at the end of the evening, she came up to us, smiling.

"So", she said, "things have settled down!"

We smiled back in relief. It seemed my misgivings had been unnecessary. Could I really have been wrong after all? Had my doubts been unjustified? It certainly seemed so, as we walked out of the school on that fine crisp, clear, November night.

After that, other parents evenings followed throughout the year; all surprising to me.

But what had occurred had only been a small storm. Just a passing squall. A violent, sudden squall, but only a squall. It had battered us around a little, and often left us puzzled. But now a time of quiet and harmony returned to our little family. Claire was making her way, and Anna seemed happy enough in her subject choices. I had obviously been wrong to have been at all concerned.

Perhaps, after all, this was just adolescence? Perhaps we had just been too confident? Perhaps we had simply just forgotten what it was like to be sixteen?

Chapter 17

The summer of 1990 was a season of contrasts. Our small town on the edge of the countryside and the capital, basked in a seemingly endless succession of warm and sunny days. Our little house too. But inside our home, the summer became increasingly brutal. A succession of cataclysmic and brutal events. And astonishing beyond anything we had experienced, or could ever have imagined.

These events propelled us forward with great speed, and yet held us stuck in a limbo that was full of pain; and eventually they led me to having to write to Dr P. at 2.30 one morning at the beginning of autumn.

As I wrote, it was in desperation:

26th September 1990, *2.30am.*

Dear Dr. P.

It is not possible for me to describe to you, by these means, at this time, the misery that we are experiencing as a family.

As I write Anna is again being treated as a missing person, this time by the Claydon police. We are quite unable to determine where she is.

During your conversation with the educational psychologist who was working with Anna, on 1st August, you assumed professional responsibility for Anna. Yet I am bound to say that your particular interpretation of the importance of the confidentiality of your relationship with our daughter has had the effect of leaving her without the support she needs.

We are not now able to feel confident about her well-being, and ask you, again, to intervene and advise her to consult the borough's psychologist whom you recommended to her so many weeks ago. It is not adequate to ask Anna to 'choose' to see him, when it is her very confusion which makes his advice so necessary. Equally it is not helpful, when she is in this state of confusion, to represent parental advice to Anna to see you, as unjustified interference.

Yours sincerely,

William Holden

If this letter seems terse, that can only be explained by my recounting the events of the summer that led up to my writing it. During this time, a strangeness entered our lives. A mystery. One about which we could indeed not easily speak, and yet could not easily keep silent. And one which I cannot write about now except by addressing the particularities that the letter refers to, and which I shall now describe more fully.

We were nearing the end of Anna's first year in the 6th Form, and she had to take end-of-year examinations: mock 'A' level exams. Just as she was about to sit them in early June, she arranged another Saturday job for herself. A familiar pattern was re-establishing itself.

The job was as a waitress in a newly opened private hospital in our village; up just beyond the church on the horizon, over the field at the back of our house. The catering manager was a neatly dressed man of middle age; now very flushed as I sat in front of his desk. As we sat talking.

"I'm very sorry, Mr Holden, I really am", he began.

I had said nothing previously, except to introduce myself, and to say that I was answering his telephone request to come to see him. I didn't really know why I was there, unless it was to listen.

We hadn't met before, yet already I felt a touch of sympathy for this man as he struggled.

"She seemed such a nice young girl when I interviewed her. But I cannot allow it. I simply can't".

He continued,

"Mrs Rivers has been with me a very long time, long before this hospital opened, And I cannot have her being treated like that!".

I listened on. As he continued, it became clear that Mrs Rivers was the cook.

Mr Tribe spoke slowly, deliberately, and out of some distress. As if he was still trying to establish to himself the events he was now relaying to me; trying to confirm to himself what had happened.

"I've never heard such language from a young girl. Really, she can't stay". He seemed to be almost apologising.

"No, of course not", I agreed. And although I was only acknowledging what was clearly inevitable, I felt disloyal. Yet by now not so surprised, as I waited to hear the details of what actually had occurred, which had brought the two of us together that morning.

What I learned was that there had been a disagreement between the cook and Anna; on only her second day in the job. During it, Anna had thrown plates of food over the kitchen floor, and after them a torrent of abuse over the older woman.

In the chaos that followed, a small fire had broken out in the new kitchen, damaging expensive equipment. The good order of the kitchen being so rudely interrupted was something for which the catering manager was held responsible; not least by the more than startled Mrs Rivers.

As I walked home across the field in the sun, over the path across the chalk hill, all that had happened since I had collected Anna from the party last year came into my mind again. And all my misgivings about the 'A' level subjects she had chosen.

Only a short time afterwards, Carol and I were sitting in front of another desk, in the new Head's office at Anna's school. Mrs Vaughan was telling us how Anna had walked into her office, unannounced, a few days earlier, and declaring.

"I don't drink you know!"

She spoke to us of Anna's violent disagreements with other girls, and how her behaviour was making her unpopular. She said that she had a suggestion, which was that Anna should see an educational psychologist she knew of.

We asked for time to think over this suggestion, but in the days that followed, it became clear that we could not afford to reject the help that was being offered. And so I rang Mrs Vaughan, and she said that she would go ahead and arrange things.

Soon afterwards, we were in Mark Hill's office; and two days later Anna met him for the first time.

The summer holidays, after the mock examinations, promised to be very full for Anna. Arrangements had been made with the school in the previous year, for an exchange visit from a young French girl. Also we had arranged for an exchange with a German student.

Before Anna's difficulties, we had assumed that these visits would be times of relaxation and special interest for her. That they were to be looked forward too.

So, at the end of June, Lisl, a young girl from Cologne, was to stay with us and attend some classes at the school with Anna. The following month a young girl from Paris would come to us. In the middle of August, Anna was due to fly to Cologne to stay with Lisl's family.

Claire would be spending time at home after the end of her term, after a concert tour to Jersey. We thought that she and Anna would work together at the farm just as last year. And so they did.

But one Saturday evening at the end of July, Carol and I were at an evening performance at the Greenwich Theatre. I forget the play; we had a season ticket for the whole season. After the performance, we walked down the stairs to the theatre's foyer, and as we did so Carol drew my attention to a message written in chalk, in large letters, on a blackboard at the foot of the stairs. I would probably have walked straight passed it.

The message read:

> ***'Will Mr and Mrs Holden please ring home as soon as possible, as their daughter has an urgent message for them?***

Just that.

The evening had been enjoyable and relaxing. We had completely forgotten recent events, but now it was the play that was forgotten, and another drama was about to unfold. Of which we were to be a part, and not only as members of an audience.

Feeling just a little alarmed, we searched around for a public telephone. We knew there were some to one side of the foyer. When we found them we saw that several were free. Carol rang, as I watched her face.

What she heard when she got through to Claire was not something we could have anticipated. Nor could we have foreseen the events which that telephone call ushered into our lives.

Claire told her that Anna had not returned home that evening; and that the police had rung asking us to collect her from Fairfield Police Station. I tried to read Carol's expression as she was talking to Claire. And all I saw on her still young face was incomprehension.

"But don't worry mum", Claire was reassuring her, "she's alright. They just want you to collect her".

We set off immediately for the police station, though finding it took us a little time. Although we must have passed it many times, we were not actually sure where it was.

When we entered the red, sandstone, Victorian building, brightly lit in the night, we did so upon a wave of imminent crisis and anticipation.

There was a young policewoman at the front desk, and I immediately noticed how immaculately white the collar of her uniform was. Sitting a little back from her, sat Anna, in deep conversation with an equally young policeman. She looked flushed, and anxious.

As we went up to the desk to explain why we had come, we had no grasp of why our visit was necessary, nor why Anna was there. We learned from the policewoman, smiling, professional, and friendly, that there had been a disturbance at the house of a school friend; in fact right next door to the house of a colleague of mine. Anna, apparently, objected to the girl's mother, an Iranian lady, telling her to go away. When she refused, the woman called the police.

Anna's response to seeing us could not have come as more of a surprise. Immediately she shouted,

"You f--- off. I'm not coming with you!"

She turned to the policewoman,

"I'm not going with them. Please don't make me go!"

We looked at each other, and then at the two police officers, in astonishment.

But Anna steadfastly refused to come home with us. The shock of this only slightly modified that which we felt at needing to be in the police station at all, at 11.15 at night. After an evening at the theatre.

Anna stood by her refusal to move for half an hour, in spite of everything the policewoman, the policeman, and we, said to try to persuade her. At last though, reluctantly and with a dismissive shrug of her shoulders, she agreed to leave, barging passed us to the door. We thanked the puzzled young woman at the desk who had done most of the negotiation with Anna – and we all left.

Astounding to us as were the events of that night, they were just an introduction to many that were to follow. To occasions when Anna would run off into the night without warning, and apparently without reason. This was to be only the first of many when we would rely upon the police to keep her from harm; and eventually to retrieve her.

We were, in the months that followed, to be instructed in the truth that there is a country between childhood and adulthood, where sometimes people become lost, perhaps for the rest of their lives. When this happens, those who love them may also become lost.

The weeks before that evening, when Lisl and the French exchange student had visited, had been difficult.

Lisl had stayed with us before; this was her third visit. Originally she had come as an exchange visitor for Claire, and that had been arranged by Claire's school. After that, her parents and we had arranged various visits privately. Two years older than Anna, she fitted easily into the household, and we all got on well together. She had become, really, a family friend.

Manu however was a different proposition, and from the beginning she and Anna did not get along well. Physically mature, she was keen to stay out late to meet boys from her own school with whom she had travelled to England. Anna's school, not unnaturally, made specific requirements of us as a host family, to ensure the safety and well-being of our visitor – especially in the evening.

With Lisl this had not been a problem; she had a serious intention to improve her English, and enjoy her stay with us. For the younger girl from Paris, however, it was different. Her priorities were not at all the same.

We had hoped, even expected, that the novelty of the day-to-day demands in ensuring the success of these visits would serve to calm and restore Anna. But although her weekly meetings with Mark Hill had begun well, her attendance at them became irregular quite quickly.

Mark and I were in regular contact; and several times I took telephone calls from his secretary, or Mark himself, at work. These calls became increasingly urgent, as Anna did not turn up for her appointments. Her excursions into the night increased; and with them the involvement of the police.

I should emphasise that as all this was going on, work had to continue – fortunately. During this time, one day I was returning from visiting a school in Barking. Two of my students were there on a second teaching practice. The train home from London Bridge that early evening, was crowded and warm, but I had found a seat and was wedged between two other people. Opposite sat three others. And the memory of this journey stays with me.

The train stopped at every station as the early evening, and dusty, South London sunshine poured through its windows and over us all. Although I hadn't realized it at first, I was sitting amongst a family of four: a young husband, his wife, and their two young children. Visitors from Austria.

I sat between the mother, a blond young woman of thirty something, and another passenger by the window – a man simply returning from work. Recent events, the warmth of the early evening, the quiet chatter of the children, and the regular movement of the train, sent me to sleep. Perhaps for ten minutes or so.

When I woke up, it was to the embarrassment of realizing that my head was resting upon the shoulder of the young Austrian woman. My apologies were met only by smiles from the whole family. Apparently the children had been told to quieten their chatter. I left the train soon afterwards at my station, still to the smiles of the little family. And still apologising.

On an evening, towards the end of our French visitor's stay with us, Carol returned home to find Manu pinned up against the dining room wall by Anna. Yet the two of them also talked very late into the night. Well into the small hours. And as this continued, Manu viewed Carol and me with increasing suspicion.

Towards the end of Manu's stay, Claire came home from the Academy, with the result that she needed her room. So, because our visitor had Anna's room, Anna slept downstairs in the dining room, her room not being big enough for the two of them.

Anna seemed to be becoming increasingly angry and distracted, and in the morning after the second night of this arrangement, we found the new, and quite substantial, portable metal bed, had been turned into just twisted wreckage in the dining room. We had bought it especially, to provide for these few days.

By coincidence Manu's departure was on the morning of our evening visit to the Fairfield police station; and we had thought that now Claire was home, and two of the three exchange visits were over, things might settle down. Perhaps Anna could now look forward to her holiday in Cologne.

On the day after Fairfield, Anna ran out of the house late at night, packing chunks of bread spread with butter and marmite, into her duffle bag. She could not be dissuaded from leaving the house, and we didn't know where she was at well past ten o'clock. Then a neighbour rang, the wife of our milkman, whom we had known for many years. They were the parents of Mary, an old friend of Anna's from primary school days. Although they went now to different secondary schools, they had kept in touch.

The two girls had played in the garden beneath the field when very young; built igloos out of snow in winter, or had water fights using garden hoses in the summer.

Jane told Carol that Anna had just arrived at their house asking if she could stay the night. She wanted to know if that was alright with us.

We were embarrassed, although relieved to know where she was, and of course we agreed. Carol thanked Jane, and arranged to call in next morning to collect Anna, and also to learn something about her unexpected arrival.

When morning came, and Carol called in, she learned that Anna and Mary had been talking for most of the night. And then Jane disclosed,

"Really Carol, if Jim and I hadn't known you all these years, we wouldn't know what to think of the things she said. We think you should know".

Carol didn't ask what things, again probably out of a mixture of surprise and embarrassment. It was quite a long time before we learned how to respond to these particular public statements of Anna's. When Carol told me about this conversation with her friend, we decided to simply ignore what Anna had, or had not, said.

There were, actually, further reasons for this decision, because events moved on suddenly very quickly. When it was time for Anna and Carol to leave the house Anna refused. In her anger and distraction, she filled a jug of water at the sink in the kitchen where they all were talking, and poured it over the floor. Jane had been describing how she and her husband had just finished decorating the kitchen. And as Anna emptied the jug over the floor, Carol saw how deliberately our daughter smiled.

When Carol told me later of all this it was with tears in her eyes, as she described Jane looking down at her new, but now soaked, carpet tiles. And she described how humiliated she felt. After this, and thanking her friend as best she could, and apologising continually, she left without Anna, and came straight home. When she arrived and told me of these events, we made the decision to insist that Anna made another appointment to visit the doctor. Such was our faith then in the medical services.

It was clear to us now that something was very wrong; there had been just too many incidents. We needed advice.

We felt that we were approaching the limit of our ability to manage; that we were drowning in our daughter's anger. And we couldn't understand.

At around 11.00 o'clock, Jane rang to say that Mary's younger sister had persuaded Anna to visit the surgery, and had just left with her. As a result of this news, we decided that it would be best if I rang the surgery to try to explain the reason that the girls were coming. Of course without giving details of the morning's events.

I was put through to one of the four doctors in the practice, a woman, Dr. L.. I did my best to explain briefly why Anna was coming into the surgery. She listened, thanked me for ringing, and the short conversation ended.

When Anna reached the surgery, she was not seen by Dr. L., but by Doctor P., the young male doctor she had seen the previous year. We were to learn in the months to follow, that Dr P. had responsibility in the practice for patients with mental health issues.

Because we were desperate to gain some purchase on Anna's behaviour, some kind of understanding, I cycled down in the sunshine that morning, in the hope of being able to speak to a doctor. I arrived just before midday, and by chance happened to meet Dr P. at the front door, as he was leaving the surgery. And so we were able to have a short conversation, which I immediately thought was a piece of great good fortune.

Yet, in this year of surprises, the response of the young doctor to my rushed and anxious enquiry, was yet another surprise; and as were to come to understand, a defining one.

His manner was off-hand and dismissive. He told me immediately that he had seen Anna that morning, but then went on,

"I'm sorry but I can't talk to you".

I looked at him, and simply asked why.

But his reply was cold,

"Anna has told me something in confidence which makes it impossible for me to speak to you!"

At the time, in an early anticipation of our getting the help we needed for Anna, I just didn't realize the significance of what the doctor had just said. Its implications.

Instead, I just felt exasperated, as he continued,

"It's not your problem!"

When I asked him whose problem it was if not mine, he answered,

"Mine".

I couldn't believe that he was asking me to accept that, and I asked,

"But what if you're wrong?"

Enough had already happened in that year for me to know that his replies did not indicate that we were easily going to get the help for Anna that we needed.

His last words to me, over his shoulder as he walked away on that warm summer morning, were

"It's not your business!"

As I returned home, I wheeled the bicycle; trying to clear my head.

Mark Hill had emphasised to me, when we last spoke, that he was coming to the view that only her GP could get Anna the help she needed. And now a GP., whom we had not even expected her to consult, had told me that it wasn't my business. I just couldn't understand it, however much I tried; and however much I stared at the path disappearing under the wheels of the bicycle I pushed.

When I got home, I found Anna and Carol in the hall. Carol was on the floor with her head by the radiator. Just moments before, Anna had attacked her, as her mother had attempted to put her arms around her. I was just in time to intervene as she was kicking her mother where she lay.

I shouted to Anna to stop, whereupon she rushed into the kitchen, with her duffle bag. Stuffing it hurriedly with bread, she then rushed out of the front door.

At 10.00 that evening we received a telephone call from one of Carol's friends. She had seen Anna outside the amusement arcade in the High Street, and said that she was worried about the way she seemed to be acting.

I drove down to the arcade immediately, and found her. But she refused to come home with me, and there was nothing I could do to persuade her. I had to return alone.

At around 11.00, she rang us, and Carol answered the telephone. Anna's message was,

"Tell Dad to come and fetch me or I'll throw myself under a bus!"

I heard Carol say,

"You know Dad will come anyway. Where are you ?"

But the phone went dead.

I went down to the High Street, but there was no sign of Anna.

Eventually she returned home at past midnight, though none of us got to bed before two o'clock.

Next door in her room, Anna was playing music, and seemed to be crashing around. The music was loud, repetitive; so loud that the walls throbbed.

And so the pattern of Anna running away from the house, and me running to retrieve her, became established. We still had Mark Hill to support her, but our hope of getting the advice we needed from the GP, upon which Mark had said everything depended, seemed to have been removed.

If we had had the time or the wit, or the opportunity, to look at our position dispassionately, and with hindsight, we would have recognized that we were now at the mercy of events. We had no control of the situation, although we were still a long way from realizing it.

ii

The summer was half spent, and Carol decided that things could not be left to run on as they were. We needed to know what to do about Cologne. Anna was due to leave on 7th August. But should she go? Was it safe now? Was she medically fit to go?

Carol therefore said that she would go to the surgery the following morning, and speak to the Senior Partner in the practice. But seeing Dr T. was not so straightforward. When she put the request to see this doctor, and gave her reason for asking, the receptionist picked up the telephone on her desk.

After the call, the woman told her briskly,

"In the light of Dr P. spending two hours talking to your husband yesterday, Dr T. is not prepared to see you. If you insist, she will see you at 12.00 after surgery".

And so with her ears ringing, and wondering how my snatched conversation with Dr. P. outside the surgery had become a two hour consultation, Carol was sent away; but not before saying she would be back at 12.00.

Then, across the doctor's desk, she said how worried we were about Anna. She explained that we had doubts about her fitness to travel to Cologne to take part in the exchange. The trip was now just five days away. At this the Senior Partner picked up the telephone and spoke to Dr. P.. When she replaced the receiver, the news was that,

"Dr P. feels that Anna should go to Germany, and that while she is away there should be news about an appointment he has requested with the Borough's Psychology Service".

And so it was decided, using the only advice available to us. We would not intervene to prevent Anna from going to Cologne. Perhaps, in spite of our fears, the change would bring about a return to a more calm state in her.

That afternoon Anna ran off again. When she had not returned by early evening, we rang around the usual places, but no-one had any news of her to re-assure us.

At midnight she still hadn't returned, and I rang the Fairfield Police Station in case she'd gone there. I had to explain about Anna's previous visit to the station, and that now she was out missing in the night. I cannot stress enough how worried we were about her by now.

The police suggested that we should report Anna as a missing person. They asked if we could provide a photograph, and I set off in the car to take one.

When I arrived, the young policewoman we had met on our previous visit was on duty, and the first thing she told me was that Anna was at Chillingstone Police Station. She said that Anna had rung the Chillingstone Police at past midnight in some distress, from a local high-rise council estate just outside the town. Apparently she had been at a party, and there had been some difficulty when she wanted to leave. The police had gone to fetch her.

I thanked the policewoman, again, and set off back to Chillingstone to collect Anna. But when I arrived, she refused to come home. Eventually she did agree to leave, but not with me. She would only return home, she said, if she could ride in a police car, with another young policewoman, who had been speaking to us both. From time to time the desk sergeant looked over his glasses at me.

The young policewoman's name was Debbie, and after I left they followed me home in a police car. Then we all sat together on our settee, until passed three in the morning, with tea, biscuits, and conversation. The rest of the night was quite peaceful, if short, though it began with some slamming of doors.

When dawn broke, it was upon another very hot day. Anna took my bicycle to visit a friend from the church choir. To our surprise, she was back home by six o'clock. She confided later that this was, " only because if I didn't, I knew I wouldn't be able to go to Germany".

That weekend, Anna went to Farnbury on the bus, alone as far as we knew. Debbie came around to see how she was, but Anna had already left. The following day, Anna went to Germany, although the journey to Heathrow by tube, was almost indescribably bizarre and alarming.

Because Carol had to be at work, and because it was the vacation and I could work at home, I went with Anna, to help her with her luggage – and to ensure that she caught her flight safely.

As I have said, the journey from Central London to Heathrow was more difficult than I can easily describe, or than I could ever have imagined. When we needed to make connections, Anna continually ran off to the wrong entrance or to the wrong platform. As she left without warning in this way, shouting out at other passengers as she did so, I was left with the decision to follow as best I could or wait for her to return. Because of this, our journey time grew and grew.

As the succession of fresh starts continued, so the chances of our making it to the terminal in time for her to catch her plane diminished. By some chance, we did catch the flight, though I really don't know how. As I sat returning alone on the tube, it was with a feeling of such relief. And yet, I wondered, whatever would Lisl's parents make of Anna, who had so obviously changed since they had last seen her?

She would be away for a fortnight. Lisl's parents were by now friends, and at least we could be grateful that she was going to people that she and we knew. Now there was time to take stock. Space to think again. Just for a while!

We had for instance to decide what to do about a letter we had received from Mrs Vaughan at the school. The first reason for her writing, was to finalize arrangements for the French exchange. But a second was to inform us that the school would be asking Anna "to retake some of her examinations before the start of the new term, on 5th September".

As the letter put it,

"...Other members of the lower sixth will be re-taking, and there seems no reason that we should exempt Anna from this. I hope you will agree that it will give her the opportunity to cope with the examination situation again and also help rebuild her confidence by improving on the very low results achieved in the June examinations".

We had tried to discuss with Anna, when the letter had arrived, what it was precisely that the school was asking her to do. That the fresh papers would be in French and German only. At the time she had not said much; and since then, events had pushed from our minds the matter of these re-takes.

Now, also, we could let Mark know that Anna had actually made it to Cologne. He had asked me to keep him informed about how things were at home.

For a whole fortnight Carol and I had the opportunity to collect our scattered senses. We were alone in the house for part of the time, because Claire was away for a few days in Spain, on a tour with the orchestra.

And yet, when Anna returned, on the 21st , she seemed really much as before. Reading between the lines of what she said, things had been difficult for everyone. Nor did our telephone conversations with Lisl's parents reveal many more details. When Anna went to the surgery, there was no news of her appointment with the Borough's Psychological Service that had been promised by Doctor P. We had been depending upon there being some.

An early conversation with Mark Hill kept returning to me, when we spoke following his initial assessment of Anna. He had said that that he believed Anna had the personality of a potential suicide, particularly in the first year of university.

I re-called also how Anna had told us, at the beginning of the summer, that after Mrs Vaughan had referred her to the school doctor, he had asked her whether she had ever considered committing suicide. Could he really have asked her that? Certainly Anna had herself appeared outraged about his question as she told us about it. We were simply nonplussed. Unbelieving.

We had begun to discuss a number of options with Mark. That perhaps Anna might return, after a break, to another school. Or perhaps to the local FE college to complete her 'A' levels if that was what she wanted to do. Ironically Doctor

T's eldest daughter had been attending the FE college after not doing so well at her 'A' levels at school.

Mark suggested that perhaps a year away in Germany, as an au pair, might be an option. It would help her German, at which she had always shown promise. We could support her in continuing with her 'A' levels after a year's break; if that was what she wanted.

We grasped at all these possibilities, although none of them seemed quite possible because of how Anna was.

When I contacted Mark's office during the fortnight that Anna was in Cologne, his secretary told me of a bruising telephone conversation he had had with Dr. P.. The doctor had rung to tell him that the matter was a medical one, and that he should withdraw; that he should no longer be involved.

During another, later, conversation on the telephone, Mark's secretary laughed down the phone to me that she had never before been spoken to as Dr P. had spoken to her. Before adding: "But then there's always a first time for everything". To which I had to agree.

Anna returned home on the 21st August, and the fresh examinations were on 3rd September. But we were no nearer knowing how to advise her to approach these, especially given her obviously still distracted state of mind. It could only be up to her. But how could she possibly decide?

Then this impasse was removed by Anna herself. She told us that she would not re-take the examinations, and wanted to leave school.

Eventually, in my final meeting at the school with Mrs Vaughan, I would tell her that we dare not let Anna re-sit the exams, for fear that she would have a complete breakdown. Indeed I had now come to believe that, and Mark's warning was never far from my mind.

She was sympathetic, and indeed she seemed nearly as close to tears as me. She laid her hand on my arm as she said,

"These girls are very privileged, and if they don't have anything to rebel against, they will often find something, whether it is by taking drugs – or whatever."

How true that is I cannot know, but she clearly meant well by the comment.

Carol and I had decided that I would attend this appointment alone. As I left Mrs Vaughan's office, I heard her say something about her recommending that the school would be waiving the next term's fees, normally payable in lieu of notice. As I left the school for the last time, I felt we had been defeated, after all. Nothing, it seemed, had worked. In spite of our believing for so long that it would. And what would we do now? What would replace Anna's previous expectations?

In the days that immediately followed, we tried to discuss with Anna what she might do next. Or rather we simply raised possibilities, and tried to reassure her. Carol suggested, that if she wanted to go to Germany as an au pair, to improve her German further, we would help to arrange things. We suggested that if she wanted to work at something in the meantime, to prepare and save for that, we would give her £1 for every £1 she saved. We didn't particularly want her to work, but we felt there would be great risks in her not being occupied during the day when we could not be around.

And it was for this reason that we offered this simplistic solution.

We suggested that she should not rush to do this. But in so far as we could get her to listen, she didn't seem at all keen on the idea of working as an au pair in Germany. Then very soon afterwards, and completely without our knowing in advance what she intended, she arranged an office job in London, through a local employment agency.

Though we couldn't imagine how, because of what we knew of how she was, things seemed to go well at first. But in the second week, Anna had a violent quarrel with her office supervisor. During this, she stood up in front of a large office and roundly abused the supervisor. As a result she was asked to leave, and the same afternoon Carol, who was working that day at home, received a series of anxious telephone call from the manager of the employment agency.

Every time he rang, which was on five or six occasions, he asked whether Anna had returned home. He had mentioned early on, that he had been informed by the employer that she had left mid-morning, and that they were very concerned about her mental state, and for her safety.

When she arrived home at the expected time, Anna didn't mention anything about being dismissed. Only that she was not going back.

Now the pressure on the whole family increased further. The running into the night started again, and we came to rely even more upon the patience and the efforts of the police.

* * *

By 26th September, and my letter to Dr P., we were all exhausted, though it would be a full week before the storm actually broke with all of its force. Everything so far was just part of its gathering.

Anna now slept very little, even when the police brought her home.

One afternoon Anna ran off again, to the local police station, and she refused to come out for three hours. She stayed, waiting, in the public waiting area. Just previously she had run through the High Street branch of WH Smith, in a distraught state as I tried to persuade her to come home with me. So bad by now was her condition, that we feared in so many ways for her safety.

As she ran through and around the shop, she screamed out to other shoppers,

"Get him away from me. Help! Save me! He's molesting me!"

Whenever I went into the shop, for some months after that afternoon, I received doubtful looks from some of the shop's staff, though at the time of the incident, and as the month drew to its unhappy close, these really were the least of my worries.

At 6.00 pm on 24th September, we received a telephone call, from the YWCA at Claydon; a town we didn't know well.

The caller told us that Anna had walked in off the street, and asked if she could stay the night. They wanted to know if we would agree to that. Of course we did agree, relieved that we knew where she was, and that she was safe.

That night the house seemed so quiet, though Claire was still at home. When we woke up next morning we felt refreshed, and ready again. We expected Anna back. But mid-morning, we had another call from the YWCA, to tell us that Anna was not "allowed" to stay another night. This only surprised us, at first, because we had not expected that she would ask to stay.

But the caller told Carol of a disturbance after Anna had got up late that morning. Apparently she had objected angrily when told that she was simply too late for breakfast. The caller asked Carol if we could collect Anna as soon as possible. We set off immediately after the call, found the YWCA building, but Anna had left.

While we were talking to the two young women who had met us, in the canteen, we were joined by another staff member, the Manager of the hostel. She looked worried, and had with her an unkempt looking man of thirty five or so.

She introduced us to this new arrival, as Anna's parents.

"Oh, right!" this visitor began, turning to me, "I've come to collect Anna Holden. And you owe me £45!"

As I adjusted to this new development, we learned that this man claimed that he arranged catering and waitress staff for Gatwick Airport. He said that he had come to take Anna there, and the money was to reimburse him for a uniform which he had provided.

As my head cleared, I responded bleakly; in keeping with how I felt.

"Well, we're off to Claydon Police Station to report Anna as a missing person, and you're very welcome to come along with us, and we can sort all this out there".

He declined this invitation, and left mumbling something I didn't catch. When he'd gone, the manager explained that he was a known drug addict, and that Anna had had lunch with him and his partner in their home the previous day.

Later that night, after I'd written the letter to Doctor P., I would go over these events in my mind, instead of sleeping. At least we could be glad that we were able to go to the YWCA branch when we had.

But for now, Anna was missing again.

A young girl who had been with us in the canteen before the man's arrival, turned out not to be a staff member after all. Rather she was a resident. Because she had seen and heard everything that had taken place when we arrived, she could tell us that she and Anna had spent most, but not all, of the previous day together.

Believing that Anna would have nowhere to stay after the disagreement over her missed breakfast, she said that she had told her of a derelict house, a squat, that she knew of. Jill said that she thought that Anna might be there, and said that she thought she could show us where the house was.

We decided that after we had been to the police station, we would return to the YWCA, collect Jill, and then set out to try to find Anna.

When we reached the police station, we discovered that we had to provide another recent photograph of Anna; and so we set off for home again to get one.

When we had returned to deliver the photograph, and from telling a fresh set of police of the recent events that led to us being so worried for Anna's safety, we collected Jill at around 3 o'clock. Claydon, with its tower blocks and flyovers, really was unfamiliar territory to us, and we depended on her to guide us to the house she had spoken of. But it turned out that, however much she tried, she couldn't be sure where it was. We drove around and around, trying to find the house, but unsuccessfully.

Although we continued with our search for the house for two hours after dark, in a town that appeared to us increasingly threatening, following Jill's directions and intuition about the location of the squat, we couldn't manage it. The more we drove around a seemingly endless succession of backstreets, all of which looked the same, the more completely hopeless the attempt felt.

As we drove with Jill, we heard from her about how the day before, Anna had seemingly intentionally attempted to step out from the pavement in front of oncoming traffic. We thought it more likely that this happened because Anna was by now worn out, and was unable to concentrate properly; though of course we couldn't know for sure.

Eventually, at about 9 o'clock we had to give up trying to find the squat. We dropped Jill off, thanked her for her efforts, and after another long talk with the manager at the YWCA, set off for home. Our only comfort was that the Claydon police were looking out for Anna, and might find her – if she was still in that town.

It was well past ten o'clock when we reached home. As Carol prepared something to eat, and as we looked back on the day's events, we waited for the telephone to ring hoping that Anna would be at the other end of it.

While we were eating, a couple of Carol's friends rang to ask after her and Anna. I decided to drive down to the High Street, just in case Anna had returned to places that she had rung us from many times before in the months since the party. Before I went, we telephoned the Fairfield police, just in case… . While in Chillingstone, I dropped into the police station, just in case …, but she wasn't there, and there was no news of her.

Shortly after I got home again, Debbie rang our front door bell. She'd learned of our visit to her station, had been in touch with Fairfield, and had come to find out what had been happening during the day. She left after about three quarters of an hour, telling us to try not to worry, and assuring us that the Claydon police would do all they could to retrieve Anna. And so we were alone again, together in the small hours.

And suddenly we felt incredibly tired. We talked a bit about the day, and waited by the telephone.

And so, it was then that we decided I should write that letter to Doctor P.. By now it was 2.30. The night was well advanced. Or was it the day?

CASSIDY, JOHN *Walking On Frogs*. Bloodaxe, 1989, pp.64. £4.95. 1 85224 089X

John Cassidy's previous collection of poems, *Night Cries*, won a Poetry Book Society Recommendation in 1982. *Walking On Frogs* deserves as much. Here is nature poetry of horror and loveliness which includes the city. Throughout this book the menace and the bounty of hidden deep down things are held in precise balance, in "*... purity clutched / from a ditch*" ('Well- heads') . None of the poems disappoint, and many are memorable.

The first section, '*Coast to Coast, fragments of America*', contains fresh effects of colour and tone. There are startling clarities everywhere as surfaces and impressions juxtapose in images across a continent. Be it the moon in *'New Orleans'* which "*... hangs like the last cantaloupe / on the market*", or a short visual journey in *'Walking in Chicago'* when "*... the street walls have a polish / to brighten the eyes' track up to where the sun strikes*". But there is more than one *"utterly undomestic possibility" ('Noon in Santa Fe'),* and we meet them again in the second part of the book.

The fearfulness of what may burst from the depths of the earth, the mind, or the future, is considered but in balance still with promise and hope. It's worth looking closely at *'Still Life'*. Other poems to be cherished in this truthful book include *'Equipoise', 'One long blue note', 'Flaw', 'At an outdoor café' , 'Windfalls', and 'Marching to Breakfast'*. I promise though that you will enjoy making your own selections.

A book to save and use. Such resolution is to be prized, and should be offered to young adult readers and writers.

William Holden

PRITCHARD, SELWYN *Stirring Stuff*. Sinclair Stevenson, 1993, pp.145. £8. 99. 1 85619 308 X

Selwyn Pritchard is a very quotable poet, who found his voice in Australia where he now lives. An angry lyrical voice counter-pointing two sides of the world, and illuminating each within the other. His celebration of Australia is the exile's complex celebration of "*...Home transplanted but* ***still*** *elsewhere*". For instance, experiences of Britain and Australia are woven together in poetry as in life, where "*... by frames memory unwinds from fifty years / railway tracks and buttons bright as tears,*" With "*the hiss of the cold cosmos*" always present, it is a memory teaching that *"Love does not stem the ruthless chance of things / nor chill indifference check the Winters' Springs"*.

This voice denounces much in contemporary culture, " *... fearing for love's trusting innocence / in futures media bland, where all the world's a stage; ... wars prime timed , edited, glossed*". Counter-pointed too are love and the *"chill keening"* of those exercising economic power over others' lives, *"beaten from parish / to slum to colony ..."*. And in acutely painful poems, love and death are counter-pointed.

Sixth formers will intuit how it is that "*... revolutions of the heart die with the first official kiss*". They may wish to quote the poem *'Haiku for a sleeping wife'*. If they recommend this collection to each other, it will be for the reasons that I recommend it to you.

William Holden

CROWE, ANNA *Skating out of the house.* Peterloo, 1997, pp.85 £7. 95. 1 871471 70 2

There are more riches in this first collection than anyone has a right to expect. It is a book of subtly inclusive poems: varied in their subjects, diverse in their forms, and often sweet in their wisdoms. Painting is one source of their inspiration, nature another, childhood another. The writing is emphatically visual, one voice of the poet confiding, *"I let my eye just rest"*. As a result, a recurrent preoccupation is how what is visible is influenced by what is hidden.

The interiors and exteriors of memory and place are distilled, by poetry, from paintings by Palmer, Raphael, Velasquez, and Stanley Spencer. Like the bird on the river they come, *"veering between what's seen and hidden ... from the out of reach ... broaching the here and now"*. ('Kingfisher on the Eden').

Among the wisdoms which we come upon here, if often too late in life, is one collected from the Arawak Indians. When they weave, they always leave a small fault in their work: *"as though they understood / how the heart, bent on perfection ends / trapped in its own web".* ('Arawak Tunic').

My recommendation of this writing is that of an admiring reader to other readers, including mature readers in the secondary school. Fine, felicitous, and full of truth.

William Holden

Chapter 18

The next day, Friday, we were up early, and the morning was again a fine one. I stood looking out of the sitting room window on to the garden where the summers of our daughters' childhoods had passed. And I remembered my young wife out there with them – doting upon them.

And I recalled how just two years previously, Carol had organized a birthday party for Anna. Girls from her class at school had come. But it had been a disaster.

Carol had described it to me in the car from the airport, as I returned from a work-related trip to Calgary.

I had thought that it would be a small joke to wear a large white hat which I had been given in Canada; off the plane when she met me. But the events during my absence had turned my attempt at this joke into a mistake. She was too pre-occupied, and worried, to laugh.

I heard in the car, driving home that early afternoon from the airport, how the girls at the party had mocked Anna. Carol told me how she realized then, for the first time, how unpopular our daughter seemed. Perhaps because she wanted so much to be liked – and by the wrong people?

Then there were the parents, mostly fathers, who did not leave the house, but who stayed and stood around in our kitchen as Carol organized things.

She had not expected so many fathers to stay. Talking about cars and the stock exchange, their houses and their jobs. Looking across to each other, amused perhaps at how small the house was. At how basic to them the kitchen and its equipment – even though it had recently been extended and re-equipped.

And as I listened I wondered, then, if this was that other price of Anna attending the school? Now as I stood at the French window, Carol came and stood beside me. She didn't speak, and I put my arm around her. And I reflected how she had always stood beside me. She was looking tired.

Today was her day to be over at Anerley, at the design firm. Freelance now, she had divided her working week into three parts to fit in with the family. Two days in the office in the High Street, one at home working for an accountant, and today.

I would work at home, and wait for news.

We were interrupted by the front door bell. Although it was still only 7.30, Debbie from the Chillingstone station, was calling to see if Anna had turned up. She left quite quickly when she learned that she hadn't.

Now there was the letter sitting on the dining room table from the night before. We had decided that Carol would drop it into the surgery on her way to work.

I somehow felt better at the thought of the letter arriving immediately. Irrationally. As if something had actually already been achieved. Perhaps we felt that we were regaining some kind of control, just by making the statements in the letter.

In the days before, we had cast around in several directions for advice. On the telephone to various agencies.

Carol had rung the 'Mind' helpline to discuss our situation, trying for advice. The counsellor had listened, and after some time she had finished the listening by commenting,

"Have you thought, Mrs Holden, how a little creative neglect might be useful?"

But how could we know? How could we dare?

Carol had only just left, and I was settling down at my desk, when the YWCA rang to say that Anna had turned up at the hostel, and that the police had collected her. Soon afterwards, the Claydon police rang asking if she could be picked up from the police station.

But now I had no transport, and I seriously doubted that Anna would stay with me during the awkward, quite long, bus journey back from Claydon. And I knew just how long it would take me to reach there without the car.

The Anerley studio was not so far from the police station, and I thought how little there was to be gained from Carol leaving her place of work so soon after she had arrived. I knew also that being at the studio for the day would give her some relief; her colleagues there were really more like friends. And now I knew that Anna was safe and secure again.

And so I made the decision, which may or may not have been a mistake.

I asked the policeman at the end of the line if it would be in order for Anna to be picked up by her mother at around 4.30 in the afternoon. And he agreed. It simply seemed much better for Carol to leave work a little early and collect Anna on the way home. I suppose I had in mind also our, by now long, experience with the Fairfield and Chillingstone police. And their support.

After waiting twenty minutes or so to allow Carol to arrive at work, I rang to tell her about the two telephone conversations, and the suggestion I had made to the police at Claydon. I said that of course the arrangement could be changed, but it seemed to me that it was for the best. And so that was how it was left.

That evening Carol would describe to me how it had been when she had arrived at the police station for Anna. How she seemed even worse; more distracted rather than at all chastened. She said that she had been locked in a cell.

Carol had to sign for various items which the police had taken from Anna. Surprising items. Things she didn't recognize. A sharpened screwdriver. A pornographic magazine. And other pieces of junk.

And she described how, as these formalities were attended to, seven or eight policemen and policewomen had stood ringed around Anna, as if they expected something to happen.

As they drove home, Anna spoke of "hearing things". And she confided:

"The only reason I'm coming home is that you've arranged a birthday party for me!"

Her birthday was nearly two months away.

I went to the front door as they drove up, and as they got out of the car I noticed how pale Carol looked.

We set about preparing supper, and suggested that Anna watch something on television in the meantime.

"You f-- off!" she replied, and then locked herself in her room.

When the meal was ready, Carol called up to tell Anna.

There was no reply, so she went upstairs.

Anna was in the lavatory opposite her bedroom. The door of her room was closed; and when Carol looked, in it was to another surprise.

All over the dressing table, on the bedside table, on her desk and on the floor, were candles. Lighted candles. There must have been fifty of sixty of them.

Alarmed, Carol called downstairs to me. When I saw them, we immediately started to put them out; and I picked up a box of matches that were on the dressing table and put it in my pocket.

Soon the room, and then the whole house was full of the smell of the extinguished candles. When Anna came out of the lavatory we expected violent protests, but instead all she did was smile. And all I could say was,

"Anna, surely you know how dangerous it is to leave lighted candles around!"

But then of course I knew she did.

She went downstairs and left the house almost immediately. On the kitchen work surfaces, she left behind roughly cut slices of bread which she had intended to make into sandwiches but had forgotten about. A jar of marmite stood on the worktop with its lid off.

Carol put Anna's meal in the oven, in case she returned soon. Pointlessly.

And so again Anna was out of the house, and we didn't know where she was.

At around 10.00 the same evening, the mother of one of Anna's former classmates at school rang. Anna had walked in off the street, and asked if she could stay the night with her daughter. Mrs Spicer wanted to know if that was alright.

So, again, we knew that she was safe. Mrs Spicer suggested that she drop Anna back home in the morning. She said that she was driving past the house anyway, though that was unlikely.

When morning came, Carol had gone to the shops nearby for food. I was working upstairs, the term still not having begun. When I heard the front door open I called down thinking Carol was back; and went to the top of the stairs. But it was Anna. She let out a loud scream, and immediately ran out of the house again.

Soon afterwards Carol returned from the shops, and a little later a friend of hers rang to say that she had just seen Anna in the High Street.

"Carol, I thought I should ring," she explained. "She was behaving so strangely and it didn't seem right. I was worried, and thought you should know".

All that day we searched for Anna, in the High Street and all around, but without success. And so in the evening, quite late, I contacted Chillingstone Police again, to say that Anna was missing.

At half past midnight, as each day merged seamlessly into the next, there was a loud crash as Anna came in through the front door. When we asked where she had been, she said that the police had dropped her off.

She said that they had picked her up in Gillett's Lane. It was a lonely spot, about half a mile away. They had told her that it was not safe to be out alone so late. We were dismayed by how she looked. She seemed to be even more distracted, and moved erratically. Dark rings framed her eyes. In spite of our pleas, she would have nothing to eat or drink, but agreed to go to bed.

I was more certain than ever that she needed medical help, and decided to try to force a response from the practice by ringing its emergency number. I was put through to a locum doctor who said that he would come as soon as possible.

Half an hour later, the remaining telephone rang but Anna reached it before we could; and she refused to surrender it. Whoever the caller was, they rang off. And no doctor came.

In her disorientation and anger, Anna began to slam the glass door into the living room. She slammed and slammed and slammed it, until finally it smashed, showering shards of glass everywhere.

The cat was normally a composed and friendly soul, but she had recently followed a policy of absenting herself when Anna was at home. Curled up on the settee as she had been, she now displayed a centuries' old impulse for self-preservation, and raced off upstairs.

As I began to clear up the glass, Anna smiled and plugged in the telephone in the dining room.

After a while, Carol tried to persuade her to come to bed, but Anna turned on her threateningly. Carol had tried to hold on to her, with her hands on her shoulders, to re-assure and comfort her. To tell her how much we loved her. But Anna re-acted badly. She pushed her mother away, and went into the dining room with the telephone. Slamming the door behind her.

Unlikely though it was, she was on the phone to Chillingstone Police Station, talking she said to a desk sergeant whom she insisted had asked her out. When after two hours or so she finally agreed to end the call, it was with the comment to whoever was at the other end,

“I’ve got to go, I’ve been told to go back to bed!” Such a reasonable and innocent-seeming comment. But for its context. And the time.

By now, as the autumn sun retained its peculiar warmth, whatever its cause and whatever form it took, fear was living with us in our home, and it was beginning to feel normal. A reign of terror was becoming established. It was as if the house was occupied by an invading army of one; or rather by our fear for Anna, and our own sense of powerlessness.

What were we to make of Anna telling us that a woman had followed her home? That everyone was looking at her on the bus? That another woman had died when she was on the bus? That she was late home because she had to go to the hospital because a woman had died in the street? That someone had stolen Carol’s bicycle which she had borrowed? Or even that a sergeant at the police station had asked her out?

Her constantly losing things, was no doubt to do with her lack of sleep. Each of these claims, alone, was credible – except for the last; yet together they were not. They were rather, and especially, a very undomestic possibly.

The next day was a Sunday. Linda, a friend of Carol’s rang her in the morning. Although Carol had never discussed how things were with us at home, Linda knew about Anna’s distress. Everyone in the village could not but know, simply because of Anna’s membership of the choir, and how she was when she was there.

The Rector had co-incidentally come to the parish at the same time as we had. Although it had meant little to us before, his previous job and ‘parish’ were that of chaplain in a large psychiatric hospital in Surrey.

Perhaps prompted by something Carol had said in her telephone conversation with her friend, maybe about our difficulties with the GP., Linda suddenly declared,

“I’m going to talk to Richard, you and William need proper advice!”

Very soon afterwards she rang again, asking,

"Carol, can you and William see Richard at around 8 o'clock after evensong? He'll know what to do!"

It has to be said that our attendance at church was not frequent, and we had not actually attended evensong since living in the parish. Yet, as with the writing of the letter to Dr P., things felt suddenly better. Perhaps because momentarily we felt less isolated.

Claire's term was beginning on Tuesday, and we had promised to take up lots of her stuff to the flat she shared with a violinist. It couldn't be transported by train or tube, and so normally we would all have driven up altogether.

We decided that I would go up to Marylebone with Claire in the evening as planned, and that Carol would keep the appointment with the Rector. We knew that Anna had arranged to be out of the house that evening, as she always was on Sunday evenings. She would be with other members of the choir at Venture Scouts. An unlikely destination, but there it was.

When I returned, Carol seemed very positive as I heard about the advice she had received during her two hour visit to the Rectory. What Richard had said was,

"You must go to the surgery. Bang on the door if necessary, and demand a domiciliary visit. Don't be put off any longer. Just insist! Don't leave the surgery until they agree!"

That someone could seem so very definite, in itself, brought a kind of comfort and relief. The meaning of the term "domiciliary visit", though unfamiliar to us, was clear enough.

But banging on doors? Insisting? Refusing to leave the surgery? I wondered about all of that, but in any case we resolved that next day, on another Monday morning, I would be at the surgery first thing. So now, a tiny suggestion of residual hope had returned.

When Anna came home from Venture Scouts with a friend at around 10.30, she ran off almost immediately – alone and into the night. And at midnight she had still not returned. And we had heard nothing.

In spite of the promise of what the following morning might bring, we felt we could not avoid ringing the Chillingstone police yet again, and informing them that Anna was out in the night. We were so concerned about her condition.

Debbie, and an older policeman, came to the house very quickly, and as we all sat on the settee talking, Anna rang.

She was in a telephone box, she said, outside the house of the friend who had left the school two years before, when the family had moved to Exeter.

The good thing was that at least we now knew where she was.

As Carol listened on the phone, Anna said "I'll ring back in half an hour!"

As we all listened, we heard Carol say in some desperation,

"No, Anna, stay where you are, and dad will come to pick you up!"

But it was too late, and the phone went dead.

The police left immediately. A little later they returned to say that when they had got to the telephone box Anna had already left, and they hadn't been able to find her.

As they left the house again, Debbie laid her hand on Carol's arm saying

"Don't worry, we'll keep looking!"

It was 1.30 when Anna rang next.

"Where are you?" Carol asked.

And the reply was,

"I'm going to school".

Wearily, Carol asked,

"Wouldn't you like to come home?"

And the reply was,

"Yes, dad can come and fetch me".

When I drove up to where Anna had said she would be, she was sitting on a low wall outside a branch of a Sainsbury's supermarket. When we got home to what remained of the night, it was to little sleep for any of us.

And now it was time for my visit to the surgery, and I arrived early to find that Dr T. the senior partner was not on duty. After I had explained the reason for my visit, I was shown into Dr. L's room. Dr L. was the woman doctor I had spoken to on the telephone at the very beginning of August.

Immediately upon sitting down, I began to explain why I was there.

The doctor straightaway told me to stay calm, which actually was hardly necessary, since I had resolved to follow the spirit but not the letter of the Rector's advice.

I explained that Anna's condition was a great worry to us. That she wasn't sleeping, or eating, or caring for herself. I said also that I had received no reply to my letter of 26th September to Dr. P..

I continued,

"I believe that Anna is now very unwell. And I would like to ask you to see her because of her physical condition. I cannot ask her to come to the surgery, and so will you please come to the house?"

The doctor looked at me from across her desk. She was a woman in her early forties perhaps.

"Mr Holden", she said, in all my career I've only ever referred two adult patients to a psychiatric hospital. Do you understand? Just twice!"

All I could reply to this was,

"I just want you to help Anna".

Her reply then surprised me in a way that I had forgotten was still possible.

"What you want, Mr Holden, I think, is to have your daughter sectioned!"

Here another unfamiliar term hit me from across the desk, and as I replied I only half understood her meaning.

"I just want you to come and see her condition for yourself".

But her reply was simply,

"No! The matter is in hand".

At this, I asked her what she meant, and received the reply,

"Dr P. is dealing with it".

When I said that he clearly wasn't, she simply said,

"Well I'm sorry!"

And so I left, because that was all I could do.

I'd not banged on any doors as the Rector had advised, but I had put our case as strongly as I felt was prudent in an attempt get a doctor to visit Anna. But it hadn't worked.

When I got home the doctor's accusation was still resounding in my head. Anna was still in bed, exhausted further by the events of the previous evening. A new month had begun, and we seemed to have made no progress.

In spite of our attempts to dissuade her, Anna left the house at about midday with nothing to eat.

While I could not get Dr L's accusation from my mind, neither could I forget Mark's repeated advice that everything depended upon the GP.. We knew of course that Anna had long since not attended her appointments with him. And I was above all mindful of the deterioration in her. So plain was it. So obvious.

And so I decided to contact Mark's secretary for advice early that afternoon. I explained my reason for ringing, and that I was doing so because of my interview with Dr L. in the morning.

The secretary left the phone, and after a short while returned. What she said then was the beginning of everything changing,

"What you must do is ring the Duty Social Worker of the day".

And she gave me a telephone number.

When I rang it, I was advised by another voice to ring the secretary of the Consultant Psychiatrist at Fenside Hospital.

When I did this, a soft, very calm, voice at other the end of the line, said that she would pass on my message.

By midnight on this first day of October, Anna had still not returned home. But we left the light on in our bedroom at the front of the house, to signal to her that we were still up.

During the previous weeks, when Anna opened her bedroom door during the night it was in a certain way. Like a violent announcement, but always preceded by a very quiet sound. And the same was true that night as she came in through the front door.

First, there was the slightest noise, and then a loud crash, at around two in the morning. She said that she had been at an underwear party along the road, with two other teenage girls.

The rest of the night was to be the worst yet.

The house had only just become quiet again with us all in bed, when Anna ran into our room. She drew back the curtains, looking up and down the street frantically. The light from the street light outside the house flooded the bedroom.

She said that she had to signal to the people outside, and then began to switch the bedroom lights on and off rapidly and persistently.

She then disappeared and returned with her tape recorder; and began to play upon the buttons as if they were the keys of a piano. Rapidly and very fast. Incessantly.

She announced that an aeroplane had just landed on the back lawn, that the flowers were talking to her and to each other, and that the police were using her radio to speak to her.

On a set of bookshelves in our bedroom, there was a small model of a Citroën C6 car. It was used as simply an ornament, and had been a present – some kind of souvenir. We had forgotten it was there, but now Anna shrieked that the police were speaking to her from it.

Now we were all part of a slow-burning nightmare, and all of us were scared, even more than before. At its centre was our daughter on her personal pyre. Then, as later, our concern was to prevent her from becoming her own bonfire.

When she was not in her room, very loud music came from it. Now as previously, yet much more than then, the walls vibrated with it; and it felt that we did too. The lyrics had a repeated line:

"*Must keep this pressure on! Must keep this pressure on!*" Their repetition persisted.

I didn't know the song – perhaps unsurprisingly.

A little later, Anna began to run around the top floor of the house, repeatedly opening and then smashing shut every door. This seemed to continue for a long time, until I intervened and she returned to her room.

Carol clutched hold of me in bed, in something like terror. I was frightened too, perhaps even frightened of Anna now, as well as for her.

At around four in the morning, the house became quiet, and when we looked into her room we saw that Anna was asleep on her bed in her daytime clothes.

In the morning at around ten o'clock, the secretary to my department at work rang, to tell me that I had as much compassionate leave as I needed. I had no idea then, nor since, how or why this decision came to be made and so coincidentally relayed that morning. And can only assume that a colleague had informed the Dean by some route.

In recent weeks, Anna had been going through a phase of evangelical Christianity. We weren't sure where this had originated, but realized that it was connected somehow with her school friend, Sally, the one who had left for Exeter. The family were fundamentalist Christians. We had heard Anna mention this former school friend again on the telephone to the police, just recently.

Large parcels of books had begun to arrive for Anna, just as parcels of books arrived regularly for me to review.

The irony of this did not reveal itself to me until much later. Anna's books were Christian-based novels for teenagers, and there were by now twenty or so of them, stacked in a neat pile on her desk in her room.

During the last few weeks, we noticed that she had been keeping a diary which she guarded jealously. She mentioned several times also, that she was writing letters to God, which she said she knew we wouldn't understand. We didn't really.

Recently she had taken to upbraiding us for our irregular attendance at church.

Then she would scream,

"You're f---g heathen. You don't believe in God!"

When I challenged her about this and tried to reason with her, she turn upon me with some menace,

"You want to watch yourself! You don't know what you're dealing with!"

Only a few days previously, Carol had walked into a similar conversation about church-going, and when she tried to remonstrate with her, Anna had pushed her hard against the radiator in the hall.

In response, Carol took Anna by the arm, opened the front door and put her outside, telling her to calm down. Afterwards, I wondered if she only acquiesced in this purely from surprise. Indeed I wondered that she acquiesced at all. Perhaps she didn't expect Carol to re-act in that way. Or perhaps at all. No doubt she had long since begun to sense our helplessness. That we were becoming powerless.

In the event, Anna immediately stepped over the low wall that separated the front gardens of the houses, and knocked on the front door of one of our immediate neighbours. She said that she'd been kicked out of the house, and had nowhere to go. Luckily Vera just laughed, and sent her home.

But now all we could do was to wait for the psychiatrist to contact us. Tired and fearful, and hoping that the secretary had passed on our message as she had promised. Though we could hardly celebrate it, this day was our wedding anniversary; our silver wedding anniversary.

In the early evening of the next day, the 3rd October, Dr H. rang from the hospital.

When the telephone rang, Anna answered it. That had become usual, for she now policed the remaining telephone receiver. We let her do this in spite of our anxiety for the call, because she had already destroyed one handset by tearing the cable from the wall. That was when we had challenged her about refusing to hand it over. We knew that we had to preserve the remaining telephone link at all costs. I have to emphasise again how this was before the time of mobile phones.

After a short while, Carol gently took the telephone from Anna – but she quickly grabbed it back. In the short ensuing struggle, Dr H. said,

"Let her speak Mrs Holden". Something I remembered later, in spite of myself, with just a trace of a sense of irony – and perhaps even bitterness.

The doctor had a short conversation with Anna, and then asked her to put her mother on.

After a very few words, for even at this stage he seemed not to see the matter as urgent, he said to Carol that he would be "back in touch".

And then, with a clear-headedness and resolve, almost unimaginable after the events of the previous night, and others before that, Carol calmly but with her voice trembling, said to the caller,

"It really is a matter of urgency. Please come!".

And at this he simply promised to re-arrange his diary, and to come the next day. Before ringing off, he asked for directions.

Dr H. came at 10.40 the following morning. Quietly, and just seeming to appear. He had left his large grey Volvo saloon two doors down the street.

It was 4th October, and we showed the consultant psychiatrist into the dining room, where he immediately picked up a framed photograph of the two girls, taken some eight years before. As he introduced himself, he examined this photograph closely.

"May I?", he asked.

We nodded, as he held the frame which had rested on the bookshelves for so many years.

As we spoke to him, it was with an overwhelming relief.

"Tell me what the problem is", he directed.

He was a large man, quietly spoken, and from somewhere in the Middle East.

We began by saying how worried we were about Anna, and how long the difficulties had been going on.

I forget now who spoke first, though it is probable that I let Carol explain.

Quite soon, since he had asked the question, I probably imprudently, and impulsively, added,

"We have been trying to explain to Dr. P. since the very beginning of August".

At this, our visitor replied,

"Well yes, the relationship between you and Dr P. has completely broken down!".

Feeling very tired, I didn't challenge this, and said only,

"Our only concern is Anna!"

Dr H. continued however,

"Dr P. is a very fine doctor, and works with us at the hospital".

He then went on to ask whether there was any history of mental illness in the family.

I had to mention of course that I couldn't say in my case because I had lost my parents very early on.

Dr H. carefully replaced the photograph on the shelf of the bookcase, and then asked if he could see Anna, who was lying on the settee in the living room next door. She had been there since falling asleep in the small hours – still in her outdoor clothes.

When he entered the room it was dark, for the curtains on to the garden were still closed. And it wasn't long before he returned to where we had remained in the dining room.

It was only a few seconds later that he was saying that Anna should be admitted to hospital immediately, and that he would arrange it.

"It would be best if she came voluntarily, but when I put it to her she refused, and became distressed". She will therefore have to be admitted under section 2 of the Mental Health Act".

His words peeled like a bell that morning, of warning and celebration alike. Celebration because I thought that now our daughter would get the help and support she obviously needed. Warning, out of the knowledge of the months that we had sought help for her. When her being admitted to a psychiatric hospital was not something we could have anticipated or expected. Indeed we would have shrunk from it.

He asked if we had any objection, and we just shook our heads in despair and relief, for ourselves and for Anna. How could we now be almost welcoming something which, had we thought about before, we would have done anything to avoid for our daughter? The daughter whose childhood image smiled back shyly at us from the photograph on its bookshelf, her fair hair plaited and shining. From the past.

The doctor explained what would happen next, though he could know of only some of the events that would follow once he'd left the house.

In a very short time, two women social workers arrived. One of them was a woman in her mid-forties, the other younger, a trainee. Both were very kindly, and gentle.

Then Dr. P. arrived, and he joined us in the kitchen, where we were being told how things would proceed.

Carol was crying quietly, gently. The older social worker asked what had been happening, and Carol then turned to Dr. P.,

So quietly, almost inaudibly, and through her tears, she asked him,

"Why wouldn't you listen to us?"

He didn't reply, and simply stood there blinking in the morning light which was shining in through the window of the kitchen door from the garden.

Shortly after that his pager sounded, and he said that he had to leave. At this the older social worker said,

"Oh great, so it's left down to us".

And so Dr. P left our kitchen and our house, without further comment; leaving behind in it the wreckage of our family. That was the last time we would ever meet him, or speak to him.

The senior social worker made a telephone call, and shortly afterwards an ambulance arrived. Two paramedics stood at our door.

Anna was upstairs in our bedroom, and she had seen them arrive through the window. We were with her. She picked up a small china ornament from the window sill, and opened the window.

"Please don't", said Carol quietly, knowing how Anna would in normal times have regretted what she was to do next. But the ornament smashed down on the path beneath the window anyway.

Then as I went down to answer the door, Anna locked herself in the bathroom and refused to come out.

The two middle-aged men from the ambulance service stood with us outside the bathroom door, and one of them suggested that we all go downstairs to join the social workers in the kitchen. And Carol set about making them all some tea. What else?

One of the ambulance men told his colleague to go into the back garden. Carol was puzzled, and asked why. His reply came:

"Because she may jump out of the bathroom window!"

But we needn't have worried. For we heard the front door slam; shortly after the quiet sound that was Anna running down the stairs. As the paramedics moved toward the door, I realized what I must do.

"No!", I insisted, "I'll do it".

And I followed Anna down our street where we had lived for twenty years. Down the street of the childhood of our two girls. Upon which they had looked from their earliest years in winter and in summer. From which they'd gone to school in the morning, and to which they had returned at night.

I knew that if she was to be taken into the ambulance against her will, then I must be there, and be taking responsibility. It could not be left to a stranger.

As I began to catch up with Anna, she cried out,

"Help!, Help!, he's molesting me!".

A young woman who as walking on the pavement towards us, called to me,

"Hey you, leave her alone!"

All I could think to reply was,

"Thank you but it's alright. I'm her father. She's not well".

And at this, the young woman said, as the ambulance cruised behind us,

"Oh right, I'll run this way! You go that!". She only wanted to help.

And by now Anna was knocking on the door of one neighbour after another, crying out as she did so,

"Help me! Help me! He's after me!"

Some of our neighbours came to their doors, and some didn't.

If they did, I held up my hand in some sort of explanation, or supplication, but by then I had no time to say anything much, before Anna had moved on, away and further down the street.

The ambulance followed, slowly and quietly; and finally drew up alongside us both. Eventually, Carol and I, along with the two social workers, were sitting with Anna in the back – with one of the paramedics.

The progress of the ambulance was very slow and smooth; it seemed to take a long route to the hospital. Perhaps that was intentional, for Anna had become more calm.

Silent now, staring straight ahead, she sat with her hands clenched tight into fists. Carol had her arms around her.

It seemed that our daughter's mind had "snapped like a summer-dry twig."

Chapter 19

We were set upon a voyage towards understanding that there could be, after all, no family idyll. Not for us.

For so many years, charm had governed our lives. But not now.

When we all arrived at the hospital that October afternoon, we were met by a male charge nurse; and soon afterwards by a female Registrar. And we had to respond to her question, "Can you describe to me the problem?" As if we could!

We started to try but she had to leave after four or five minutes. Before she did, she handed us back to the male nurse, and we tried again to describe to him some of the events of the previous months. But there was simply no time, and we were asked to leave in order that Anna may be settled in.

Before that, we learned that we could visit Anna every evening.

Now we felt a mixture of relief, deep tiredness, and a sense that we had betrayed our daughter. Deserting her by protecting her. But at last someone would be able to help her in a way that we couldn't.

As we drove the two miles or so home from the hospital, we passed a fish and chip shop at the end of the High Street. We had never gone in, largely because the food never looked that inviting. But we hadn't eaten all day, and it was past 6 o'clock.

That night we did go in, to sit down to a meal that we had seldom eaten, after a day we could never have imagined. As we returned from somewhere we could not have anticipated needing to visit.

As we ate, we discussed how things would be better; now that Anna was safe. We told each other that life would soon return to how it had been. We were quite sure of that.

The next evening our regular visits to the hospital would begin. The part of the hospital caring for Anna was called 'The Priority Health Unit'. In the morning I would return to work, and as Carol was working from home that day, Anna would ring and speak to her twice at least. This pattern of Anna ringing from the hospital soon became established; for by now the telephone had become her instrument.

On our first evening visit to Anna I had to remain outside in the car, because she refused to allow me into her room.

For the first five weeks of her stay in the hospital she was given her own room; and it would be only later that she would be moved upstairs to share with three other patients.

It would be a week before Anna would allow me to visit her with Carol; and so the burden of entering the hospital, and all that entailed, fell entirely upon Carol at first. I had to wait in the car.

When I eventually went into the ward, I saw for myself how many young staff there seemed to be around. We learned only gradually however that these were not medical staff, nurses or doctors; but care assistants. We actually met very few nurses, and fewer still doctors.

Later we were to wonder just how many of the details of the conversations we had with these young people, which we believed so crucial at the time, were ever passed on. Or even actually heard.

The day after Anna's admission I received a letter from the Health Authority, from the Services Manager, informing me that my 'relative' had been admitted to hospital under Section 2 of the 1983 Mental Health Act. It suggested that if we had any questions (or 'complaints') we should speak to the hospital doctor, making an appointment first.

On the evening of our second visit, Carol and a care assistant sat with Anna in her room. Carol asked,

"Your dad's in the car outside. Won't you see him?"

Anna simply said,

"No!"

The care assistant asked,

"Why won't you see your dad, Anna?"

And she replied,

"Because of what happened".

With her usual insight into how this answer might be interpreted, Carol asked,

"Do you mean what happened in Claydon?"

And apparently with reluctance, Anna answered, "Yes".

During the summer of 1990, the radio and television news bulletins, along with the newspapers, were full of reports of events in Cleveland, and the Orkney Islands.

They spoke of parents accused of cruelly ill-treating their children, and of the authorities removing many children into local authority care for their protection.

Intense debate raged around these events in the press, and indeed it would continue long into the future. In Cleveland, doctors took the lead, while in the Orkneys it was social workers.

Nobody could be unaware of all this at the time, and neither were we. In the previous year 'The Children Act' was passed into law, to improve the protection of children.

As Carol told me of that conversation on her second visit to Anna, when she returned to the car, the implications of the question asked by the care worker, and Anna's response, were clear enough. And as I listened to what Carol was telling me, I thought back to my conversation with Dr. P. on 1st August, and his mentioning "something" Anna had told him; and his refusal even to talk to me.

I thought upon all this, and I dismissed it.

It would not be true to say that Anna's admission to hospital resulted in any obvious or immediate change in her. From the beginning, she harried and bullied her mother. Both in the hospital, and in her frequent telephone conversations when she rang home.

But after a week, Anna agreed that I could accompany Carol into the ward on our visits.

Then I saw, and was impressed by, the eyes that watched visitors from the staff office which we always had to pass. These eyes watched as we entered, and as we left. Apart from the care workers, we saw no one at this time to whom we could talk to about Anna.

She had been in the hospital three days, when on the Sunday morning as we were discussing our visit in the afternoon, the telephone rang. The call was from the hospital. When I answered it, it was to learn that Anna had run away – with a middle-aged male patient.

I broke the news to Carol as gently as I could when I got off the phone.

Early in the afternoon the police rang. Anna had turned up at a local 'Free Church' service, and apparently alone. The minister had informed the hospital immediately upon her arrival. And now the police were ringing us. They suggested that we meet them at the church, and so we set off.

The church was a modern building, with a deep gabled roof. When we arrived, we discovered that Anna was refusing to leave, and would only talk to a young policeman with whom we found her in conversation. He could not have been much older than Anna, and was from the Chillingstone station, though we had not met him before.

It would not be until after 5.00 in the afternoon that he eventually persuaded her to return with him to the hospital.

And as she left with him, I saw how the sudden grey of his young face was in strong contrast to the gleaming white of the collar of his shirt. He seemed puzzled at the way that he'd spent his afternoon.

When he left Anna in the car for a moment with a female colleague, and came over to talk to us, he seemed uncertain of what to say as we thanked him.

His only reply, at around twenty one or so, was,

"But she seems just like any other young girl!".

The police car drove off, and we followed. At the hospital we were met by a charge nurse who thought it best if Anna was left to settle back in by herself. And so we left, visiting time being over for the day!

Later we learned that her errant companion had been retrieved much earlier, and from then on spent his days in his pyjamas. Apparently he refused to speak to Anna, and would have nothing more to do with her. From that Sunday. Our impression was that it had been Anna who had instigated their excursion, although she remained in her usual clothes in her room.

Except that she was not so very often in her room; for when we arrived for our visits we discovered that it was empty. She wasn't there. Rather she was away visiting other patients, attending a succession of what seemed to us grim soirées in their rooms. But then sometimes her own room would be full of other patients visiting her.

Anna was turning her stay in hospital into a social round which we understood often extended late into the night. Turning it into a succession of scenes from a boarding school novel. And so by this behaviour she was beginning to dominate her hospital environment, just as she had come recently to dominate life at home.

Anna though was completely unaware that she had been admitted to hospital for assessment. As indeed were we at first. And we quickly came to realize that it wasn't only Anna who was being assessed.

On the following Thursday I had to work late. It was for a meeting of the MA group. Carol would therefore be visiting the hospital alone, even though in that first week I would still have been waiting in the car.

Anna was still very angry, and as soon as her mother arrived in her room that evening began to demand money.

The weekend was still all too fresh in her mind, and Carol

therefore thought that giving Anna more money than she already had, was not such a good idea., and so she refused. And at this Anna became furious,

"'I want some money', she said.
'Give me some money
You cow!
Get out of here!.
I don't want you here.
What kind of f----g mother are you?"'

As Carol retreated along the corridor under this onslaught, Anna pursued her, swearing and cursing.

When he heard the commotion, a charge nurse came out of the office. He had seen and heard much of what had been said in the corridor.

It was then that, as Carol told me later, she experienced an act of kindness. She said how she almost treasured it, because it was the first time that anyone had spoken to her in that humane way since Anna had been admitted.

Adrian was from a Chinese family, and as he approached Carol he was obviously concerned.

"Are you alright?" he asked her.

As she fought with her tears, she tried to explain,

"She's not usually like this!"

But Adrian didn't seem to hear, and continued,

"However have you coped with Anna in this state, Mrs Holden? But I'm not the person you should be telling. You should write all of this down".

A little earlier that evening, I was in my room at work after a day of catching up and getting things back into some kind of order. I had been occupied with seminars throughout the day.

At 5.00 I had a meeting with an MA. student, for a tutorial on her dissertation.

As she knocked on the door, I was finishing a conversation

with Mark who had rung shortly before to enquire about Anna. I rang off, with apologies.

"Sorry, Margaret, please come in!"

She was a young woman of about thirty five, in the second year of the part-time course. I knew she had young children, with a busy English department to run along with family life. Like everyone on the course, she approached her work for the higher degree with concentration and industry. I respected and liked her for that.

We sat down opposite each other on chairs, with her in the regulation visitors' armchair, and I reached for her draft chapter which I had placed on the desk that morning, and along with it my notes.

I was glancing at the notes, when I heard her say quietly,

"It happened to me also, William!"

I looked up, not having grasped fully what she had said, and asked,

"Mm, what did?" After what must have been a pause.

"I had to go into a psychiatric ward as a patient. In fact it was the same hospital. Don't be offended!"

I hesitated, as the worlds of home and work suddenly collided. All my energy seemed to be ebbing away, and I felt hopeless and tired.

She went on,

"I was eighteen. It was bad at the time, but it passed".

Above all though, I felt grateful for this confidence. For what seemed an act of extreme kindness. And I wondered how she knew about Anna.

Of course there was the fragment of the end of the telephone conversation with Mark, which she would have overheard. But that couldn't have been it. Most likely she had heard on the efficient bush-telegraph in the department – from other students.

'Who knows?', I thought.

Perhaps one of my colleagues on the course had made

some mention of it to one of the other members of the course. I had after all been away from work for some days. And the Faculty, although large, was close knit.

As she finished speaking, I looked out through the window upon the fading light on the rooftops towards the city.

"Thank you for mentioning it", was all I was able to reply; inadequately, as I tried to collect myself.

She smiled.

The details of the business of the half-hour tutorial were easily dealt with. I had only enthusiasm for her draft chapter which I had read carefully, and knew well. So I had only positive things to say.

We left together for the evening seminar downstairs. I locked my room, and we walked along the corridor to the stairs.

"Thank you again", I said, and then the conversation turned again to the evening's business, and the paper she would be giving at the meeting. And I wished her good luck.

The meeting passed quickly, as I became immersed in the work of the group of fourteen students, whom by now I knew well. All serving teachers, attending the course on their two evenings a week.

When I got home, it was around 9.15 as we had supper. Carol told me of how Anna had behaved, and of her own conversation with the charge nurse in the corridor. I told her about my meeting with Margaret.

* * *

Eleven days had passed since Anna had entered the hospital, and we were anxious to meet Dr H. again to get news about her progress; to find out what he had learned. What he thought.

She had just been home for the weekend for the first time, but we couldn't see that she seemed much different.

On the Saturday afternoon she went into Farnbury alone

to do some shopping and, she said, to meet a friend. But when she returned she was distraught, and talked of being chased by police cars. She seemed distracted still, and angry.

On Sunday she was on the telephone for much of the morning, and we left her to it, keen not to make the situation worse. We sat on our bed upstairs, chatting about how she seemed, and in truth we were glad to be out of the way. And we were discussing something that Anna had told us the previous day.

She had mentioned that she had news that Dr H. wanted to see us first thing on Monday morning. Obviously this had been what we had hoped for, but why had he or someone else at the hospital not contacted us to arrange the meeting? How could we know the time of it, or where it was to be? Anna said that she had no knowledge of these details.

She seemed vague, and said simply that we had to be at the hospital at 9 o'clock on Monday morning. Carol had rung the hospital on Saturday afternoon, but there was no-one who could confirm that we were expected. Nobody seemed to even understand the question, or why we were asking it.

We decided that we must be there whatever. So Carol rang her employer to say that she'd be late in, and I contacted my head of department at home, to explain that we needed to be at the hospital early on Monday, and that I would therefore be delayed in the morning.

Anna returned to hospital on Sunday evening at 6.00, morose and reluctant; and we were there the following morning at a quarter to nine.

We found a nurse by knocking on the office door, and explained that we believed that we had an appointment with Dr H. that morning, but that we were not sure of the time, or where we should meet him. And although the nurse said she didn't know about the meeting, we were shown into the patients' common room which was empty. It was a sad and soiled public area, dilapidated and with exhausted furniture.

We sat down and waited. Uncertain, but expectant.

After half an hour Carol asked me, "Do you think we should check again? Nobody seems very certain that we're even expected!"

So I walked out into the corridor and found another nurse eventually, who promised to try to find out what was happening. I returned to the common room, and the minutes ticked by, but no-one came.

At 10.15, when we had been at the hospital for an hour and a half, a brisk woman, a nurse, appeared and said simply,

"Will you come with me please?" Just that. Polite and to the point.

But we were relieved. We were expected after all. As we followed her our spirits rose; and we were optimistic suddenly that at last we could discuss Anna's progress with the psychiatrist who had visited us on the 4th October. Elated almost, and feeling grateful that we would at last be meeting him again – for the first time since he had come to the house.

We arrived at a set of double wooden doors, and were shown into a very large room.

Dr H. was there … but he was not alone. He sat facing us in the centre of a semi-circle of six or seven other people, arranged either side of him. And Anna was also there sitting in front of them – a little to one side.

And directly in front of this assembly, were two empty chairs. These were for us. Although there were no formal introductions, and although at the time we had no understanding at all of its significance, we were being introduced to "the team". We later learned that this was a ward-round meeting.

Dr H. got up, and spoke,

"Oh do come in Mr and Mrs Holden, please come in!" he said, as we entered the room struggling with a complete astonishment.

"Thank you for coming. Please sit down".

After we had sat down on the two empty chairs, Dr. H

continued, but very precisely,

"We would like to hear about your weekend together. Anna will speak first, and then we would like to hear from you Mrs Holden, and then from Mr Holden".

As he spoke, and as we nodded our understanding of what he had said, my head was clearing, and my astonishment at our being in front of this assembly had largely dissipated. Carol touched my hand, as we sat next to each other.

The consultant psychiatrist continued,

"If at any point, as you speak to us, Anna does not want you to continue, you must stop".

My surprise returned when I heard this further instruction, and as I looked around at the impassive faces flanking the doctor. I remember just that I determined upon a need to be concise in what I would say. To try not to display the uncertainty that was still engulfing us both, in the face of what felt like an arraignment.

"So", Dr H. continued, "Anna, can we hear from you please?"

She spoke very clearly, about going shopping to Farnbury on the previous Saturday. And she spoke of her time at home on the Sunday. She went on,

"I didn't see much of mum and dad, because they were in the bedroom for most of the time".

I winced slightly at this, as I looked at the unsmiling faces all around. I felt Carol also stiffen at what Anna had just said.

After a short while, Anna finished, and so it was Carol's turn.

She began by speaking of how Anna had returned from Farnbury on the Saturday, anxious and in disarray because she thought that police cars were following her.

Suddenly, Anna sprang to her feet,

"Right!", she said. "That's it. I don't want her to carry on. Get her to stop!"

I looked at Carol, at Anna on her feet, and at the watchful

faces in front of us.

Carol stopped immediately, and said nothing more.

Anna continued,

"I want my dad to speak!"

"Perhaps, Mr Holden, you could tell us about your weekend ?" the psychiatrist then said, as Anna sat down again.

At that point, in spite of Anna's interruptions, and the faces, I was quite clear how I would describe the events of the weekend. After all there was very little to tell; and in any case I would simply do as I had been asked.

And so I began. "When Anna came back from Farnbury quite distraught and worried, she seemed concerned about police cars".

I continued,

"We were discussing that in our room on Sunday morning while Anna was on the telephone".

Anna stood up again.

"Okay, I want him to stop!"

Dr H. then thanked us, and asked us to leave, which we did. Anna remained.

We were now outside the room again, with the large double doors closed behind us. We could not have been in there for more than ten minutes. And now, stunned, we stood outside in the corridor.

Carol turned to me, and asked quizzically,

"Now what do we do?"

Someone, perhaps a nurse, was passing, and I quickly introduced myself and explained why we were standing there. I said that we had been in the meeting, and then I asked her if were expected to wait, because we were completely at a loss. Could she please find out if we should stay to speak to Dr H. when the meeting finished?

She looked nonplussed and said she didn't know. She left to enquire, though not in the room we had just left.

After a short while, she returned to tell us,

"No, you're not expected to stay!"

Just that! And so we left.

Whatever the many surprising characteristics of that meeting on the 17th October, it introduced us to one principle that was to govern all our dealings with the hospital. This principle was never to be departed from. It is simply stated, although it only became fully apparent to us very gradually.

It was that we were not permitted to speak to any doctor, or to any member of the hospital team, without Anna's permission. When we requested a meeting or information, we were always asked immediately if we had consulted Anna.

This interpretation of the primacy of "patient confidentiality" was one that Anna came to embrace; and she was, from that meeting on, insistent that she would not give permission for us to discuss her progress with any doctor, or anyone connected with the hospital, unless she was present. And she refused that also.

The reason that we found this requirement immediately so difficult was that we had naïvely assumed, and truly believed, that we had important information which was relevant to the hospital's treatment of Anna; and we had also important questions that we needed to ask hospital staff. But none of that mattered. Whatever information we thought we had to offer privately, and whatever questions we had to put, were not a priority for anyone but us.

In repeatedly seeking information, a kind of access, and a necessary permission, all of which were always refused, the enchantments of life were gradually banished. And we became slowly informed rather by a sense that we needed to defend ourselves – though we were not sure from what.

So, within these terms, our evening and weekend visits to the hospital to see Anna continued. But a few days after the meeting on the 17th October, one evening Anna again asked, on the telephone, for me to remain in the car when we visited that evening. And I had to agree, however unwillingly.

When we arrived at the hospital, and Carol went in, Anna

asked her immediately, “Do you want me home?”

Carol’s reply when confronted by the question was not measured nor diplomatic; at the time we neither of us had enough energy for politic responses. And so she said directly,

“Not while you’re in this state, Anna, no I don’t”.

At this, Anna began shouting, chanting almost:

“She doesn’t want me home,
She doesn’t want me home -
The bitch!”

Carol’s response was, “Anna, I’m not putting up with this! I’m going to find a nurse”.

But there was no-one around, and she came outside to the car, quietly crying to herself. As she left the room, Anna had followed her down the corridor, swearing and cursing.

A short while later, Anna had been in the patients’ recreation room at some point during the day. She told us that Dr H. was also there:

“Oh you!” she called out
Across the room,
“Dr H,
Come over here!”

Apparently he replied,

“‘No, Anna,
You come over here.
I don’t think you have a problem
With examinations, Anna.
I think it’s relationships
You have a problem with!’”

When Anna told her mother of this incident, she had added,

“He can’t speak to me like that, I’m f----g clever I am!”

And she said this with a prosaic, and incredulous, seriousness.

Carol was beginning to realize that while Anna was like this, it was useless to reply.

One morning, soon afterwards, Anna was not dressed, not ready for a visit from Dr H.. When he realized this as he arrived, he said:

"Oh, so you don't want to
Speak to me Anna.
Very well, I'll see you next week!"
"No! No! I'll speak to you now",
And she ran after him.
"That's alright Anna,
I'll see you next week".
And he left.

When she spoke to Carol of this incident, Anna confided to her, gravely, confidentially,

"I'm too beautiful to be in here
Everybody says so.
They say,
What's a young girl like you
Doing in here?
It's not right!".

When Carol described this incident to me, she was crying quietly, softly; sobbing lightly to herself. And as I saw this, I thought how she was learning so many new and different ways to cry. How misery may have many textures.

On 24th October, Anna's "section" became voluntary. We only came to know this because Anna told us. She had agreed to stay in hospital, and less than a week before being discharged, she was moved upstairs to a small dormitory. To share with three much older patients.

There were no locks

On the bathroom door upstairs,
Unsurprisingly.
And it was always noisy.
Anna couldn't stand that.

Downstairs, being observed, assessed,
She was never in her room.
The one she had to herself.
Surprisingly.
Or more often it was full of her
New friends.
A very special soirée.
And a bit like a boarding school.

Upstairs though, here,
She shared.
"They banged their heads,
Muttering.
Shouting out in their sleep."

Every afternoon before we left for our visit, and also after we returned in the evening, Anna rang Carol. And she rang often during the day when Carol was working at home.

On 2nd November, I answered the telephone. And she seemed different. Changed. Somehow calmer.

Friday 9th November was Anna's 18th birthday, and she came home for the weekend, Carol had asked members of the choir to arrange a party for her at the village pub. She had spoken to the landlord about a bottle of champagne and sandwiches; and she ordered a large cake from a local events' shop.

We didn't attend; the evening was just for Anna and her friends. Though she was very reluctant to go.

This was the choir, some members of which in the summer had walked through the kitchen as we sat talking, sometimes speaking to us as they went through, sometimes not. On their way upstairs to Anna's room. Always urged on by Anna, "It's okay. Just go through!"

One member, a young man, had rung the bell one weekend that summer, calling on Anna. When I opened the door to him, he had announced:

"I thought I'd call on Anna, and see her parents for myself!"

He was about eighteen, and his name was Rob. I didn't respond to his comment, but simply showed him into the living room. At the end of the garden the church spire gleamed in the afternoon sun, at the top of the field. And Carol went upstairs to tell Anna that she had a visitor.

While we waited for Anna in the sitting room, Rob walked across to our somewhat ancient hi-fi system, and peered down at it dubiously. He went to the record cabinet and took out an LP, and placed it on the turntable. Then he fiddled, at some length, with the balance and the tone controls, before sitting down opposite me on the settee – from where he stared back at me defiantly. I gazed back, wondering; but not so surprised, for this was simply a part of the nature of that summer.

When Anna came in, I left them to it.

Just as friends of Anna's had come suddenly unannounced, and announcing, into our home back then, now we found ourselves meeting her new acquaintances in the hospital, just as unexpectedly and reluctantly.

One of the closest of these new friends was Sharon. And one late afternoon, Carol and I were sitting in the hospital canteen chatting with Anna, when Sharon came in with her mother.

They joined us, and as we all sat together, Sharon showed us a drawing she had in her hand, which she had produced in the occupational therapy class from which she had just come. It was a drawing of the head of a horse. She asked Carol what she thought of it.

Mindful of the plight of the tall sallow girl who had just

joined us, Carol praised the drawing. Sharon was in hospital because she had some kind of depressive illness; Anna said it was 'clinical depression'. The drawing was obviously competently done; but was stylized in a way that these kinds of drawings often are.

As always Carol wanted to be encouraging, and so perhaps because she was tired also, and rather without thinking, she said,

"Have you ever thought of applying for entry to an Art School?"

It was a comment which she almost immediately regretted, for the girl turned aggressively upon her mother.

"See!", she exclaimed, "Anna's mother thinks I should go to Art School!"

The comment was boastful. Defiant.

Sharon's mother was a older than us, in her late fifties; but looked older still. Indeed, she looked exhausted. Worn down. Anna told, us a little later, that she had three other children – all sons. And that the family had a farm.

Carol had only meant to be encouraging. Now she felt uncomfortable at having added to the woman's suffering.

The other mother smiled a very tired smile. She said nothing immediately, but simply gazed at Carol. It was a look of resignation mixed with pity. Later, in the following year, Anna would tell Carol that Sharon's mother had killed herself. She had left a note, Anna said, and a car.

When she had read the note, Sharon had told Anna,

"We never knew she felt like that!" And later she drove around in her mother's car.

On 12th November Dr. H. rang us at home. It was the first time we had spoken since the ward round meeting at the hospital, although I had written, unsuccessfully requesting a meeting on a number of occasions. I answered the phone.

He asked me if we were willing to have Anna home for good. Of course I agreed.

And so it was that Anna came home to us that November.

When I collected her from the hospital one evening, she was sitting in the lobby on the stairs; alone and with her suitcase beside her. There was no-one for us to speak to as we left.

Chapter 20

I was standing, again, one morning at the window of the living room. Looking out on the back garden. Watching a pair of blue-tits, and their journeys to and from a nesting-box.

They made their cautious broken journeys to the box which I had placed high up in an ornamental cherry tree. The tree had been a gift from me and the children to Carol, one Mothering Sunday many years before.

Anna had made the nesting-box in occupational therapy classes at the hospital. She had attended them for some months after returning to us.

Her return occasioned the beginning of a series of broken journeys for Carol and me also. The details of these journeys would take another lifetime to record and understand. As if either were possible, for they are not yet completed.

But to return to the story.

The day after she came back home, and over breakfast, Anna asked us,

"Would you like family meetings?"

We had no idea what she meant.

She explained that the hospital wanted us all to meet there on an afternoon every week. For a year.

We still weren't sure what this could mean, and what was expected of us. The uncertainty was the same as back in October when she had told us that Dr H. expected us to meet him at the hospital on that Monday morning.

Now, as then, the suggestion was put to us by Anna, and not by medical staff or any other member of the hospital team. Now, as then, the suggestion was surrounded by uncertainty and doubt. Now, as then, we had a simple choice to make: "Yes" or "No."

Of course we eventually agreed; because as we reasoned, perhaps it would help. Perhaps we would receive some information about what the hospital thought was causing Anna's difficulties. Perhaps it would help us all.

We didn't decide immediately. I was very sceptical at first. Reluctant. But Carol talked me round.

A little afterwards Anna said to her mother,

"I knew you'd agree. You want them to think we're a problem family don't you!"

And so the meetings began, though they would actually only last until the following May.

They were, from the beginning, very structured. Stylized. Run by Gwen, a young female behavioural psychologist, they were also surprisingly painful – and for yet more surprising reasons.

Gwen was never without her clipboard, and often raised her eyebrows in conversation, particularly when I said anything. Jack, a psychiatric social worker also attended each meeting. We fitted the meetings around our work commitments; not always very easily.

Gwen also met Anna at the hospital at a different time every week. Just for an hour. Just the two of them.

Our meetings lasted an hour also, and were always divided into two parts. About halfway through, Gwen and Jack would withdraw for ten minutes, leaving the three of us alone together.

At the end of each meeting we would be set small tasks for next time. For instance, that we should all sit down all together for a meal; or that we should go shopping together on a Saturday morning; or that we should sit together and talk about how to consider each others' wishes.

We often felt bewildered at the assumptions Gwen was making about our family life. Puzzled because she obviously didn't realize that we usually did these things anyway. At least we believed we did; though getting Anna to sit down for the last one was not as easy as it might sound. We hadn't been successful with that recently.

Inevitably, during the fifth or sixth meeting, at the point in the afternoon when we were to be set our tasks for the week, I pointed out as tactfully as I could that much of what she was asking us to do were things which were normal for us anyway. I forget the specific task that prompted this response.

At the same time, and no doubt out of some frustration, I asked Gwen about the theoretical underpinning of these meetings. I suppose I was keen to discover what lay behind her preoccupations and assumptions in setting us these tasks. My question was not intended to cause avoidable conflict. And perhaps I could have put the question better.

But I learned, unsurprisingly perhaps, given the evidence from the meetings so far, that this challenge was not helpful. And indeed was very unwelcome. From that moment Gwen's eyebrows were almost permanently raised.

I recall, how some time before, as early as the second meeting, after we had been set our tasks for the week and were leaving together, Anna remarked in a loud voice, though thankfully only when we were outside,

"Silly cow! Doesn't she realize that's what we do anyway?"

But this wasn't really a question, and it was not in our interests for us to respond to it. The reason we attended these meetings was that we had little option; quite simply we depended upon the professional skill of Gwen and Jack.

Then Anna suddenly announced that she wouldn't attend them any more. This was potentially very serious. We had been told that they could not continue without Anna, and they were our only contact with the hospital.

Perhaps in an attempt to encourage Anna to keep coming, Jack ran the meetings without Gwen present, and this seemed to work. Anna still came. But then a slightly different pattern emerged. She began not to turn up without giving any notice.

When she failed to appear the second time, and because as I've said they could not proceed without her presence and permission, the meetings ceased finally. She continued, however to see Gwen by herself every week.

On the first occasion that Anna did not arrive, and as the meeting therefore almost immediately broke up, Jack remarked to us, quietly as we left, and out of the blue,

"All I can say is that we don't necessarily believe everything that Anna tells us".

By now our threshold for being surprised was pretty high, but nonetheless as we drove home we wondered and discussed what he could be referring too. Of course I asked him at the time what he meant, but he'd say nothing further. Inexplicably, I felt grateful for this smallest of confidences; though we were still just as helpless as before.

Then he repeated this assurance a second time, as the final family meeting broke up without Anna; and then it entered our consciousness for ever.

And so our own link with the hospital was severed. And just as we could not speak to Jack or Gwen officially, or unofficially, without Anna's permission, so we continued to have no success in our attempts to speak to Dr. H. face to face. We failed to achieve a private meeting with him from that very first day when he had come to our home.

Our requests, whether on the telephone or by letter, were always refused; and the reason was becoming clear. Anna did not wish it. When on one occasion, on the telephone, I asked for a meeting, Dr H. said, with polished politeness,

"When you speak to Gwen and Jack you are speaking to me!"

At the end of the year following her discharge from the hospital, when I had made another request to see him, this time by letter, he wrote back briefly, promptly, and courteously, thanking me for writing.

His reply began by saying that he assumed that we had spoken to Anna about our request; although it was because of her continuing disarray that I had written. The letter went on to say that he understood from Gwen and Jack that she was doing very well. Further, he wrote that because he hadn't seen Anna for some time, he felt that there was little point in our meeting.

But we needed information and help, to know how we could support Anna; not least in how she should best approach choosing a career. How could school be replaced? And how could her lost expectations upon leaving it be replaced?

Immediately after her discharge, and as she was still attending the hospital periodically as an outpatient, Anna decided that she wanted to be a nurse. The hospital team encouraged her in this, although we were privately doubtful that this choice of career was realistic. Naturally we did not express our doubts to Anna. Nor to anyone else.

Some years later, Anna would show us a copy of an open testimonial to support this application for nursing training, written jointly and signed by Dr H., Gwen and Jack.

The college to which she applied asked for a report from the Senior Partner at our local surgery, Dr. T..

The doctor had already provided us with a brief letter when Anna had come out of hospital. It spoke of behavioural disturbance during mock 'A' level examinations, and it mentioned that Dr H. believed that there was no evidence of mental illness. It ended by saying that when Anna was discharged, the "team were unanimous in the decision that she had no need of medication".

Carol went with Anna on the day of her interview at the nurses' training college, which was not near where we lived, nor in London. This was a time when the training of nurses was being re-organized nationally. The college was further down in the centre of the county, and Anna was insistent upon choosing it.

The result of the interview was that no offer of a place on the course was made.

And so we had to help Anna somehow to find herself a career; and yet as we did so, we had in our minds Dr T's warning, that

"There should be no more examinations!"

* * *

During the next five years, Anna left home twice and she returned twice. She seemed desperate to leave, perhaps because Claire had done so just in the normal course of things. Her sister shared a student flat, and that was a very big thing for Anna.

Soon after she came home from the hospital, we began to get a series of telephone messages from adult voices asking to speak to her. We would answer the telephone to discover that the callers would only to speak to Anna.

At first, when they learned that Anna wasn't around, they simply rang off.

But the calls continued, and eventually the callers relented and they began to give us messages to pass on, which naturally we did. It was then that we learned that these calls were from the managers of local hostels for young people. Anna had asked the hospital team to arrange hostel accommodation for her.

In the event she did not accept a hostel place, but rather she joined a placement in Langley, at a school for children with learning difficulties. This was something that she arranged for herself. But things didn't work out, and she left.

At around this time, as her course at the Academy was coming to an end, Claire received an invitation to continue with postgraduate study of the oboe in Cologne; and we encouraged her to accept it. Her teachers were enthusiastic about the idea, and we were relieved that she was making her way. We would miss her, but I set about helping her in making applications for funding, and scholarships.

It was just after Claire left for Germany that Anna left home for the first time. When she did so, she stripped her room completely bare. Everything was removed. But as I mentioned, the job with the children did not work out, and she returned home after about three months.

The work she arranged next, was at a centre for mentally disadvantaged adults, where she again had a small flat. However this job also came to an abrupt end, and she returned home. She then organized for herself a job at a nursing home for the elderly.

This was very difficult to reach by public transport, and the hours were long. So we lent her the money for a second-hand Škoda car. So that she could get to work, and return less tired.

A mechanic, we knew, came to the house periodically to keep a close eye on it. To make sure that it was always safe and roadworthy.

We were right at the beginning of a sequence of jobs begun over decades by Anna. And ended. Some very quickly. Some not so quickly.

One day, a little after she had begun at the nursing home, Anna told us that the matron had said to her,

"Right, I think the time has come for you to see a dead body!"

Could this really be true? we wondered.

We were simply unable to decide. Just as we couldn't decide whether the school doctor had really asked her whether she had considered killing herself, as she had claimed. We just couldn't know.

The mention of the matron's statement at the care home was around the time of Dr H's reply to my letter. With all of this going on in the background, with the matter of a suitable career or occupation for Anna unresolved, we could draw no comfort from his assurance that Anna was "doing very well". We could see that she was not, and further that she was being ground down by physical tiredness, if by nothing else.

During the year following her discharge, in the summer, I received an invitation to talk at a conference in Taiwan, which naturally I had to decline. I did however accept two other invitations, much nearer home. This was work. I was expected to accept these offers from other institutions, especially if they were for events in the summer.

Unfortunately these periodic invitations, though flattering, did nothing to contribute to the family budget. I would just receive a small fee, along with travel and accommodation costs.

One I accepted was at a conference for head teachers in Wales; and the other was to read a paper at a teacher educators' conference in Osnabrück. Luckily the dates were very close together. A week contained them both, and I could be home again.

Yet it would be misleading if I denied that the demands of that week did not come to me as a relief. It was only work, but work was important too! It was encouraging to have to meet specific demands, perhaps even successfully. Even, to be honest, the attraction of these goals was that they were not determined by Anna's seemingly endless difficulties. They were short term, and might actually be met.

When I got home to Carol, it was with a renewed determination that Anna's disclosure about the matron and dead bodies was something that we had to address; though quite how was another question. Somehow we had to help Anna to find a career choice that was suitable, and had more optimistic outcomes.

And then an opportunity presented itself as a result of Carol's friendship with the owner of a nursery for young children. A friend who was a client at the Chillingstone office where Carol worked. Marion offered Anna a job, on condition that she prepared herself for the necessary on-the-job qualifications.

Three years after leaving hospital, Anna had met Steve, though it would be another five years before they would marry. At the time of their meeting, Anna was going through a calm time, and seemed generally more settled.

Steve was about to begin a three year Business Studies course in Southampton, and she visited him there several times during that first term.

When he returned for a sandwich-year working at a national brewing firm in London, they seemed happy together.

All she had wanted, we reasoned, was someone for herself. And now she had settled into her job at Marion's nursery.

But then the time came for Steve to return to Southampton for his final year. And Anna began to unravel again.

On the day that he left she sat down, crossed-legged, in the middle of the road outside our house. She refused to move for ten minutes as traffic slowed and picked its way around her. She shouted, and wailed and cursed. And said that Steve was deserting her.

After his departure, Anna's demeanour worsened. She behaved in the house increasingly like an occupying army of one. Sometimes I felt that there was no part of the small house to which we could escape. Our experience with the hospital meant that we could not even feel the optimism of that earlier time; buoyed up as we were then by a confidence that we eventually would get the advice we needed.

Now it was quite usual for Anna to burst into the living room without warning, where I might be listening to music, and simply turn off the player.

"I don't know how many times I have to tell you!", she would rail,

"I don't want to listen to that rubbish!"

Or she would suddenly jump up and switch off a programme we were all watching together on the television, simply because she didn't like it. And she began to do this repeatedly.

It was clear that things were building again towards a crisis; and with it our despair was returning.

In this fresh time of unreason, she demanded of Carol,

"'You should have stopped me
Sucking my thumb
When I was small.
Why didn't you?
How do you think it will feel for me
Waking up next to my boyfriend
With my fingers in my mouth?
You are such shit parents!'"

When these outbursts occurred, Anna would smile during them. As if she was noting their effects.

But now Marion intervened, and she did so directly and insistently, breaking into Anna's hurrying descent into a new and violent turmoil.

In the time that she and Steve had known each other, Anna had decided to change her GP., to one just a little further away. It was a move to the practice used by Steve's family. We thought this was a good decision, though we had to remain with our practice. We made certain, however, that when we needed to consult a doctor, we saw Dr S..

One evening, a little time after Steve had left for Southampton again, Marion insisted that she and Anna visit the new doctor together. Perhaps Anna's mounting difficulties were becoming clear at work, and no doubt Marion guessed at the situation at home. She certainly knew that all the time Anna refused us permission, we couldn't consult a doctor on her behalf.

Whatever the reason for Marion acting, it was perhaps because of this new authority in her life that Anna agreed to go with her employer to the new doctor.

At the surgery, Anna apparently made a tremendous fuss. Ranting and shouting at Dr B..

After the meeting, that same evening, Dr B. rang us at home. This was a quite new development. Truthfully, it was a revolution! Carol answered the phone, but before she had time to say much, Anna walked into the room and attempted to grab it. The conversation could not therefore continue, and Carol had to ring off. The familiar pattern was becoming re-established.

After that, partly in explanation of what had happened that evening, I wrote a long letter to Dr. B.. I did so because it felt it important that we should not allow Anna, yet again, to prevent us getting her the help that she needed. My letter dealt in detail with the time that she had spent in hospital, the time before, and the years since.

And then, no doubt because of Marion's influence and no-nonsense approach, Anna agreed to visit the doctor once more, this time with Carol; who witnessed again the aggression and rudeness that Anna had so often displayed. Now in a new setting.

But at last, Anna had a GP. who seemed willing to speak to us at the same time as speaking to her. And she agreed to continue to see him.

He would be able to observe, I reasoned, the nature and results of Anna's difficulties for himself. And it was by reminding her of this, that I tried to comfort Carol later that evening. To try to stem her tears when she described Anna's anger at the doctor's response to her question,

"Will I have to go into hospital again?"

His reply had been,

"Well yes Anna, unless you gain control of yourself and your situation, that is possible".

Two days later, I received a written reply to my letter. Here was a doctor who was actually willing to write a letter to us! In it he promised to do everything he could to help, and said that he had held a number of meetings with colleagues already about Anna. He said that he had carefully reviewed her notes, and the information I had provided in my letter. And then his letter ended with a familiar emphasis:

> *"You will be aware that I am unable to enter into any correspondence, or conversation, with you about Anna's medical state, without her express written permission. I trust that you will understand that I take this matter very seriously, and will do my best to procure a satisfactory outcome".*

And so we were definitely not simply back where we were before; we had made some progress. This GP's approach was very different to Dr P's. He had rung us, and written, and actually spoken to us; and seemed genuinely anxious to help. Also Anna now had an employer who knew about her problems, and was also more than willing to take positive steps to help her. Because of the friendship with Carol.

These were reasons for optimism. They offered new possibilities. Gave us renewed energy to press Anna to give us the written permission that the doctor's letter referred to. The permission which she had always denied us.

At first she flatly rejected the idea, telling us that it wasn't any of our business, and that we had no right to talk to the doctor. This refusal, along with the angry tirades that accompanied it, lasted for a week.

Then, one evening, she burst into the dining room where I was sitting, and said to me,

"Alright you dictate the letter, and I'll sign it. I'm missing Steve!"

Hardly able to believe what she had said, I had to refuse this sudden offer.

Trying to sound unconcerned, I replied,

"Yes, I understand, but I can't write the letter. If you want us to have it, you must write it. You have to give your own permission. I can't do it for you".

"Okay then, you won't get it!" she shouted, and she left the room – slamming the door as she left.

Eventually though, and almost to our astonishment, she did write the letter – though she didn't give it to us immediately. Rather on two occasions, she came up to me with it in her hand, dangling it before me; holding it out to me, before withdrawing it and leaving the room laughing.

Finally, late one Thursday evening she came upstairs to where I was finishing some work task, and threw the letter on to the floor beside me, before leaving the room. For some seconds I left it where it had fallen, not daring to pick it up in case she returned and demanded its return. But the door stayed shut.

'*At last!*' I thought.

After nearly six years we could now speak openly to a doctor, with some chance of getting help for Anna. Could this really be possible?

When the appointment was made with Dr B., we decided that I should go alone. Carol had already met him, and it was I who had written. But more importantly it was imperative that every second of the appointment should be used to gain the doctor's professional opinion, advice, and support. We wanted to avoid those unnecessary diversions which can so easily occur in conversations between three people.

This decision, which might appear so over cautious, was prompted and guided by our mounting despair about Anna's condition. We had a sense that this was another chance, but very likely a final one.

Her terror seemed to be returning. And so was our own. Her manner was becoming detached. And she was adopting ways of speaking, of shrieking, which presented statements as if she were a client of her own advocacy. As when she insisted,

"This girl needs understanding!"

At this time Carol and I had lain in bed chatting about these new developments. And as we examined them, Carol said,

"You know, Will. I feel so scared sometimes".

And after a pause she continued,

"I'm scared of getting old. We've got to live into old age".

I turned to look at my wife, who certainly still looked young to me in spite of everything. And I tried to re-assure her.

"But we're not old", was all I could say.

However she seemed not to have heard me,

"There'll be no one to protect us", she continued.

Although I recognized the fear she was expressing, I said,

"They'll be Claire, perhaps". This was inadequate, and not what I really meant.

"Oh, but she'll have a life of her own".

And I couldn't, at that time, think of anything more to say to her. To try to comfort her.

But still, Anna had written the letter, and there was enough that was different in her responses, and in those of the new doctor, to give us hope again. Above all, perhaps, there were the residual effects of Marion's direct interventions.

We could never know the full details of these. We only got a sense that they were being made at work. From small things that Marion and Anna said from time to time.

When I walked into his consulting room, I discovered that the Scottish doctor was just as his letter had indicated: softly spoken, meticulous and very straightforward in his manner.

The meeting lasted half an hour and as soon as I could, I pressed him for his opinion, which he gave clearly and openly. The tone and content of his answer were careful and measured,

"Well from what I've seen from reading her notes, and from what I've observed, and now from what I've learned from you, I think Anna exhibits massive hysteria, which overlays a personality disorder of some kind".

He continued,

"I think her only hope is to meet an older, kindly, man. In the meantime ...", and here he smiled, "keep your cheque book handy!"

As I left his consulting room that evening, I thanked him for his time and efforts; and we shook hands. As he showed me out, he added,

"I will do everything I possibly can. But just remember that this Wednesday will not come again. Remember your own lives!"

As I drove the short distance home, I felt more optimistic than at any time since Anna had left hospital. Comforted, somehow, by the balm of the doctor's promise. Eager to tell Carol of the outcome of the meeting.

To cheer her with hope.

Chapter 21

(i)

The new doctor was as good as his word.

He quickly arranged for a psychiatric nurse to visit the house. And he referred Anna to a counsellor at a nearby Mental Health Centre, who wrote to her within a week.

When the nurse came to visit he actually had very little to say to us, spending the time with Anna. As we were showing him out, he said simply,

"This will take a long time".

That was all, and then he was gone; taking some of our newly discovered optimism with him.

When Anna visited the Health Centre, she found that her counsellor was a woman. She decided that she didn't want her counselling sessions to be run by a woman.

Everything depended upon Anna making and keeping these appointments. But she refused.

And so we were left only with the nurse's prediction.

Anna was in charge of events again, though she was not in charge of herself.

Uncertainty and doubts came to be woven into the decades that were to follow; our remaining decades.

This uncertainty took many forms, had varying levels of intensity, and would often engulf us. It was flavoured by Anna claiming not to being able to remember, when friends or members of the family referred in passing conversation to painful things she had said and done.

If, among all its wonders, life is inevitably a sad song, I had always been optimistic that the sadness could be deferred. And at least it was a song. But we could never quite have anticipated the nature of the undomestic possibilities which Anna's struggles would present to us.

Her moods swung between a docile over-dependency with an incessant need for re-assurance, and uncontrollable rage at being with us. At times she would appear happy and relaxed; but later we wondered if when she had seemed most happy she was really at her most depressed.

It was most noticeable that her physical state oscillated; as she rapidly gained and then lost weight over just a few months.

When Steve left again for Southampton to begin his third year, Anna visited him a couple of times before Christmas. However that Autumn her erratic and distressed behaviour grew in intensity again, until it settled back into a familiar pattern. Or so it appeared to us. Her anger was expressed mainly in a renewed obsession with leaving home, and an insistence upon staying; although in truth neither she nor we had an alternative solution. And so her anger was born of rejection and dependency alike.

Steve came home for Christmas. And when he left for Southampton again in the January, he left behind an ultimatum for Anna. He said that he wanted to concentrate upon his course, and didn't want to see her before it was finished. And she gave us this news in wild desperation.

She claimed again that he was deserting her. And privately Carol and I thought the relationship was over: and that he had had enough.

As he left our house, for what we thought was the last time that January, he was sobbing quietly and regularly. I walked home with him offering what comfort I could, with an arm around his shoulder.

Spring and Summer that year were difficult. But we managed to settle into a regular work-pattern again; adjusting to Anna's demands as best we could as our experience of them increased.

Then, at the beginning of July, Steve returned as he had said he would.

He and Anna moved into a small house together in early March the following year. Soon afterwards they became engaged, and were married in October 1998. Their first child was born in March 2005; a little boy, who came into the world smiling – heart breakingly. On a cold day, as a light snow fell from the sky.

Thus should have begun the very best of Anna's and her young husband's domestic possibilities.

But Anna's crises increased during these years, and seven months later came the diagnosis that she was suffering from bi-polar disorder. The illness at this stage was managed by her new health authority; not by hospitalization but by a psychiatric team visiting her at home.

Her second child was born on Valentine's Day in 2008; and then in the summer, two years later, she was again admitted to a psychiatric hospital. This was a slow and harrowing process for everyone, although we were not directly involved in the decision or the process. In the end she went into hospital voluntarily; supported by two young woman friends of her own age.

By now, Anna and her small family had moved into a slightly larger house in Westerford, a town which I had I thought that I had left forever, but which now I would visit very regularly again with Carol in the years that followed.

Our earlier uncertainty continued but now it was differently composed. The original questions and doubts were replaced by others, immediately Anna was diagnosed as suffering from a mental illness rather than being seemingly simply unwell.

Previously many of our assumptions had rested upon Dr H's insistence that he had found no evidence of mental illness in Anna. Surprising as we had thought that conclusion, we were cheered by it; and it had become the platform upon which we had built our lives. Now that platform had been dismantled finally, and now there were very young children to consider.

With the diagnosis came the prescription of a combination of different sorts of medication, which she resisted taking. She said that they made her fat. It is true that it took a while to get the balance of these drugs right. And of course ideally it would have been best if she could have done without them.

The new psychiatrist struggled to meet Anna's demands by reducing the doses gradually. Yet it became obvious, as the months and years passed, that when she was suffering from an 'episode' it was only the medication that enabled her, and her family, to experience any shred of harmony in their lives. Anything that resembled peace; anything offering a space to think. To live.

Yet when the news of Anna's diagnosis sank in, I couldn't help reflecting what all our lives might have been like had Dr H. diagnosed Anna's condition all those years before. Could he indeed have acted out of a cautious humanity, and a necessary optimism? How would Anna's life have turned out had he not decided as he did?

"Maybe Dr H. thought he could delay the worst possibilities. Mitigate them.

And I thought almost immediately also, what my own life as a child would have been like without the foster home. It is difficult to imagine, given Anna's state and attitude at the time, that it would have been possible for her to find any kind of hopeful occupation, any sort of career. And marriage? And a family life?

We all need miracles, indeed we depend upon them; and miracles are not always so easy to recognize. They may come in unexpected forms.

As I reflected upon these things, it was to confirm to myself at least, that what I wanted for both our children was the warmth and colour, the harmony and the wonder, that I had found in my own childhood. After all, it was that which had made love possible, and above all I wanted it for

Claire and Anna. After childhood, with adolescence comes the need for the guidance and the altruism of education in schools. Carol and I had surely recognized that also, and striven to make it possible, year by year.

Yet it had always been at Carol that Anna had directed her venom; and, as I have said, it was upon her that the greatest majority of our daughter's impossible demands fell. If my supposition about Dr. H's optimism was correct, they would be the price. And for me to describe the details of these fully, as I have tried to explain, would take another lifetime. Or even longer. And what would be the point?

Of course the two of us had expected and hoped to grow old together, but it was Anna who turned this into something menacing. Back in 1990, she had shrieked in her torment,

"One day you'll be old, and then you'll see. You have one week to put this right!"

Her stipulation of a week was a grim irony, though at the time she would probably have thought it generous. Perhaps the grimmer irony still, was that throughout so much of the time we had, we so often believed that putting it right was possible. That our naïve assumption in the fish and chip shop at the end of the High Street, about life returning to what it had been, could ever have been justified.

In making this comment at eighteen, Anna was referring specifically to having a flat. And she had gone on, when we tried to explain that we were not in a position to provide one,

"You're just old. You're just pathetic old people. I've got my whole life in front of me!"

At this time Carol was not quite forty six, and I was forty nine.

In truth Claire's flat in term time, in Marylebone near the Academy, with Sophie and Sophie's violin was not much of a place, but Anna provided her own commentary upon it. Spitting out,

"I hate her,
She's got everything I want.
I want a flat.
You took me out of school
And ruined my life,
You bastard!
Call yourself f----g parents?
You're f-----g useless!"

I recalled how at the first hospital, we had not mentioned the violence at home when speaking to the care assistants, or Jack, or Gwen. Better we thought, and resolved continually, that they should think ill of us than Anna. For if they knew more of the details of what was going on at home, they might be less inclined to help her.

How often did we find ourselves, during that time, saying to whoever might listen,

"She's not normally like this. She will be astonished when she realizes!"

What we were remembering then, of course, was Anna as a child, the one in the photograph that Dr H. held in his hand for so long when he visited our home before going into the living room at the back.

From that moment, it was we who would be astonished.

So, on occasions, we came to view eventual old age through the prism of the psychological dominance which Anna had established. A dominance over us that was built upon our attempts to achieve help and support for her.

We came to sense, and anticipate, a peculiar fear of old age in addition to the usual ones. And always it was Carol who most fearfully anticipated it.

As this fear became more evident, our uncertainties in the years before her diagnosis were only increased by her repeated claims that she had no recollection of what she had said and done. During what she and her doctors would later describe as an 'episode'.

Increasingly we had no-one but each other from whom to get advice. Yet throughout all the years, while Anna could not remember, our lives were governed by so much that could not be spoken of to anyone else, in or outside our small family. Nor be kept silent about either.

That was the paradox around which our lives came to turn; a version of the rule of confidentiality which surrounded Anna's condition. Our attempts to cope had to be confidential as well.

And throughout the years, the parcels of books for review continued to arrive – even though review editors came and went. Producing the reviews to a deadline, with as much care as I could muster, became a part of life, though a tiny part.

It became a small, self-imposed, discipline. I suppose a bit like my consultant's insistence upon completing the 'Times Crossword' before breakfast.

And yet not like that. For one thing I had to work slowly and methodically. Because of the sheer numbers of books that arrived in those brown parcels, I was able to choose to review only those that I admired. And the process of selecting these, demanded a careful and continuous programme of reading. One determined entirely by chance. By what arrived.

The only exception to my rule of only reviewing in admiration, was the occasional book about the teaching of poetry in school; when I thought it offered a too easy, superficial, fashionable, and ultimately damaging, analysis of what was entailed. Then, although always looking for positive things to say, I sought to offer an alternative set of possibilities and outcomes.

Fortunately these occasions were few; and since such books were usually written by best-selling authors, offering just the right formulae to tempt hard-pressed classroom teachers, I knew they would sell in large numbers anyway. Whatever I said.

However to join the debate by explaining my reservations as clearly as I could, in the hope that some readers might agree, and consider, seemed worthwhile. Anyway I thought it was. And I knew that there was always the option for the editor not to print what I sent in. For the most part they printed it. But as I say the instances were few anyway.

At the same time, invitations to run workshops on poetry teaching, from around the country, increased in number. And sometimes I even went further afield.

My preparation for these tasks had to be meticulous, for I knew the risks; whether when speaking to serving teachers or to students in the Education Departments of other universities, who were preparing for a working life in the classroom. Whether in a single school, with teachers from a group of schools, or at the National Poetry Centre, I had always to work 'with' the audience.

My intentions and rewards were always the same. These were to focus upon, and somehow attend to, the grain of childhood itself. And the nature of language. If with young teachers, to seek to conjure a recollection in them of the children they had once been. Mostly it worked, and the invitations continued to arrive steadily. And I accepted them whenever possible.

Poetry, I found myself constantly reminding listeners, was not in the beginning about literariness, important as that would become; just as education is not in the end about examination passes, important though they may be. The trick was to show how all of this is true, or rather just to remind them how it is.

Of course, therefore, my real concern was the nature of educational activity; teaching poetry just happened to be the focus.

So these workshops, here and there, were as much about the point of schools as the value of poetry to my listeners. For me it was a serious if entertaining business, underpinned by the theory of poetics which I have already referred to. Of course I didn't always say this explicitly – it wasn't necessary.

I remember how one summer I was returning by train from Liverpool, after running the second of two weekly workshops at one of that city's universities. These visits had become a regular annual event, at the invitation of a teacher-poet who worked in the English Department.

The visit had gone well, and my friend's second-year students had been welcoming – and saw the point. They laughed a lot. Proof enough that they understood.

Just as in Jacksonville, all those years earlier, when I was at the beginning of working things out, I had used the recorded voices of children to build my argument; voices recorded from working in schools. What children said plotted the direction of the message.

My listeners had sat up and showed every sign of remembering, when they heard a nine year old say,

"When you read lots of poems, and listen to other peoples', I find it really helps me to write mine".

They laughed when another young voice said,

"Say I went on something at a funfair, and I thought, 'This is really exciting. I think when I get home, or at another time, I've definitely got to make a poem about it'. I just think about it and make sure I've got it. If I think I'm enjoying myself too much, so I might not remember, I get a piece of paper from my pocket and I write it down. So when my mum washes my coat, she takes all these pieces of poems out".

I dozed as the train measured its way south, reflecting upon the two sessions.

Remembering another nine year old saying,

"It's very different when you're able to write at home as well as at school. The more time you get the more ideas you get."

And I must have smiled, when I remembered another replying,

"You can let your imagination run wild. I think it's important that you shouldn't always do what you're told in writing. I think you ought to be allowed to write what you want. If you don't, you'll find that you won't have anything to show that's really yours!"

At this, my audience had laughed again, but this time just a little more softly. Some of them even began to clap.

And my thoughts had switched to Anna, and I wondered if she would ever have anything to show that was really hers.

'*Such a good way of putting it Sam*', I thought.

Sometimes I felt that I didn't really know who Anna was, and wondered if she ever remembered the child she had once been. All the sense of wonder that we thought she had, seemed lost. Swamped by her anger and turmoil. And this, in spite of everything that we had planned and hoped for her.

But all this brought me back to the day, and I decided that I must put these thoughts away. Just be glad that the workshops were over, and had gone well; and that I was on my way home – and on schedule. No mishaps. Be grateful that it didn't seem that I had let anyone down; that the friendliness and hospitality I had received had been somehow justified. That no-one seemed to think that what I had to say "was contemptible".

So I reached for a book from my case. I had brought it along for just this journey home. It was a new book of poems in translation, from Hungary. I had thought, after a first reading, that it might be a good one to review. As usual, time was short, and this train journey was a good opportunity to look at it again – and perhaps make some first notes. And so I settled down.

I'd hardly begun, when I realized that a quiet voice opposite was speaking to me. A young woman, not so unlike those in the audience I had just left, was leaning forward. She was from Japan.

"You're reading poetry!", she said. "Why?"

Although this might seem a surprising question, coming out of nowhere, it didn't appear so at the time. It was, after all, fair enough, and there were a large number of good answers available to me. Further, that she had bothered to ask it, so directly, meant that she was likely to be able to understand any number of the possible answers.

So I simply, and plainly, attempted to explain my interest, and how I was returning from a work engagement.

My questioner then began, and very enthusiastically, to tell me about the New Year celebrations which took place in her family in Japan when she was a child. And how they continued still. About the game of 'Ogura Hyaku-nin-isshiu'. *One Hundred Poems from One Hundred Poets*, which she had played every year with her family since she had learned to sing – and speak.

This young traveller seemed so immediately natural and open in her enthusiasm, as she spoke to a total stranger, that I completely forgot my foreboding about Anna. And I decided, as she spoke, to try to pick up the cards and the book of poems which she described, from the Japanese Cultural Centre in Piccadilly. It would be useful to learn more about the game, and to be able to refer to it perhaps in workshops; and in the teaching sessions on my little course at college.

This chance encounter with the quiet and enthusiastic voice which left the train at Birmingham, was one that I recall easily. By the time the train had reached Kings Cross, I had made the decision to review the book of Hungarian poems.

Before catching the train home from Charing Cross, I dropped in on the Japanese Cultural Centre, and there sure enough were the boxes of cards, and the book of '*One Hundred Poems from One Hundred Poets*' just as my young travelling companion had described them. It had been a productive journey home.

Nor was this kind of encounter so rare, in fact it occurred quite frequently.

I recall another one, again on a train, on the way to Groningen in Northern Holland. This time my informant was an older woman, a grandmother. And again a conversation began because of a book I was reading. And again I was able to incorporate what she told me into meetings of the poetry course at college which was still running.

She told me of her recollection as a young child of making a '*Poesy Album*', and this was interesting because she told me how all of her friends also made them.

She said that her grandchildren still did, and that the shops in her town still sold empty books just for this purpose. She said that she thought that young children still made poesy albums throughout the Netherlands, and that it had nothing to do with what was going on in their schools.

It occurred to me that here was a very early example of a bridge, provided and encouraged by parents, between the world of playground rhymes, and songs, and children's own writing and reading at school. Definitely relevant to the detail of the poetics upon which my course at work was built.

When I arrived at the university, I asked my hosts immediately about poesy albums, and they confirmed what my elderly informant had told me. Certainly, Dutch children still made them, and they remembered making them themselves. They were amused at my interest in the practice.

Willy, my contact at the conference, asked his students if they could bring in their own examples from when they were children. Later in the week, there was a very large pile for me to examine, all of them very full, and elaborately decorated. All in very good condition still. These twenty year olds were happy to answer my questions, but also diplomatically keen that I would be returning their collections saved from childhood. Keen that I shouldn't take them away.

And so our family life continued as well as it could among Anna's difficulties. This duality, our attempts to retain momentum in our own lives at the same time as trying to give Anna the support she needed, is what defined those years; binding them together in a tense unity.

Years later, when we had left our home on the edge of the city and the country, where we had known such happiness and unhappiness, Anna and Steve were visiting us at our new home on the south coast. By now Claire was married and living in Germany. Anna and Steve lived some fifty miles away from us. It was actually before the birth of their children.

This visit would lead to another unexpected conversation, which I could hardly forget, but which Carol and I would seldom discuss either. It was between Anna and her mother.

During part of the afternoon, Steve and I were watching a cricket match on the television. Anna and Carol were visiting Dover, walking on the pier in the sun.

Anna was going through a quiet phase. Withdrawn and dependent, but allowing everyone some space and peace. Mother and daughter had walked to the end of the pier where there was a café. If you went there you might still find it. Like Tatlebury Corner.

They sat chatting over coffee, and as they talked Anna confided in Carol; without warning. Suddenly she was referring to her stay in hospital in 1990. The topic came from nowhere. It was as if, Carol said, she was suddenly driven by some compulsion.

"I may have said things about Dad at the hospital", she blurted out. "But", she added, "I told them quickly afterwards that it wasn't true!"

Carol told me of this some weeks later; and how she had then asked,

"What wasn't true?

But Anna wouldn't give more details, and would only reply,

"Oh, I can't remember! You won't tell Dad will you?"

The conversation moved on, no doubt swamped by Anna's panic, so Carol didn't have to answer the question. Didn't have to give that undertaking.

When I heard about this from Carol, of course I was angry; but most of all what I felt was resignation. A kind of hopelessness certainly, and indignation too; but mostly just a controlled resignation.

And was it just an indulgence to notice the irony of how Dover Pier had been the venue for Anna's confession? To think of Matthew Arnold again. Of his lines from 'Dover Beach'. Wave after wave of, "Let us be true to one another!" So I thought of the two locations. Unaccountably too, I thought of how Arnold had been an Inspector of Schools. And then I recalled how Anna had said to her sister so many decades before,

"I have to tell mummy or my head hurts".

I wondered why Anna had disclosed this to Carol on that particular day, and decided that there was probably no reason which was available to us. That it was likely that she would have not known why herself.

Was she seeking comfort by some act of contrition? Probably. Was she asking for forgiveness? Perhaps. … Absolution?

I remember pondering how even Dr B. might have not expected me to provide quite such an open cheque. Though perhaps he would have understood also.

Whatever the reasons for Anna's disclosure, so freely given then among all the permissions she had withheld from us for so many years, it would certainly explain some of the responses of other people – responses we had collided with continually in earlier years.

Could this be the reason for our not being allowed to meet Dr H. face to face, and privately, a second time? For Anna's refusal to allow it? Perhaps she was fearful that any conversation might turn to what she "…may have said". Perhaps Dr H. and 'the team' were all the while having to assess the truth of what Anna had claimed. Of what she now said she had claimed. I have mentioned already how they were working in the context of what was going on in the Orkneys, and in Cleveland.

If that were so, then we had another reason to be grateful for the doctor's caution. I particularly had a reason to be grateful for it. Obviously, whatever Anna had claimed, they had discounted. For when the police knocked, it was only to offer us help and support.

What Anna had told Carol at the end of the pier could offer the key to a whole list of puzzles which were aligned in our memory, explanations for so much that had happened in our struggles with Anna.

For instance, about what Janet, in her swamped kitchen, "wouldn't have known what to think ..." .

It could inform us about why Dr. P., in his inexperience and arrogance, had acted as he had.

And about an incident that Anna had told us of in the hospital, at the beginning. How, when she and Sharon were returning from an occupational therapy class, her companion had said, "Something must have happened to you in your childhood!"

Perhaps the lie had grown from the young care worker's question, while I waited in the car because Anna refused to see me, "Why don't you want to see your father, Anna?"

Could it go some way towards explaining the twenty year old choir member's impertinence as he visited us; when he mentioned casually,

"I thought I'd come and see Anna's parents for myself!"

Could it be what Jack was referring to when he had said, that they " ... didn't necessarily believe ..." ?

And what of Gwen's permanently raised eyebrows now?

Could what Anna had just told Carol make some sense of all of it?

Had Anna, back then in her turmoil, built barriers to our getting the help for her that was so vital, out of a fear that what she had claimed about her home would be uncovered and discovered as false? And what was the effect of that fear upon her? Over so many years? Upon her still?

And what did it tell us now about our daughter's motivation and personality. And what did it tell us about what the future might hold for us all? What could I do about it now?

Did this 'confession' of Anna's make the truth of it all any clearer? Or did it raise further questions? Was Anna, then and now, in the grip of an illness that she just could not break without seemingly unavailable help? Held by something that was beyond her control, that had caused her to smile at the mayhem she caused as our family crumbled; sometimes suddenly and dramatically, and later just slowly. Gradually, a little at a time.

Could we now be quite certain that Carol's fears of our growing old near Anna had substance? Were those fears actually a perceptive response to a sense of real menace?

Now, even more than when Carol first voiced those fears, I could only focus upon the qualification she referred to. I had to hope that it was only "sometimes" that she felt so frightened. And that it was only sometimes that we could think the fear was justified. For it was only sometimes that Anna behaved as she did.

As from the very beginning, from that evening when I picked Anna up from the pre-examination party, I could only hope. We could both of us only trust in a benign fate.

Yet, undeniably, so many years before, Carol had mentioned to me quietly one evening,

"Sometimes, I think I'm in chains!"

(ii)

I last met William, just for a couple of days, when I visited the ancient cathedral town near where he lived. And we had a chance to catch up on each other's news over a weekend.

He was still writing, and accepting occasional invitations, rather like me I suppose. He looked older, no doubt as I did also. Many of our former friends, the best of them, were already dead.

What I learned during those two days saddened me. As Carol was the attentive hostess, at what was for them a particularly difficult time for them both.

Just previously, Carol had reached her 71st birthday, and it was almost to the day that Anna began her third stay in a psychiatric hospital. William was in his 75th year.

In fact, because of the parlous state of mental health provision in our country at that time, Anna was not admitted to one hospital but to two. Irony upon irony! And I'll explain how that came about in a moment.

Now it was winter, and a time of not just one but three birthdays. Anna's two children had birthdays around this time also. Her little girl would become seven, and her son ten.

By now Anna had suffered eleven severe episodes of mania over a period of twenty six years. Six of these had occurred from that early school party to when she was eventually diagnosed as suffering from bi-polar disorder in 2005, at the time of the birth of her first child. And there had been five more since that diagnosis.

Now the children were becoming the mirror which reflected the effects of these attacks, though when she was suffering an episode she could have no sense of that. She spoke only of how beautiful her children were. And she kept them increasingly close.

William seemed pre-occupied with the pain and mystification that he saw in their young faces. And the fear.

As he spoke, he reflected upon how the effort and life which had been spent in supporting Anna and Steve during the sixteen years of their marriage, particularly since the birth of the children, had apparently come to nothing.

At this time, as on so many previous occasions, it seemed that it was Anna's desire to work which was the focus and context of a renewed decline. But this along with an apparent complete inability to deal with even the smallest demands which working made. Which having a paid job made.

Carol had recognized how the tension had been building again for a couple of months. At first Anna did voluntary work, which she handled well. Then came the part-time agency work which had seemed so ideal. And to be going well too. Just two part-days a week, easily fitted in with the children at school. With the nursery making no administrative demands. And with, importantly, no paper-work.

Then they offered her more hours, over four days. And quite quickly the signs of the approaching hurricane again became impossible to miss. And then impossible to ignore.

Now it was the children's half-term, and Carol had agreed to drive Anna and the children to the dentist. It wasn't an emergency; just a six monthly check-up. And the dentist was in Farnbury. William and Carol had long since transferred to one nearer to where they lived on the south coast.

But Anna had insisted that she and the children stayed with the practice, even though they now lived sixty miles away. She said that the dentist was good with the children.

So, for three years or so, the pattern of Carol driving them all up to Farnbury had become established. By doing this, she felt that she could save Anna the two and a half hour return drive, or a difficult train journey. And of course Carol would see the children.

And it was the latest of these car journeys which would be a fresh, grim, theatre for Anna's returned mania.

It was from then that her young daughter began to develop an involuntary facial tic.. At first it was hardly noticeable. But increasingly her face was pulled first to one side and then to another. William noticed it first, and he saw too that the child seemed quite unaware of it.

Carol's journeys in the car that day were desperate, from when she reached Anna's house in the morning.

When she arrived, she found Anna in disarray. Anna screamed at her, almost immediately, following something her mother said,

"Get out of my house! Get out now!"

Recognizing how things were, Carol said she would wait in the car with the children, while Anna completed what she had to do. And so she shepherded them outside with her. To wait.

During the thirty mile drive, the crashing, shrieking, tide of Anna's massive hysteria washed around the inside of the small car. Around and over the children in the back.

In her raving, she shouted at Carol that her daughter had inherited her condition. With the children in the back.

Carol immediately replied that she thought that very unlikely. What else could she say? She said what she believed was true. There was no evidence for such a conclusion. And every reason not to state it. There, or at all.

But this only provoked Anna.

"You don't know anything!" she screamed. "I've been doing research. It never skips generations!" With the children in the back.

"Anna, that's just not true".

But Anna would not be silenced.

"What do you know? You're just an old person, and I'm strong".

And at this, Carol saw the rest of her days near Anna stretching out before her.

"Anna, try to calm down!"

But she would not calm down.

"You shut your f…g mouth. You had me locked up. I won't forget that. You're both such shit parents!"

With the children in the back.

Then … "Stop the car. Stop this car now!", she yelled. As foreign lorries thundered past them, and around them, on the motorway. And with the children in the back.

"I'm getting out! I'll jump out! I'll do it, and it will be your fault!"

Until this, the children had been silent. In the back of the car. Completely. None of their usual chatter. None of the guessing games which they usually played in the car with Carol.

But now the boy, not quite ten, said quietly; very quietly and slowly,

"No mummy, if you jump out it will be your fault".

As a precaution though, probably unnecessarily, Carol had applied the electronic door-lock, from the dashboard.

Anna made as if to struggle with the door to open it. And the seven year old's voice announced from the back,

""Mummy, if you talk like that, you'll have no friends".

And as she did so, her young face twitched. Pulled first to one side and then to the other.

The inside of the car vibrated with Anna's screaming and rage. Outside the surrounding lorries roared; pulling out from the inside lane to overtake each other, and then slowly back again. Always very slowly.

And as they did so, as she was to tell William later, Carol thought

"This is just too dangerous!"

But the journey continued. And Anna was just as distracted, and not much quieter, in the dentist's, at lunch, and during the afternoon's shopping which she insisted upon.

In the waiting room, and in the shops, people stared at Anna and the children – and at Carol.

Anna was much the same in the car as they all returned to Westerford. As her mother strove to concentrate at rush-hour on the motorway.

Carol reached William, back home, at around 9.00 o'clock that evening, and as she came through the door he saw how pale she looked.

She asked him rhetorically, over supper, about the effects upon the children of hearing all that in the car. Would they grow up thinking it alright to behave as Anna behaved? She seemed troubled by that.

William said that he didn't know. I think she knew he didn't.

He told me how during the rest of that week, Anna visited her GP. a number of times.

In the days before the car journey, she had already been referred again to the County's Psychological Services, which were based in Westerford. But from what her parents could tell, nothing much had happened, though it was difficult for them to get proper information.

At the instigation of one of her friends, who was herself suffering from clinical depression, Anna had gone to the hospital with her case packed, with the same friend, and asked to be admitted. But they had sent her away.

She said that they had told her,

"The system has changed. You're not ill enough".

And then the following weekend it was Carol's birthday. A Sunday. As was usual, Anna, Steve, and the children would be going to her parents' for lunch, and a birthday celebration at tea-time. It happened like that every year.

That was the plan.

On the Sunday morning, Carol and William were in the kitchen preparing for the visit, when the telephone rang. William answered. It was Anna, and she was angry. Very angry.

"You just turn round my husband and children, and send them straight back, she screamed at him down the line. "Or else", she threatened, "you'll see what will happen!".

As William started to respond to this new development, trying to understand what she was saying, Anna screamed,

"Don't you think you're taking my children".

About an hour later, Steve arrived with the children. William saw that they were without Anna.

Once in the house, Steve told them how Anna had refused to get into the car as they set off. And that he had driven away without her.

William wondered, but he wondered to himself, whether leaving her behind was the wisest thing to have done.

Steve told his parents-in-law that he had done it to protect the children.

Apparently during the week, Anna had claimed in front of the children, that she was getting a divorce. That she loved Keith. Keith was a member of a voluntary bi-polar support group which Anna attended every week. She said that Steve was an unsympathetic person.

The afternoon was punctuated by desperate and very threatening telephone calls from Anna, which Steve at first refused to take. Her small daughter asked William, as they played snakes and ladders,

"Mummy and Daddy aren't splitting up are they?"

He tried to re-assure her, as he negotiated a snake unsuccessfully, and she seemed to forget her own question. William spluttered theatrically at going down the snake and almost to the foot of the board again. And the child laughed.

Her face twitched as she spoke, and William reflected with irony at the appropriateness of the game they played.

Carol saw how little the ten year old said. Normally a gentle and optimistic child, he now was very quiet, and stared ahead into some distance of his own. Lost in thought. Or perhaps simply lost. He usually loved to help Carol in the kitchen. But not today.

The wild telephone calls from Anna to her parents filled the afternoon. She, raging that they were taking her children from her, as they tried to divert the children's attention by playing charades.

Through the wall of a titanic mania, William tried to re-assure her that they were not. But she couldn't listen.

He tried to reason with her that the children had come expecting a birthday celebration, and that it was out of the question to turn them back. Their grandson had brought down a cake he had made. But it was hopeless. In her rage, Anna put the phone down on her father.

She immediately rang back and demanded to speak to Carol; and then her relentless hysteria was directed at her mother,

"You f---g witch from hell!", she railed. "You are a disgusting mother!".

She wanted to speak to Steve then, but he refused to come to the phone; and so she rang off again.

Steve announced to them that he wasn't "going back". His reason was that he had to protect the children. Nor would he allow Anna to speak to them. When William tried to persuade him to allow that, he brushed him aside angrily.

As the children were preparing to go to bed in the evening, Anna continued to ring. And Steve continued to refuse to let the children speak to her.

And William persisted in his view that it would be better if he were to allow it.

Then Anna rang to tell Steve that she had called a taxi, and that she would be leaving immediately for her parents', unless she were allowed to speak to the children. She offered the information that the fare would be seventy five pounds; and William somewhat bizarrely thought to himself that he was surprised it was so little.

Steve could hear that the driver was in the house, and at this he relented. Anna spoke to the children before they went to bed.

Since the Monday was an extra day's holiday for the children, because of a staff-training day, their staying at their grandparents' unexpectedly presented no problems. But Steve refused to return home that night while Anna was there. He said that he wasn't going back the next day either.

When the children realized that they might not be returning home, and therefore would actually begin to miss school, they became very anxious. And they wanted to know why.

So William and Carol were caught in an impasse.

However, Steve had learned previously that 'a crisis meeting' would be held at the Mental Health Centre at 11.00 o'clock on Tuesday morning, which Anna was meant to attend also. Previously, also, Carol had said to Steve that she thought that he really should attend it too, – in the teeth of violent protests from Anna.

Now it seemed unlikely that anyone would be attending the meeting. It seemed that events had intervened. Carol put it to Steve again that it was now especially important for Anna to be at the meeting, and that if that happened he should be there too. And in this she was successful.

It was arranged that the children would remain with their grandparents. As simply the best solution available.

In the park that day, on its swings, in its café, and fishing for sticklebacks in its handsome lakes, the children remained very unhappy at not being at school. But they cheered up when Steve rang to say that he and Anna had decided to meet them halfway down the motorway from Westerford, at a Kentucky Fried Chicken outlet. And to take them home. If, that is, her parents could drive the children up to the café.

So, as things turned out, they would only have missed a day in school.

In the days immediately following, William and Carol drove up to Westerford repeatedly to be with the children at various points. To cover the necessary absences of their parents.

Finally Anna was admitted to hospital, or rather to those two hospitals I have mentioned, on the very last day of the month. Sadly, rather too late in both cases! The procedure for this was confused and confusing.

She was admitted to Westerford Hospital in the early afternoon. But the hospital didn't have a bed for her.

Thus she had to wait there while another hospital was found that could accept her. At 4 o'clock in the morning of the following day, she arrived at a hospital in Cheldondene, in SW London. It was a private hospital.

William was told of all of this when he rang the Westerford hospital. But the administrative assistant he spoke to would only say that Anna was no longer there. And that she could tell him nothing further, because of Anna's right to confidentiality.

The next day was Sunday, and he rang the Cheldondene Hospital, and was put straight through to the ward that had admitted Anna. The nurse he spoke to confirmed that Anna was admitted "some time after midnight", and added that she could not discuss her further.

After four days, Anna was transferred back to Westerford Hospital. When he learned of this from Steve, William rang Cheldondene again, and asked another nurse on the ward if there was anything she could tell him.

To his surprise, she replied that she would ask the psychiatrist who had been seeing Anna twice a day during her stay, whether he would ring back to answer his questions.

And they arranged a possible time for this to happen.

When the call didn't come, William rang again to check whether it might be more convenient for him to ring the psychiatrist. It was the same nurse. Perhaps, he asked, she could contact the psychiatrist and he could suggest a time for William to ring? She suggested that he ring back in an hour, when it should be possible to speak to a charge nurse.

When he did this, he explained again his reason for ringing, to Michael, the charge nurse, who seemed hopeful that the psychiatrist could still ring that same day. He said that he would contact him, check, and then ring William back.

The return call came very quickly, but the news wasn't good. Michael said, before ringing off very soon, that the psychiatrist had said that he couldn't speak to William, even though Anna was no longer at the hospital. And the reason was that Anna had expressly forbidden it – formally; insisting upon her right to confidentiality. She had apparently signed some document to ensure that.

Over the decades, William had grown used to this. He and Carol had long since given up the idea of achieving detailed information about Anna from those treating her. Momentarily he had become more hopeful, simply because of the nurse's optimistic response to his question about the psychiatrist being willing to speak to him.

So there it was. Just as before.

Two days previously, while she was still in the Cheldondene Hospital, and still in extreme turmoil, Anna had rung her mother, and informed her that the psychiatrists at the hospital had told her that she had been subjected to emotional abuse by her parents and her husband.

Nothing had changed. Things were much as they had been for so long. They had made very little progress in penetrating the maze of the medical services.

This third period in hospital ended after four weeks. A new regime of drugs was prescribed, but when Anna was discharged she seemed little better.

She told her parents of the violent and distracted behaviour of some of her fellow patients. And she told them that she'd never forgive them for not immediately turning Steve and the children around on Carol's birthday. And she demanded an apology.

It was clear that this episode was the worst yet. Because of the close involvement of the children. And it was continuing.

Apart from these declarations on the telephone, she actually rang very little at this time.

Indeed from her going into hospital, she rang little. When her parents visited her there, she didn't want to talk; and cut the visits short. She asked them just to send massages by mobile phone. These were often left unanswered, or her replies were very short – perhaps just one word.

During this period they felt that she was slipping away from them, just as they felt their own resilience ebbing away. For the most part, now, her behaviour exhibited a complete absence of restraint, and often very publicly. They felt that now what they were seeing were the symptoms and effects of plain old-fashioned madness.

On one evening when Anna was still in the Westerford hospital, she rang to tell Carol that Steve had to visit a local hospital's 'A an E' department because she had broken his arm. When they checked with Steve, they discovered that her claim was untrue. There had been no visit to an 'A and E' department.

This could actually have been possible, because although she was an in-patient, she was often around in the town, or in a café nearby, in the local branch of Tesco near the hospital, or even briefly at home. There would therefore easily have been an opportunity for fresh conflict between Anna and her husband away from the hospital environment.

On a night when Anna was still in hospital, William and Carol spent an evening at the cinema belonging to the university town that I was now visiting. It was to hear the digital screening of a concert from Berlin.

The concert programme included Beethoven's 'Pastoral Symphony'. They had bought the tickets long before. And now amid this new chaos, the concert was a temporary, small, refuge.

The 'Pastoral' had been the very first piece of music they had listened to together. In William's little flat which was really just one room. In the town on the Essex coast where he worked in his first school after leaving Goldsmiths'. Over fifty years before.

He had an LP of the symphony; same orchestra, different conductor.

Again, music itself was a refuge. Music that promised life, just as Anna's turmoil and terror presaged and threatened death.

Anna had given instructions to Steve from hospital. On no account were the children allowed to visit Carol and William without her.

So they could only do what was possible to re-assure the children by visiting them, and playing with them in their own home. Just trying to distract them, or cheer them up.

That home had become dilapidated by neglect under the pressures of Anna's illness. From the effects, for instance, of not being thoroughly and regularly cleaned. Anna had never done much housework; and now their little house seemed over-used and shabby. More like a public area than a home. Increasingly undomestic.

When they visited, they gathered up armfuls of clothes in need of ironing. The clothes were everywhere in the house. On the floor of the landing upstairs, draped over the banisters, in all the bedrooms, and even piled up in the living areas downstairs.

When the ironing was done and ready to be returned, Carol at the same time took meals for the children. They always asked about what they termed 'granny's roasts' when they visited their grandparents.

One of the things Anna demanded during her increasingly infrequent calls and texts, was that her mother should not remove clothes from the house. Perhaps she had heard from Steve about the ironing.

I cannot know of everything that occurred at this unhappy time. In any case it is impossible to describe and re-tell unreason accurately. It really is true that some stories can be too large to tell.

I know that Anna spoke occasionally of periods of violence between her and her husband. Recently, and at other times. I know that William and Carol worried about the effects of it all upon the children. And it led them to fear for them.

I know how when that episode was eventually passed, and Anna had returned to a quiet and so surprisingly lucid state, she seemed again remarkably clear-headed, apparently sophisticated, and socially aware. And so, then, she could ring her mother and say, plaintively:

"You won't give up on me mum, will you?"

Just in conversation, and with such sincerity.

And at this time a card arrived. Large. A photographed scene of bluebells with sunlight glancing through tall trees and full upon a flood of flowers. Sharp shafts of light through trees just beginning to find their leaves. Pastoral. Idyllic.

Plain, against the snowy white, there was a message from Anna inside, written in her familiar at once bold and unsteady hand, and beginning by speaking of some small gift for one of her sister's children:

Dear Mum and Dad,

Just posting the £10 cheque for you to pay into Claire's account. I appear to keep forgetting to give it to Steve.

Don't really know what to write, apart from I love you and hope that you know I'm a good mum and don't behave the way I do to hurt you, either of you.

I have never experienced overwhelming sadness like this before. I'm sorry.

Anna

x

And yet, more often, before that episode and later, when she and her family were with her parents she seemed detached. Made absent by the drugs she had to take to make life possible for them all. In one way she was so right to resist and complain about having to take them. Over the years William and Carol had both come to realize just how much of their daughter the medication was removing. Had already removed.

And I know about the effects of it all upon William and Carol. As we talked, just the two of us, that last weekend in their garden, I reminded him of the words of the one doctor who had been allowed by Anna to speak to him:

"Remember your own lives!"

I'm not sure it helped. And William confided to me how, of all the aspects of the fear that had grown over all the years, the biggest he had now was that in the end he would let Carol down. Somehow. At the end of everything.

I know that sleep was becoming less easy for them both. It was that time in life when, in the dead of night, the radio can become a very peculiar solace. When the detail of the BBC World Service, the shipping forecast, or music, simply that, could conquer sleeplessness.

As you will realize, I know a great deal about the life of my friend, and because it seems of wider interest I have attempted to tell of it. There is much I do not know. And much of what I know I cannot understand.

I do know, and I think I do understand, how Carol and he realized that it was Anna who in her despair, was most "in chains". How she was in the grip of something that she could not shake herself free from, whatever she did.

It is quite beyond me to understand the nature of what that something was, given the advantages she had. I know that there are wise souls who will understand it; to a greater or lesser degree.

Could Anna's doctors, down the years, be counted among those wise souls? Well, the reader must judge.

From my close acquaintance with what happened, my doubts swirl around the way that the medical profession seemed constrained in its interpretation of the important principle of patient confidentiality.

I cannot but doubt that the medical support for the mentally ill is sufficiently intelligent and humane in our country. That, for whatever reason, medical decisions are helpful enough to the patient and those they care for, and who care about them.

I think I know that it is unworthy for "patient confidentiality", so often quoted, to be allowed to be practised for any other purpose than protecting the patient. And that has surely to be demonstrated and interpreted. It should not be invoked for any other purpose. For instance to protect professional interests, or to hide ineffective practice from view. Or simply quoted daily, as a mantra, by those in administrative posts.

It is already the case that mental illness is a mystery. To hide away its treatment, from the kind of scrutiny which is demanded for every other example of public policy, is not helpful.

Why was Anna enabled so consistently to invoke a spurious right to confidentiality, when there had to be a doubt that it was in her best interests? And when her condition made her unable to be the only best judge? Could my friend have reasonably have expected her doctors to ask, and investigate for her good, why she insisted upon it?

As it turned out, a slavish and crude interpretation of "patient confidentiality" as a resource rather than a principle for good, left Anna isolated while threatening further the quality of the lives of those around her – upon whom her well-being depended in part at least. And along the way, it hid from scrutiny the possibility that mental health provision in our country is worryingly ineffective. And for many other families than Anna's.

Or perhaps Anna and her family were just unlucky? Again, the reader must judge.

On that last occasion that I met my friend, I remember expressing my frustration at what I had learned of his situation over the years. And I tried to impress upon them both that it was important that they protect themselves. And this because we all knew that Anna could not always help what she did.

I tried to remind them, yet again, of what the good Dr. B. had said so many years and tears before. That "older man", he spoke of, hadn't turned up. But he was right about the cheque book. And their Wednesdays? They had a right to them surely – and to the rest of their other days.

At the end of that last weekend, I was walking with William along Dover seafront. With our most recent conversations behind us, he raised something which had obviously come to pre-occupy him. To be increasingly in his thoughts.

We stood together at the end of the pier and watched a cruise ship leaving for St. Petersburg. As we watched it, he reminded me how when Dvořák had been in New York he had gone down to the docks every day to watch the liners leaving. Homesick for Bohemia.

He then continued, almost to himself:

"I wonder now whether it was Anna who was waiting for me, for us, when I was thirteen. Behind that door with its blue paint peeling, all those years ago in Westerford. And whether after all, in spite of everything I tried, it just wasn't possible for me to walk away".

And he added,

"I think that perhaps I've already let Carol down."

And it was then that I realized how William had become preoccupied by this thought. That it had come to govern him.

Chapter 22

LEVERTOV, Denise *A Door in the Hive; Evening train*. Bloodaxe, 1993, pp224. £8.95. 1 85224 159 4

This makes easily available to us, in one volume, two recently published collections by an American poet who began as English. It is a volume which we might usefully introduce to any sixth-former.

These poems speak to the reader of being human, and of the consequences of inhumanity. Of the self-destructiveness of spoiling the loveliness of the earth; and of the obscenities of human cruelty in so-called war situations, for instance currently in El Salvador.

Denise Levertov's reverential love of the physical world has a spiritual origin. Only the poems themselves can reveal just how '*... the body being savaged / is alive./ It is our own.*' How resonant in this work, is the assertion that '*... Surely we were to have been / earth's mind, mirror, reflective source.*' Flowering into a delighted and delightful lyricism, if often in lament, it is a poetry that elevates reading to singing.

Another American poet who began life in England, Anne Stevenson, reminds us that '*no artist can be optimistic in days of spiritual decay, but it is possible to be honest. And joyful.*'

Levertov shows us just how. These collections are a gift to us, to pass on – in case '*... there might be open to us, even now, / a chance to evolve ...*'.

William Holden

STEVENSON, Anne. *Granny Scarecrow*. Bloodaxe. 2000, pp.80, £7.95. 1 85224 534 4

Anne Stevenson's is a distinctive poetry, developed over a long period. More than a collection, this book will beguile the receptive reader, by its completely mysterious blending of loveliness and truth. In the secondary school and later.

Much of its loveliness is its musicality; inherent in such questions as, '*Why does what is known of happiness / like sadness find insignia in harmony?*' Yet, its effects are a combination of 'sounding' and 'looking'. And so, much of its truth lies in its peculiar intelligence.

This insight is often expressed in seeming paradox. Children may be brought up *'too carefully'* ; the human tendency, aware enough of life's transience, is to love best retrospectively: *'Consciousness walks on tiptoe through what happens. / So much is felt, so little is said'*. Betrayal is as often as unintended as intended; and epiphanies may make life *'a very sad song'*.

The connections between the imagination and everyday living are rigorously defined. The living and the dead know each other as well as the living. Perhaps better. The sadness waiting at the end of everything, is as much the result of our best efforts as in spite of them. The loveliness and the truth describe *'unendurable riddles ... resolved in ... remorseless ascent'*.

William Holden

FANTHORPE, U. A.. *Consequences*. Peterloo, 2000, pp.75, £7.95. 1 871471 83 4

Oscar Shumsky, the recently deceased violinist, insisted: "I've learned ... about the violin by thinking what the painter thinks and talks about". Good poets have a similar inclusiveness, and these poets demonstrate its merits.

In a collection about *continuities*, its forms have strikingly tuned endings, which propel the reader on into the book. Audenesque, and from within the mainstream of English poetry, yet likely to quote Sinatra, the poems look always outward as well as forward. Given their subjects, this is significant; for *'Truth is hard to translate / When our only machinery is words'*.

The long poem *'Consequences'*, and the contents of the remaining three quarters of the book, are a necessary rebellion against the prevailing values in contemporary England. Against the narrowing of choices: *'theme park or business centre?'*.

This poet's voice is ironic and humanising, *'taking notes around the corner'* upon a wilfully de-humanising society. One in which the caring impulse is transformed into a complaint against the needy: *'You've come here for help; that's what you're getting'*.

The collection speeds, in reverse, towards ignored but ultimately more durable values; and so may yet be a contributory antidote for the reader in the secondary school, and later. Upon which note, see the exquisite third of the '*Four Christmas Carols*'.

William Holden

Chapter 23

COTTON, John and SEDGWICK, Fred, *Hey!* and *The Biggest Riddle in the World*; illustrated by Paul Cox. Mary Glasgow (Two by Two), 1990, pp.64. 1 85234 294 3 (one ISBN).

These two books remind me of the horse chestnuts of Autumn, fresh in their husks, about which John Cotton writes in one of his poems. They look especially new, go together naturally, invite collection, and seem made for exchange – all of which will appeal to eight to twelve year olds, and their teachers.

The writing of these two poets is easily complementary: containing much fun, but expecting children to be serious about features of their common experience which deserve recording and celebrating. Another stunning complementarity, is the almost liquid exchange between the texts of the poems and the black and white drawings of Paul Cox. The books really are well designed.

Their slightly unusual size makes it as desirable and easy for children to store them in pockets and bags, as on bookshelves; which is just how poetry books for children should be used – whether in or out of school. The books will help children to be, to borrow a word from one of Fred Sedgwick's poems, 'de-silenced' about poetry – and like conkers, children will value them.

William Holden

Brownjohn, Sandy, *The Ability to Name Cats*. Hodder, 1989, pp. 90, £3.75. 0 340 50339 4

In this new book about teaching children to write poetry, Sandy Brownjohn's skill and commitment are as palpable as in her previous books on the subject. It does well what they do well. It describes a collection of 'exercises' designed to stimulate children to write; ending with a chapter, 'Credo', which defines her teaching approach.

There is, indeed, much to believe in, and to agree with, in the introductions of these innovative classroom strategies. Teaching intentions which confirm to children the value of playing with words, of gaining access as writers to a large number of techniques, of recognizing purpose and gaining confidence in writing, and of becoming autonomous as writers, are all valuable beyond question.

I have a doubt though, and it is that the teaching methodology recommended will often enough deliver these results by themselves. There seems to me a need, in these teaching strategies, for a greater acknowledgement of the origin of metaphor in young children's play, and of the origins of integrity in their writing.

There are risks in an approach which concentrates so much upon what the teacher should direct, and so much upon writing; and that in the classroom so exclusively, and during a period of only a year. One risk is that children's satisfaction in completing the 'exercises' may supplant other activities which are also important in enabling them *'to grapple with the demands of a strict form'.* Form gets into children's writing too when they become habitual readers and listeners at the same time as becoming committed to being writers. Much of this activity cannot take place only in the classroom, and often involves important people in their lives other than the teacher. The achievement by children of all the things that will lead to their autonomy as writers, depends as much , 'I believe', upon these other activities, in other places, with other people (including other children), as upon our directing them to specific written tasks in the classroom. My hope is that the many colleagues who will buy this book may believe so too.

William Holden

PART 5

AUSKLANG

What makes an overture sound like an overture?
What makes a conclusion something more than an ending?

FITZMAURICE, Gabriel The Village Sings. Peterloo Poets, 1996, pp. 82, £6.95. 1 885266 29 4

This collection ends with sonnets about a teacher and a musician, introducing neatly what I have to say about it. From another poem comes, *'The true test of the artist / Is that he perseveres'*. Perseverence is necessary, too, when arguing the case for the arts in school curricula today; for it is indeed easy to feel that we are '... *playing music / For empty pockets*', or compiling a cv. that will never be read (see 'The Interview' p.26). Yet ... *'freedom isn't granted , / We win it from ourselves'*. And now, as ever, the teacher is *'bound to pass along / The values inherent in our language'*.

The best poems here speak of our language, be it Gaeilge or English; and about the conjunctions and collisions of private and social worlds, within rural communities in Western Ireland. Drawing upon material from Irish fairy tale and history, in humour, despair, and hope, the symmetries of Fitzmaurices's art are composed from the beauty and pain of the everyday.

Poet, reader, teacher, reviewer, become pre-occupied with *'things insufficient till they're sung'*. Read this book for what it attempts, and the poems it achieves. Their large audience, including readers in the secondary school, will recognize the hazards inherent in not "persevering" ! (see 'Port na bPucaf', p.62).

William Holden

Chapter 24

Bonn

So, perhaps we recognize much too infrequently how common it is for people to become lost on the journey from childhood to adulthood. Marooned in some hostile country in between; losing any chance of maturity, and lacking a creative and joyful recollection of their earliest years.

The Saturday morning was very warm and sunny as I sat outside the café in the square, with these thoughts and a cup of coffee. I wished I could escape the thoughts, and I knew I shouldn't be drinking the coffee.

The square of the little Rhineland town where Claire and Bernardt lived with their three very young children, was full of activity and people.

Carol and I had taken the by now familiar E40 route, this time from Dunkerque; and were in Germany visiting our daughter. And as so often happened, I also had a small work engagement to fulfil. I had agreed to give a twenty five minute talk at the 'graduation ceremony' at a large independent school in Bonn.

It wasn't something that I was actually keen to do, and I'd only agreed to it because the invitation came from a source that made it difficult to refuse. The task had no genuine teaching, learning, outcome; and perhaps it was this reluctance that had caused me to delay my preparation.

The occasion was a kind of Speech Day, and as we know Speech Days and I had history. The difference, and problem, was that there would be no books to go with the speeches.

But I was stuck with it. I had a favour to repay to someone on the staff of the school who knew that I was quite frequently in Bonn for family reasons. So that was that. When she suggested my name to the Director, who then had passed it down to the Principal, a letter with the formal invitation quickly followed.

And so, while Carol was helping Claire with the children, and catching up on family news, I was sitting in this sunny square attempting to finalize the content of my talk. With my notebook and the morning, here was an opportunity to decide what to say.

As I sat there, I reflected upon how Hermann Kesten had remarked that "the café is the waiting room of poetry". A good line, I thought, and I took the point. A certain idleness, or space at least, is necessary for any kind of writing. But then the waiting room of a hospital clinic can be a spur also.

But whatever the truth of all that, I had a small job to complete; and this was a very agreeable place to settle down to it.

And yet the scene before me was not conducive to quiet reflection, for at just past 10 o'clock the sun-swamped square was very full and very noisy. And the reason for all the activity was that polling day for the post of the town's mayor was fast approaching. This was to be the last weekend of election campaigning.

At the stroke of 10 o'clock, the team of the governing national party had begun establishing their stall. Five or six of them were already busy, and their candidate had arrived. A shortish man, neat and tanned, and a little overweight; looking part estate agent, and part conjurer.

His team had installed amplification equipment around their stall and, ironically, a popular song was being played in English: "I'll be there to love and comfort you!" trilled the message.

"L----- K----- für Burgermeister!"

declared a large poster pinned to the front of a table.

"Ein Herz für dein Stadt" read another.

Four or five large red umbrellas shielded his team from the already strong morning sun, as they worked at trestle tables, unloading and arranging piles of pamphlets explaining the wonders and achievements of the national party in government.

On one of the tables stood a coffee urn, and a member of the team was serving free cups of coffee to passers-by. At another, a small group of helpers was blowing up large balloons – in the party's colours of course.

For quite a while this was the only show in town. But then after about twenty minutes another group began to form. Just four or five metres from the first. This team represented the other candidate for the post of mayor, who belonged to the party which at the time formed the opposition in the German Parliament in Berlin.

At first, this group had just one table. There was no urn for free coffee; just the table and a single orange umbrella. Nor was there any sign of music at this table, nor the candidate.

And now the Saturday morning shoppers had to pass between the two groups; on their way to the two bakers' shops, the two cafés, the butcher's shop, the post office, or the greengrocer's.

The two groups did not acknowledge each other as they worked on in close proximity. It was as if they and their attendant audiences had the whole square to themselves. I saw not so much as a glance pass between them, as I sat warm in the morning, under one of the café's umbrellas at my table. Drinking in the scene with my coffee. It was all very slick, and workaday.

I wondered if the free coffee was as good as mine.

Suddenly there was confusion all about. One of the town's dustcarts had stopped noisily in the square, blocking all other traffic nearby and indeed all around it. Two of the operatives in their orange, and somewhat soiled, overalls jumped down from the cab, and the driver made straight for the governing party's candidate to shake his hand. And I detected some mischief in this approach.

The candidate tried to look pleased as the dustman very considerately removed a seriously besoiled glove, before doing what the candidate had been doing since ten o'clock to everyone else. The neatly tanned, fixed, smile became a little more firmly fixed in place as the dustman shook his hand vigorously, no doubt assuring him all the while of his support.

As these newly arrived employees of the town helped themselves to the free coffee, the refuse collection vehicle's engine was left running, noisily pumping out black fumes.

While I had been engrossed with these developments, activity had greatly increased at the second stall. More trestle tables had arrived, along with two more orange umbrellas – and the candidate.

The women shoppers who crowded around him seemed to be rather older, prosperous looking, but still mothers of young children. The children were all clutching the coloured balloons of the other party.

The stall had now been transformed by the arrival of two large crates of single orange roses, which had already been partly unloaded; with the result that people began to wander past me, old and young, male and female alike, clutching the long stem of a handsome single rose.

Each of these had been handed out personally by the opposition candidate. He also was just a little overweight, with the same foxy expression on his face as his rival. Quite short, with a tie, he seemed to have resolved that he should appear tidily but not too smartly dressed. Forty eight or so, with a goatee beard, he had the same eyes as his rival: alert, ever watchful, and intent upon smiling. A little suspicious, perhaps, of being found out?

I realized that the noisy dust cart had left, and the square was now quieter. Suddenly tranquil even. Though the fumes it left behind still drifted around.

Now, this little town had a countess. A real countess. And that morning she passed through the square on her way to the post office. She stopped to speak briefly to the opposition candidate. She didn't actually shake his hand, but then neither did he offer her one of his handsome orange roses.

She had a castle a little way from the square, down next to the river. I had met her a few times during the previous three years, at the town's summer music festival which was held in the castle. Claire and Bernardt always played in its concerts.

I reflected upon how, over a very few years, Bonn had become for us a city of oboe concertos, as we listened to Claire playing in various concerts halls and churches. In every season, a city of Richard Strauss and Marcello, Bellini and Cimarosa. Kalliwoda's Opus 228 had become her haunting signature in various halls around the now dispossessed former capital city.

But now my thoughts returned to the countess. Her castle was not large, but the handsome room in which the concerts were held was gracious and more than pleasant; on the first floor overlooking the Rhine. As the evening light faded on the river outside, and the temperature cooled, and the candles were lit inside, and the music and the summer evening became one. All of it quite implausibly romantic.

The countess did not have the conventional, popular, appearance of a countess. By that I mean she wasn't young or tall, not dazzling in her presence; nor was she at all ostentatious in manner. Certainly I reflected, as I looked out on the square, not Tolstoyan!

She was already over seventy, quite small, and her dress and general deportment were almost studiedly workaday.

Yet, although slim, she had the easy, casual, solidity, of the very wealthy. She was used to it, and as comfortable with it as with the cardigan she wore. Her eyes were calm, certain, neutral and detached, quite in contrast to those of the two candidates. Unlike them she had nothing to prove, certainly not on this square; and importantly she had nothing to hide. Quite the contrary.

As she moved away and out of the square, she nodded to me as I looked on. She missed nothing around her. Noticing everything effortlessly, calmly, without appearing to concentrate.

She had another castle, near Stuttgart.

As men and women passed through the square, they expressed their support by shaking the hand of one or other of the candidates. Greeting one, and mostly ignoring the other. The respective groups of helpers grew ever busier, and I noticed how those of the governing party's candidate were, perhaps surprisingly, all young women; and I noticed how, unlike the countess, they seemed rather haughty.

And now the square was blocked again; this time by two delivery lorries trying to reach the cafés or perhaps the hotel, with beer and bottled water. All around, motorists were stuck. One woman driver got out of her Mercedes to give the lorry drivers the benefit of her Saturday morning opinion. With advice about where each might re-position his lorry.

Her opinion made absolutely no difference to the impasse, as the crowd flowed around the marooned lorries.

A Korean nun carrying a governing party's balloon in one hand and a rose from the opposition party in the other, walked by wearing a serene smile.

Yet the effect of this engaging scene was that I made slow progress in preparing for the ceremony to be held on the following Thursday afternoon. The ceremony in the large and rather famous gleaming white hotel, perched very high up above the Rhine, a few kilometres along from the café in which I sat.

And then the idea came to me, from who knows where, that I could usefully introduce to my audience a particular custom of the Arawak Indians of South America: which is to intentionally introduce a fault into cloth they are weaving.

They do this because they believe that the thoughtless pursuit of perfection is a snare waiting for a rabbit. This memory came into my mind as I reflected upon the likely composition of my audience on Thursday. And its possibilities danced around each other in my head, growing in their appeal. In the sunshine of that morning.

Perhaps, after all, the morning had not been wasted – the entertainment aside. I thought of the wealthy and ambitious parents who would make up the bulk of the audience.

And I pondered upon how I could make the idea palatable to the young people. And I thought of the town officials, the nervous Principal whom I had met when I visited the school, and the school's assiduous Director. And I thought again of how the difference between this event and a Speech Day was that on this occasion there would be speeches but no books as prizes. Perhaps this story might be their prize.

But all of that must wait, for I had promised to collect fresh rolls for lunch, and now it had become late. The morning had almost passed. I had to leave the square, calling at the bakery on the way.

* * *

The last few days had been enormously hot. On Sunday the temperature would pass 35c, and as so often in that part of the Rhine Valley at that time of year, it was very humid. In the evening there were violent thunderstorms. On Monday it was slightly cooler, but overcast with light rain. Carol and I planned to go Bonn in the late morning, on one of the shiny river boats which called at the little town. For an hour-long journey to the former capital city.

In the early afternoon, as the river boat drew near to the city which had once been the home of Beethoven, he who had so filled Dvořák with awe, and where Schumann finally rested, the rain began to clear away. But the temperature was rising again. Carol had arranged to collect some shopping for Claire, and since I still had work to do for Thursday, we decided to meet at 3 o'clock at the ice-café in Kaiserplatz. Under the lime trees.

I'd go straight there, and find a table with my notebook; to settle upon a final shape for what I would say. An hour should be enough now.

When I reached the square, the rain had become heavier again in the heat. I knew the ice-café well, for we had been there quite often when Claire and Bernardt had lived in Bonn. When they were first married.

It was owned by an Italian family. There were two married daughters who both worked at their parents' café with their husbands; both had very young children, and were friends of Claire's.

I sat down outside, under the shelter of a large umbrella; the rain meant that there were not as many other customers as usual.

Maria, one of the daughters, immediately recognized me, and we chatted for a little about the young families. She told me how the children were growing, the youngest being already nineteen months old.

The waiters, when serving the tables outside, used their personal umbrellas against the rain, but soon it began to get underneath them; and then under the tables' umbrellas; dripping down through the leaves of the trees. Someone at the next table to me lit a cigarette, and the wind was in the wrong direction. So I moved inside to a quiet table, just inside the door and near the counter.

As I settled down again, I noticed a poor apparition of a man outside, though perhaps no more than fifty years old, moving slowly from table to table. Asking for change.

Unshaven and emaciated, he also seemed scarcely able to speak, and was clearly dying. Perhaps Aids or Cancer, or some other illness of the sort was the cause of his woeful condition.

Whatever it was, it had already made a wreck of him, so that he appeared almost the mediaeval representation of death itself.

I noticed him again as Maria brought over some more coffee, and I saw the effect of his presence upon the four or five young men waiters, two of them the young fathers of the young families.

They were working behind the counter, and at the kiosk which served customers from the street who just wanted to buy ice cream as they passed. Kugeln of scoops of ice-cream to cool them as they walked on in the heat.

The visitor now stood at the window of the kiosk, and abruptly all conversation between the young men quietened, and then ceased altogether, as did the talk amongst customers at the tables seated nearby. It was as if death itself was visiting Kaiserplatz on that stiflingly hot, wet, June afternoon.

His speech and movements were almost imperceptible. He was static, encased in his long, old, and somehow ragged leather coat. This figure was such a contrast to the usual customers who appeared at the open kiosk window of the ice-café. So different to the faces of young children peering, excited, wondering and always undecided, at the vast array of coloured pots of ice cream laid out before them.

The young men, in particular, were solemn in the presence of this visitation at the open window. The dying man pointed a long finger at a large container of ice-cream; and was handed, in total silence, a scoop of ice-cream in a cornet.

The young husband who served him did so methodically and very carefully. Almost in fear. And the unexpected, unfashionable, customer handed over some coins which were immediately declined. The older man's face moved into what might have been a smile, and he gave the young man what might have been a wink.

Then painfully, and slowly, he ghosted away from the window; along the pavement and away from the shelter of the lime trees. And out into the rain.

For a while, everyone near me in the café, and behind the counter, remained very quiet. I returned to my task of preparation; and then about half an hour later, Carol came smiling through the open door.

A rush of greeting and kissing immediately followed when the family recognized her. After a short while, though, we decided to leave. Walking across Münsterplatz, with the heat and the rain continuing, we headed for a Sicilian pizza and a glass of red wine in another café we knew in Bottlerplatz.

At last it seemed that the rain was clearing away for good, and the afternoon promised to become hot and sunny rather than hot and wet. And we easily found a table outside under some plane trees.

I told Carol about the sick man at the ice-café, as the afternoon's heat fell on us from the trees above. And light, bright and green, pierced through the leaves on to our table, before fastening itself on to the damp pavement all around.

The waitress who came smiling up to us could hardly have presented a greater contrast to the man we had been discussing. No more than twenty two years old, blond, relaxed, and shiningly alive in her white blouse and black apron, her smile felt as welcome as the bright sun over our heads.

At first she appeared entirely conventional in her dress, but when she turned away with our order, and had her back to us, her wheat coloured legs were revealed naked to a long way above the knee. And we laughed. About her remedy to the heat. In the sun under the trees.

It was impossible not to reflect, Faust-like, upon the sick man and the waitress, who like so many young people working in the restaurants, in the town, in the summer, was probably a student at the university.

Her presence seemed to coincide with Carol's arrival and the re-appearance of the bright sunlight. And then as the tables all around began to fill up, our wine came.

I had finally decided upon the direction of what I would say on Thursday to the eighteen year olds, about to leave school for universities or whatever, around the world.

The message would have to be disguised, in order to avoid disturbing some parents, not to mention a few of the great and the good who would be in the audience. But I could do that; I just had to make them laugh first.

The practice of the Arawak Indians was the key, and I decided just to trust that those members of his audience I could reach, would understand. And immediately. Perhaps the ceremony might be fun after all!

Before we caught a tram and the train back, for it was now too late for the river boat, we passed a large bookshop on the market square. And when we looked in, we saw that at the back were three shelves full of the books of Stefan Zweig. Among them were the novels and short stories, published only after his suicide.

And on the train back, I recalled what Bernhardt had said to me on the previous evening, as the conversation had turned to Anna and her difficulties,

"You know, William, Claire has her problems too!"

I had not asked him to explain further, for I really didn't know how to take the comment. Perhaps he thought simply that too much time was spent discussing Anna's problems, and certainly Claire had suggested as much to us on a number of occasions. Or perhaps he could have meant any number of things. And after all, I thought, I had not raised the topic of Anna.

Whatever, I had not pursued the comment, and not mentioned it to Carol. But now it returned to me, if only fleetingly.

PEACOCKE, M.R. Selves. Peterloo Poets, 1995, pp.47, £5.95. 1 871471 57 5.

I should want to own this book just for access to the poem 'Towards an Elegy' alone; but there is much more, besides, to admire in this collection which is indeed a conjunction of differences. It contains two separate but not separated kinds of writing, which draw upon quite different linguistic resources.

There are poems which look back into a life – finding '*the several compartments / to memory's box*'. And there are others which look into places, country places, and the lives which belong there: into for instance, '*fields sharp with lambs*', and the old farmer's '*grin / like a bagful of ferrets*'.

Outside these categories is the ironic 'Mr Henry in Retirement', who when '*the nurse came*', and as '*the condiments were quiet as mice ... was managed quite away*'.

The exquisite 'Towards an Elegy', where '*we lived upside down, slung by the knees / dangling from parapets of lies*', however, combines the differences. As does a poem about the gory days of the making of George Stubbs' art.

M.R. Peacockes's previous collection, ***Marginal Land*** was justly praised; and this new collection has enough in it, that is fine, to justify the same appreciation. Readers in the secondary school can join in.

William Holden

CALDWELL, Roger *This being Eden.* Peterloo. 2001, pp 63, £7. 95. 1-871471-88-5

CUNNINGHAM, Tim *Don Marcelino's Daughter.* Peterloo, 2001, pp 68, £7.95. 1-871471-89-3

These two first collections, from the inimitable Peterloo, have exceptional appeal. Fresh and distinctive, each has a diversity of subjects, is often quotable, and contains fine individual poems: humane and serious, sometimes funny – sometimes grimly.

Roger Caldwell's writing has a precise and winning way with thoughtfulness; a philosophical yet poetic concern for 'mind'. Thus, '*If I lost a finger or a toe / would a little piece of mind then go?*'. Poems such as '*Limits*', '*Images*', '*Judas: His Apology*', '*Bad Weather for Some*', *and* '*Chinese Walls*', express kinds of inner-exile, as presaged by the collection's title. They are in '*the other side of joy*', where '*Bach lasts years / and is the silence at the heart of things*' . Within a '*bouquet of secrets*' where '*the wilderness outside had met / the wilderness within*'.

Around this theme, and variously, philosophical, literary, biblical, historical, mythological, and theological perspectives are lightly drawn, and complement Tim Cunningham's '*pencil sketch of love, / Of life disappearing / Like wrens into a bush*'.

Cunningham's is a collection of contrasts. Flashing and darting, they lie within colours and music. In '*Magnolias*', the whole of a resplendent countryside is conceived as the inside of a church. '*Old Coins*', '*Corrections*', *and* '*Bridget*', are memorable poems of ageing and loss.

In the poems and lives of this luxuriantly imaged collection, '*Sometimes the music stops / But mostly they accept the score / And play the harmonies / That exorcise the demons at the door.*'

Both books belong on library shelves in secondary schools, where their benedictions will fall where they may.

William Holden

Chapter 25

Prague

I wander through Theresienstadt
my heart as heavy as lead
Till suddenly my way ends
right there by the rampart.
I stand there on the bridge
and look down into the valley:
I'd like so much to go further
I'd like so much to go home!
Home! – You strange word,
you make my heart feel heavy.
My home has been taken away from me,
now I no longer have one.
I turn away, saddened and weary,
how hard it is do so!
Theresienstadt, Theresienstadt,
when will our suffering end?
When shall we again be free?

Ilse Weber

Above all else, a teacher must be optimistic. Every kind of teacher. And it is equally important for a parent to be optimistic; for how can we know what may come to us in the future, or burst upon us from the past? Or what may be repeated, da capo?

As I sat in the café in the square of the small Rhineland town, watching democracy in action, I had also reflected with pleasure, and some admiration, upon how Claire was making her way in life. As we had wrestled with the unrelenting destructiveness of Anna's problems, this thought had quite often comforted me.

Claire, at least, seemed to have successfully negotiated the journey to maturity. Her life, I thought as I sat there, was interesting and fulfilled. And I think I probably smiled as I thought of that in the Saturday morning sunshine.

Yet, this history has actually scarcely touched upon Claire and Bernhardt's lives. Their distinctive, peculiar, and inevitable mixture of wonder and terror and error, had somehow become excluded from the story I told myself about our own lives.

They were still at a stage of happiness in their marriage. Neither of our daughters' young husbands had yet felt the full force of their wives' voracious sense of entitlement. And I had yet to wonder, with Lear, whether there is some cause in nature that makes hard hearts.

I had yet also to have cause to ponder upon whether the question might as justly be asked of Claire as of Anna. Or so it has often seemed, and painfully.

Whatever, Claire would have no sympathy for her sister's difficulties, and instead channelled all her energy to creating and meeting the demands of her children.

It had been twenty one years since Claire had first left for Germany, to continue her oboe studies at the Musikhochschule in Cologne. And sixteen years had passed since, after being married in a little church in the hills of Kent, she and Bernardt had settled in the small Rhineland town; up river from Bonn where Bernardt had been born.

Eighteen months after that Saturday morning in the square, a surprise invitation would eventually take me to Prague, a city of accumulated and shocking contrasts, of horrors and harmonies; for so long cut off in the centre of Europe. Not for nothing was it the home of 'black light'.

I have often thought, since, that in life's voyage towards me preserving my reason, I had instinctively looked for new territories; with new wonders and new mysteries. And of course that is probably true for many people. So Bohemia gradually became my new Weald. A territory to browse in if not to own for ever; full of wonder and threat, fears and celebration.

But this was my first visit to Prague.

Long after Kafka had laid bare the peculiar oppressions of that city, and history had intervened to create fresh ones, it had without doubt become, if rather quixotically, a place of fascination for me.

And so I was already prepared for what Paul Leppin describes as its "rat catcher's beauty". And I was prepared to find it as much in the alley ways towards Smíchov as in the courtyards and palaces of Mála Strana; in its fragrant orchard parks as in its picturesque spires lit up at night. Though not in its mean and dusty liquor stores.

Of course it was the city of Mozart as well as Dvořák – he who loved pigeons as well as he loved Mozart above all other composers. The city of Janáček too in a more roundabout way – convinced as he was that the harmonies, tunes, and melodies of music, owed everything to the sounds of human speech.

Prague, the adopted city of Roman Jakobson, whose writing on linguistics and poetry had so beguiled me when I began teaching at Goldsmiths'. Whose name became identified with the 'Prague School of Linguistics'. And then also of Jaroslav Seifert, a native of the city; the maker of songs in spite of everything, and Jakobson's close friend.

But it was Ilse Weber's city too. Poet and musician – and prisoner. In nearby Theresienstadt she "wandered through" a concentration camp that was large enough to be a town, before wandering off into eternity. As music was misused to tell the most inhuman lie of all, to serve the greatest of evils. And fool the Red Cross.

When she left Theresienstadt, it was for Auschwitz. Volunteering to be with sick children on a transport. To sing to them quietly as they were carefully gassed.

The camp was liberated three years after Stefan Zweig killed himself in despair. At around the time I entered my first school.

When I eventually heard a recording of Weber's poem and song: "I Wander through Theresienstadt", I knew I had heard it somewhere before, a very long time ago. It sounded so familiar, as if it had somehow been with me from the beginning. But I had no recollection of where or when that could have been. I just knew that this was not the first time. Could that be possible? That it was part of some buried memory?

And so I took all of these associations and imaginings with me on the plane, as I set out for the mysterious destination, And when I said goodbye to Carol, it was from Cologne/Bonn airport, for we had decided to combine this trip with a visit to Claire and her family. I would be away for seven days.

As I think I may have already mentioned, I was not an enthusiastic frequenter of conferences. But this invitation to Prague followed a paper I had given at one which I had been to three years before. It was later published in a collection of essays on teacher education; and what it argued for had obviously somehow resonated with someone in central Europe.

I was invited to give a lecture, though I preferred to call it a talk leading to conversations, at the Viola Theatre on Národní, just a little along from the National Theatre. The Viola Theatre is known in Prague as the 'Theatre of Poetry'.

When I arrived at my hotel in Mála Strana, I found it was basic yet comfortable; typically 1970s' Prague. On Mělnická, just across from the Bridge of Legions, and around the corner from the elegantly restored Savoy café.

On one of the hotel's front walls was a small plaque commemorating the spot of the death of a Prague citizen, murdered by the Nazis as they left to escape the advancing Russian army. A final present among many. A little further along Mělnická was another plaque, and another commemoration.

At one end of the street, lay the foot of Petřín Hill and the modern sculpture of a succession of fractured, skeletal, metal figures commemorating the victims of fifty years of Communist rule. Hollowed out, with the sky peeking out through their ribs, climbing up from Újezd, towards but never reaching the orchards and rose-beds far above on the top of Petřín.

I had planned a series of small pilgrimages while in Prague, to provide a personal context for my talk at the theatre. They would be a rare and fortunate opportunity for some explorations of the city. Some browsing.

It would take me to the house where Seifert had lived in his apartment, in virtual exile at the end of his life. Now, in summer, up another hill from the tram-stop in dusty Bělohorská, the whole house was azured in wisteria.

And to Dvořák's tomb in the National Cemetery at Vyšehrad, upon which I would see a red squirrel frolicking about, and then away when it saw me. To Vila Amerika, the museum dedicated to the composer's life, to ponder upon the faded ribbons of his medals and honours – awarded by an Emperor of an Empire now quite disappeared.

To a little second-hand bookshop, discovered by accident, tucked away on Myslikova; at 8.30 one morning, where the owner and her daughter showed me, with eyes alight, a pristine copy of a biography of Janáček, which I bought immediately for its price of CK100.

Nor was this the only book I bought at that little Myslikova bookshop, for I found too a surprising paperback copy of A. G. Macdonell's *England Their England*. That lunchtime, I re-read Chapter 7, and Donald's description of the village cricket match at Fordenden. In the 'Slavia' café opposite the National Theatre, where the Velvet Revolution had probably been planned.

Quickly immersed in Fordenden again, I had to stop reading because I could no longer see the pages in front of me through the tears which filled my eyes. On the brink, as I was, of being loudly and publicly convulsed with laughter.

I remembered how it had been the same when I had first been read this chapter at my second school, when I was about fifteen. During the last week of the summer term, when the set texts could be laid aside and examinations forgotten, my English master had read to the class from this book – just because he thought it was something that we would enjoy!

I had certainly, and the effects of doing so then, were the same as now in this Central European café . As I considered cricket in the 'Slavia'. Several times, fifty or so years on, I could only narrowly avoid laughing out loud, sitting as I was – alone at my table. Tears of mirth clouding my vision, and making further reading impossible.

I sensed that I was attracting the attention of other customers seated nearby. And warning glances from bustling waitresses, who would very likely not know their 'forward short-leg' from their 'silly point'!

So I had to put the book aside, replacing it carefully in the bookshop's bag. Wondering as I did so, thinking again of Fordenden, what a Kentish village could possibly be without the long since vanished hop-gardens. Perhaps much like Spring without the call of the cuckoo to announce it? Something I no longer heard.

I discovered in that tiny bookshop that the working day in Prague began early, and I found further proof of this as I became absorbed by the city's strangeness.

Soon after I arrived, I had made a quiet and secretive visit to the theatre where I had been invited to meet my hosts for the first time on Thursday evening. I saw its little terrace-café reached through an arch of stained glass. And when I'd seen it, I left without waiting around.

As I did so, so, I thought of Carol back in Germany, and what I could take back for her from Prague. What might I find just as the sensations of the strange city were at their freshest? And in a side-street just off Národní, near the Viola Theatre, the Theatre of Poetry, I found the answer. In a small Vietnamese shop selling traditional art and craft pieces. An ornamental box covered completely with the many colours of mother of pearl inlays. And it seemed just right.

The letter I'd received before setting out from London, had emphasised that most of my audience would not be native speakers of English. I thought this a useful reminder. And perhaps that letter, along with the residual anxiety which must always attend accepting this kind of invitation, was the reason for a menacing dream I had on my very first night in Prague.

In my dream it was Friday night at the theatre, and I'd arrived for the lecture; and after the usual formal introduction and welcome, I got to my feet to begin. And as I did so, everything I said was turned instantly into gobbledygook. It was as if my speech itself was encrypted. The dream ended there, and I woke up with a start.

However the following morning was full of sunshine, and as I stepped out into the street I saw that, unaccountably, all along it were scattered pages of sheet music. Somebody had obviously dropped them the previous evening. Perhaps just as I was having my nightmare.

The music really did lay all along the pavement and the street, and some of it had blown up on to the windscreens of the lines of parked cars, sticking to them. Better than a parking ticket certainly. And so I took these scattered pages of music to be a good omen, on this my very first morning in Prague. I still think of that morning and its images.

I had decided to visit Dvořák's birthplace at Nelahozeves. For this I must catch the train at Masaryk Station, which on this morning of suddenly bright prospects appeared run-down and shabby. My destination was the tiny station of Nelahozeves Halt, just under an hour's journey time away.

The carriage of the train I joined was dirty and neglected. The vinyl seats were ripped and torn. And it seemed that the whole of the inside of the carriage was smeared with black graffiti. Soiled. It was a slow train, which would stop at Kralupy – twice, for that now sad town still has two stations.

And so my journeys of pilgrimage had already begun to reveal the nature of Prague; of the reality and the dream, of its history and modernity, of its grinding dullness and poverty, of its filth, menace, and glitter – and genuine and startling visual beauty. They had begun to reveal other aspects too. Of my imagined Prague: the frozen music of its architecture, and the echoes of its energy and confidence in the 1920s. And, something still of the glories that Dvořák would have known another thirty years before that.

And all around, too, there were the traces of everything that had come afterwards.

Much of all this was in my mind as the train pulled out of the station. Opposite me sat a middle-aged woman and her two young children. The young girl was nine years old or so, and her brother was perhaps twelve. The scene I was to witness, in spite of myself, would play out all the way to Kralupy, where the little family would get out. The action was slow, quiet; often silent, and cruel.

She sat between her two children, with the boy on her left directly opposite me. The children didn't chatter, indeed they didn't speak to each other at all, and their eyes were full of pain. Mostly they looked straight ahead into nothing, as if they could see things that I couldn't; and not see things that were all around them outside. They avoided my gaze, intentionally or not, and they didn't smile.

Occasionally the boy looked at his mother, and said something to her very quietly. Just in a whisper. Whenever he did this, she snarled back almost inaudibly, and in this way signalled a careless lack of interest in whatever it was that he'd said.

Both children seemed quite lost, perhaps the boy the more so, since it was he who attempted to speak the most. I was startled by their expressions of resigned loneliness as the train trundled through the fields of Bohemia in mid-morning, sometimes along the banks of the Vltava, sometimes away from it. Although the sun shone down upon everything outside, whatever there was to see seemed to be of no interest to them.

They paid no attention to what was there, as if they already understood that it could mean nothing to them.

The mother was no more than forty, and stocky. She was dressed in a simple, printed, and soiled frock with short sleeves. Her face was sweating, and her eyes were bloodshot, their lids red and swollen; and her lips were blue as they closed repeatedly around the neck of a plastic litre-bottle of orange liquid. The bottle was re-cycled, and had obviously originally contained something other than liquor. Probably lemonade.

Little trickles of spittle ran down her chin as she drank and perspired in the growing heat of the morning. And as she drank, her manner became increasingly sullen. Increasingly unaware of the children, except when she sneered at the boy's attempts at conversation.

Behind my book, I felt an unwilling participant in the scene, yet all the while feeling drawn to it. And I would recall again those small dusty liquor stores, which seemed to be everywhere in Prague once the visitor found themselves outside the scenic splendour of its centre.

And I remembered immediately something I had witnessed the previous afternoon when walking through the small park on Wilsonova, near the State Opera House. The same opera house where Klemperer had begun his conducting career – after receiving a letter of recommendation from Mahler.

As I had walked through the park, I heard a clicking sound of disapproval from a young woman as she passed. New in the city, having only arrived a few hours before, I quite unreasonably thought that this phatic and involuntary gesture was somehow directed at me. And so I followed her eyes enquiringly and automatically.

Then I saw that they were actually resting upon a young man of twenty or so, who was stretched out upon a bench under a tree in the sun. He was injecting himself from a syringe, openly in the afternoon. And then I saw that there were others on the grass in the little park doing the same thing. Scattered around like sheep in a pasture. This wasn't a dream.

My reflections upon that earlier scene, were interrupted by the train's arrival at the first of the Kralupy stations. A square was visible from the train, and the town appeared grey, dusty and forbidding, as I looked again at the departing faces of the young boy and his younger sister.

Their mother walked unsteadily towards the door clutching her bottle of orange liquid, now considerably reduced; and her children walked behind her, quietly and respectfully. She had hardly spoken to them during the thirty minutes of their journey together.

And now she left, silent still, with her children, and they were all swallowed by the dismal, depressed, town in the dusty sunshine. The drunken mother, and her bewildered, silent, watchful, and disappearing, children.

When soon afterwards, I crossed the track at the tiny station of Nelahozeves Halt, it was to find the little museum, which had been Dvořák's birthplace, closed. Its gates festooned with geraniums were definitely shut; but not locked. Peering over and behind them I could see the neat courtyard of the former inn.

In mediaeval times, there would have been a green wreath at the entrance to the inn. There would then have been a green wreath also on coffins. For it was believed that the dead would first assemble in an inn, before descending into hell. So perhaps, I reflected, better a closed museum than an old inn. Better too that this was just a flying visit – and that I was alone!

But it was not the museum that I had come to see; rather the place in which it stood, alongside the lonely little station.

Nearby was a small church, and standing over the station and the church was the elegant château of Nelahozeves, with its black and white sgraffito walls luminous in the sun. It seemed likely, at any second, to fall upon everything below and embrace it. Near the church there was an hospoda, with cool gardens and beer. But that was a visit for later.

I walked up to the château, the only caller that morning. To look at its galleries, its paintings and halls; to visit eventually its excellent and reasonably priced restaurant for lunch. And before that to discover the modern, well-stocked, and inviting bookshop; containing many Czech books in English translation. And there I noted with a smile how a 1960s' anti-war song, '*Where have all the flowers gone?*' was playing in English. I remembered it well from student days. I'd not heard it since.

Neither the station nor the great house seemed a tourist attraction that day. Perhaps because the museum was closed.

When I returned to the hospoda and the little station at the end of the day, to wait for a train back to Prague, I saw how derelict the station actually was. The waiting room was locked and full of rubbish. The windows were mostly broken, and its walls were besmirched with very inelegant graffiti.

So here was the contrast again: the sgraffito and the graffiti: the wonder and the squalor, the celebration and the neglect, the past and the present – though I knew that later judgement wasn't quite fair. For when the train arrived, it was a double-decker express from Dresden. Modern, sparklingly clean and fast, dramatically different from the morning train.

There was only one other passenger to join the train with me that early evening, a young woman. She was greeted on board by a smiling young man of her own age, who was obviously expecting her. They kissed in greeting, and immediately started to chat quietly, confidentially, with shining eyes, perhaps anticipating their evening in Prague.

The train did not stop at Kralupy, not even once; and they had no reason to notice. They were pre-occupied with other things, just as the morning's silent children had their pre-occupations. For very different reasons each couple was unaware of the fields of Bohemia, shining and swiftly slipping almost silently past into the evening sun.

Walking, quite late now, back across the Bridge of Legions in the warmth of the evening, I was suddenly in a whole crowd of people on their way home, and walking along with me. The castle gleamed up on our left, and I heard the steady tread of steps behind me. Not a secret policeman, but only a confident, beautiful, twenty-one-year old woman – just returning from work.

I was walking to the Louvre café, for dinner.

After the first morning in the hotel, I had stopped having breakfast in its dining room. Instead I went to the Louvre, on Národní, just up from the National Theatre. Indeed just a little across from the Viola Theatre.

Breakfast in the hotel dining room, a kind of basement cellar, had been hot, crowded and noisy that first morning. There was a large group of young, female, and loud, British tourists on an extended hen-party. And while the food was plentiful, it was also unappealing and dull.

In contrast, breakfasts at the Louvre café were fresh, varied and peaceful. Sitting there with the sun streaming through the windows of the spacious, cool, second floor restaurant, it was easy to imagine Kafka, many years before at the next table. The table linen was immaculately white, as no doubt it had been for him.

The calm rooms of the large café were free of tourists at that hour; and just a few of the tables were occupied by youngish local people who were seemingly having working breakfasts together. Breakfasts that were for me, happily, not at all expensive because of the favourable exchange rate.

And so this café would become a favourite of mine during my very first week ever in Prague. One of the practical advantages it offered, was easy access to toilet and washing facilities, which I could even visit sometimes without necessarily having to enter either of the restaurants. Still wrestling, as I was, with the after-effects of recent radiotherapy treatment, this was not a minor consideration.

So, the Louvre café was not only a place of gradual awakening at the beginning of the day, but it became a base from which my daily small pilgrimages and explorations began.

And one of these resulted in a series of unlikely discoveries about the war-time popular song: ***'Roll Out the Barrel'***.

I had previously had no interest in this song. I knew of it, but that was all. Had I known it in its original form, before the many alterations and adaptations had befallen its lyrics and the arrangement of the original music, I would I think have been very interested in it. These alterations were fashioned by the contexts and purposes, the preoccupations and privations, of a world war. A war which had only just ended when I was waiting with my small, limp, red, warm notebook and chewed pencil, for the bus edging around the bend in the road in front of the church. In my first village. Making notes.

And it all happened because another bright sunny morning found me on a small bus to Zbraslav, to visit another château on the Vltava river. It housed an exhibition of oriental art which had been widely praised. And then again, I was also very curious about the flavours and colours to be found in at least one small Czech town on the immediate outskirts of Prague. What could be better than seeking them out on a short bus trip into the completely unknown?

SMITH, Ken and BENSON, Judi (Editors) *Klaonica: poems for Bosnia*. Bloodaxe, 1993, pp. 128, £7.95. 185224 283 3

So, we have an international anthology of 113 poems to raise funds for Bosnia.

As here, one of the functions of poetry is to record the unspeakable, and with a few exceptions each of these poems makes its own terrible contribution in this book. Its record is of a multi-faceted despair; when hope itself can seem a greater cruelty. A record of what occurs when civil society ceases to exist; and individual lives lose significance and purpose. When everyone, instead, belongs to a community that has become the cauldron; mesmerised , looking in, and struggling to secure belief.

This is a poetry '*to voice the daily grief*'; 'of *learning to live without dreams*'. Where language makes its record, '*bent double / crossing into death*'. When the child realizes that '"*There is no-one left to forgive me.*"'

And yet to record is to affirm the need for truth; to re-affirm, also, a need to make art: for '*only love can lighten things ...*'.

I wonder if there can be a justification for this book not being on the shelves of the library in every secondary school, and institution of further, and higher, education?

William Holden

I left the bus in the centre of the little town by its war memorial, with not the slightest idea which direction to take to the château. I had looked out for it from inside the bus as we had sped into the town, but could get no clue. As I was examining the details on the memorial, I saw a quite elderly lady approaching, along the street towards me; and it was to her that I put my enquiry about directions for the château.

Her response was to take my elbow, and to guide me in the opposite direction to that I'd been taking. She insisted on taking me to the very entrance of the château itself, a little way back along the street that the bus had brought me.

This short journey was full of conversation, as in excellent English she told me how, when young, she had stayed with a family in Brighton as an au pair. She was very curious about why I was in Zbraslav.

When I explained that I'd come to visit the exhibition at the château, she seemed quite extravagantly pleased at such an idea. Then she interrupted what she had been saying about Brighton, by gripping my arm tightly again and directing my attention to the town restaurant as we passed it. Its Czech name was '**Škoda Lásky**,' which I later discovered translated into 'Unrequited Love'.

"When you have finished at the museum", my guide confided in almost a whisper and still holding on to my arm, "that would be a very good place to have lunch!"

If my mentioning this incident seems still a long way from what I was saying about the war-time song, '***Roll Out the Barrel***', I must ask you to be patient for just a little longer.

For now, as my guide and I said goodbye to each other at the gates of the château, she ended our short and pleasant meeting by saying,

"Well, I never thought that I should meet an Englishman in Zbraslav!"

And with that she turned back, with a quiet chuckle, to the tasks of her morning shopping which my question out of a fine clear morning had interrupted. Three hundred yards and twenty five minutes before.

I was the only visitor to the exhibition that morning, and perhaps this unlocked the displays of pride shown by the elderly female attendants in their place of work. Only my lack of Czech, and their lack of English, prevented further long, informative, conversations as they directed my attention to first one exhibit and then another.

And so, eventually and inevitably, I returned to 'Unrequited Love' for lunch, and having ordered something large and Czech, and actually delicious, my attention was drawn towards the many surprises and puzzles which were in frames all around me on the walls of the little restaurant.

These puzzles took the form of framed photographs of the owners of the restaurant, the Vejvoda family. They were standing alongside George Bush Snr., the former President of the United States. All of them smiling out together upon the diners' tables.

That was the puzzle. Why, I wondered, had the President of the U.S. come to visit this tiny restaurant in this small Czech town? And it was then that I began to stumble a little further towards a musical discovery which has a central if minor place in recent European history, and in modern Czech history. One which then, as now, lay in the loneliness and vulnerability of a small country at the very heart of the continent.

And moreover, it was a discovery which would provide an ironical commentary upon the life of my own small family.

Sometime afterwards, I would gradually piece together how Jaromiv Vejvoda, a local band leader, had written his 'Modřany Polka' in Prague in 1929; and how it was only later when the Czech lyrics were added, that the song was called 'Unrequited Love'. And that the family restaurant gained its name.

The full and original version of the music and the lyrics were haunting and subtle in ways that were entirely absent in the revised, much more widely known, popular wartime version. It was a love song, in a way that ***'Roll Out the Barrel'*** was definitely not. How could it be, when it had been changed into a soldier's drinking song; made to serve the purposes of war for both sides in the conflict?

Not only was the sad music of the original, adapted and re-arranged, but the lyrics of the Czech song were replaced – and nearly lost.

They had originally asked:

"*What happens to all our wasted love?*" And concluded, "*What a pity about love, our wasted love!*"

Not at all the sentiments of a war-time marching song.

And so it was that this accidental discovery in Zbraslav reminded me of how, in such ways, a life is constructed as in a dream, from accidents, meetings along the way, questions, and conversations. From things said and heard, or not, as circumstances allow or dictate. All of them providing meaning, and meanings, to a life; or to dreams from which we may eventually wake up – or not.

As I sat on the bus on the half-hour journey back to Prague, I reflected upon how unrequited love may be experienced just as much by parents for their children, as by young people driven by desire. And, especially upon how the love of ageing parents for their grown-up children may be unrequited, and often is. And I knew too that the natural fear of ageing may be amplified by other fears; and that the years, as they pass, may quite easily turn our fears for our children into a fear of them.

How common, may I ask you, do you think are the kinds of fears and forebodings I felt that evening as I returned to Prague on the bus? Do you know? Is it a matter of secrets necessarily well kept? Too well kept? Of silences too well maintained? Or perhaps these questions just seem nonsense to you. Actually I hope so. Really.

As the bus approached Smíchov bus station, these questions, and the whispered confidence of my guide as we had passed the restaurant that morning, led straight to a recollection of some lines of a long poem by Jaroslav Seifert; "from all the verses in the world to which (he'd) added just a few" – another whispered confidence:

"The worst is over now,
I tell myself: I'm old.
The worst is yet to come:
I'm still alive."

And yet I knew, on that bus as now, that more than one death may await us all; for instance if we lose someone we love.

And so another small pilgrimage, a tentative if excited exploration, had led me deep into the territory of my own and my family's life. And as I waited on a platform of the metro station at Anděl, on my way back to the city centre, I saw that inset in a tiled wall was a large concrete sculpture of a hammer and sickle. Not yet removed.

On the metro train, as throughout that week, the Slav language was strange to my ears, as each approaching station was announced over the public address system. Foreign sounds combined into words. A stranger in a strange land, I heard the music of the tongue. And it was something approaching that first poetry of speech, experienced by every infant when they first hear people around them talking – and talking to them. No wonder their eyes open wide.

My fellow possibility of passengers, young and old, many with pale and tired faces, had by now heard their language too often to be interested in more than the messages it contained; so important for them as they were. I heard the sounds but not the words. And they heard mostly the words and not the sounds.

They had appointments to keep, and they needed to know where they were. People were waiting for them. Their concern was, for the most part, only with the outcome of the message, with information; as proof of their progress through the day. They were not at this point concerned with the sounds of the words as they had once had heard them, as they had both once been. As they once were: both the sounds and the hearer.

All of these thoughts and reflections from when I had first set out for Zbraslav that morning, led me once again to the Louvre café. To a light supper, a very white tablecloth, and a glass of Moravian wine. Deep and red.

And now only a day remained before my Thursday evening appointment in the little café on the theatre's terrace, under its arch of stained glass. I planned to spend most of it at the Vila Amerika, the museum dedicated to Dvořák; in the evening I had a ticket for a performance of 'Rusalka' at the National Theatre. And as usual, I set out from the Louvre, this time along Janackovo nábřezí, at around 9.30, and when the new day was already quite hot and sticky.

As I walked back across the Bridge of Legions, I seized another opportunity to look up at the castle, resplendent in the still soft morning. And then I turned along the bank of the river, by the channel past 'Children's Island'. On the opposite bank, facing the sun, were the imposingly handsome houses of Masarykovo nábřezí, the frozen music of their facades flaunting its charms to the morning. These so grand houses, which had long since been divided into apartments.

I walked on, by two barges moored to each other. On one, a young man was swabbing the deck, and on the other his friend was watering roses in a trough. And the gardener laughed as he suddenly turned the hose upon his friend, who complained – though mostly for effect.

My new exploration took me back across Jiráskův bridge and into Resslova, where a young boy was standing precariously on some railings reaching for plums with a long pole. Beneath him on the street below, the interminable Prague traffic rushed past both ways. And as I walked, I noticed how the humidity of the day had insinuated itself into my watch, so that the dial and the hands were barely visible beneath its glass.

The way took me on past the gleaming white church of St Cyril and St Methodius where, not so long before, SS troops had cornered the two Czech airman who had assassinated the brutal Reichsprotektor Heydrich. Then further on, into the morning, along Ječná, to find the dark red and elegant, Vila Amerika; just off Katěrinská, resting peacefully in the dusty heat of the still quite young day.

I walked around to the back of the building, which was easily accessible, to look at the garden; and to discover a group of gardeners on their morning break. Like the bargeman, they too were spraying each other with water from a hose.

At one moment, the oldest man in the group, stripped to the waist, trained the hose on himself. 'Paradiso!" he called out when he saw me, mistaking my nationality.

They all stopped for a second, and the older man laughingly offered me the hose. Cupping my hands I washed my face with the deliciously cool water.

When I stumbled out a 'děkují' of thanks, their laughter tumbled all around the garden. And then they returned to their plants and the brown lawn; and I turned back, retracing my way to the front of the building.

It was hugely hot in the museum, and the attendant at the desk was about to leave, perhaps for an early lunch. He was straight from central casting. His face might have been chosen for its obvious Slavic, if gloomy, antecedents; eyes and hair as if he'd stepped out of a picture by Mucha.

I hurried to buy my entrance ticket, and a CD of Dvořák's 'Gypsy Songs', from a little display of discs on the desk. Just to celebrate the morning, and having met the gardeners, seen the boy stretching for plums above the traffic, and the young bargeman watering his roses. And being there.

I would play the CD long after that visit, redolent as it is of the wilting plants in the parched garden of the villa. Redolent also of the recording of the composer's 'American Quartet' which, along with others, played during that afternoon on the hi-fi system in the salon. Among the faded and fading memorabilia of the dead composer, in its glass cases.

The salon had a little stage, for sometimes it was used for recitals. But not today. Today I was the only visitor, and only the recorded music played; while outside violent thunderstorms raged for most of the afternoon. Cleansing the day of the heat and dust of the morning.

At one point I stood looking at the threatening sky, watching the lightning, and listening to the thunder crashing all around the deserted salon in the temporarily isolated museum. And I thought of how I'd read of Dvořák's own nervousness about thunderstorms, and how this had led to some distracted behaviour in later life. To his immediately closing the shutters, lighting the lamps, and playing the piano loudly to shut out the crashes.

And now in the background the 'American Quartet' played on, in reply to the thunder.

And as I listened to its sad and isolated beauty, I remembered how I'd also read in the same source, that even as he was being lauded in New York, Dvořák could not afford to pay for a seat at the Metropolitan Opera House. Such were his family responsibilities.

And I thought how it is that, quite naturally, contradictory truths may combine to make a larger one. That Dvořák could write with insistence how his early poverty had fed his determination as a composer. But that he could write also, at about the same time, how much he regretted that this same poverty had resulted in his being unable to attend the National Conservatory in Prague. How he believed that "a more thorough musical training" which his doing so would have made possible, would have enabled him to have achieved "so much more".

And I wondered, as I stood at the window. So much more than the beauty and joy of this music? And so much more than all that he left behind in this world? And I remembered how I'd first heard his Prague Waltzes. On a coach I should not have been riding on. So many years before.

And I thought of how the joy and colour in those waltzes was expressed also in the many other national dances, around and within Dvořák: in the dumkas and the sousedskás, the furiants and the skočnás; the sp̌acírkas, odzemeks, kolos, mazurs, and polkas.

It was late in the afternoon before the heavy rain moved away, and I was able to hurry back to the hotel, and shower before leaving for the theatre. The performance, I'd noted, began at seven o' clock which was earlier than I would have liked. So, there would be no time to eat.

Sitting at the opera among the prosperous looking members of the Czech audience, I couldn't help wondering what role each of them might have played only ten years before. Which would have been the informers, and which the informed upon; and how many would have been both, in the so subtly comprehensively oppressive regime; so recently and surprisingly swept away?

Was it just my imagination that here was a people still cut off in the centre of Europe? And more than that, still cut off from each other? What was there to be read in those pale faces, all of whom had played out their own especial roles for so long until recently? Difficult to tell, for they seemed to have learned to wear a particular expression. And was it in my imagining also that they seemed so seldom to smile?

What appeared so clear, to even the casual observer, was that for many here the transition from totalitarianism had been easy enough. Many of my companions, that evening, had been successful before and would be still. Well placed to carry on making the best, and taking the best, of everything.

Earlier in the week, I had from curiosity, and following the information provided by my excellent guidebook which I'd learned to trust, attempted to find the former headquarters of the StB., the former Czech secret police. I had walked up and down the street so clearly described by the guide book, looking for the building. But I could find no sign of it where the book said it should be. The young woman at the British Council enquiry desk couldn't help either.

I asked several local people, but they all said they knew nothing about the building, or where it could be. I went into one of the two new smart hotels on the street, and asked at the desk, and my enquiry caused some consternation. Eventually a middle-aged man from the hotel came up to me, insistent that he had lived in Prague all his life and knew the street well. And he had never heard of the building I was enquiring about, and couldn't think where it could be anywhere in Prague. He had also never heard of the StB!

A mystery then among other mysteries, which it was fruitless to continue to pursue. So I gave up asking my naïve question.

And this was the first time that I had heard, or seen, the whole of Dvořák's opera. This tale of the water nymph, a 'rusalka', who having fallen in love with a prince, traded her power of speech for the chance of having a human soul. So confident was she of experiencing the fidelity of human love. And in the production this evening, the stage design created the illusion of water washing over the stage and even into the orchestra pit. Even into the stalls!

I knew that there are many rusalkas, water nymphs and wood nymphs, in Slavic folklore. Nor, no doubt, are they confined to Bohemia. I mused during the opera, how they could well have been found around the wealden ponds of my childhood. Disappearing into the shadows and the silences of the little woods, laughing and fading behind the willow trees. It was inconceivable that they were to be found in my second village. For that belonged to a different set of pre-occupations; and in any case, I joked to myself, the sandstone ridge had few woods. And no ponds. Obviously!

Always found in natural and therefore potentially lonely places, rusalkas are representative of the beauty of nature, and as a result are never able to interact fully with human society. When interaction does occur, it is often with dangerous and unpleasant consequences for everyone involved. And so it is in Dvořák's opera, his music, Erben's story, and Jaroslav Kvapil's libretto.

As I followed the English, electronic, translation of the action, on the discreet monitor above the stage, and in thrall to the music, I could not help thinking of 'illegitimacy'. That the illegitimate are by definition representative of nature, and again by definition, can yet never interact automatically with society. Not in the 1950s anyway.

I remembered how I'd never found it possible to deal with those simple questions, which were both inevitable and unremarkable to most people around me at the time. About mothers and fathers. How it had been impossible to avoid giving answers to enquiries which were only approximations to serve the moment. Impossible not to lie by small degrees; so adding to my sense of shame, as if it was all my fault. How it was impossible not to be mute, silent, about not belonging to a tribe.

Again, by definition, the illegitimate have limited claims upon human society. Inevitably therefore, this is a condition which takes a lifetime to manage. The illegitimate are outside the law in quite specific and well defined ways, which was where Rusalka found herself. Love can in the most miraculous circumstances actually be the remedy, if we are fortunate – even though it wasn't for Rusalka.

I knew that for me it was, though none of us can be free of the ill-chance that may suddenly threaten us from the past.

As I sat, near the end of the opera, and as Rusalka sank into the lake, yet destined always to lure innocent souls to their deaths as a punishment for her misjudgement, I read the monitor as Rusalka's restored speech addressed her dying prince:

"For your love, for your beauty,
For your inconstant human passion,
For all that condemned me to my fate,
May God have mercy on your human soul.
May God have mercy on you".

These final words from the stage fell into a long, deep, silence in the theatre; a silence which was still part of the performance. A musical silence which was a further ironical commentary upon Rusalka's loss of speech; and after her attempt to gain human love.

And I recalled that when we were young, it had been in a theatre that I had asked Carol if she would marry me.

The silence of the human souls around me in the audience, the silence of their shared exposure, swallowed the theatre, as the spell of the story and the music remained – until finally it was broken by thunderous applause.

That long silence had reminded me of a lesser silence forty nine years before, after I'd finished reading extracts from Arnold's poem to that very first class of young people – having first told them the story of Sohrab and Rustum. The silence of those fifteen year olds, who now were nearly old themselves, returned to me; as did the memory of that one girl's repeated comment to her friend as they left the room:

"That's really sad!"

The extracts from Arnold's poem and the narrative relayed from the stage to the monitor created similar silences. The one, because the young audience had gradually realized that the father could kill his son only because Sohrab stayed his hand having realized whom he was fighting. The other, because a mature and worldly wise Bohemian audience realized afresh, in spite of knowing the story by heart, that, after all, the contest could not be won. And the key to this alchemy … was Dvořák's music.

Suddenly hungry now, I rushed out of the Opera House and into the cleansed summer night, with no thought for the young men still stretched out on the seats and grass of the nearby park. I found a restaurant on Vítežná that was still open; where a waiter took pity on me and brought me food – just as the establishment was about to close after its usual long day.

My short explorations and pilgrimages were nearly over. All that remained were tomorrow evening's meeting at the theatre's café, a final rehearsal by reading through the headings on my lecture cards in the peace of the Louvre café – and giving the talk itself.

And I would explain again how the approach to preparing teachers to teach poetry in the classroom which I had introduced in the paper that had brought me to this city, echoed Octavio Paz's reminder that we all of us not only use language, but "*are language which produces language*". That children's loss of poetry is comparable to Rusalka's loss of speech. Its removal will result in their being unable to live properly.

Indeed I would try to illustrate, again, that the whole story of poetry and schools now, is not only about our failing to give children something, but rather it is too often about taking away from them something which they already possess. Something which defines their nature, just as it defined the nature of their forbears.

Its loss is a kind of dying – and one of the consequences of our moving against a secret of nature: the community of childhood.

I would set out, in the talk, to demonstrate yet again how children can give each other models for reading poetry, for listening to it, for talking about it, and offering it to everyone they know, at school and at home. Models for writing it and thinking about it. That when we see this as part of all the other composing that they are capable of, we find them informing each other, not as experts to the inexpert but rather as the increasingly expert to the increasingly expert.

As usual I would ask a series of questions: Is it possible that our education systems are becoming de-humanizing again? Is that necessary? Do they oppress children? Do they have to? Must schools be so utilitarian? And empty competition be so enshrined? Can they not concentrate again on the best possibilities? Why does it matter?

Rhetorical questions only of course, and intentionally mischievous. As usual I would let children's recorded voices suggest the answers. Let them insist upon them. Let them remind us that poetry as well as music makes it possible for us all to sing. If we have a voice. Just as we can dance if we can walk.

The meeting with my hosts at the theatre was easy, and the few remaining organizational details were quickly dealt with over a quiet meal. After I'd said goodbye, I wandered a little again around a few of the very strange streets that I had come to know just a little, and which had assumed some small familiarity. I wanted to use this time as a way of making final preparations for tomorrow evening, and my journey home.

On my way back to my own hotel, I passed the old Europa Hotel on Wenceslas Square. Two old men were absorbed in a game of chess outside at one of the tables; silent and unaware of all else in the evening bustle, and slight sleaziness, which was all about them.

Friday was my last proper day in Prague, and I determined that it would be a gentle one; in preparation for the evening. I spent the morning in the orchards at the top of Petřín Hill, walking quite accidentally past the bust of the Czech poet Karel Mácha, who wrote a bloodthirsty and popular poem: 'May'. About, of all things, unrequited love! And whose father had hop-gardens. Proof of the popularity of the poem still, is the custom for lovers to make a pilgrimage to the spot on 1st May every year.

Before I left, to be at the theatre by six o'clock, I packed for the following morning's departure, showered, and changed my clothes. My first visit to Prague was almost over.

I knew that the night ahead was likely to be a long one, extending well after I'd finished my conversations at the theatre. I had an early start the next morning, because of needing to be at the airport before seven. Sadly, there would be no time for breakfast at the Louvre.

My flight for Cologne/Bonn left from Ruzyně Airport at nine; 'Ruzyně', where very close by and not long before, Václav Havel had been imprisoned for speaking and writing. Just for speaking and writing. Just for refusing to be silent.

Only the final tasks remained that afternoon before leaving for the 'Theatre of Poetry': to pay my bill and book an early taxi at the hotel desk – for the morning.

At around eleven o'clock on Saturday morning, I met Carol at Cologne/Bonn airport, only a little hung over. She had always been my lovely girl, and that's how she was that late summer morning; as we kissed just before noon. And as we anticipated our afternoon and evening in Bonn.

DOBIE, Kirkpatrick *Selected poems*. Peterloo, 1992, pp.63, £6.95 1 871471 31 1

This is a book of poems which quietly demonstrates the necessity of poetry. Their quality reminds us how its value, and origins, lie elsewhere than in literariness. The voice here speaks plainly and musically out of a long life, often to protest; and the poems that result are unpretentious but reflective, vigorous and very appealing. Their freshness will appeal directly to the young adult reader.

Kirkpatrick Dobie's sharp eye and balanced ear scan far and wide – and if their judgements are summary, they always seem just. An example is in the poem 'Aberfan' which condemns, without compromise, the routine betrayal of ordinary souls by those protesting virtue. Thus, *'The Church saw nothing wrong / They only wanted to belong / Their only horror was the fate / of seeming to be out of date'.* Another poem, 'The Voice of Divinity' reminds us how *'God is a very common thing like bread / There's loss in ordination'.* This is equally true of poetry of course, which the poem is also about.

We need this kind of writing of social commentary, and the young need it particularly to reassure them. If it is true in a way, and I think it is, that *'poetry has few friends, though many flatterers'* ('Ça Ira'), those friends will admire this book.

William Holden

RUTHERFORD, Maurice. *And Saturday is Christmas: Collected Poems.* Shoestring Press, 2011, £10.00. 9870 1 907 35621 6

The effects of love, and the dilemma of death, are sharply juxtaposed in Maurice Rutherford's New and Selected poems drawn from a long life (see TSL vol. 37, no.4, and vol. 43, No.2).These distillations from *Slipping the Tugs* (1982), *This Day Dawning* (1989), *Love is a Four Letter World* (1994), and *After the Parade* (1996), offer prescient rewards for returning to the original collections.

Not for nothing does a quatrain from the *Rubaiyat* appear on the frontispiece, introducing poems that are conflations of the pastoral and place, joy and loss, the domestic and the universal.

In the large number of new poems, the intensities of ageing lay bare the fear that '... *time's riptide is far too strong / for both the singer and his song*'. But look again at this luminous poem, 'Look Twice'; and you may recall *'the two young lovers ... / each watching the other grow old*' ('Love Story', 1989). And see the valedictory poem 'Light', beginning: *'When the sun bleeds over the edge / of the world one last time / for me – or for you – may our pledge / have been kept ...*'.

If , in this last section, the physical condition and conditions of ageing are in yet clearer focus, so also is poetry – and writing it. Thus, '*age peels away, reveals a young man's brain / and maybe, on the page, a poem again*' ('The Fertile Year').

Just as new poems are welcomed as '*guests*', so are other poets – many other poets – in this poetry of softly nuanced truths. As *'the linnet on the laburnam / shows poetry to the other birds'* ('Poem on Saturday' 1982), in the poem 'Lights Out', addressed to Vernon Scannell, poetry's power *'to captivate the mind'* is spoken of by a poet to another.

Remaining undeceived, and still enchanted, the engaged and engaging voice in these pages will captivate the mature reader in the secondary school – and beyond.

William Holden

Epilogue

> He who can drown out a spring thunderstorm,
> on whom laughter was bestowed in the cradle,
> who is not inclined to cry without cause,
> who knows love and is cherished,
> ...
>
> Karel Švenk

I really don't believe that William ever regretted his decision that afternoon, when he was thirteen, to turn away from the blue door in Westerford. The blue door with its paint peeling in the summer sun. Ever believed that it wasn't for the best.

When he told me of that incident, I confess I wondered whether perhaps there might have been a patient behind that door. And that the person who opened it could have been a nurse.

After his foster father died at the good age of eighty three, I believe William lost touch with the family; though Evelyn, Arthur and Christine had all been at his wedding two years before. Christine was a bridesmaid; by then the shock and pain of her injuries from the fire had brought on diabetes.

Dorothy died at well over eighty in a psychiatric ward, following a second admission. Hers is one of the stories that he was not able to tell in this history, just as Claire's is another.

Anna suffered repeated attacks of mania after her diagnosis; and so it was that one of William's discoveries was the strangeness that, for their daughter, the many opportunities she had been given became a very special kind of burden to her. This strangeness, at times, resulted in ever violent and desperate attacks upon her parents, in which she involuntarily involved her young children. I believe that these were more intense than anything I'd heard about before.

Stefan Zweig hated his secondary school. And if those years of formal schooling were a burden for him, it was the opposite for William. Without doubt his two schools saved him.

He had a quiet belief that schools could save others also; that they can offer 'best possibilities'. He never revised that view either. Nor his understanding that being educated was a means of travelling rather than a state at which to arrive.

When he decided to retire early, there were two leaving parties for him – in the Faculty and in the College's Senior Common Room. Sadly, I attended both of them.

He died suddenly one afternoon, not from his illness but in a car accident. In a village near his home. A driver from Lithuania thought he was still at home, and hit William's car on the wrong side of the road. There was no-one else involved.

The car radio was on, as usual, and before help arrived and it was turned off, music accompanied the noise and chaos at the scene of the impact. Schubert's '*Winter Journey*' was just starting. '***Goodnight***' played on regardless, with no-one nearby to listen.

"I came a stranger, ...

I cannot choose the time
Of my journey:

Softly, softly, the door closes!
..."

And so William finally came face to face with the Hurdy-

Gurdy Man. The same who had been playing always. Just around the corner.

William told me at some point, when well passed seventy, how he had become aware, in despair, that physical love making had eventually become expunged even from his dreams. As a result of the effects of the drugs which he had to take continuously as his cancer progressed.

When neither he nor Carol could sleep, for whatever reason in the middle of long nights, they checked very often with each other: "Are you alright?" Or, "Do you want to cuddle me?"

They hardly ever missed the shipping forecast.

He loved her above everyone and everything, and he admired her and wondered at her, right to the end.

Another of his particular loves, also allowing him a lesser silence, was the poetry of Czeslaw Milosz; not least, he said, because it contains hope against the evidence. Hope, to put with the admiration and love. He told me how he thought it could help us to understand our own story. Without interrupting it.

Wherever he is now, I like to think that he will remember Milosz's poem:

Meaning

– When I die, I will see the lining of the world.
The other side, beyond bird, mountain, sunset.
The true meaning, ready to be decoded.
What never added up will add up,
What was incomprehensible, will be comprehended.
– And if there is no lining to the world?
If a thrush on a branch is not a sign,
But just a thrush on the branch? If night and day
Make no sense following each other?
And on this earth there is nothing except this earth?

– Even if that is so, there will remain
A word wakened by lips that perish,
A tireless messenger who runs and runs
Through interstellar fields, through the revolving galaxies
And calls out, protests, screams.

1991

translated by the poet and Robert Hass

Notes

page xiv — the A. E. Housman lines are from A Shropshire Lad. The poem begins: "Loveliest of trees…".

page 3 — "sun-heated doorsteps" is adapted from a line in Tomas Tranströmer's poem 'Five Stanzas to Thoreau', translated by Robin Fulton.

page 4 — the Vita Sackville-West line is from her long poem 'The Garden'.

page 5 — "… the sun / smooth its hand across the corn", is adapted from a line in David Scott's poem 'My Best Hatt'.

page 6 — the mention of a tank is a reference to the Czeslaw Milosz lines in his poem 'Preparation':

"… the cannon of a tank/Growing immense at the corner of a street."

page 11 — "When June in festive garb/pushed jasmine under our windows" are lines from Jaroslav Seifert's long poem 'The Plague Column'.

page 14 — "… what rustled in the fern?/I feel my flesh divide" are lines from Theodore Roethke's poem 'The Small'.

page 46 — "Don't shoot me soldier!". This is a young women's plea to the invader; perhaps a little more likely to succeed than her avoiding other even more obvious threats. The line is from

Alexander Solzhenitzen's long poem 'Prussian Nights'.

page 46 Milosz. Ibid. Note as for p.6.

page 59 "The cuckoo shouts all day at nothing/In leafy dells alone..." are lines from A.E. Housman's Last Poems; from a poem beginning:

"Tell me not here, it needs not saying,
What tune the enchantress plays
..."

page 60 "The Bird of Time has but a little way/To flutter – ..." are lines from The Rubaiyat of Omar Khayyam, 2nd Edition. Edward Fitzgerald.

page 60 "... huge and mighty forms ..." , from Wordsworth's 'The Prelude' .

page 60 "Drink! for you know not whence you came ...", from 'The Rubaiyat ...' . Ibid..

page 60 "But see! The rising Moon of Heav'n again " from 'The Rubaiyat ...' . Ibid..

page 65 the day became "saturated with the light of hops" refers to a line from Milosz's poem 'Annalena'.

page 98 the Octavio Paz insight is to be found in his collection of essays, Convergences: essays on Art and Literature.

page 102 "... fewer friends than flatterers." A reference to Kirkpatrick Dobie's line in his poem 'Ca Ira', which is: "For poetry has few friends though many flatterers".

page 103 "… a little courtesy glows / like lemons on the underside of leaves" are lines from Andrew Greig's long poem 'Western Swing'.

page 108 The line "… between summer and the end of summer" is from Ted Walker's poem 'A Celebration of Autumn'.

page 109 "… when youth lay sleeping on the breast of youth …" are lines from Vita Sackville-West's long poem 'The Land'.

page 109 The note about heaven is a reference to Sheenagh Pugh's lines in her poem 'Earth Studies': "… If you really want to know/What I think about heaven, the truth is/I think I lived there".

page 112 "Fields of snow and tranquil trees in snow…" are lines from 'The Land'.

page 132 "… much goes to little making …" . Ibid.

Page 145 Roman Jakobson. Influential Russian linguist and anthropologist. Moved to Czechoslovakia and later to the United States.

page 149 Richard Peters was a seminal international influence upon the Philosophy of Education within teacher education at the time.

page 149 Pat Wilson was a creative proponent of the Philosophy of Education at Goldsmiths'. His important book Interest and Discipline in Education (Routledge) had just appeared.

page 156 Grantly Dick-Read's book was at the time a popular and rational guide to pregnancy

page 161 for a clear description of the unique place then of Goldsmiths' within the University of London, see Chapter 7 of Richard Hoggart's An Imagined Life and Times 1959-91, entitled 'The Great Tradition Re-visited: Goldsmiths' 1976-84'.

page 170 The Garden of Alcinous. Homer's mythical, and forever luxuriant, garden. His invitation is to "Take a seat there!"

page 238 The reference is to Iris Murdoch's book The Sovereignty of Good.

page 239 "… the hiss of the cold cosmos" is from Selwyn Pritchard's poem 'New Zeal'.

page 241 "… the ruthless chance of things" echoes lines from Selwyn Pritchard's poem 'Washing Up'

"Love does not stem the ruthless chance of things nor chill indifference check the Winters' Springs."

page 316 The lines, "Her mind snapped like a summer-dry twig / And fell in pieces at her feet / To be trampled on by people going to work …" are from Brendan Kennelly's poem 'Litter'.

page 397 'Kugeln'. Roughly translated as a ball of ice-cream, for cones.

page 404 Paul Leppin (1878 - 1945) was a controversial Bohemian writer, who spent most of his life as a postal clerk in Prague. Well represented in his collection of short stories about characters and life in Prague: Others' Paradise, Twisted Spoon Press, 2003. After his death his work fell into obscurity, but recently there has been a renewed interest in it.

page 419 Seifert's lines beginning "The worst is over …", are from 'The Plague Column', translated by Ewald Osers.